CONSTANCIA
AND OTHER STORIES
FOR VIRGINS

Constancia
and Other Stories for Virgins

Carlos Fuentes

TRANSLATED BY

THOMAS CHRISTENSEN

FARRAR STRAUS GIROUX

NEW YORK

CONTENTS

Constancia

Seal me with your eyes.
Take me wherever you are . . .
Shield me with your eyes.
Take me as a relic from the mansion of sorrow . . .
Take me as a toy, a brick from the house
So that our children will remember to return.

> Mahmud Darwish, cited by Edward Said
> in "Reflections on Exile"

For Sadri and Kate, the refuge of friendship

1

The old Russian actor Monsieur Plotnikov visited me the very day of his death. He told me that the years would pass and I would come to visit him on the day of my own death.

I didn't understand his words very well. The heat of Savannah in August is like fitful sleep: you repeatedly seem to shudder awake, you think you've opened your eyes, but in fact you've only introduced one dream inside another. And, inversely, one reality adheres to another, deforming it until it seems a dream. But it's nothing more than reality baked at 101°. At the same time, it's nothing less than this: my deepest dreams on summer afternoons are like the city of Savannah itself, which is a city inside another city inside . . .

This feeling of being caught in an urban maze is a result of the mysterious plan that gave Savannah as many squares as stars in the heavens, or so it seems. A gridwork regular as a chessboard, beginning with a square from which four, six, eight streets lead off to three, four, five squares from which, finally, twelve, fourteen streets radiate, leading in turn to an infinite number of squares.

The mystery of Savannah, in this respect, is its transparent geometric simplicity. Its labyrinth is the straight line. Its clarity produces, paradoxically, a most oppressive feeling of disorientation. Order is the antechamber of horror, and when my Spanish wife once more opens her old book of Goya prints and stops at the most famous of the *Caprichos*, I don't know if I should disturb her fascination by remarking:

—Reason that never sleeps produces monsters.

The immediate reality is simply this: the only solution (for me) is to sit on the porch of my house, in a rocker, with a round fan, trying to see off to the green, slow, fraudulent river, and not being able to make it out, consoling myself with the argument that since I'm in the open air, I must feel cool.

My wife, wiser than I, understands that these old Southern houses were designed to keep out the heat, and she chooses to close the shutters, take off her clothes, and spend the afternoon hours between cool sheets, under a silently revolving ceiling fan. That is something she has done ever since her childhood in Seville. Still, we do have one thing in common—air-conditioning gives us colds and sore throats; so we have agreed never to allow in our home one of those devices that stick out like pimples or scarred stumps from one or two windows of every house in the city.

They are ugly and they make the houses ugly. Savannah's domestic architecture dates from a period between the end of the eighteenth century and the third quarter of the nineteenth century; that is, the years between the independence of the Union and its severing in the Civil War, when our pride was greater than our sense of reality. The noble edifices of our city are symbols of two commerces, one famous, the other infamous. Cotton and slaves; blacks imported, white fibers exported. As an old Southerner, I appreciate the chromatic irony of this exchange. We sent out messengers as fresh and ethereal as clouds to the world, and in exchange we received flesh charred on the coals of hell. Still, irony is better than guilt, or at least I prefer to cultivate it, especially now that everything for which my ancestors so nobly and stupidly fought has been lost. Some statues survive, it's true, but now there's a Hyatt Regency next to the river and a De Soto Hilton behind my house on Drayton Street—proof that the Northern carpetbaggers, the mercenaries who profited from our defeat to annex us to their commerce, their values, their vulgarity, are still winning.

No one escapes these mercantile imperatives, not even I, who have so cultivated an understanding of my region and its history. Every week I travel to Atlanta to minister to my medical clientele, and from the airplane I see that there is no trace of the capital of Georgia, burned by Sherman in 1864. Skyscrapers, supermarkets, urban beltlines, elevators like cages of glass rising, brittle ivy, up the frozen skin of the buildings: plastic magnolias; defeats tasting of strawberry ice cream; history as television miniseries. I spend my Tuesdays, Wednesdays, and Thursdays in Atlanta, and Fridays I return to enjoy the weekend at home. It is my refuge, my asylum, yes. It is my dwelling place.

I return home with the feeling that for us this remains the city we built ourselves (despite the commercial incursions I have mentioned), where we received, to help in its construction, those refugees despite themselves, the blacks, who did not flee freely from Africa (if one can speak in that way about a refugee), but were dragged, in chains, out of their continent. Sometimes, rocking and trying to overcome the heat by thinking of the slow-moving river, or flying over Atlanta and trying to discover a single charred vestige of the past, I ask myself, old and somnolent now, if we have finally atoned for our guilt. How can we be done with it? Or does our well-being depend on our learning how to live with it forever? How long a vigil, I ask myself, does historical violence impose on us? When will we be allowed to rest? I seldom see the blacks of Savannah; I speak to them only when I have to. But I never stop asking what my history all comes down to: how far can or should my personal responsibility extend for injustices I did not commit?

2

I say that rocking in the open air is my strategy for feeling cool. I know that I am lying to myself. It's just a kind of autosuggestion. But anyone who has lived in extreme climates before artificial climatization knows full well that heat and cold are, more than anything, mental states that, like sex, literature, or power, are accepted or rejected at the very center of your existence, which is the mind. And if the head won't help us, then let us drink hot coffee in hot climates. That way, the inside and outside temperatures balance out; but, in hot weather, cold upsets the balance and we pay with hours of discomfort for a minute of

relief. Would the inverse be true, in cold climates? Does eating
ice cream help you through a Russian winter? I must ask Mr.
Plotnikov, the next time I see him.

The reader of these hurried notes, which I'm jotting down
with the strange sense that I must do so now, before it's too late,
must understand that to say I saw or visited Mr. Plotnikov is to
dignify what was really no more than a series of chance encounters. Sometimes there was an element of surprise in them. One
time, in a shopping mall, I stopped to take some ID pictures in
an automatic photo booth. The curtain was closed and I waited
a long time. Some old-fashioned, laced-up black boots attracted
my curiosity. When the curtain parted, Mr. Plotnikov appeared.
He looked at me and said:

—They make us choose our roles, Gospodin Hull. Just look,
an actor obliged to have his picture taken to get a passport, what
do you think of that? Don't you want to wait with me for the
four photos to come out of the slot?—he said, taking my arm
with his gloved hand. —Whose pictures do you think they will
be? The actor? The private man? The Russian citizen? The
apprentice set designer? The refugee in America? Who? He
laughed, and feeling a little uneasy, I smiled as one smiles at a
madman to placate him, for I must say that the old man, despite
his apparent calm, also seemed uneasy.

I wondered if I should give in to my curiosity and wait for
Mr. Plotnikov's photographs to appear. I laughed, thinking how
we sometimes make ridiculous faces without realizing it, staring
at the hidden, shuttered, aggressive eye of the camera. But his
question pursued me. Which of our multiple personalities is
caught, at any given moment, by a photograph?

Once I met him in the cemetery where I sometimes go to pay
a visit to my ancestors. Dressed, as always, in black, he was
picking his way gingerly over the red earth. I asked him if he
had relatives here. He laughed and, without looking at me, murmured that nobody remembers those who died fifty years ago,
no, not twenty, not even ten years lasts the memory of the dead

. . . He walked away slowly, before I could tell him that I was proof to the contrary. I visit and remember two centuries of dead people.

Another summer I ran into him in the shopping mall by the Hyatt Regency, where his old-fashioned mourning clothes were in sharp contrast with the neon lights, the electronic games, the movie marquees. I saw he was very tired and I took his arm; the up-to-date flashiness of the mall, the heat outside, the artificially cooled air inside, seemed too much for him. It was the only time we sat down to talk. He told me about his Russian past, about working as an actor and set designer, how he couldn't be several things at once, which was why he left Russia, they wouldn't let him be all he wanted to be, they wanted to compartmentalize his life, here the actor, here the citizen, here, very secretly, the sensual man, the father, the keeper of memory . . . He made the remark on that occasion, as he incongruously ate pistachio ice cream, that, no matter what, asylum is temporary, one always goes home again, despite popular sayings: —Remember, Gospodin Hull, our past is always with us.

He was playing with a strip of I.D. photos, still damp, waving them gently to dry them. I told him with understandable awkwardness that he was certainly welcome in the United States. He replied that he was tired, very tired.

I reminded him that I was a doctor; if I could help him, he shouldn't hesitate . . . I didn't look at the photographs when he finally put them on the table. But I did notice, out of the corner of my eye, that they weren't pictures of him but of someone else—I could not see clearly—who had long dark hair. Man or woman? It was during that unisex period when one couldn't be sure. Another reason to avoid an indiscretion.

He shook his head and acknowledged my kindness not simply by declining my offer but by responding in the same tone: he said no, his problem was not the kind a doctor could cure. He smiled pleasantly.

—I understand—I told him—the distance, the exile. I could

not live far from the United States. More precisely, far from the South. As a young man, I studied in Spain, and I love that country. But I could only live in my own.

—Ah—. Mr. Plotnikov looked at me. —And living in your country, do you look back to the past?

I told him that I thought I had a fair sense of tradition. He looked amused and said that North American history seemed overly selective to him, it was the history of white success, but not of the other realities. The Indian past, for example, or the black, or the Hispanic . . . All that was left out.

—I am not a chauvinist—I told the old Russian a little defensively. —I think that amnesia has a price. But at least our society has been a melting pot. We have admitted more immigrants than any nation in history.

He shook his head good-naturedly to show that his observations were not meant as a reproach. —No, Gospodin Hull, I myself am the beneficiary of that generosity; how can I criticize it! But I'm talking about—he stopped manipulating his spoonful of pistachio ice cream for a moment—I'm talking about something more than physical immigration, I'm talking about accepting the memory of others, their past . . . and even their desire to return one day to their homeland.

—Why not? That's the way it is.

—What you don't understand is how hard it is to renounce everything, to face the loss of all that we are, not just our possessions but our physical and intellectual powers as well, to leave everything behind like a suitcase and begin anew.

—I hope that everyone who comes to our country feels that we want to give them, in our own way, the strength to make a new beginning.

—And also a grace period?

—Pardon, Mr. Plotnikov?

—Yes, I'm not talking about starting over but of earning a reprieve, do you understand? I'm talking about someday receiving, as a gift, an extra hour of life. Yes, exactly that: don't we deserve it?

—Yes, of course—I agreed emphatically—of course.

—Ah, that's good. —Mr. Plotnikov wiped his lips with a paper napkin. —Yes, that's good. You know, after a while one lives only through the lives of others, when one's own life has run out.

He put the photos in his jacket pocket.

That was not the first or the last time, over many years, when an unexpected snowfall would cover the red earth of the cemetery or when thunderstorms would turn its paths to mud, that I chanced upon my neighbor the actor Plotnikov walking along the cemetery paths, repeating a sort of litany of names that I sometimes caught snatches of, as he passed near me . . . Dmitrovich Osip Emilievich Isaac Emmanuelovich Mikhail Afanasievich Sergei Alexandrovich Kazimir Serafimovich Vsevelod Emilievich Vladimir Vladimiro . . .

3

Now it was August and Mr. Plotnikov (Monsieur Plotnikov, I sometimes call him; whether out of respect, a sense of difference, or mere affectation I know not) came (I remember: it was an unannounced visit) to tell me of his death, but neither the heat of summer outside nor the heat of the hell that according to popular legend awaits actors, who are denied burial in consecrated ground, neither of those seemed to oppress that gentleman, white as a transparent host—white skin, white hair, white lips, pale eyes—but dressed entirely in black, in a turn-of-the-century-style three-piece black suit, a Russian overcoat too big for him, as if another actor had given it to him, with the hem dragging through the dust, the Coca-Cola cans, and the chocolate Mars Bars wrappers. He managed all this with dignity. Making a unique concession to the climate, he carried an open umbrella, black also, as he proceeded with slow and dusty tread: I noticed his sharp patent-leather shoes with little bows on their tips, a detail that gave Mr. Plotnikov the air of a perverse ballerina.

—Gospodin Hull—he greeted me, pointing his umbrella in my direction like a bullfighter taking off his hat to salute the fatal act that will follow the formula courtesy. —Gospodin Hull, I have come to say goodbye.

—Ah, Monsieur Plotnikov—I replied, half asleep—you're going on a trip.

—You are always joking—. He shook his head disapprovingly. —I have never understood why Americans are always making jokes. This would be very badly received in St. Petersburg, or in Paris.

—Pardon us, sir. Blame all our failings on our being a country of pioneers.

—Bah, so is Russia, but we don't spend our time guffawing. Bah, you act like hyenas.

I decided not to respond to this last allusion. Mr. Plotnikov snapped his parasol shut, very theatrically, so that the mid-afternoon sun shone straight down on him, accentuating the cavities of his narrow, transparent skull, barely covered by skin growing ever thinner, like a worn-out envelope, finally to reveal the contents of the letter within.

—No, Gospodin Hull, I have come to say goodbye because I am going to die, and I feel it is a basic courtesy to say goodbye to you, who have been a courteous and polite neighbor, in spite of everything.

—I'm sorry that, living right next door, we never . . .

He interrupted me without smiling: —That is what I am thanking you for. You never imposed unwanted formulas of neighborliness on me.

—Well, thank you, then, Mr. Plotnikov, but I'm sure, to para-phrase a more famous American humorist than me, that you greatly exaggerate the news of your death.

—You can never tell, Gospodin Hull, because my condition is the following . . .

I had stopped rocking and fanning. I didn't know whether to give in to my first inclination, which was to laugh, or surrender to the deeper feeling engendered by the sight of this man—so protected by his clothes and yet so mercilessly exposed by a sun that allowed him no more shade than the bony ridges over his eyes and the wrinkles of his aged skin—which was to take his words seriously indeed.

—Yes, sir?

—Gospodin Hull: you will come to visit me only on the day of your own death, to let me know, as I have done today with mine. That is my condition.

—But you will be dead then—I began, logically, almost happily, although I quickly abandoned that tack—I mean, the day I die you will no longer be living . . .

—Don't be so sure of that—now he opened the umbrella with nervous haste and shaded himself with it—and respect my last wish. Please. I am so tired.

As I relate this, I recall many of our chance meetings at the corner of Drayton Street and Wright Square, in the cemetery, or in the mall. We never exchanged many words (except the afternoon of the pistachio ice cream), but we were neighbors, and without ever paying each other a formal visit, we passed along snatches of information, like the pieces of a puzzle. What did I know about him, really, on that day when he predicted his death in such a strange manner? What did I know about him? Two or three vague facts: he was a theater actor in Russia, although he really wanted to be a set designer and stop acting. It was the era of Stalinist terror, life was difficult for everyone, as bad for those who submitted as for those who resisted the madness of personal power posing as collective power. Who didn't suffer? Even the executioners, Mr. Plotnikov said one day, they, too, breathe, and their breath was like a forest felled. He left Russia and found asylum in the United States, which offered it to so many refugees from a Europe convulsed by ideology, in those generous years when America was America; he smiled at me, recalling some Jews, some Spaniards, who couldn't get through the doors of our democratic refuge. But what could you do; we received so many more, Germans, Poles, Russians, Czechs, French . . . Politics is the art of limits. Art is the limit of politics.

—Respect my last wish. Do not come to my wake tonight or

accompany my funeral procession tomorrow. No. Visit me in my house on the day of your death, Gospodin Hull. Our well-being depends on it. Please. I am very tired.

What could I say, seeing him there on that street-scene stage, with the garbage beginning to distract us from the colonial grandeur of Savannah; what could I tell him, that the day of his funeral I was going to be in Atlanta taking care of patients less lucid, more impatient than he? What could I tell him, to show my respect for something that I understood, I appreciated, I was grateful for, that this was perhaps his final performance, the final act of a career brutally interrupted—I deduced—by political adversity and never taken up again outside Russia.

—I needed—he explained to me one day, or I imagined or dreamed, I'm no longer sure of the truth—the Russian language, Russian applause, to read the reviews in Russian, but above all I needed the test of the Russian heart in order to present myself in public, acting; I couldn't communicate as an actor apart from the Russian language, space, applause, time, testimony, intent. Did I understand that, in my country of wild syncretisms, of political pastiche and migratory melting pots and maps stuck up with chewing gum, could I possibly understand?

What could I tell him, I ask again, except, yes, Mr. Plotnikov, I agree, I will do what you say.

—Very good. I thank you. I am too tired.

With that, he bowed and walked stiffly away in the blazing sun to his house next to mine, near Wright Square.

4

Almost in spite of myself, I went into the house. I wanted to tell my wife what had happened. I wanted to tell her how deeply Monsieur Plotnikov had disturbed me, enough to make me take the unusual step of interrupting Constancia's nap. I was beyond observing that tacit prohibition, so great was the turmoil my Russian neighbor had caused in me. But my astonishment grew when I realized that Constancia was not in her bed, that it had not even been slept in. The shutters were closed, but that was normal. And it would have been normal, too, if Constancia, finding she had to leave the house—I looked for her on all three floors and even in the unused cellar—had wanted to tell me she was leaving, but saw me in the rocking chair and, giving me a fond smile, went out without waking me. In that case, a note would have been enough, a few scribbled words, saying:

—Don't worry, Whitby. Be back soon.

And, on returning, what pretext would she give me?

—I don't know. I decided to lose myself in the plazas. This is the most beautiful and mysterious aspect of the city—the way one plaza always opens onto another, like a Russian doll.

And other times: —Remember, Whitby, your wife is Andalusian and we Andalusians don't accept age, we fight it. Look, who dances *peteneras* better than an old lady, have you noticed?— she said, laughing, imitating a sexagenarian flamenco dancer.

I imagined her lying down, nude, in the shade, telling me these things: Sometimes, on dog days like these—understand, love?—I go out looking for water, shade, plazas, a maze of streets, ah, if you knew what it was to be a child in Seville, Whitby, that other city of plazas and mazes and water and shadows . . . You know, I walk through the streets seeking my past in a different place, do you think that's madness?

—You've never tried to make friends here, you haven't even learned English . . . Even my name gives you trouble— I smiled—

—Hweetbee Howl— She smiled in turn, and then said to me:

—I haven't criticized your Savannah, we've made our life here, but leave me my Seville, at least in my imagination, my love, and tell yourself: It's a good thing Constancia knows how to find the light and water she needs here in my own American South.

I would laugh then, pleased to think that the South, the South with its names full of vowels—Virginia, Georgia, the Carolinas— is the Andalusia of America. And Spain, I tell her, as an old reader of Coustine and Gautier, is the Russia of the West, just as Russia is the Spain of the East. Again I laughed, observing to Constancia that only Russia and Spain had come up with the idea of changing the width of their train tracks to forestall foreign invasion; that is to say, the aggression of other Europeans. What paranoia—I laughed in mock amazement—what love of barriers, whether the steppes or a mountain chain: to be *the others*, Russians and Spaniards, unassimilatable to Western normality! But, after all—I defended myself against Constancia—perhaps normality is mediocrity.

I think, naturally, of our neighbor, the Russian actor, when the conversation takes this turn. With the skilled touch of the bibliophile, I run my hands over the dark spines and gilded, dusty edges of the books in my library, the coolest and darkest place in the house on Drayton Street, and I secretly pride myself that the flexibility of my hand is a perfect reflection of the quickness of my sexagenarian mind. I was—I am—a man of letters, part of an inheritance that does not flourish in the United States and is kept alive mainly in the South, the land of William Faulkner, Walker Percy, Robert Penn Warren, and its Dulcineas with a pen, Carson McCullers, Eudora Welty, and Shirley Ann Grau. I often think that even self-exiled Southerners—I'm talking about diabolically self-destructive gnomes like Truman Capote as well as painfully creative giants like William Styron—are like the carriers of a literary aristocracy that is unwanted in a country that craves proof that its Declaration of Independence is right, that all men are created equal, but what this equality (proposed by a group of exceptionally learned aristocrats, Hamilton, Jefferson, Jay, Adams—the golden youth of the colonies) really means is the triumph of the lowest common denominator. Why do we elect retarded presidents like Reagan if not to prove that all men are equal? We prefer to recognize ourselves in this idiot who talks like us, looks like us, makes our jokes, shares our mental lapses, amnesias, prejudices, obsessions, and confusions, justifying our own mental vulgarity: how consoling! A new Roosevelt, a new Kennedy would force us to admire them for what we *are not*, and that's an unsettling feeling. Still, I'm a quiet American who sticks pretty close to his library, almost to the point of neglecting my practice, doesn't need many friends, has chosen to exercise his profession in a modern and impersonal city that shuts down at five, the blacks given over to lassitude and nocturnal violence and the whites locked away in their mansions surrounded by savage dogs and electric fences. And I spend three nights of the week in a hospital room so as to perform heart operations early on Wednesdays and Thursdays. In our time, it is impossible to be a surgeon without the support of a great medical center.

Yes, for all this, I'm a quiet old American who votes Democratic, of course, and lives in a secret city where he sees no one, is married to an Andalusian woman, talks about death with a Russian, and goes into his library to confirm, within its shadows, the Hispano-Russian eccentricity of the American South: countries with non-standard railway gages.

—Did you know, Constancia—I say, appealing to her marvelous sense of popular culture, magical and mythic—did you know that Franz Kafka's uncle was director of Spain's national railroad in 1909? He was a Mr. Levy, Franz's mother's brother, and he heard that his nephew was unhappy in the insurance company in Prague and invited him to come to Madrid to work for the Spanish railways. What do you think, Constancia, of a man who imagines himself awakening one morning transformed into an insect, working for the Spanish railways? Would it have been literature's loss or the railway's gain?

—The trains would have arrived on time—mused Constancia—but without passengers.

She had never read Kafka, or anything else. But she knew how to use her imagination, and she knew that imagination leads to knowledge. She is from a country where the people know more than the elite, just as in Italy, Mexico, Brazil, or Russia. The people are better than the elite everywhere, in fact, except in the United States, where Faulkner or Lowell or Adams or Didion is superior to its crude and rootless people, stultified by television and beer, unable to generate a cuisine, dependent on the black minority to dance and sing, dependent on its elite to speak beyond a grunt. Exactly the opposite, if you ask me, a Southerner married to Constancia, exactly the opposite of Andalusia, where culture is in the head and hands of the people.

Constancia and I have been married forty years and I have to confess right off that the secret of our survival, in a society where seven out of ten marriages end in divorce, is that we do not limit ourselves to a single fixed mental attitude in our daily matrimonial relations. We're always ready to explore the full range of possibilities in each of our ideas, suggestions, or preferences. In this way, nobody imposes on anyone or harbors lasting grudges; she doesn't read because she knows, I read because I don't know, and we meet as a couple in a question that I pose from literature and she answers from wisdom: the trains would have arrived on time, but without passengers.

For example, when she returns at six o'clock to our house on Drayton Street, the first thing I notice—being a longtime reader of detective novels—is that the tips of Constancia's shoes are covered with dust. And the second thing I note, in the best Sherlockian tradition, is that the red dust—just the finest film— covering her shoe tips comes from a place I know quite well, a place I visit because my glorious ancestors are buried there, a place I explore because someday Constancia and I will rest there, in that earth colored by Atlantic silt: my land, but facing hers, Georgia on a parallel with Andalusia. And my Georgia, I think, recalling the old exiled Russian, is also parallel with his Georgia.

And the third thing I notice is that Constancia notices I've noticed, which immediately makes me aware that, as she is aware of everything, she can leave nothing to chance. Which means, in other words, that she wanted me to notice what I noticed, and to know she knew.

5

But there was still one thing I didn't know that August afternoon when Mr. Plotnikov announced his death and asked me to reciprocate by visiting him the day of mine. And that was the most essential thing: what was Constancia trying to tell me by all her unusual activity on that singular day? That, and not the color of the dirt on her shoes, was the real mystery. I looked at her standing there, at sixty-one still an Andalusian, protecting herself from the fading rays of the sun, Constancia the color of a yellow lily, Constancia of medium height, with short legs, her waist still narrow but her ankles thick, a full bosom and a long neck: deepset, dark-ringed eyes, a mole on her lip, and her graying hair done up, as always, in a bun. She doesn't use hair combs, although she does use silver hairpins, of a rare sort, in the shape of keys.

Constancia, at this late-afternoon hour, keeps her back to the window, which, like every other space in the library, is surrounded by books—above, on the sides, and below that opening in the corner of the house that looks across to the opposite corner of Drayton Street and to Wright Square, where Monsieur Plotnikov lives.

I am a bibliophile, as I've said, I not only look for the finest leather bindings but I also have my discoveries specially bound: the golden spines were like an aureole around Constancia's white face, when suddenly, behind her, in Mr. Plotnikov's house, all the windows, which had been completely dark, lighted up at the same moment.

Constancia had not turned her head, as if she had divined what had happened by my shocked look.

—I think that something has happened in Mr. Plotnikov's house—I said, trying to sound calm.

—No—Constancia replied, with a look that made my blood

run cold—something has happened in the house of Whitby and Constancia.

I don't know why, but I felt sickened and aged by my wife's words, which were followed by her flight from the library, up the stairs, to the bedroom, with me frantically trying to catch up with her. Something inside me told me to stop, to go slowly, that Constancia was to blame, forcing me to run upstairs this way, despite my physical condition, but I couldn't slow down; her speed, her anxious haste, spurred me on: Constancia entered her bedroom, tried to close the door and remove the key, and then gave up and simply knelt at the Spanish prie-dieu that she had brought to our house forty years ago when I completed my postgraduate medical studies in Seville and returned to my home in Georgia with a young, beautiful Andalusian fiancée.

She knelt before the bleached, triangular, wide-skirted image—white gold, silk, and baroque pearls—of our Lady of Hope, the Virgin of the Macarena; she knelt on the worn velvet, clasped her hands, closed her eyes. I cried: Constancia! and ran toward her just as her head bowed down, falling lifeless on the opulent swelling of her breasts. I caught her, took her pulse, scrutinized her vacant eyes. We were in the darkened bedroom; only a votive candle dedicated to the Virgin burned in front of Constancia's pallid face, and behind her, in the Russian actor's house, all the lights went out, just as they had come on, all of a sudden.

Constancia took my hand, half opened her eyes, tried to speak the words *My love, my love.* But I knew, beyond any doubt, that for a few moments, between the time she knelt down and the time she revived in my arms, my wife was, clinically, dead.

6

She slept a long time. Her pallor, icy as a tin roof, kept me at her bedside all that night and the day after. On Monday I forgot to call my office in Atlanta to ask my secretary to cancel my appointments. The telephone never stopped ringing. Constancia's illness turned my promise to the Russian into something more than a duty, it assumed a strange fatality that I couldn't help connecting with that obligation. I forgot my own responsibilities.

Keeping watch over my wife, I thought how her illness began when the lights in Mr. Plotnikov's house went on. Did the lights and her illness also coincide with the death of the actor? I told myself that this was nothing but superstition; I was deducing; simple logic said the Russian actor was dead for two reasons: first, because he predicted it, and second, the signs—lights coming on, then going out, Constancia's attack—seemed to bear a symbolic spiritual value. From this confusion of cause and effect, I concluded that Constancia's illness had something to do with the presumed death of Monsieur Plotnikov; I smiled, sighed, and began to think of things that might have escaped me when I was preoccupied with my professional responsibilities, which flowed slow and steady as the river to the sea.

First, over the years, whenever I saw Monsieur Plotnikov he was alone: in the streets and plazas of Savannah, in the pantheon of red earth, occasionally (strange, freakish meetings) in a shopping center near the Hyatt Regency that smells of peanuts, warmed-over pizza, popcorn, and tennis shoes.

Second, I never met Mr. Plotnikov indoors, as the shopping mall has a false interior (as well as a false exterior): it's a street of glass. I had never been inside his house, across from ours, and he had never been to ours.

And—the third thing—for perfectly natural reasons, as natural as the fact that Constancia had never accompanied me to the hospital in Atlanta and I never had gone with her to a beauty salon, she had never been with me when I met Mr. Plotnikov, either inside or outside any wall.

There was one last fact, the most difficult to reconcile with the rest: Constancia had been dead in my arms for several moments; it was that fact that forced me to ask: Had Mr. Plotnikov died exactly as he had foretold, and, if so, did his death coincide with the play of lights in his house and with the fleeting death of Constancia? Why did I see our neighbor only outdoors, and why had I never run into him with my wife? I will admit to my share of sentimental egoism—these questions had never disturbed my sleep before, they only interested me now because of the melancholy terror I felt on holding Constancia and knowing, *with scientific certainty*, that Constancia was dead.

But no longer: she lived, she returned to me, to herself, to our life, little by little. And the telephone never stopped ringing.

7

I devoted myself to her for several days. I canceled my appointments and operations in Atlanta. It was an exceptional step. As long as we had been married, Constancia had insisted that only in the most extreme case should I care for her professionally. It would be better if I never saw her as a patient. She would obey any doctor who told her to undress, spread her legs, get on all fours. But she would obey only one lover who told her to do those things: that man was me, her husband, not her doctor. And, as for me, what maddened me from the beginning was that passion for obedience in Constancia, as if my commands became her own desires, as if I merely guessed her own most passionate desires and eagerly and ecstatically followed her lead.

In our forty years together, however, Constancia had never had to see a doctor. She had suffered only minor ailments: colds, digestive upsets, mild insomnia, nose bleeds . . . It was therefore an emotional experience to have her in my hands (I mean, in my care) for the first time: my patient.

I was waiting for her to regain her lucidity and strength—she spent several days in that half state between trance, prayer, and a sudden smile—so that, together again, like one as before, we would regard what had happened according to our unwritten rules: There are many possibilities; let us weigh them all, one by one, without rushing headlong to any conclusion. But during

these first days of her convalescence—what else can I call it?—
Constancia was not a woman but a bird, with a bird's nervous
movements, unable to turn her head without her movement's
being cut short by a sort of ornithological tremor—the movement
of a winged creature that cannot look ahead, eyes to the front,
but only to the sides, confirming with a rapid movement of the
left eye some fact suggested by the right. Like an ostrich, or an
eagle, or . . . ?

What was she looking at that way, during those days when I
asked myself so many questions—Had the actor died? Did the
lights announce his death?—and came increasingly to one conclusion, that those phenomena coincided with the fleeting death
of Constancia. I took her pulse, pressed my stethoscope to her
breast, pried her eyelids open (eagle, ostrich, or . . . ?). With her
bird movements she looked at the window that in turn looked
toward the house, dark and silent, of Mr. Plotnikov. She looked
at the image of the Virgin of the Macarena, immobile, mournful,
in her triangular paralysis. She looked at the flickering light of
the votive candle. She did not look at me. I looked at her
reclining body, her open gown exposing the breasts of a sixty-
one-year-old woman who, however, had never had children, her
nipples still voluptuous, gifts for my senses, perfect spheres for
my touch, my tongue, and especially my sense of fullness, of
pregnant reality. They say that we North Americans attach too
much sexuality to the breasts, just as South Americans do to the
buttocks. But in my house, since I never saw her pregnant, her
ample breasts seemed to concentrate that sense of pregnancy that
men like to contrast with the ethereal (her face, her eyes) in a
woman: earth and air. But Constancia always told me: I am water,
I am the source. She was Andalusian. And Andalusia is an Arab
land, a land of nomads who arrived from the desert and found
the refuge of water. Granada . . .

I couldn't leave her. I couldn't abandon her. In other circumstances, I would have called in another doctor, nurses, an am-
bulance. But that wasn't possible. If the phenomenon repeated

itself, I, only I, should be its witness, nobody else had that right, nobody else—just as Constancia could offer herself erotically on all fours only to me, though she might present her ass to be examined for evidence of cancer. Now I was her lover and I was her doctor, too. She was my case. She couldn't be admitted to an impersonal hospital. Constancia would not enter any hospital; I saw her, across the passage of time, lying there, lily-white, deep-set eyes, mole, her hair loose—I kept her silver hairpins in my jacket pocket—and I told myself that I would have to be admitted for her, with her, in her. But her look—which I followed—was still not for me; it was for the Virgin, the votive candle, the window.

Since I couldn't leave her, I couldn't resolve one of the more important questions. Her apparent death, in my arms, for several seconds, displaced the other question: Had Mr. Plotnikov died? I didn't notice any further activity at his house, but that was not unusual. I never had noticed anything about that unremarkable house, except the night the lights blazed and then went out, all at once in each case. Normally, nothing happened at the house across from ours. It might as well have been vacant. The newspaper was delivered each morning as usual, but there was no mention in it of Plotnikov's death. Perhaps he had requested that. If he had died, who would attend his wake? I supposed that the Russian actor would keep beside him an icon of the Virgin, fashioned from hammered silver, in which the reality of the metal itself would be more vivid than that of the faint, distant figure of the smiling Virgin, pale ocher, with the Child in her arms, both looking at the faithful old man from the eternal background of orthodox religion, which refuses to come down and tread the earth. Who would bury him?

I cast a quick look at our Virgin, by Constancia's bed, the Andalusian madonna, Virgin of bullfighters, processions, tricks, outrageous blasphemies, gypsy dances, ardent bodies. The Russian Virgin never said anything, anywhere; the Andalusian Virgin shouted, here, now. Constancia always said: Andalusia: water, source, and reflection. Alhambra . . .

She knew how to speak beautifully, gracefully, with passion and tenderness, but now, in her trance, I set aside our discussions and considered matters on my own account. Her conversation had kept from me many thoughts, which were rendered insubstantial so that they floated away from me like so many little birds, the barest of possibilities in place of the certainties that pin us down. So now one thought weighed on me heavily, horribly, through my long vigil, again and again, despite my conscious and unconscious denials:

Constancia, tell me, please, how many times have you died before?

8

(I sound like the survivor of some catastrophe. It's not true. Constancia and I are alive, the heat is intense, soporific, I'm sixty-nine, Constancia sixty-one, and now we're both shut up inside a shuttered room. She is better than I am at beating the heat of these dog days. Can you overcome the heat by showering your floor with wood shavings, like those Constancia has strewn around her bed and prie-dieu?)

I don't know how much of what she says without looking at me, as if I weren't present, during the long week of her recuperation, is a response to my question: —Constancia, tell me, how many times have you died . . . ?

I don't know, I repeat, because I don't even know if she is talking to me. She says (not to me, she simply speaks) that she only gives voice to dreams and prayers. Of that I haven't the slightest doubt. She will announce: Last night I dreamed that . . . ; or sometimes she will even say: —I am dreaming that . . . ; and sometimes she will unsettle me by announcing: —I am going to dream that . . .

She dreams that: She was a mannequin in a shop. Two wild young men, perhaps students, stole her from her window and took her to live in their studio. They threw dinner parties in her honor. Nobody knew if she, Constancia, was dead or alive, neither the jokesters nor the targets of their prank. The students fell in love with her, argued over her, but in the end destroyed her: or perhaps (the dream is ambiguous) abandoned her to save their masculine friendship. But she triumphed, *Madre Ana, madre mía* (delirious, she calls this name for the first time), and dominated those poor impure lovers, *madre mía*, slaves to male sexual vanity, which is the worst vanity of all because it excuses everything if you're a man, but you get away with nothing if you're a woman, nothing, *madre*, but she triumphed, she reappeared and looked at them as if *they* were the wooden dummies; she is alive; she is in her place: *Blessed art thou amongst women . . . you hear me, Mother?*

She dreams that: She has been born again, far away, a dark girl, ignorant, almost mute, silenced by centuries of servitude, misery, abuse, rape, violation, contempt, lack of charity, oh, *madre mía*, this dark girl in a faraway place has nothing, not even hope for all that you and I give unto the world: she has only the tracks of her tears like scars on her face: *Full of grace, the Lord is with thee, He sees my bare legs exposed to the sun.*

She dreams that: She is giving birth illicitly, knowing that a virgin birth can occur but once, without sin, not twice or three times, like a bitch's, but she is giving birth again because they killed her son, they didn't let the poor boy live out his life, and now she wants to have another child secretly, surrounded by women just as secretive as she is, and, thanks to the carpenters, the bricklayers, the architects, who have constructed a secret place, she can have her son there and this time protect him from death: *And forgive us our trespasses . . . Now and at the hour of our death . . .*

She dreams that: She is crossing a bridge during Holy Week and sees her reflection in the water . . . That the bullring is empty because the matador's servants have swept away the blood of the bull, so the beast will not return to his refuge in the arena . . . That a bloody specter follows her from the depths of the tomb where he had been hiding, headless, he who watched and painted the others, she and her lover . . . That . . .

Constancia wakes with a cry, murmuring feverishly:

—*And blessed is the fruit of thy womb* . . .

She looked at me terrified, without recognizing me, asking me: Why did you abandon me? Why did you leave without me? Why do you make me follow you? Why . . . ?

I comfort her, I take her head between my hands, I reassure her, I haven't left you, Constancia, here I am, I'm not forcing you to do anything.

9

When Constancia, after two weeks of this, felt well enough to sit up in bed, propped up among her pillows, she slowly regained her sense of my presence.

I didn't want to let go of her hand, which I had held in mine all the while, as much to express my devotion as to make sure of detecting any sign of what had frightened me previously.

Gradually, we began to discuss our by this time long-standing marriage and, without intending to, the events that might have threatened it. We recalled together, for example, the first time that one of us, then the other, and finally both of us together, realized we were no longer young. It started when she misinterpreted a suggestion of mine, purely professional, about her periods. Since we were not able to have children, I suggested that she could avoid—and, frankly, spare me—the monthly nuisance by having a simple operation. I knew an excellent doctor in Atlanta who would take care of it discreetly . . .

Constancia stopped me unexpectedly, without attempting to disguise her anger. So that's how I saw her, as a menopausal old woman, sterile, like a . . . She screamed and ran to shut herself in her room, and stayed there, without food or water, not letting me enter, for more than twenty-four hours. Days later I made it up to her, in a sense, by giving up the cigarettes I had enjoyed as I worked, was lost in thought, or relaxed after dinner . . . I told Constancia I was doing it because of a slight heart murmur. Gradually I developed new habits, never asking her to follow my example. I stopped drinking, gave up tennis and squash, even though I knew those sports were good for my circulation: Constancia felt games should be left to the young and were dangerous for older people. Nor did I dare propose a program of jogging (besides, a number of my acquaintances had died with their Adidases on, in the course of those untimely trials).

In that way, I tried to show Constancia that old age is a series of renunciations of what we loved when we were young. I made myself into an example, but when I had done so, I realized that Constancia refused to follow my lead, and, in fact, she gave up nothing. She was always the same, or it might be better to say she still led the same life. She kept house, complaining about the lack of good servants in the United States but making no real effort to obtain domestic help; she saw no one but me, so she did not speak English (and had never wanted to learn it); she punched the buttons of the television set, without watching any particular program for very long; she went to Mass, said her prayers at night, and then delivered herself to a sexual pleasure that would have seemed almost indecent if it hadn't been preceded by hours of prayer, Constancia kneeling before the votive candles and the image of the Macarena . . . She broke too many rules, only to convert the exceptions into routines. It annoyed me sometimes, made me ask myself: Why not get a servant and stop complaining? For me, though, staying out of domestic affairs left me time to read, and reading transforms everything, raising it to a higher level of existence, beyond stupid routines.

There's an entire library here, don't you realize? I said to her one day, a first-rate library, I assure you, really choice, there are things in it that would interest even an uneducated woman. Has it ever occurred to you to go into the library and read a book, Constancia? Do you believe I'll always be satisfied with your daytime domesticity and your nighttime passion? When we are old, what are we going to talk about, you and I?

She screamed, ran to her room, again the cloister, and now, twenty or thirty years after my affront, here we are holding hands, both of us old now, and talking, not of books, but of our life together.

This unshakable faith in love, love, our love, might it not be just as much an affront as suggesting that she anticipate her menopause or make a little effort to fill the gaps in her vast Andalusian ignorance? I have said that she was not prepared to give up anything in exchange for my ever-increasing discipline, and in this disparity I saw a profound reflection of our religions: discipline (mine) in return for nothing (hers). And yet, without ever exchanging words on the subject, she acted as if I should thank her for her unreserved availability, her freely giving of herself. This exasperated my Calvinist genes, even though I knew that it was precisely this quality that made my woman so attractive to me. Her library was her prayer, or an exceptional song, or an unexpected danger.

I saw her from a distance one afternoon, seated on a bench facing the river in Emmett Park. I had been at the hotel buying a pack of cigarettes and was returning home along River Street. I saw her sitting on the bench facing the river and thought, what luck, I will surprise her. Then a young black man, about thirty years old, strong, vigorous, sat down beside Constancia. She looked at the river. He stared down at his tennis shoes with a fixed look. I went a little closer, clutching the cellophane of my cigarette pack. They didn't see me. The black man spoke to my wife. She looked at the river. I said to myself in a low voice, hoping she might somehow hear me at that distance:

—Don't show fear. By all you hold dear! If he senses you're afraid, he might attack. Fear incites them.

Now the black turned to face Constancia, speaking to her insolently. I was going to run to her. Then I noticed that she was answering him, without looking at him. He grabbed my wife's hand. She did not pull away. She didn't show fear. Or familiarity. That's good, I told myself, don't take chances. I had decided to approach them at a normal speed, give Constancia a kiss on the cheek; we would go back to our house together, along

Lincoln Street. Then another black man approached the bench, a younger man, and seemed to ask the other for something. The first man got angry, stood up, the two faced each other wordlessly, the only sound was their hissing, that's what I particularly noticed, they were hissing like snakes, two black snakes glaring with fury, with blood in their eyes. Never have I seen so much hate concentrated in two human beings, they were trembling, both of them, not touching each other, just looking, the two bodies leaning close to each other.

Constancia got up from the bench and left by Factors Walk, on the other side from where I was standing. I decided to watch her go while the two black men faced each other with a wild tension, though, as far as I could see, no violent consequences. When Constancia disappeared from sight, I lost interest and returned home. She came in a few minutes later. I preferred not to mention the matter. I would end up asking for an explanation, and a marriage is weakened when a spouse has to make explanations. Who excuses accuses. The best course was to maintain a sympathetic silence.

Now, on this dying August afternoon, as the scissors of autumn slowly, mysteriously begin to snip through the heavy air of summer, and it's not worth the trouble to recall that remote incident in the park, I can almost understand her feeling that love that has complete certainty is not true love; it's too much like an insurance policy, or, worse yet, a certificate of good conduct. And indifference is the price you pay for it. So perhaps I am thankful for the moments of conflict that Constancia and I experienced in the past; they show that we had to test our marriage, we would not consign it to the indifference of perfect security. How could it be, when something of no importance to me—having a child— was a constant source of frustration and argument throughout the first twenty years of our life together, always raised by her: So you don't care about having a child? No, I care about having you. Well, I do care about it, I need a child, I can't have one, you're a doctor, you know that perfectly well, I can't, I can't, and you don't care at all, or else you care so much that you feign this horrid indifference that hurts me so much, Whitby, that hurts me so . . .

10

Conscious of the most obvious biological signs, I resigned myself to not having children. Her suffering was clear, but she refused to have any tests done. I urged her to see a doctor to have the problem diagnosed. We couldn't go on blaming each other. But her determination never to see a doctor was stronger than her frustration, pain, and unhappiness. That's a perfect example of the hermeticism of our marriage, which couldn't avoid what might be called intramural problems, even though all outside contacts—friendships, doctors, shopping, social calls, trips— were zealously avoided. On the other hand, we were capable of exploring, usually with good humor, such other possibilities as adoption (but the child would not be of our blood, Whitby, it has to be our blood) or artificial insemination of a surrogate mother (But what if she falls in love with the child and refuses to give it up to us? —We'll choose a poor woman, so if there's a dispute the court will award the child to us, since we can assure it a good future . . .).

—Children don't need money to have a good future.

—Constancia, you're your own worst enemy, you're the devil's advocate. You think like a gypsy! I laugh then.

—The Virgin was Blessed, she didn't have to fornicate to bear a child, the Holy Spirit passed through her sex like light through a crystal.

I kissed one of her ears and asked, laughing, if she would like that better than the way we did it. No, she answered, without hesitation, wrapping her arms around my neck and caressing it with her long fingers, proportionally the longest part of her body.

—Don't think about having children (typically, I resorted to a joke, just the sort that Mr. Plotnikov accused me of); think, rather, that Herod was probably right when he ordered all the male children of Israel to be killed.

At that she tore away from my embrace, screamed, ran to shut herself in her room to fast for an entire day, and then came out, contrite, but I am not inclined to cede my authority, much less my literary authority.

—All right. Where should I start to read your famous library?

—You can begin at the beginning, which is the Bible.

—Never. Only Protestants read that.

—And Catholics?

—Christ, we know it all! We know all about the Holy Virgin, and you, you know nothing about her.

—Very well, Constancia—I laughed then—very well said, my love. You see what heretics we are.

—Come on, Whitby, next thing you'll have me read the dictionary from A to Z, or something just as stupid.

—So what would you like to read?

—Maybe the stories of all the fallen women.

—You would never finish. And you would have to begin, again, with Eve.

—Then I want to read everything about a fallen child, a sorrowful boy.

That's how she started reading Kafka, and she threw herself into it, reading the books again and again, moving from biography to fiction and discovering, finally, that he had no better biography than his fiction, and so accepting Kafka on his own terms, as a man with no life other than literature. She said, half in jest (I think), that she would have liked her son to be like him, like that thin, sickly boy with the ears of a bat, who . . . who could have gone to work for the Spanish national railways.

—A child, please, even one who would be sad . . .

—Let's flee to Egypt, Constancia, so Herod can't kill him.

Then she ran to shut herself in her room and this August afternoon, taking her hand, I'm finally reconciled to this questioning: had Constancia died each time she fled from me and shut herself up for a full day in her bedroom, before coming out, renewed, radiant, to make up, play, and *improve* our love that would have died of pure perfection, of pure distance, of pure suspicion, of pure incomprehension (—*An old woman.* —*Ignorant.* —*Sterile*) if not for those incidents? Perhaps our arguments were more than just domestic tiffs; they were more like personal sacrifices made by my delicious Spanish woman on the altar of our domestic, solitary love in a ghostly city—the most ghostly— of the American South. Did Constancia die for me and did our love, so enduring, require nothing, here and now, but that death without end?

11

Constancia doesn't travel anywhere. We were married in Seville in 1946. I had to return to Atlanta to take my exams. She asked me to go ahead and get the house ready. She would follow me. She had to arrange her papers, say her farewells to family and friends in the four corners of the peninsula and gather the furniture she had left with aunts and cousins, and so forth. I found the house in Savannah and waited for her here, gazing out at the sea that would bring her to me: there was only one thing I could think of in the entire world, and that was the Andalusian girl, so fresh and graceful, so amorous and wild, who smelled of earth and balm and lily and verbena, who sunned herself in the plazas of Seville, as if throwing down a challenge to death, because Constancia, like the stars, was *enemy of the day*, and it was in bed, in the darkness—nocturnal or artificial—that her games flowed forth and her games drove me mad.

She arrived in Savannah in a freighter forty years ago and has not moved from this city since. The only thing she brought with her was the prie-dieu and the image of the Macarena, not a single other piece of furniture, not a photo, not a single book, although her trunk contained dark clothes and many religious pictures and prayers to the Virgin Mary. Now, late in her life, she reads

Kafka—her sick child, her sad child, as she calls him. She imagines trains that arrive on time but without passengers. Monsieur Plotnikov, on the other hand, never stops moving. It occurs to me that I have never seen him when he wasn't moving: hurrying out of an automatic photo booth; walking with an almost ethereal slowness along the red paths of the cemetery; looking nervously, as if in flight, at the shops in the commercial gallery of the Hyatt Regency, as if afraid; walking the neighborhood streets that link our houses: walking. Surely he was playing a role, as he said to me one day, before announcing his death to me. Or, indeed, he was playing too many roles; the world wanted him—he told me, or led me to understand, I can't remember—to be too many people. He was tired, he said before disappearing. I imagined his shoes, worn out from so much walking through the streets and galleries of Savannah, worn shoes covered with the dust of the cemetery.

I asked him once if he shouldn't resume his acting career in the United States, as so many exiles had done. Mr. Plotnikov was visibly taken aback. Hadn't I seen them on the videocassettes I rented to escape network programs and commercials? My neighbor didn't give me time to answer.

—Haven't you seen them, the greatest interpreters of Piscator in Berlin and of Meyerhold in Moscow, reduced to bit parts, playing waiters, hotel concierges, Russian shopkeepers, and kindly doctors? Gospodin Hull, I am talking about actors like Curt Bois, who electrified Germany in *The Last Emperor*, a staging by Piscator in which a gigantic shutter framed the action, so that it was possible to enlarge, reduce, or frame the action of the drama, a drama played in front of backdrops that the director had filmed especially, among them a storm on the high seas, a gigantic sea, waves breaking, flooding over the stage, the theater, and the actor, who was the key, the point of reference of this gigantic aperture of the theater to the world. Curt Bois, Alexander Granach, Albert Basserman, Vladimir Sokoloff—do these names mean anything to you, my dear Doctor? Well, they were the greatest, they reinvented acting in Europe. They had no right to play old men on a little screen between two beer commercials.

—They had the right to survive in exile.

—No, Gospodin Doctor. Their only right was to die, executed like Meyerhold or Babel, or in a concentration camp like Mandelstam, to commit suicide like Esenin and Mayakovsky, or to die of despair like Blok, or be silenced forever like Akhmatova.

—If they had waited, they would have been rehabilitated.

—A dead man cannot be rehabilitated. A dead man has to make do with the life that was once his. A dead man lives on the charity of memory. A dead man rehabilitates himself, Doctor, finding life where he can . . .

—Well, all right. He can find that life in an old film shown on television at 2 a.m.

—No, better to be seen no more than to be seen diminished. That's why I decided to give up acting and take up stage design, which is by definition essential but transitory. It is the comprehension of the moment, Gospodin Hull, as instantaneous as the lighting invented by Meyerhold, movable lights, now here, suddenly there, displacing the action, showing us how quickly the world can be changed, forcing us to give up a little of ourselves and submit to the diversity, the rapid changes, of the world; ah, to have worked with Meyerhold, Dr. Hull, a man whose superior intelligence put us all in touch with a better world; is that why they killed him? Tell me, you are a doctor, is that why they killed, censured, and drove the best to death? Because we knew how to achieve what they only proclaimed, because if we obtained it, they would no longer be able to promise it? How politics become exhausted, how the arts renew themselves, these are things they didn't know. Or perhaps they did know and they were afraid. That's why I wanted to give up acting and become a stage designer. I didn't want my heart or my voice to survive. I wanted my works to survive for a moment, Mr. Hull, and then disappear, leaving only *a memory*. But it doesn't matter. Someone said that being an actor is like sculpting in snow.

Relieved that Constancia was improving, and affected by the memory of my talks with the Russian actor, I collapsed in an easy chair in my living room and began to watch old films. When the library tires me, I relax by watching a nostalgic old film. No doubt, I was unconsciously influenced by thoughts of the Russian stage in selecting the cassette I put into the VCR. It was *Anna Karenina* with Vivien Leigh. Either I was careless or the machine didn't work properly, and the film began to run backwards. The first thing I saw was the word END, then a screen full of smoke, suddenly a train pulling into the station (on time, without passengers), then the actress reborn from the smoke and the wheels of the train, miraculously revived on the platform where her unforgettable, melancholic face, worldly but pure, like her wine-luminous eyes, said goodbye to the world, and Vivien Leigh portraying Anna Karenina ran quickly backwards. Fascinated, I pushed the pause button on the eternally frozen face of the dead actress. I was stunned by the power I held in my hands to keep life at a standstill, move it forward, return it to the beginning, to give these images a second-level life, an energy that, while it cannot restore Vivien Leigh, the forever dead magnolia, to life, can nonetheless restore these images of her sadness and her youth. I give life every time I push the button. Vivien Leigh is dead; Vivien Leigh lives. She lives and dies playing the role of a Russian woman of the past century. The film is an illustration of the novel. The novel lives each time that it is read. The novel has the past of its dead readers, the present of its living readers, and the future of its readers to come. But in the novel nobody interprets the role of Anna Karenina. When Anna Karenina dies in the Moscow rail station, the actress playing her doesn't die. The actress dies after she interprets the role. The interpretation of death survives the actress. The ice of the actor Plotnikov becomes the marble of the architect Plotnikov.

I remember my peripatetic conversations with Mr. Plotnikov, and I ask myself if he was right to prefer the theatrical container—stage design—to the contained—the action, the movement, the

words, the faces. Turning off the television set, tonight, I reject
my own thoughts, I tell myself that it's distinctions like the ones
I've just formulated—form, content; glass, water; dwelling, inhabitants; inn, guests—that destroyed my exiled neighbor and
his generation of artists. Better to save the cassette of *Anna
Karenina* for another, better occasion, I decide, reflecting on the
fact that what seems to be form if you look at it one way is content
if you look at it from a different perspective, and vice versa. I
admit that none of this really makes up for or reduces the pain
of the old actor's sad speech, one day, on the incongruous stage
of the commercial center by the Hyatt Regency:

—What harm did they do, Gospodin Hull? Whom did they
hurt, tell me? Never had there been such a constellation of talent!
What tremendous power for a country! To have at the same time
poets like Blok, Esenin, Mayakovsky, Mandelstam, and Akhmatova, to have filmmakers like Eisenstein, Pudovkin, Dovzh-
enko, and Dziga, my friend Dziga Vertov, Dziga Vertov, Dziga
Kaufmann, the *kinok*, Dr. Hull, mad about movies, so likable!
and novelists like Babel and Khlebnikov and Biely, and dram-
atists like Bulgakov, and my teachers, the creators of all the new
forms, my friend Rodchenko reinventing lighting, my friend Malevich exploring the limits of color, my friend Tatlin inviting us
to construct parallel forms of the world, not imitations of the
world, but new worlds accessible to everyone, unique and un-
repeatable, within that other world; all, Gospodin Hull, enriching
the world that contained them by offering new perspectives.
What harm did they do? How strong my country could have
been with all that talent! What madness caused them to be sacrificed? I died in time, my dear Doctor. Meyerhold was the
greatest genius of the theater. He was my teacher. He created
marvels, but did not go along with a theory he considered sterile,
the vile product of three factors: bureaucratic lack of imagination,
desire to make political theory coincide with artistic practice, and
fear that exceptions would weaken the institutions of power. Was
that a reason for arresting him, carrying him off to a Moscow

jail, and shooting him there, without a trial, on February 2, 1940, a date I will never forget, Dr. Hull? I ask you again: Was that a reason to kill Meyerhold, for not accepting a theory of art that would have prevented him from creating? Maybe so, maybe Meyerhold was more dangerous than he or his betrayers suspected. It's the only explanation, Gospodin Hull, why the slashed and mutilated woman, Meyerhold's lover, was found in the couple's apartment the day Meyerhold was arrested. Such cruelty, such sorrow. And such fear. A woman knifed to death only to augment her lover's pain.

He remained silent awhile, before saying to me, in the calmest voice in the world: Why, Dr. Hull, why, why so much pointless suffering? Your profession is to heal, perhaps you can tell me.

12

If Constancia had died a little after each of our conjugal quarrels, it was also true that she always recovered quickly and that our love had grown each time. We discussed how we didn't need to justify ourselves; we respected the reciprocal intimacy that the demand for justification would have violated. She always recovered.

But in every instance my wife's recovery took longer than before. September found the invalid still not out of bed. The situation was becoming difficult. I didn't dare, for all the reasons I've mentioned, to put her in a hospital. The perfectly mortal calm of a summer in Savannah only increased my indolence. After the first Monday of September, Labor Day in the United States (which, unlike the rest of the world, does not celebrate May 1, the day the workers were martyred in Chicago: in the United States there are no unhappy days, one doesn't celebrate death, one doesn't remember violence), a buzz of activity returned to the city and I felt my spirits stirring dangerously. I had to do something. My passivity, which may only have prolonged Constancia's illness, was beginning to tell on my own health.

To leave her alone would be an act of abandonment. That, at least, is how she would see it, and that's what her sorrowful and increasingly hollow eyes told me whenever I went out for a few minutes, perhaps half an hour, or went to the bathroom, or got something to eat, milk and cereal, toast with jam . . . The night I allowed myself the luxury of watching Julien Duvivier's *Anna Karenina* on television, I fell asleep for a moment and woke with a start to see Constancia's face superimposed on that of the British actress on the screen. I gave out a strangled cry. There was a crackling noise and the screen went black, but I was sure that Constancia was in the room, that she had come down from her bedroom, and that the face on the screen was her reflection, not my imagination playing tricks on me. I reached out for her in the darkness, afraid that she had fainted: Constancia hadn't spoken. I touched her. She withdrew from my touch when I reached out to her, but then she touched me, several times, in an unwanted manner, vulgar, forward even . . . She touched me, but I couldn't touch her; it was as if she could hear me without seeing me. I heard the soft sound of beating wings, and when the lights came on, I went up to the bedroom and found her kneeling before the full-skirted image of the Virgin. I came up behind her. I embraced her. I kissed her neck, her ears. Her eyes darted nervously, as if they had an alien life of their own . . . As I knelt beside her, my knees became covered with wood shavings.

Every day the newspaper and the milk arrived at my doorstep, the mail was delivered, nobody called me from Atlanta, everything went on as always, but our diet lacked fresh vegetables, we'd run out of toothpaste, the bar of soap was just a sliver.

She would sleep at unexpected times. Then, before falling asleep, she would say: —I am going to dream that . . . or, on waking, announced: —I dreamed that . . .

I wanted to surprise her in the act of saying: —I am dreaming that . . . to absent myself and make her believe that my absence was only part of her dream. Now I understood that dreaming, along with sex and religion (prayer and love), was Constancia's true literature; apart from that vast oneiric, erotic, and sacred novel which she dreamed herself, she needed only one story in her life, the story of that unfortunate son who, sorrow of sorrows, pity of pities, could wake up one morning metamorphosed into an insect.

—I am dreaming that . . . the insect begged for mercy, and nobody granted it, except me, I am the only one to come to him and . . .

That was my justification for leaving her; my cue for abandoning her, hearing her say *I am dreaming*; I would go downstairs to the vestibule, open the mahogany door, its beveled glass covered by a cotton shade, tiptoe over the wooden porch, cross Drayton Street to the corner of Wright Square, go up the stone steps of the house where Monsieur Plotnikov lived, trip over the bottles of milk piled up on the porch—curdled milk, yellowed, with greenish mold on the top—the newspapers, carelessly tossed, and though carefully folded into rubber bands, their big Cyrillic characters visible . . .

(I don't understand why milkmen insist on carrying out their job so inexorably, so mechanically, even though they can see that the milk already there is going bad. The person who delivers the newspapers—I've seen him—is a boy who goes by on a bicycle and expertly tosses the paper onto the porch. His careless haste is understandable, whereas the milkman is announcing to the world that the house is uninhabited. That anyone could go in and rob it. Milkmen are always accomplices: in adultery, in robbery.)

I touched the copper doorknob apprehensively. The door opened. Nobody had locked Mr. Plotnikov's house. I walked into a perfectly ordinary foyer, no different from ours: an umbrella stand, a mirror, the stairs to the second floor right by the door, inviting one to go up. It was a house in the so-called Federal style, symmetrical in design but secret in its details: an old window unexpectedly looking out over an impenetrable tropical garden of bamboo and ferns; a window protruding like a mysterious

island from the rest of the continent; the plaster eagles, escutcheons, victory banners, and military drums. And on each side of
the narrow vestibule, a salon, a dining room.

I went into the Russian's dining room, with its heavy furniture,
an ornate samovar set up in the center of a table with massive
legs and a white tablecloth; its dishes with popular Russian decorations, and the walls holding not the icons I had imagined
there but two paintings in that academic style that was equally
popular with Czarist nobility and Soviet commissars: one of the
paintings depicted the quintessential outdoor scene, a troika, a
family going out for a ride: excitement, overcoats, fur rugs, caps,
covers, the snowstorm, the steppe, birch trees, an endless horizon
. . . The other painting, all interior, showed a dim bedroom, a
bed in which a young woman lay dead. By her side, standing,
a doctor, his satchel on the floor, feeling for her pulse. The
composition called for her pale arm to be extended, for the doctor
to hold her long, thin hand. In a film (for example, *Anna Karenina*
with a different ending) the doctor would have shaken his head
sadly. Here, the dramatic commentary was provided by a ba-
bushka sitting in a wing chair in the foreground, consoling a
child in a nightgown who stares heavenward with angelic eyes
to the infinite that infuses the bedroom.

The room on the other side of the foyer was the reception
room and it was decorated in a conspicuously Spanish style.
There was a piano with a lace shawl tossed over it. The furniture
was Moorish and the painting, in the style of Romero de Torres,
showed bullfighters and gypsies, gold flowers and red satin capes.
On the shawl were a group of photographs in silver frames. I
didn't recognize their subjects; all the photos, I realized as I
looked at them, were from the period before the Spanish Civil
War. There were men in the uniforms of the Imperial Russian
Army, and others in uniforms of the Moroccan infantry. The
women, all dressed in white, belonged to a generation caught
between the virtues of the past century and the unavoidable (and
anticipated) sins of the new one; they resisted giving up their

bustles, cameos, and elaborate hairstyles, just as Monsieur Plotnikov clung to his old-fashioned clothing.

The dancers were the exception: there were two or three por-
traits of a spectacularly beautiful woman, all long legs, narrow
waist, filmy clothing, smooth arms, swan's neck, bright makeup,
dark gemstones in equally black hair cut short: her body arched
passionately and gracefully toward the ground, poised to give
life or to lose it: who knows. I couldn't identify Mr. Plotnikov
in these photos; who knows, who knows. There were no photos
of the man acting such and such a role. I understood the reason.
He wanted a complete life, not a fragmentary one, he had told
me. History wanted to divide it; he resisted. There would be no
photo of him in *Uncle Vanya* or *The Seagull* (was he blessed with
the self-critical humor necessary to play Konstantin Treplev?).

I heard an invisible wingbeat in the salon, as my attention was
drawn to a photo: Mr. Plotnikov standing, in almost the same
pose as the ballerina, but this time he was the one leaning—gray
hair, his youth gone—over Constancia, dressed in white, my wife
at fifteen or sixteen, radiant, holding a child in her lap, a child
whose features were difficult to make out, blurry, as if he had
moved just as the photo was being taken—but also blurry, I
suspected, because of his unformed youth: his age was impossible
to determine, but he seemed to be about a year or fifteen months
old.

The three of them, I thought to myself, all three of them, I
said over and over again, as I ran upstairs, just as Constancia
does when she is mad at me.

I say *ran*. It's not true. The deeper I penetrated into Monsieur
Plotnikov's nineteenth-century house, the more completely I was
gripped by torpor, an unaccustomed sluggishness that possessed
and divided my body and soul. My body seemed to go in one
direction and my soul in the other, a strange mood rose within
me as I climbed the stairs, as if the vapors given off by the two
rooms, the Russian dining room and the Spanish living room,
had united to create a thin but suffocating atmosphere, height-

ened by the constant noise, a sound of wings beating against the roof of the house. I climbed to a height greater than the distance from one floor to the other, I was aware that I was entering another region, another geographic zone, unexpectedly cool, with the air so thin that I was filled with a false euphoria, though I knew that this signaled the advent of something horrible.

13

I needed a rest. I informed my office and the hospital that I would be taking a long vacation. Nobody wanted to point out to me that I could have retired years ago; but I knew what they were thinking: a man like me, so reserved and unsociable, married to a woman no more outgoing, needed his work to feel alive. Retiring is almost redundant for a man like me. Besides, I'm still an excellent surgeon.

Those mornings, I examined myself in the mirror as I shaved, something that I had not done before; I had always shaved mechanically, without really looking at myself. Now I seemed to be seeing myself for the first time with a clarity brought about by my feeling of abandonment, a feeling that might be Constancia's way of punishing me for having dared to violate the secret of her friend, Mr. Plotnikov, her friend before I knew her, if the photo in the Spanish room could be believed.

I looked at the old man in the mirror who was finally seeing himself as others saw him. The old man was me.

How often we refuse to recognize the advent of old age, putting off what is not only inevitable but also obvious; with how many lies we reject what others can see perfectly well: these eyelids permanently sagging, the dry, bloodshot eyes, the thinning, graying hair that no longer can even feign a youthful virile balding, the involuntary rictus of disgust with oneself; what has become of me, my neck was never flabby, my cheeks were not covered with a web of veins, my nose didn't used to hang this way. Was I young once?

Was I once Dr. Whitby Hull, native of Atlanta, Georgia, student of medicine at Emory, soldier in the invasion of Sicily and the Italian boot, student at the University of Seville, on the G.I. Bill, husband of a Spanish woman, resident of Savannah on the shores of the Atlantic after my return, surgeon, man of letters, passionate man, secretive man, guilty man? Old man. A man surrounded by mysteries, things he can't understand, trying to see across the ocean to the other shore through a bathroom mirror that repeats its accusation: *Old man*; trying to look past the steam on the glass to the other side of the Atlantic, a razor in my hand.

Was I once a young Southern doctor doing postgraduate work in Seville? A young man, twenty-eight, with black hair, a strong jaw, tanned and toughened by the campaign in Italy, but revealing his background (his weakness, perhaps) by his baggy blue pinstripe seersucker suit, its pockets stretched out of shape by what I imagined a good American took to Europe in the postwar years: sweets, chocolates, cigarettes. I ended up eating them or smoking them myself. I never even managed to offer them to the Andalusians; the look on their faces stopped me.

As I shaved in front of my mirror, looking at an old face but picturing it young, I felt that I wanted to go back there. The key, if not to the mystery, at least to my life with Constancia, had to be there, in her native country, in the period after the war. A Southerner, a reader of Washington Irving and the *Tales of the Alhambra*, I decided to go to Andalusia. That's where I met Constancia, when she was twenty and I was twenty-nine or thirty. That's where we fell in love. What did she have when I met her? Nothing. She served tables in a café. She had no family. They had all died in the war, the wars. She lived alone. She tended her room. She went to Mass every day. Was it chance that I met her in the middle of the plaza of El Salvador, sitting with her face to the sun, sunning herself, legs stretched out in front of her on the hot paving stones—not looking up at me. Why did I feel so attracted to this unusual creature? Was she a symbol of Andalusian youth, this woman sitting in the street, facing the sun with her eyes shut, her open palms pressed against the hot ground of summer, inviting me with her closed eyes to sit beside her?

She lived alone. She tended her room. She went often to Mass. Nobody knew how to make love like her. She waited tables in a neighborhood café in Santa Cruz. But I already said that. She was my Andalusian Galatea, I was going to shape her; excitedly, I felt myself the agent of civilization, the bearer of spiritual values, which did not conflict with prosperity, with the practical dimension of things. I was so sure of myself, of my country, my tradition, my language, and therefore so sure I could transform this virtually unlettered girl, who spoke no English: I decided— with a nod to the ghost of Henry James—that Pygmalion would be an American for a change, bringing to life the European Galatea, plucked from the banks of the Guadalquivir in the oldest land of Europe: Andalusia, the Tartessus of the Greeks and the Phoenicians. Andalusia was pure because it was impure: a land conquered, ravaged. We returned together and I set up my practice in Atlanta and my house in Savannah. The rest you know.

Only now, flying first-class from Atlanta to Madrid, surrounded by the aseptic terror of airplanes, the universal scent of petrified air and inflammable plastic and food heated in a microwave oven, did I hazard a look down from my height of thirty thousand feet, first at the fleeting earth, then quickly at the eternal sea, and try to think, with some semblance of reason, about a scene that assailed me with memory's peculiar lucidity, the scene that was waiting for me when I reached Monsieur Plotnikov's second floor. A narrow window faced the street. The other walls were covered with a pale yellow paper, a thin silver thread running through it; light from the window revealed a single door (I pressed my feverish face against the cool window of the airplane): a single window at the end of the hall. I said thank you: they'd brought me a Bloody Mary I didn't ask for; I said thank you stupidly, removing my cheek from the window; I didn't have to choose, like saying I didn't have to suffer.

There was a single door, with the light shining on it (I looked at the pilots' door, which opened and closed incessantly, it wouldn't shut properly, it opened and closed over an infinite space), and I walked toward it. Suddenly I caught a glimpse (I closed my eyes, not wanting to see what the pilots see) of the strangeness of the life that Constancia and I had led together for forty years, an entirely normal life, completely predictable (as normal as going to the airport in Atlanta and boarding a jumbo jet to Madrid). The strangeness was precisely that, the normality of my practice and my operations, my skill with surgical instruments, and in compensation for my hours of work, the time I spent reading at home or, before I gave it up, playing tennis and squash with men I didn't know, who accepted me because I am what I appear to be.

I don't know whether it was stranger to be flying over the Atlantic on my way to Madrid, as if released from a long spell, or to be a Southern doctor of solitary habits, to have a wife who never goes anywhere with me, who, as you know, doesn't speak English, who is very Spanish, very Catholic, very reclusive—we don't have children, we don't see neighbors—but who gives herself to me completely and gratifies my vanity perfectly, a vanity not just male but American (I admitted it then, flying on the wings of our domestic technology)—taking care of a helpless person—and Southern (I told myself with the silent, hermetic eloquence distilled from a mixture of vodka and tomato juice)—having a household slave. (And the murmur from the wings of the plane resembles the murmur of the invisible wings in Plotnikov's funereal home.)

All these strange things were the regular features of my life, they didn't even begin to seem strange until that moment, when I was beginning to connect my presence in the cabin of a jet with the remembrance of my equally present presence on the landing of my neighbor's stairs this morning, slowly approaching the only door on the second floor of the house on Wright Square and pulling it open, having left my slave Constancia at home, my Andalusian slave, in exchange for . . . what?

In exchange for my life, because without Constancia I was dead.

14

I open the door in the silence.

I open the door to the silence.

It is so absolute a silence that, as I open the door, all the sound in the world seems suspended.

The wings cease beating.

Now there is no noise: nor will there be ever again, the gray emptiness seems to tell me—the luminously gray emptiness that receives me.

The floor of the bedroom is dirt. Black earth, silt, river mud.

In the center of the earthen floor stands a coffin, resting on a circle of red earth.

I know that it is a coffin because it is shaped like one, and is large enough to hold a human body, but its baroque construction reveals a rare level of woodworking skill; the box of worked wood is fashioned to pick up and reflect the pearly light of this region—every surface is cut, angled, opposed to another surface, the infinite surfaces shattering light as if to carry it to some mysterious dimension, the edge of the light of death itself, I don't know, a supreme point that contains and rejects everything, an awesome place, one that I can't begin to describe even today, flying thirty thousand feet over the Atlantic.

But one thing is recognizable, one thing is unmistakable: on the lid of the coffin is sculpted the same image one sees in the royal necropolises and cathedrals of Spain, the reclining figure of a woman, with the loveliest, the largest eyes, the saddest expression, her hands crossed over her breasts; she is dressed in cowl and mantle: popular iconography makes me see this as blue and white, but here all is worked wood and whitewashed walls, black earth and red earth. There are no icons; no full-skirted Virgins, or crucifixes, nothing: only my feet covered with red earth, which I stare at stupidly.

I come to. I try to raise the lid of the coffin. I can't do it. I run my avid fingers over the decorations covering that horrible monument, feeling, without wanting to, the woman's feet, her shoulders, her icy features, the sides of the coffin, the wood carved in facets that break up the very light, and each facet contain a single name, carved in the wood, a Russian name, and I have heard all the names before, in the litany Mr. Plotnikov recited as he followed the red earth paths of the cemetery, names that I am finally beginning to place, names of dead men, executed, driven to suicide, imprisoned, silenced, in the name of what? For what? A powerful sense of hopelessness overwhelms me as I read the names carved on that coffin: MANDELSTAM ESENIN MA-YAKOVSKY KHLEBNIKOV BULGAKOV EISENSTEIN MEYERHOLD BLOK MALEVICH TATLIN RODCHENKO BIELY BABEL, in exile, sur-viving, dead or alive, I don't know: I only know that this con-dition of suffering, which seems so normal, such an essential part of life, as normal as going to the cemetery to read the names of our forebears, becomes upsetting when we see it on the marble wall of the Vietnam war memorial or at the entrance to Ausch-witz; but this thought is driven from me by the discovery of a small lock, a tiny hole waiting for the key to open the lid of the coffin in the house of Mr. Plotnikov: in the keyhole's shape I recognize the echo of a form I have seen every day of my life, at least of my life with Constancia, Constancia and her sick dream: her hairpins shaped like little keys, the keys I put in the pocket of my jacket the night Constancia died in my arms, that I pulled out of her hair to keep them from getting lost when she fell, when I carried her to her bed, her hair streaming behind her.

The hairpin shaped like a key fits perfectly in the lock. There is a creaking sound. The lid, with its sculpted figure of a reclining woman, carved in silver, shifts slightly. I get to my feet. I raise the lid. Monsieur Plotnikov, for once dressed completely in white, lies inside the wooden tomb. He holds the skeleton of a child no more than two years old.

I quickly shut the lid and leave the place, feeling the full weight

of my sixty-nine years in my knees, my shoulders, the tips of my
shoes reddened by another earth, not mine, not ours; I want to
be back at Constancia's bedside, even though I know, in the
saddest, the most secret part of my heart, that Constancia, my
beloved Constancia, my companion, my own sensual, pious Spaniard, my wife, will not be there when I return. Monsieur Plotnikov's warning was like a painful throbbing in my head.

—Gospodin Hull, you will only come to visit me the day of
your own death, to let me know, as I have done today on mine.
That is my condition. Remember, our well-being depends on it.

Without Constancia, I was dead.

15

Two, then three days passed and she still hadn't returned home.
I didn't want to go back to Mr. Plotnikov's house. I was afraid
of finding Constancia in the arms of the old Russian, holding the
skeleton of the boy (or girl): it was an image I couldn't bear:
another mystery, not a rational solution to one. I didn't want
another mystery. I knew that any explanation would only be
converted, in its turn, into an enigma. Like the obsessive names
of the Russian artists of Plotnikov's generation. The enigma reveals another enigma. In this, art and death resemble each other.

I looked at myself in the mirror: I accused myself: I had abandoned Constancia; I had visited Mr. Plotnikov—violated his
tomb, defied his prophecy, since it was not the day he had told
me to visit him, the day of my own death. I was still alive, despite
Constancia's disappearance, still able to study my lathered face
in the bathroom mirror. I—I wrote my name on the mirror with
shaving cream, *Whitby Hull*—am not dead; neither the death of
my old neighbor nor my forbidden visit to his singular tomb nor
the flight of Constancia had killed me. So what would my punishment be? When, where would it strike? Now I watched the
blacks of Savannah from my window; I had never been particularly conscious of them before. There they were, the visible

manifestation of my sins; they were not where they should have been, on the other side of the ocean, on another continent, in their pagan land, and the fault was mine. I searched in vain for the faces of the two blacks who had approached Constancia in the park that day, who spoke to her, touched her, seemed to fight over her. I searched in vain for the face of my youth in the bathroom mirror or in the scratched window of the airplane.

I am returning as an old man to the place I visited as a youth; perhaps I should have waited, let things run their course, rather than trying to force a solution. I shrug off the question. Whatever I find, it can hardly be more peculiar than the way I have lived my life, reducing all my odd, private, socially unacceptable habits to normality, without even realizing it.

I shrug again. Americans can't bear a mystery, not even someone else's, much less one's own; we need to do something—inactivity kills us—and what I was doing was to visit the city archives of Seville, to find out about Constancia, to verify what I already knew: our marriage record is on file there, I carry a copy of it with me, and I know it by heart: on one side there is information about me—my date of birth, the names of my parents, my profession, my place of residence—and on the other side, information about Constancia Bautista, a single woman, about twenty, parents unknown, thought to be a native of Seville.

But now I went to the clerk's office in Seville to look at the original on file, and when the record book was set down in front of me, I made a discovery: my half of the form was the same as my copy, but Constancia's was not.

I found that while my record was still there, the record of the woman I had undoubtedly married on August 15, 1946, had disappeared. Now my name, my birthdate, my genealogy appeared alone on the form, orphaned, just as Constancia had always been orphaned. Facing my completed column was a blank one.

I was gripped by an inner despair that didn't show in my motor abilities or my exterior demeanor—it was a private feeling of dismay that could be remedied only through more action; my way of reacting complementing Constancia's, my constancy complementing hers (I couldn't help smiling a little—I had started to say *theirs*, instead of *hers*; without intending to, I thought of *them*, the three of them). I opposed action to inaction and it made me feel both righteous and guilty, righteous for accomplishing something, guilty for not leaving things in peace. If the marriage certificate I had carried with me for forty years was false and the original record in the clerk's office of Seville was the true record, who had made the criminal alteration? Again, who else could it have been, it must have been her—or, indeed, *them*. Against whom were my enemies conspiring? For God's sake, why was I being played with this way? My confusion kept me from seeing the facts: nobody had changed the record; the original on file in the clerk's office in Seville was blank; my copy of Constancia's record had simply been filled in. I slammed the register shut and thanked the clerk, who had helped me without noticing a thing.

I'm not a man who can simply accept mystery. Everything must have an explanation, says the scientist in me; everything must have an inspiration, says the frustrated humanist that I am. My only consolation is that I believe the two attitudes complement rather than exclude each other. Seville is a city of archives. I resolved to follow the faintest lead, like a bloodhound, to examine every scrap of paper (like a bloodhound; yet I was uneasy, I had a constant sensation that the air was stirring over my head, as if a bird of prey were hovering there).

Ah, the world was in such turmoil, the young Sevillian archivist was telling me, we're just now beginning to put together the records—there were so many people killed, he sighed, guiding me through the maze of boxes covered with peeling labels, in the pale light of the high church windows, all I know is that so many were bombed, murdered. Come back tomorrow.

I was in a hurry. It was the same old story, and I had already spent too much time in Seville. There's an old saying: See Naples

and die. I would change it to Seville, but with this variation: See
Seville and never escape from it. There was something urging
me on, telling me to find out whatever I could, until I had learned
what I wanted to know. The young archivist—who was very
proud of his job, and claimed to be eager to help a visitor, a
foreigner, an American—showed me some papers that had been
sealed, and told me I needed to talk to a certain solicitor, who
would have to provide the authorization to open them. I made
no attempt to hide my irritation at this bureaucratic complication.
The clerk turned off the charm and adopted an official tone, an
extremely cool manner. —I have already gone way out of my
way for you. Go see the lawyer tomorrow. The matter is entirely
in his hands.

Which I did. The lawyer raised some trivial objections and
said the same things as the young clerk: —It's so long ago! But
I believe, Dr. Hull, that the best way to heal the wound is to
talk about how it was made. Not everyone agrees with me: some
people think that if we don't mention the horror, it will not come
back to haunt us.

I looked across at him, sitting in his office with its gray walls
and its high ceiling crisscrossed by the sort of light you see in a
convent or an old courtroom, likewise high and gray; he had one
of those mustaches that only the Spanish know how to cultivate:
two thin grayish lines that met precisely above his upper lip, like
two trains approaching each other head-on. I thought of Constancia and her fantastic story: the trains arrive on time, but no
one is aboard. The official had a dog lying at his feet, a huge
mastiff, pure gray, which he kept reaching out to, rubbing the
back of its head or offering it something to eat—I couldn't tell
what—from his half-open hand.

The official looked at me sadly, an hidalgo more interested in
his own honor than in someone else's. At least, he was good
enough to be specific:

—The people you are interested in, Dr. Hull, came to Spain
from Russia in 1929, to escape the political situation there, and

then tried to get out of Spain in 1939, to go to America, to flee
from our war. Unfortunately, they were detained at the port of
Cádiz; Nationalist forces took one look at their Russian passports
and decided they had certain political sympathies. The three
people—the man, his wife, and the sixteen-month-old child—
were murdered in the street by the forces I just mentioned. It
was one of the ironies of war.

—They were killed—I repeated stupidly.

—Yes. Forty-nine years ago—said the official, aware that we
were both saying the obvious. He shook his head—he seemed
to be an intelligent man—and added: —It makes me think of
my own family, Dr. Hull. There was no justice to it, the innocent
were struck down, the guilty spared.

—Do you at least know where they were buried?

The lawyer shook his head. The war was so terrible; when
you think that in Badajoz alone, two thousand innocent people
were killed, herded into the bullring and executed. I saw so many
senseless murders, Dr. Hull, the gunshot wound between the
eyes, that was the signature of certain groups. Do you know the
story of the death of Walter Benjamin, the German writer? He
was stuck at the French border and his death there was a mistake
caused by bureaucratic apathy and terror. That is the most tragic
thing of all, Dr. Hull, the number of lives cut short accidentally,
by errors, by . . .

He stopped short; he didn't want to be found guilty of in-
dulging in personal feelings or personal anecdotes.

—The only reason we know what happened to the couple and
their child is that the party that won kept their identity cards.
That's why I'm able to give you any information. You must see
the irony in their story, I repeat. Just imagine: the family you
are interested in had arranged to have their belongings, their
trunks and furniture, shipped to America. And all those things
made the journey—they left this ancient land of Andalusia, Doctor, and traveled to the new land of America. Here are the documents. Their belongings arrived, but without their owners. I

am truly sorry to have to tell you this, it's such a sad story . . .
and such an old one.

—It doesn't matter—I said. —I'm grateful to you. You've been
a big help.

He waved away my thanks and stood up. —Dr. Hull, so many
people tried to get out in time, to escape, to go to America . . .
Some made it, others didn't . . . He shrugged. —Too bad your
friends did not make it. I'm sincerely sorry.

He was shivering, as if he felt cold, and I noticed that the
purebred dog shivered along with its master.

—Fortunately, times have changed, and we are at your service.

—Where was the furniture shipped to? I broke in to ask.
—Pardon me? —The family's furniture. Where do the documents
say that . . . ? —The port of Savannah, Doctor.

16

I have to know. I cannot rest. I scrutinize all the signs. I wander
the streets of Seville. I go back to all the places we had been
together. The café where she worked, waiting tables. The plaza
where I first met her, sitting on the pavement, sunning herself,
her bare legs stretched out in front of her. The house in the Calle
de Pajaritos where she had a room and where we made love for
the first time. The Church of San Salvador, where she went so
often. I did not meet her again, as I secretly hoped I would.
There was new life now in all those places. In the patio of Constancia's house an older woman was walking among the orange
trees, dressed in an old-fashioned wedding gown. She did not
turn to look at me. In the church Constancia went to, another
woman discovered a sparrow's nest in a dark corner and cried
out in surprise. And in the café where Constancia used to work,
a barefoot gypsy began to dance, they insulted her, she insisted
she had a right to dance, they told her to leave, and the young
woman walked past me, grazing against me, giving me a sad
look, and all the while the waiters dressed in coarse white shirts

and black bow ties that made them look like pigeons were throwing her out of the café, she kept screaming at them in her peculiar accent: they had no right to persecute her, they ought to let her dance a little more, they should show compassion, and she said it again in her shrill, plaintive voice, they should show some compassion, compassion, just show a little . . .

I sat down to drink a cup of coffee that autumnal afternoon at the busy corner of Gallegos and Jovellanos, where it meets the bustle of the Calle de Sierpes. She ran into me there; she didn't recognize me. How could she recognize me in the gray-haired old man who bore no resemblance to that American boy, his pockets stuffed with cigarettes and caramels? I still wore the American summer uniform, a lightweight, absorbent seersucker suit with thin blue stripes on a pale blue background, but now the pockets were empty. I would like to emulate the elegance of the Spanish official with his dog, his coolness, his precise mustache, but I am hot, I shave every morning, and I keep no pets; she never wanted animals in the house. I am sixty-nine years old and my head is full of questions that have no answers, that are nothing but loose ends. If Plotnikov died in 1939, how could he know that his mentor, Meyerhold, was killed in 1940 while in solitary confinement in a Moscow prison? How old was Constancia when she married him, if that is what happened, and when she had his son, if the skeleton that I saw was their child and that child was the one whose picture was on the piano with the mantilla? Who was Constancia, daughter, mother, wife, refugee? I had to add, child-mother, child-wife, child-fugitive? The girl I met at twenty aged normally while we lived together. Perhaps before she met me her youth had a different rhythm; perhaps I gave her what we call "normality"; perhaps now she had lost it again, returned to that other temporal rhythm that I knew nothing about. I don't know. The pockets of my summer suit are empty, my eyebrows are white, at six in the afternoon my beard is full of gray bristles.

17

I returned to the United States weighed down by more than sadness, by an ever-growing pain. The Spanish lawyer's reference to Walter Benjamin had led me to the Vértice bookstore in Seville, where I bought a volume of his essays. The illustration on the frontispiece excited my interest: a reproduction of *Angelus Novus*, a painting by Paul Klee. Now, as the plane flew over the Atlantic, I read Walter Benjamin's description of the angel in Klee's painting, and I was filled with emotion, with wonder.

"His face is turned toward the past. Where we perceive a chain of events, he sees one single catastrophe which keeps piling wreckage upon wreckage and hurls it in front of his feet. The angel would like to stay, awaken the dead, and make whole what has been smashed. But a storm is blowing from Paradise; it has got caught in his wings with such violence that the angel can no longer close them. This storm irresistibly propels him into the future to which his back is turned, while the pile of debris before him grows skyward. This storm is what we call progress."

I read those lines in a Jumbo 747 flying from Madrid to Atlanta and I tried to imagine the death of the man who wrote them. On September 26, 1940, a wretched group arrived at the border post of Port Bou, the entrance to Spain from a France that had fallen to the Nazis. The group consisted of people seeking asylum. Among them was a nearsighted man with the wild hair and mustache of a Groucho Marx. He had escaped on foot, over the mountains and through vineyards planted in red earth. And all through that journey the nearsighted man didn't let go of the black suitcase that held his final manuscripts. He kept one hand free to hold on to the thick, metal-framed glasses that rode on his long, thin nose. The refugees presented their documents in Port Bou to Franco's chief of police, who rejected them: Spain did not admit refugees of unknown nationality. He told them:

—Go back where you came from. If you don't leave by tomorrow, we'll hand you over to the German authorities.

The man with the glasses, blinded more by his distress than by the heat, clung to his black suitcase and looked down at his shoes, which were covered with red dirt. His manuscripts mustn't fall into the hands of the Gestapo. He had three companions, three women who stood near him and wept in despair, Jews (like him), part of a group that had fled from Germany, from a Central Europe devoured by indifference and denial and the utopias of the powerful. As he gazed toward the Mediterranean, Walter Benjamin thought of the Atlantic, which he had planned to cross to America; perhaps the Mediterranean became for him a symbol of a past reduced to ruins that can never be restored to their original state. The first homeland, the heart that cradled the dawn. He wanted to hurl himself toward the Atlantic that I, the American Whitby Hull, am now crossing on wings that are frozen but free, reminding me of the immobile wings of the Angel Benjamin, who saw history accumulate its ruins and was still able to realize his final vision: the ruin reveals the truth because it is what endures; the ruin is history's permanence.

Flying back over the Atlantic, I stop trying so hard to reconstruct chronologies, to tie up all the loose ends and solve all the mysteries. Have I learned nothing, then? We are surrounded by enigmas, and what little we understand rationally is merely the exception in an enigmatic world. Reason astonishes us; and to be astonished—to *marvel*—is like floating in the vast sea surrounding the island of logic—so I tell myself, sitting thirty thousand feet in the air. I remember Vivien Leigh in *Anna Karenina*; I remember the stage setting for Piscator's *The Last Emperor* in Berlin, which my neighbor, the actor, described to me, and I understand why art is the most precise (and precious) symbol of life. Art presents an enigma, but the resolution of the enigma is another enigma.

I'll go further. What has been taking place in the sea surrounding my rational island is the rule, not the exception: people causing other people to suffer. Happiness and success are as rare as logic; the most basic human experience is defeat and despair. We Americans cannot remain untouched by that fact. We cannot. The destiny of Walter Benjamin or of Vsevelod Meyerhold is not exceptional. Mine—protected, reasonably happy—and that of my neighbors, is.

Perhaps that is why they joined me. I let a loud laugh escape, breaking a silence greater than the sound from the wings of the new technological angel: they saw me so well, so healthy, that they attached themselves to me so as to go on living forty-one years after their deaths, the dead child cared for by the father, who drew life from the mother, who was taking her life from me, from me . . . and now, I considered a tentative explanation, the father had reached his end, and she has gone to rejoin her family, to care for them . . . tentative, I said. What new mystery surrounds this temporary solution?

While I fly over the Atlantic, I make the greatest effort of my entire life, and I try to imagine Walter Benjamin contemplating the ruins of the Mediterranean; I'm given a package of peanuts, a Bloody Mary, a perfumed napkin to freshen up with, a hot napkin, which I put over my face to keep the stewardess from constantly bothering me, and I think of something else, not a ruin but an endless stream, a gray river, flowing from the Old World to the New, a current of emigrants, fleeing persecution, seeking refuge, and among them I make out a man, a woman, and a child I think I recognize, for an instant, before I lose sight of them, swallowed up in the flood of refugees: the flight from Palestine into Egypt, the flight of the Jews from Spain to the ghettos of the Baltic, the flight from Russia to Germany to Spain to America, the Jews driven into Palestine, the Palestinians driven out of Israel, perpetual flight, a polyphony of pain, a Babel of weeping, endless, endless weeping: these were the voices, the songs of the ruins, the grand chorale of asylum, to escape death in the bonfire of Seville, the tundra of Murmansk, the ovens of

Bergen-Belsen . . . this was the great ghostly flow of history itself, which the angel saw as a single catastrophe.

—Here are your earphones, sir. Classical music on Channel 2, jazz on 3, comedy on 4, Latin music on 5, the movie soundtrack in English on 10 and in Spanish, if you prefer, on 11 . . .

I plug in the headset and flip around the dial. I stop at a grim voice that is saying, in German:

"His face is turned toward the past . . . He sees one single catastrophe . . . A storm is blowing from Paradise . . ."

I open my eyes. I look at the wings of the plane. The clouds are perfectly still below us. I turn my head and look behind me. There I see the little man with the thick glasses, the mustache, the shoes covered with red dust, the black suitcase full of manuscripts, gazing toward the sea of our origins from the land that expelled the Jews in 1492, the same year America was discovered, the land I am returning to, alone; and on the channel I have selected I hear a voice I recognize from my reading, a voice from the letters written by the Jews expelled from Spain, and also the voice of Constancia, my lover; and, borne on high by a silver angel, unfeeling and blind to both the past and the future, I desperately want Walter Benjamin to hear this voice, the words of my lost wife, to hear it as he takes the fatal dose of morphine and falls asleep forever, history's orphan, progress's refugee, sorrow's fugitive, in a tiny room in a hotel in Port Bou:

> *Seal me with your eyes.*
> *Take me wherever you are . . .*
> *Shield me with your eyes.*
> *Take me as a relic . . .*
> *Take me as a toy, a brick from the house . . .*

When Walter Benjamin was found dead in his room on September 26, 1940, his flight was ended. But his papers disappeared. As did his body: nobody knows where he is buried. But the Franco authorities felt threatened by the incident, so much so that they allowed the three Jewish women who wept by the bed of the writer, who was also Jewish, to enter Spain.

18

How many more managed to escape death? I imagine people would do anything to save themselves, even commit suicide. Anything to reach the other shore. Pardon me, Constancia, for having waited so long to bring you to America . . . I said it over and over, trying to sleep (despite the stewardesses' offerings); but whenever I shut my eyes, I saw a series of images of brutal death, flight, of the will-to-live morbidly prolonged.

Those were my nightmares. One thought rescued me from them, the thought that, when all was said and done, I still had my home to return to, a haven, and that my trip to Spain had been a thorough exorcism. I thought of Constancia and was grateful to her; perhaps she had assumed all the sins of the world so that I would not have to suffer for them. At least, that's what I wanted to think. I wanted to be sure that when I got back to my house she wouldn't be there, and I swore, as I saw the coast of North America approaching, that I would never again visit the house on Wright Square, that I would never succumb to a desire to find out who rested there. My peace of mind depended on that.

It was already the end of autumn when I returned to Savannah, but a mild Indian summer still lingered in the South, touching everything with a soft glow very different from the colors of the images that filled my mind: blood, powder, and silver; gilded icons, gypsy Virgins, metal wings, red shoes, black suitcases.

Waiting for me was the maze of Savannah, Seville's warring twin, both labyrinthine cities, repositories of the paradoxes and enigmas of two worlds—one called New, the other Old. Which was really the older, I asked myself, as a taxi took me home, which is the newer, and the synthesis of the images that tormented me was a fleeting voice that seemed to speak to me from the sea, between the two worlds:

> *Seal me with your eyes*
> *Take me wherever you are . . .*

When the taxi stopped in front of my house I took a deep breath, got out my key, and deliberately turned my back on the house on the corner of Drayton Street and Wright Square. Out of the corner of my eye I saw the accumulation—inexplicable— of papers and milk bottles in front of the mud-splattered door of Monsieur Plotnikov's house.

My porch, by contrast, was empty, not a single bottle or paper. My heart skipped a beat: Constancia had returned, she was wait- ing for me . . . I just had to open the door. I must have given the door a push as I put the key in the lock (I couldn't help thinking of Constancia's hairpin), because it seemed to open by itself, and at once all my nightmares came flooding back. But I could no longer think of Constancia alone. *They* were waiting for me here, inviting me to join them. Never again Constancia by herself:

—Visit me, Gospodin Hull, on the day of your own death. That is my condition, our well-being depends on it.

In that instant I accepted the fact that this—the day of my homecoming—would be the day of my death. I was overcome by vertigo, I realized that all the spirits (what else can I call them?) that haunt this story were granted just one thing, a grace period, a few more days of life: in Port Bou, in Moscow, in Seville, in Savannah: why should I be any different? All I needed was the humility to kneel on the shore of the Mediterranean or the Atlantic, and pray: Please, one more day of life. Please . . .

It took a terrible noise to bring me back to reality; a noise that had to be dishes crashing, glass breaking, confusion . . . I ran into the house, leaving my suitcase outside. The noise came from the cellar. Constancia, again I thought of Constancia: it was all a nightmare, my love, you have come back, we are together again, it was nothing but a series of coincidences, delusions, misconceptions, Constancia . . . the only enduring thing is our love. You want us to be together again.

I ran down the wooden stairs to the cellar. It smelled of smoke, scalded milk, sawdust, and something spicy. I shaded my eyes with my open hand, covered my nose with a handkerchief. They were crouching there, huddled together, their arms around each other, surrounded by the piles of newspaper accumulated during the month I had been away.

The man—dark, young, mustached, with coarse, wild hair and eyes like a raccoon's, innocent and suspicious at the same time, wearing a blue shirt and blue pants and old boots—held a doe-eyed woman, her hair pulled back in a bun, her belly swollen, her dress loose, expecting a second child, for she is already holding one, a fifteen- or twenty-month-old, a dark, cheerful child whose big white smile shone out despite the dark terror of his parents.

Señor, please don't turn us in.

Señor, we saw this empty house, nobody was going in or out.

Señor, for the love of God, don't report us, don't send us back to El Salvador, they've killed everyone else, we're the only ones left, we three were the only ones who managed to cross the Lempa River.

Señor, all the rest were murdered, if you had seen how the bullets rained down on the river that night, lights, planes, gunshots, so that not a single one of our people would be left alive, not a single witness who could raise his voice, would escape the massacre.

Señor, but we were saved by a miracle, we are the only ones who were spared, so that our child could be born, and we hope someday to go back, but until then we have to live, to bear our children, before we can return, now we cannot live in our country.

Señor, do not turn us in, look, all these weeks we've been here I haven't been idle.

Señor, look here, right here, I found your woodworking tools,

I was a carpenter in my village, I have been repairing things in your house, there are many chairs with broken legs, many tables that oh! that creaked like coffins.

Señor, I fixed them all, look, I even made you a new table and four new chairs, the way we used to make them back home, so nice, I hope you like them.

Señor, look, my wife and the little one haven't drunk your milk for nothing, I haven't eaten your bread without giving you anything for it.

Señor, if you knew. They would kill you just as a warning, that's what they said, nobody knew when they would come to kill us, they killed children, they killed women, and old people too, they didn't spare a soul, only we escaped: don't make us go back, for the love of God, by what is dearest to you, save us.

Señor . . .

I don't know why I hesitated, discomposed and irresolute, thinking confusedly that I was no more than a mediator between all these stories, a point between one sorrow and another, between one hope and the next, between two languages, two memories, two ages, and two deaths, and if for a moment this minor role—my role as an intermediary—had upset me, now it no longer did, now I accepted and welcomed it, I was honored to be the intermediary between realities that I could not comprehend, much less control, but which appeared before me and said to me: You owe us nothing, except that you are still alive, and you cannot abandon us to exile, death, and oblivion. Give us a little more life, even if you call it memory, what does it matter to you?

I saw the refugee couple with their child and I wanted to tell them about Constancia, but that wasn't important now, it no longer mattered to me that I had been used in that way. I am glad that every day you were able to take a little more life for yourself and that you were able to cross the street and go up the stairs to Mr. Plotnikov. I only regret that we were unable to save the child. Or perhaps he was already dead when he got here,

one small box among the larger ones containing pianos and furniture and coffins, the boxes you sent from Spain, before they
killed you . . . As I stand next to the Salvadoran couple and their
child, I picture the overhanging windows of the port of Cádiz,
the old women hiding behind the curtains, secretly watching the
ships departing for America, bearing the sailors, the fugitives,
the dead. I see the glass-enclosed balcony in Cádiz, one bloody
afternoon when the wind from the Levant is bending the bare
trunks and thick branches of the pines, as a ship departs carrying
the furniture, the shawls, the photographs, the paintings and
icons of a Russian family, departs with a dead man and child
hiding among their possessions, which arrived in Savannah and
were moved into the house across the way during the night,
while a girl lies among the shriveled sunflowers of the end of
summer and the Levantine breeze ruffles her black hair, as the
voice of the father, lover, husband, son, tells her, Stay here, be
reborn here, let us die, but you must go on living, Constancia,
in our name, don't let yourself be vanquished, don't let yourself
be destroyed by the violence of history, you must live, Constancia,
you mustn't yield to exile, you must stem the tide of fugitives,
at least save yourself, dear daughter, mother, sister, don't let
yourself be pulled under by the current of exile, you at least
remain, grow, be a sign: *they survived here.* Protect us with your
memory, seal us with your eyes . . . Now, looking at the new
refugees from a country near my own, I remember the conversations I used to have with Monsieur Plotnikov and I see Constancia slain among dead sunflowers and quiet tidal flats at the
gates of Cádiz, and she is answering, Take me wherever you are,
take me as a relic from the mansion of sorrow, take me as a toy,
a brick from the house . . . Imploring.

   I imagine, I can only imagine; I do not know anything, even
though I have felt the pain of separation, being far from the one
I love, have felt it deeply, to the point of tears. But now I can
only imagine them—Constancia, Plotnikov, the dead child—because I finally see them as part of something greater, something

I had not understood before. How long, Constancia, did you give life—my life—to your dead? It doesn't matter. I am living now. Perhaps you didn't die in Cádiz near the end of the Civil War— ah, said the young Sevillian clerk, the world was in such turmoil, we are just beginning to reconstruct the facts, there were so many killed, so many survivors, too, so many resurrections, so many who were officially dead who were really only in hiding— you may have been waiting patiently, for me or someone like me to come and take you to America, to be near what really mattered to you: the two of them, who were already here.

How long, Constancia, did you give life—my life—to your dead? It doesn't matter. I am alive now. You are where you wanted to be. Comfort your dead. Hold fast to them.

As I hesitated, I thought about these things before doing what I had to do, which was to walk toward them slowly, approach them slowly, go toward the man, the woman, the child, sur- rounded by their poor bundles and my old newspapers, the saw- dust on the floor, the hammer and saw, the sawhorses, the images of the Virgin tacked up on the wall: my house, lived in forever, lived in again.

19

Every night, the lights of Mr. Plotnikov's house come on. I stubbornly ignore them. The brightness comes in my windows and reflects off the gilded spines of my books. I try to close my eyes. But the summons is perpetual: they call to me. Later the lights go out.

And I will go to rejoin Constancia only on the day of my own death. The old actor warned me: Come to visit me, Gospodin Hull, on the day of your death. We are waiting. Our well-being depends on it. Never forget!

Now I devote myself to the family that asked me for asylum, I reach out to them and hold them tight, don't worry, stay here, we will do woodworking together, it's something for an old man to do, a retired surgeon, I have some skill with my hands. Stay here, but take these pencils, some paper, pens; if they come for you, remember that these things cannot be confiscated, so you can communicate with me if they put you in jail, so you can demand legal aid; pencils, paper, pens: carry them with you always. What else can you do? Ceramics? Ah, the soil here is good for that, we'll buy a potter's wheel, you can teach me, we'll make plates, vases, flowerpots (for lemon balm, verbena . . .), my hands will not be idle, pottery makes use of the senses, my hands need to feel, don't worry, stay here, don't go yet, hold on to me, there are still so many things we have to do.

Trinity College
Cambridge
July 6, 1987

La Desdichada

To the friends of the Sabbath table,
Max Aub, Joaquín Diez-Canedo, Jaime García Terrés,
Bernardo Giner de los Ríos, Jorge González Durán,
Hugo Latorre Cabal, José Luis Martínez, Abel Quezada,
and, above all, to José Alvarado,
who made me understand this story

Toño

. . . In those years we studied at the National Preparatory School, where Orozco and Rivera had painted their frescoes, and we went to a Chinese café on the corner of San Ildefonso and República Argentina, we dipped sweet rolls in café au lait and discussed the books that we bought in the Porrúa Brothers Bookstore when we had the money or in the used bookstores on República de Cuba when we didn't: we wanted to be writers, they wanted us to be lawyers and politicians; we were just a couple of self-taught guys who had been delivered onto the imagination of a city that, high though it was, gave you the secret sensation of being buried, even though it was then still the color of marble and burnt-out volcano and was filled with the ringing of silver bells and smelled of pineapple and coriander, and the air was so . . .

Bernardo

Today I saw La Desdichada for the first time. Toño and I have taken a small apartment together, the local equivalent of the garret in Parisian bohemia, in the Calle de Tacuba near the San Ildefonso school. The good thing is, it's a commercial street. We didn't like going out to shop, but two single students have to take care of themselves without letting on that they could use a mother figure. So we alternated domestic duties. We were from the provinces and we had no women—mothers, sisters, girl-friends, nurses—to take care of us. Not even a maid.

Tacuba was an elegant street during the viceroyalty. Today the most hideous commercialism has taken hold of it. I come from Guadalajara, a city still unspoiled, so I notice it. Toño is from industrialized Monterrey, and that makes everything here seem romantically beautiful and pure to him, even though there isn't a ground floor on this street that hasn't been taken over by a furniture shop, a mortuary, or a tailor's. You have to look higher up—I say to Toño, his introspective eyes shielded by eyebrows thick as beetles—to visualize the nobility of this street, its serene proportions, its façades of soft red stone, its escutcheons of white stone inscribed with the names of vanished families, its niches acting as a refuge for saints and pigeons. Toño smiled and called *me* a romantic, for expecting beauty, even goodness, to descend from spiritual heights. I'm a secular Christian who has substituted Art with a capital *A* for god with a lowercase *g*. Toño said that poetry is to be found in the shoe-store windows. I looked at him reproachfully. Who in those days hadn't read Neruda and repeated his credo of the poetry of the immediate, the streets of the city, the specters in the windows? I prefer to look up at the ironwork balconies and their peeling shutters.

The window I was distractedly looking at closed suddenly, and when I lowered my eyes they were reflected in a store window. My eyes, like a body apart from me—my Lazarus, my drudge—dove into the water of the glass and, swimming there, discovered what the window hid: what it displayed. It was a woman in a bridal gown. But whereas other mannequins in this street—which Toño and I walked through every day, hardly noticing it, accustomed by now to the plurally ugly and the singularly lovely of our city—were made forgettable by their struggle to be fashionably up-to-date, this woman caught my eye because her dress was old-fashioned, buttoned clear to the throat.

It was a style from a long time ago, nobody recalls the way women dressed then. They will all be old tomorrow. But not La Desdichada: the sumptuousness of her wedding gown was everlasting, the train of her dress splendidly elegant. The veil that covered her features revealed the perfection of her pale face, softened by gauze. In her flat satin slippers she appeared proud and proper. Elegant and obedient. An incongruous silver lizard ran out from beneath her motionless skirt, scooting away in trembling zigzags. It was looking for a sunny spot in the display window, and there it stopped, like a satisfied tourist.

Toño

I came to see the dummy in the wedding dress because Bernardo insisted. He said it was a rare sight, in the midst of what he called the crowded vulgarity of Tacuba. He was looking for an oasis in the city. I had long since renounced such things. If one wanted rural backwaters in Mexico, there are more than enough in Michoacán or Veracruz. The city must be what it is, cement, gasoline, and artificial light. I didn't expect to find Bernardo's bride in a window, and so it turned out: I didn't find her, and I wasn't a bit disappointed.

Our apartment is very small, just a sitting room where Bernardo sleeps and a loft that I go up to at night. In the sitting room there's a cot that serves as a sofa by day. In the loft is a bed with metal posts and a canopy, which my mother gave me. The kitchen and the bath are one and the same room, at the back of the flat, behind a bead curtain, like in South Sea movies. (Two or three times a month we went to the Cine Iris: we saw Somerset Maugham's *Rain* with Joan Crawford and *China Seas* with Jean Harlow—the sources of certain images we share.) When Bernardo talked about the dummy in the window on Tacuba, I got an odd feeling that what he wanted was to bring home La Desdichada, as he christened her (and I, letting myself be influenced by him, also started calling her that, before I saw her, before I even had proof of her existence).

He wanted to decorate our poor home a little.

Bernardo was reading and translating Nerval back then. He was busy with a sequence of images in the poem *El Desdichado*: a widower, a heavenly lute, a dead star, a burnt tower; the black sun of melancholy. As he read and translated during our moments of student freedom (long nights, rare sunrises), he told me that in the same way that a constellation of stars shapes itself into the image of a scorpion or a water carrier, so a cluster of syllables tries to form a word and the word (he says) painstakingly seeks its related words (friendly or enemy words) to form an image.

The image travels through the entire world to embrace and make peace with its sister image, so long lost or estranged. This, he says, is the birth of metaphor.

I remember him at nineteen, thin and frail, with the compact body of a noble Mexican, delicate, Creole, the child of centuries of physical slightness, but with a strong, solid head like that of a lion, a mane of black wavy hair, and unforgettable eyes: blue enough to rival the sky, vulnerable as a newborn baby's, powerful as a Spanish kick in the depths of the most silent ocean. Yes, the head of a lion on the body of a hind: a mythological beast, indeed: the adolescent poet, the artist being born.

I saw him as he couldn't see himself, so I could read the plea in his eyes. Nerval's poem is, literally, the air of a statue. Not the air around it, but the statue itself, the air of the voice that recites the poem. When he asked me to go see the mannequin, I knew that actually he was asking me:

—Toño, give me a statue. We can't buy a real one. Maybe the dress-shop mannequin will strike your fancy. You won't have any trouble picking out the one: she's dressed as a bride. You can't miss her. She has the saddest look in the world. As if something terrible happened to her, a long time ago.

At first I couldn't find her among all the naked mannequins. None of the dummies in the window was wearing clothes. I said to myself, this is the day that they change their outfits. Like living bodies, a dummy without clothes loses its personality. It is a piece of flesh, I mean, of wood. Women with painted faces and marcelled waves, men with painted mustaches and long sideburns. Fixed eyes, colored eyelashes, cheeks like candy glazes, faces like screens. Below those faces with their eyes forever open are bodies of wood, varnished, uniform, lacking a sex, lacking hair, lacking navels. Though they didn't drip blood, they were exactly like chunks of meat in a butcher's shop. Yes, they were pieces of flesh.

Then, looking more closely, I examined the window my friend had indicated. Only one of the women had real hair, not painted on wood, but a black wig, a little matted down but high and old-fashioned, with curls. That, I decided, was she. And besides, her eyes could not have been sadder.

Bernardo

When Toño entered with La Desdichada in his arms, I couldn't bring myself to thank him. That woman of wood embraced the body of my friend the way they say the Christ of Velázquez hangs from his cross: much too comfortably. Toño, who is a typical man of the north, tall and strong, could easily hold her with one arm. La Desdichada's backside rested on one of Toño's hands; his other hand was around her waist. Her legs hung down and her head was on his shoulders, her eyes open, her hair disheveled.

He entered with his trophy and I wanted to show him I wasn't angry, just vexed. Who had asked him to bring her home? I had asked him only to go look at her in the window.

—Put her wherever you like.

He stood her up, her back to us, as if to demonstrate that she was our statue now, our Venus Callipygia of the shapely ass. Statues rest on their feet, like trees (like horses that sleep on their feet?). She looked indecent. A naked mannequin.

—We have to get her some clothes.

Toño

The store on Tacuba Street had already sold the bride's gown. Bernardo didn't want to believe me. What did you expect, I said to him, that the dummy would wait for us forever in that display window, dressed as a bride? The purpose of a mannequin is to display clothes to passersby, so that they buy them—the clothes, mind you, not the mannequins. It was pure chance that she was dressed as a bride when you walked by. She might have been showing off a bathing suit for a month without your noticing. Besides, nobody cares about the dummy. What they're interested in is the outfit, and it has already been sold. The dummy is wood, nobody wants her, look, it's what in law classes they call a fungible object, one's as good as another, it's all the same . . . Besides, look, she's missing a finger, the ring finger of her left hand. If she was married, she isn't anymore.

He wanted to see her dressed as a bride again, and if he couldn't, at least he wanted to see her dressed. La Desdichada's nudity bothered him (it also attracted him). Nonetheless, I set her at the head of our humble table, the sort you'd expect of students of "limited resources," as one said euphemistically in Mexico City in the year 1936.

I gave her a sideways glance, and then I threw over her a Chinese robe that an uncle of mine, an old pederast from Monterrey, had given me when I was fifteen, with these premonitory words: —Some clothes anyone can wear. All of us girls want to look cute.

Covered by a blaze of paralyzed dragons—gold, scarlet, and black—La Desdichada half-closed her eyes, lowering her eyelids a fraction of a centimeter. I looked at Bernardo. He wasn't looking at her, now that she was dressed again.

Bernardo

What I like best about this poor forsaken place where we live is the patio. Every neighborhood in the capital has a place to wash clothes, but our own house has a fountain. You leave behind the noises of Tacuba Street, go past a tobacco and soft-drink stand, and enter a narrow alleyway, damp and shady, and then the world bursts into sunlight and geraniums, and in the center of the patio is the fountain. The noise remains very far away. A liquid silence imposes itself.

I don't know why, but the women of our house all choose to wash their clothes somewhere else, in other washing places, in the public fountains perhaps, or in the canals that are the last remnants of the lake city that was Mexico. Now the waters are drying up little by little, condemning us to death by dust. There is a constant come-and-go of laundry baskets, piled high with dirty clothes and clean clothes, which the strongest but least agile women clutch tightly, and the most atavistic carry proudly on their heads.

The large circles of woven straw, the clothes colored indigo, white, and brown: it is easy to bump against a woman holding a basket on her head so she can't really turn to look, knock over the basket, excuse yourself, extract a blouse, a shirt, whatever, pardon me, pardon me . . .

I loved the patio of our student home so much, its soothing mediation between the noise of the street and the isolation of the apartment. I loved it as years later I would love the supreme palace: the Alhambra, a palace of water where the water, naturally, has disguised itself as tile. Back then, I hadn't yet been in the Alhambra, but in my fond memories our poor patio possesses the same charms. Except that in the Alhambra there is not a single fountain that dries up from one day to the next, revealing at its bottom sluggish gray tadpoles looking up for the first time at the people who gaze into the fountain and see them there, doomed, without water.

Toño

He asked me why she was missing a finger. I told him I didn't know. He wouldn't let the subject drop, as if I were responsible for La Desdichada's being maimed, through some carelessness of mine in carrying her home, Christ, he just stopped short of accusing me of mutilating her on purpose.

—Be more careful with her, please.

Bernardo

The toads that have taken over the beautiful fountain in the patio won't be without water for long. A big storm is approaching. When you go up the stone stairs to our apartment, you look out over the low, flat roofs toward the mountains, which, in the summer light, seem to move closer. The giants of the valley of Mexico—volcanoes of basalt and fire—are accompanied in this season by a watery retinue. It's as if they had awakened from the long sleep of the highlands, as though from a parched and crystalline dream, demanding a drink. The giants are thirsty and they make their own rain. The clouds that all through the sunlit morning have been accumulating, white and spongy, suddenly stop moving, their grave grayness become turbulent. Each afternoon, the summer sky swells with storm, punctual, abundant, fleeting, and attacks the accumulated light of the dying day and the morning that succeeds it.

It rains the whole afternoon. Falling from the apartment to the patio. Why doesn't the fountain fill with water? Why do the dry, wrinkled toads, under the stone moldings of the old colonial fountain, look at me with such anguish?

Toño

Today these are ghostly spaces: deserts born of our haste. I resolve not to forget them. Bernardo will know what I mean if I say that the city's vacant lots were once our pleasure palaces. To forget them is to forget what we had: a little happiness, one time, when we were young and deserved it and didn't know what to do with it.

He laughs at me; he says that mine is the poetry of the lower depths. Fine: but someone should recall the aroma, poetic or not, of the Waikiki on the Paseo de la Reforma, near the Caballito, the nightclub of our youth. Inside, the Waikiki was the color of smoke, although outside it looked more like a cancerous palm tree, or a sickly stretch of sand turning gray in the rain. Never has a place of entertainment looked gloomier, more forbidding. Even its neon signs were repellent, square, you remember? Everything about them established a precise hierarchy of attractions: the singer (male or female) at the head of the marquee, then the band, then a pair of dancers, finally the magician, the clown, the dogs. It was like a list of political candidates, or a menu for an embassy dinner, or even a death notice: here lies a singer, a band, two ballroom dancers, a magician . . .

The women were like the place, like the color of smoke inside the cabaret. They were the reason we went there. The closed society denied us love. We believed that, having left our fiancées at home, those maidens whom we couldn't seduce physically without ruining them for marriage, we could come to the capital to study law and meet—as in the novels of Balzac or Octave Feuillet—an experienced lover, rich, married, who would introduce us to the ranks of the wealthy and powerful, in exchange for our virile services. *Hélas*, as Rastignac would say, the Mexican Revolution did not extend to sexual liberty. The city was so small then that everybody knew everybody else; groups of friends were exclusive, and if within one of the groups some member made love to another, not even the crumbs of that banquet reached us.

We thought of our provincial fiancées, preserved like apricots, maintained in a state of purity behind the iron grilles on their windows, barely within the range of a serenade, and we wondered if our identity as provincials only put us in an even more sordid position in the capital: either we got ourselves a virginal fiancée or we went to dance with the tarts of the Guay. They were almost all small, powdered, with the blackest eyes and the cheapest perfume, flat-chested, without hips, with skinny legs and shapeless asses. They had thick lips and limp hair, sometimes bullied into place with clips; they wore short skirts, mesh stockings, kiss-me-quicks smeared on their cheeks like question marks, their every other tooth was gold, their every other pore was marked with smallpox; their heels tapped the dance floor, the tapping of their heels resounded as they went out to dance and returned to their tables, and between those heelbeats you heard the sound of their feet dragging, in the slow steps of the *danzón*.

What were we looking for, if these cheap hetaeras were so ugly? Only sex, which wasn't so great either?

We were looking for a dance. That's what they knew: not how to dress, or speak, not even how to make love. Those jokers of the Guay knew how to dance the slow *danzón*. That was their trick: to do the *danzón*, that ceremony of slowness. They say the best dancers of the *danzón* can dance in a space the size of a postage stamp. Second prize goes to the couple who can dance in a space the size of a single tile. Two bodies glued together, their movement almost imperceptible. Clothed bodies, flesh palpitating but almost still, the reflection of a dream as much as of a dance.

Who would have thought that those beaten-down girls possessed the genius of the *danzón*, responding as they did to the flute and the violin, the piano and the maraca?

Those hot little tamales from the venereal barrios of a city where nobody even used toilet paper or sanitary napkins—a city of dirty handkerchiefs before Kleenex and Kotex, just think, Bernardo, this city where the poor clean themselves with corn husks—what poor, biting poetry would their tragically restrained feelings produce? Because something else came from their world of rural misery, transferred from the destroyed haciendas to the city, the fear of making noise, of bothering the rich and being punished by them.

The nightclub was their answer. The music of the bolero allowed those women, rescued from the fields and exploited again in the city, to express their most intimate feelings, vulgar but concealed; only when dancing were these enslaved bodies given the luxury of immobile movement: these women had the scandalous elegance of the servant who dares to sit down, that is, who asks to be noticed.

Bah, let's go to the Waikiki, I said to Bernardo, let's go sleep with a couple of whores, what else is there to do? If you want, you can pretend you spent the night with Marguerite Gauthier or Delphine de Nucingen, but let's go steal what we need for La Desdichada's dowry. We can't have her dressed in a robe all day. It's indecent. What will our friends say?

Toño and Bernardo

—How would you prefer to die?

Bernardo

My mother was a widow of the revolution. Popular iconography is full of images of the woman warrior who accompanied the fighters into battle. You can see them riding on the trains, or around the campfires. But the widows who didn't leave their homes were another matter. Like my mother: serious and resigned women, dressed in black ever since they received the fateful message: Your husband, madam, fell with honor on the field of Torreón or La Bufa or Santa Rosa. Perhaps that is what it means to be the widow of a hero. But you might think it would be different to be the widow of the victim of a political murder. Really? Aren't all fallen soldiers the victims of a political crime? And isn't every death a murder? It took us a long time to accept the notion that the dead person was not murdered, before we ascribed the death to the will of God.

My father died with Carranza. That is, when the First Chief of the Revolution was murdered in Tlaxcalantongo, my father, who was his friend, was killed in one of the many acts of revenge against the supporters of the president. An undeclared war that took place not on the fields of military honor but in the back rooms of political terror. My mother remained loyal. She laid out my father's uniform on his bed. His tunic with rows of silver buttons. His kepi with two stars. His riding pants and his heavy belt with its empty holster. His boots at the foot of the bed. This was her perpetual domestic *Te Deum*.

There she passed the hours, in the orange-colored light of votive lamps, brushing the dust from his uniform, polishing his boots. As if the glory and the requiem of one faded battle would stay with her forever. As if this ceremony of mourning and love guaranteed that her husband (my father) would someday return.

I think of all this because, between us, Toño and I have gotten together a wardrobe for La Desdichada, and we've spread it out on display on the four-poster bed. A white linen blouse (from the washerwomen of the patio) and a short black satin skirt (from the tarts of the Waikiki). Black stockings (courtesy of a little trifle named Miss Nothing-at-All, says Toño, laughing). But, for some reason, we couldn't get shoes. And Toño maintains that La Desdichada doesn't really need underwear. This made me doubt his Don Juanesque tale. Perhaps he didn't get as far as I thought with the Waikiki girl. I, on the other hand, only aver that if we intend to treat La Desdichada with respect, we musn't deprive her of panties and bra, at the least.

—So where are we going to get them from, man? I've done my part. You haven't exactly put yourself out.

She is sitting at the table, wrapped in the Chinese robe from my faggot uncle. She doesn't move her eyes, of course—she has her gaze fixed, fixed on Toño.

To escape that annoying look, I quickly take her by the arm, pick her up, and say to Toño that we have to put some makeup on her, dress her, make her comfortable, poor Desdichada! to see her always so distant and solitary—I force a laugh—a little attention wouldn't hurt her, or a little fresh air.

I open the window overlooking the patio, leaving the dummy in Toño's arms. There is no respite from the sound of the frogs croaking. The storm builds over the mountains. I am oppressed by the small noises of my city, which seem all the more piercing in the lull before the storm. Today the knife sharpeners sound sinister to my ears, the used-clothes venders even worse.

I turn back, and for a moment can't find La Desdichada: I don't see her where I left her, where she should be, where I had set her at the table. A cry escapes me: "What have you done with her?" Toño appears alone, parting the beads of the bath curtain. He has a long scratch on his face.

—Nothing. I cut myself. She's coming right away.

Bernardo and Toño

Why were we afraid?

Why were we afraid to invent a life for her? The least a writer can do is give a person a destiny. It wouldn't have cost us anything; we wouldn't have had to account to anyone. Were we incapable of giving La Desdichada her destiny? Why? Did we really feel she was so dispossessed? Was it impossible to imagine her country, her family, her past? What was stopping us?

We can make her a housekeeper. She'll keep the apartment clean. Run our errands. We would have more time to read and write, to see friends. Or we can make her a prostitute. That would help pay our household expenses. We'd have more time to read and write. To see friends and feel like big shots. We laugh. Do you think anyone would be interested in her as a whore? It would challenge the imagination, Bernardo. Like fucking a Siren: how?

We laughed.

A mother?

What did you say?

She could be a mother. Neither servant nor whore. Mother, give her a child, let her devote herself to taking care of her child.

How?

We laughed even harder.

Toño

Today was La Desdichada's dinner party. The dummy was still dressed in the Chinese robe from my uncle the fruit. Nothing suited her better, Bernardo and I decided; not only that, but it was her name on the invitations, so, like a high-class courtesan or an eccentric Englishwoman in her castle, she could entertain in her dressing gown: Cast aside convention!

La Desdichada is receiving. From eight to eleven. Punctuality

required. She is never late, we inform our friends: British punctuality, eh? And we sat down to wait for them, one on each side
of her, I on her left, Bernardo on her right.

It occurred to me that a party would clear away the little cloud
in our relations that I noted yesterday, when I cut myself shaving
while she was watching me, sitting on the toilet, her legs crossed.
Seated there, totally insouciant, one knee over the other. What
a flirt! The toilet was just the most convenient place to sit her
down to watch me shave. She made me a little nervous, that's
all.

I didn't explain this to Bernardo. I know him too well, and
maybe I shouldn't have taken the mannequin into the bathroom
with me. I'm sorry, really, and would like to ask his pardon
without giving any explanation. I can't; he wouldn't understand,
he likes to verbalize everything, starting with his feelings. The
fact is that when he turned his back to the window and looked
for us, without finding us, I took a quick look into the living
room and saw him looking at nothing. I thought for a moment
that we only see what we desire. I had a fleeting sense of terror.

I wanted to clear away the misunderstanding with a little joke,
and he was agreeable. That's another thing we had in common:
the taste for a type of humor that, although we didn't know it
at the time, was in vogue in Europe and was associated with the
games of Dada. Of course, Mexican Surrealism didn't need the
European imprimatur; we are Surrealists by vocation, by birth,
as all the jokes we have inflicted on Christianity prove, confound-
ing the sacrifices of blood and host, disguising whores as virgins,
constantly moving between the stable and the brothel, creation
and calendar, myth and history, the past and the future, the circle
and the line, the mask and the face, the crown of thorns and the
crown of feathers, the mother and the virgin, death and laughter:
for five centuries, Bernardo and I tell ourselves with stern humor,
we've been playing charades with the most exquisite corpse of
all, Our Lord Jesus Christ, with our vessels of bloodstained glass,
why shouldn't we do the same with the poor cadaver of wood,
La Desdichada? Why should we be afraid?

She would be the hostess. La Desdichada is receiving guests, and she will receive them in her robe, like a grand French courtesan, like a geisha, like a great English lady in her castle, taking advantage of her privilege of eccentricity to act freely.

Bernardo

Who sent these dried flowers an hour before dinner?
Who could it be?

Toño

Not many people came to the dinner. Well, fine, not many people would *fit* in our apartment, but Bernardo and I felt that a huge party with lots of people, the kind that's usually given in Mexico (there are so many solitudes to overcome: more than in other places), might give the event an orgiastic tone. Secretly, I would have liked to have seen La Desdichada lost in a restless, even a mean crowd: I nourished the fantasy that, surrounded by a mass of indifferent bodies, hers would cease to be so: moved about, handled, passed from hand to hand, a party animal, she would go on being a mannequin but nobody would know: she would be just like everyone else.

Everyone would greet her, ask her name, what she did, wish her well, and quickly move on to chat with the next person, convinced that she had replied to his questions, how spiritual, how clever!

—My name is La Desdichada. I am a professional model. I'm not paid for my work.

The fact is, only three men accepted our invitation. You had to be *curious* to accept an invitation like ours on Monday night, at the beginning of the school week. It didn't surprise us that two of our guests were fellows from aristocratic families whose fortunes had been reduced in those years of tumult and confusion. Nothing lasts longer than half a century in Mexico, except the poor and the priests. Bernardo's family, which was very influ-

ential when the Liberals were in power back in the nineteenth
century, does not have an ounce of influence today, and the
families of Ventura del Castillo and Arturo Ogarrio, who obtained their power under the Porfirio Díaz dictatorship, had now
lost theirs as well. The violent history of Mexico is a great leveler.
The person who's on top one day shows up the next, not on the
heights, but in the flats: the mid-level middle-class plateau composed mainly of the impoverished remnants of short-lived aris-
tocracies. Ventura del Castillo, self-proclaimed "new poor," was
more afraid of being middle-class than he was of being poor. The
way he escaped was by being eccentric. He was the school clown,
something his appearance helped him in. At twenty, he was fat
and prim, with a tuft of hair over his lip, red cheeks, and the
eyes of a lovesick sheep behind a ubiquitous monocle. His role-
playing allowed him to rise above the humiliating aspects of his
social decline; his exaggerated style, instead of making him a
laughingstock at school, earned him a startled respect; he rejected
the melodrama of the fallen family; with less justification he accepted the idea, still in vogue, of the "fallen woman," and, no
doubt, when he walked into our apartment, that's what he
thought Bernardo and I were exhibiting: a cheap Nana, taken
from one of the red-light nightclubs that everyone, aristocrat or
not, then frequented. Ventura had his commentary ready and
the presence of La Desdichada gave him license to say:

—Melodrama is simply comedy without humor.

Our friend was not disturbed by La Desdichada's appearance,
wrapped in her Chinese dressing gown, her unchanging painted
face giving her a rather Orozcoan look (Expressionist, we called
it then), but it carried his innate sense of the grotesque to new
heights. Wherever he went, Ventura became the festive center
of attention, eating his monocle at dinner. Everyone suspected
that his eyeglass was made of gelatin; when he swallowed it, he
made such an outrageous noise that everyone ended up laughing,
repelled and pained, until the wag ended his joke by rinsing his
mouth with beer and eating, as a sort of dessert, the flower
eternally in his buttonhole—a daisy, no less.

For all that, the encounter between Ventura del Castillo and La Desdichada resulted in a sort of unexpected standoff: we were confronting him with someone who was vastly more eccentric than he was. He looked at her and asked us with his eyes, Is she a dummy, or is she a splendid actress? Is she La Duse with an expressionless face? Bernardo and I looked at each other. We didn't know if Ventura was going to see us, and not La Desdichada, as the eccentrics of the affair, challenging our fat friend's supremacy.

—Such rakes you chaps are! laughed the lad, who affected the verbal mannerisms of Madrid.

—She's a paralytic for sure!

Arturo Ogarrio, by contrast, wasn't as lighthearted about his family's decline. Having to study with the masses at San Ildefonso Prep annoyed him; he never resigned himself to losing his chance to enroll at Sandhurst in England, as two preceding generations of his family had done. His bitterness showed in his face. He saw everything that took place in this world of "reality" with a kind of poisonous clarity.

—What we left behind was a fantasy—he told me once, as if I were the cause of the Mexican Revolution and he—noblesse oblige—had to thank me for opening his eyes.

Severely dressed, all in dark gray, with a waistcoat, stiff collar, and black tie, bearing the grief of a lost time, Arturo Ogarrio had no trouble seeing what was going on: it was a gag, a wooden dummy presiding over a dinner of prep students where a pair of friends with literary inclinations were throwing down the gauntlet to the imagination of Arturo Ogarrio, new citizen of the republic of reality.

—Are you going to join our game? Yes or no?

His face was extremely pale, thin, without lips, but with the brilliant eyes of the frustrated aesthete, frustrated because he identified art with leisure, and since he didn't have the one, he couldn't conceive of having the other. He refused to be a dilettante; perhaps that is all we offered him: a breach of quotidian reality, an unimportant aesthetic diversion. He was almost con-

temptuous of us. I considered that something I could interpret
as his refusal of concessions, like his rejection of dilettantism. He
would not take sides—reality or fantasy. He would judge matters
on their own merits and respond to the initiatives of the others.
He crossed his arms and watched us with a severe smile.

The third guest, Teófilo Sánchez, was the school's professional
bohemian: poet and painter, singer of traditional melodies. He
must have seen old engravings or recent films, or simply have
heard somewhere that the painter wears a floppy hat and a cape,
and the poet long hair and florid neckwear. To be different,
Teófilo chose to wear a railroad engineer's shirt without a tie,
and a short jacket, and he went about with his head uncovered
(in that age of the obligatory hat, his head appeared offensively
naked, it was practically shaved, in a cut that at that time was
associated with German schools or the lowest class of army re-
cruits). His careless features, resembling a loaf of rye before it's
put in the oven, his lively raisin eyes, the spontaneous abundance
of his poetic language, seemed a commentary on Ventura's remark, which I had rewarded with a sour smile a moment before:
Melodrama is comedy without humor.

Was that remark directed at me, since I was still writing little
chronicles of the *fait-divers* of the capital and the minor poetry,
unquestionably vulgar, of the popular dance hall, the tart, and
the pimp, the couples of the barrio, jealousy and betrayal, abandoned gardens and sleepless nights? Don't overlook the classical
statues in the gardens and the forgotten idols in the basements,
Bernardo commented very seriously. Ventura laughed at Teófilo
because Teófilo wanted to provoke laughter. Arturo saw Teófilo
as what Teófilo was and would be: a youthful curiosity, but a
disappointment as an older man.

What was the bard of bohemia going to do, once we each sat
down with our cuba libres, but improvise some awful verses on
the subject of our lady, sitting there wordlessly? We saw Arturo's
grimace of disdain and Ventura took advantage of Teófilo's sigh
to laugh good-naturedly and say that this *donna immobile* would

be the best Tancredo at a bullfight. Too bad that woman, inventor of the art of bullfighting in Crete (who continued to delight circus audiences as *écuyère*), is not able to play the central role in the modern bullring. The man who plays the Tancredo—the fat, rosy-cheeked Ventura began his imitation, first licking his rosebud lips and then anointing a finger with saliva and dramatically running it over his eyebrows—is put in the center of the ring—so—and doesn't budge for anything—so—because his life depends on it. His future movement depends on his present immobility—he stood stock-still in front of La Desdichada—as the gate opens—so—and the bull—so—is released and seeks movement, the bull is attracted by the movement of the other, and there is Tancredo, unmoving, and the bull doesn't know what to do, he awaits a movement, an excuse to ape and attack it: Ventura del Castillo motionless before La Desdichada, who is sitting between Bernardo and me, Arturo standing, watching what is going on with the most correct cynicism, Teófilo confused, his words starting to burst out, his inspiration starting to perish: his hands in front of him, his pose and his speech suspended by Ventura's frozen act, the perfect Tancredo, rigid in the center of the ring, defying the fierce bull of the imagination.

Our friend had been converted into the mirror image of the wooden dummy. Bernardo was sitting on La Desdichada's right and I on the mannequin's left. Silence, immobility.

Then we heard a sigh and we all turned to look at her. Her head fell to the side, onto my shoulder. Bernardo stood up trembling, he looked at her huddled there, resting on my shoulder—so—and took her by the shoulders—so—so—and shook her, I didn't know what to do, Teófilo babbled something, and Ventura was true to his game. The bull was attacking and he, how could he move? It would be suicide, caramba!

I defended La Desdichada, I told Bernardo to calm down.

—You're hurting her, you prick!

Arturo Ogarrio let his arms drop and said: Let's go, I think we are intruding on the private lives of these people.

—Good night, madam, he said to La Desdichada, who was being held up with one arm supported by Bernardo, the other by me. —Thank you for your exquisite hospitality. I hope to repay it one of these days.

Toño and Bernardo

How would you prefer to die? Do you see yourself crucified? Tell me if you would like to die like Him. Would you dare? Would you ask for a death like His?

Bernardo

I watched La Desdichada for hours, taking advantage of the heavy sleep Toño fell into after dinner.

She had returned, still in her Chinese dressing gown, to her place at the head of the table; I studied her in silence.

Her sculptor had given her a face of classic features, a straight nose and nicely spaced eyes, not as round as those of most mannequins of the time, who looked like caricatures, especially since they were usually given fan-shaped eyelashes. The black eyes of La Desdichada, on the other hand, were melancholy: the lengthened lids, like a lizard's, gave her that quality. In contrast, the mannequin's mouth, tiny, tight, and painted to look like a ribbon, could be that of any store-window dummy. Her chin, again, was different, a little prognathous, like that of a Spanish princess. She also had a long neck, perfect for those old garments that buttoned to the ear, as the poet López Velarde wrote. La Desdichada had, in fact, a neck for all ages: childish nakedness, then silk mufflers, finally pearl chokers.

I say "her sculptor," knowing that this face is neither artistic nor human because it is a mold, repeated a thousand times and distributed in shops all over the world. They say that store mannequins are the same in Mexico and Japan, in black Africa and the Arab world. The model is Occidental and everyone accepts it. Nobody had seen, in 1936, a Chinese or black mannequin. While they always stay within the classic mold, there are differences: some mannequins laugh and others don't. La Desdichada does not smile; her wooden face is an enigma. But that is only because I am disposed to see it that way, I admit. I see what I want to see and I want to see it because I am reading and translating a poem by Gérard de Nerval in which grief and joy are like fugitive statues, words whose perfection is in the immobility of the statue and the awareness that such paralysis is ultimately also its imperfection: its undoing. La Desdichada is not perfect: she lacks a finger and I don't know if it was cut off purposely or if it was an accident. Mannequins do not move, but are moved rather carelessly.

Bernardo and Toño

He throws me a challenge: Do you dare take her out on the street, on your arm? Take her to dine at Sanborns, how about that? Test your social status, let them see you in a theater, a church, a reception, with La Desdichada at your side, mute, her gaze fixed, without even a smile, what would they say of you? Expose yourself to ridicule for her. I wouldn't count on it, friend: you wouldn't do anything of the sort. You only want to keep her here at home, for you alone if possible (do you think that I don't know how to read your glances, your looks of violent impotence?); otherwise, the three of us together. Whereas I will take her out. I'll take her out for a stroll. You'll see. As soon as she recovers from your abuse, I'll show her off everywhere, she is so alive, I mean, she seems alive, just look, our friends were almost fooled, they greeted her, they said goodbye to her. Is it only a game? Then let the game continue, because if enough people play it, it will cease to be one, and then, then maybe everyone will see her as a living woman, and then, then, what if the miracle occurs and she really comes to life? Let me give that chance to this . . . to our woman, that's right, *our* woman. I'm going to give her that chance. I think then she can be mine alone. What if she comes to life and says: I prefer you, because you had faith in me, and not the other, you took me out and he was embarrassed, you took me to a party and he was afraid of being laughed at.

Toño

She whispered in my ear, in a rasping tone: How would you like to die? Do you see yourself with a crown of thorns? Don't cover your ears. Do you long to possess me and are you unable to think of a death that will make me adore you? Then I will tell you what I will do with you, Toño, tony Toño!

Bernardo

La Desdichada had a very bad night. She groaned dreadfully. I had to watch her closely.

Toño

I see my face in the mirror, on waking. It is scratched. I rush to look at her. We spent the night together, I explored her minutely, like a real lover. I didn't leave a centimeter of her body unexamined. But when I saw my own wound I went back for another look, to discover what I saw last night and then forgot. La Desdichada has two invisible furrows in her painted cheeks. No tears flow over these hidden wounds, repaired rather carelessly by the mannequin maker. But something flowed down that surface once.

Bernardo

I remembered that I didn't ask him to buy her or bring her here, I only asked him to look at her, that was all, it wasn't my idea to bring her here, it was his, but that doesn't mean you have the right of possession, I saw her first, I don't know what I'm saying, it doesn't matter, she must prefer me to my friend, she has to prefer me, I'm better-looking than you, I'm a better writer than you, I'm . . . Don't threaten me, you bastard! Don't raise your hand to me! I know how to defend myself, don't forget that, you know that perfectly well, asshole! I'm not maimed, I'm not wooden, I'm not . . .

—You're a child, Bernardo. But your perversity is part of your poetic charm. Beware of old age! To be puerile and senile at the same time: avoid that! Try to age gracefully—if you can.

—And what about you, asshole?

—Don't worry. I'll die before you do.

Bernardo and Toño

When I was carrying her, she whispered to me secretly: Look at me. Think of me, naked. Think of all the clothes I have left behind, every place I've lived. A shawl here, a skirt there, combs and pins, brooches and crinolines, gorgets and gloves, satin slippers, evening dresses of taffeta and lamé, daytime clothes of silk and linen, riding boots, straw hats and felt hats, fur stoles and lizard-skin belts, pearl and emerald teardrops, diamonds strung on white gold, perfumes of sandalwood and lavender, eyebrow pencils, lipstick, baptismal clothes, wedding gowns, mourning clothes: be capable of dressing me, my love, cover my naked body, chipped, broken: I want nine rings of moonstone, Bernardo (you said to me in your most secret voice); will you bring them to me? you won't let me die of cold, will you be able to steal these things?, she laughed suddenly, because you don't have a dime, right, you're just a poor poet without a pot to piss in, she laughed like crazy and I dropped her, Toño ran over to us furious, you're hopeless, he said, you're an ass, even though she's only a mannequin, why did you have me get her if you're going to mistreat her this way? You're a hopeless bastard, a shithead forever, how could anyone put up with you, much less make any sense of you!

—She wants to dress luxuriously.

—Find her a millionaire to keep her and take her on his yacht.

Toño

We haven't spoken for several days. We have allowed the tension
of the other night to solidify, turn bitter, because we don't want
to say the word: *jealousy*. I am a coward. There is something
more important than our ridiculous passions. I should have had
the courage to tell you, Bernardo, she is a very delicate woman
and she can't be treated that way. I have had to put her down
in my bed and the shaking of her hands is awful. She can't live
and sleep standing up, like a horse. Quick. I've fixed her some
chicken soup and rice. She thanks me with her ancient look.
How ashamed you must be of your reaction the day of the party.
Your tantrums are pretty ridiculous. Now you leave us alone all
the time and sometimes don't come home to sleep. Then she and
I hear the music of a mariachi in the distance, coming through
the open window. We can't tell where the sounds are coming
from. But perhaps the most mysterious activity of Mexico City
is playing the guitar alone the whole night long. La Desdichada
sleeps, sleeps by my side.

Bernardo

My mother told me that if I ever needed the warmth of a home,
I could visit my Spanish cousin Fernandita, who had a nice little
house in Colonia del Valle. I would have to be discreet, Mother
said. Cousin Fernandita is small and sweet, but her husband is
a terror who takes revenge at home for his twelve hours a day
behind a counter of imported wines, olive oil, and La Mancha
cheeses. The house smells of it, though cleaner: when you walk
in, you feel as if someone just ran water, soap, and a broom over
every corner of that pastel-colored stucco Mediterranean villa set
in a grove of pines in the Valley of Anáhuac.

There is a game of croquet set up on the lawn and my second cousin Sonsoles can be found there any hour of the afternoon, bent over, with a mallet in her hand, and looking out of the corner of her eye, between the arm and the axilla, which form a sort of arch for her thoughtful gaze, at the unwary masculine visitor who appears in the harsh afternoon light. I'm sure my cousin Sonsoles is going to end up with sciatica: she must keep up that bent-over croquet pose for hours at a time. It lets her turn her ass toward the entrance of the garden and wiggle it provocatively: it shows off her figure and makes it stand out better, stuffed into a tight dress of rose-colored satin. That was the style in the thirties; cousin Sonsoles had also seen it on Jean Harlow in *China Seas*.

I need a space between Toño and me and our wooden guest. Wooden, I repeat to myself walking along the new Avenida Nuevo León almost to the pasture that separates the Colonia Hipódromo from Insurgentes, walking across that field of prickly heather until I reach the leafy avenue and from there cross over to the Colonia del Valle: La Desdichada is wooden. I'm not going to compensate for that fact with a Waikiki whore, as Toño would, or would like to, cynically. But if I go on believing that Sonsoles is going to compensate me for anything, I know that I am making a mistake. The tiresome girl stops playing croquet and invites me into the living room. She asks me if I would care for some tea and I answer yes, amused by the British afternoon invented by my cousin. She skips off coquettishly and in a little while comes back with a tray, teapot, and teacups. Such speed. She hardly gave me time to sneer at the Romero de Torres-style kitsch of this pseudo-gypsy room, full of silk shawls on black pianos, glass cases, with open fans, wooden statues of Don Quixote, and furniture carved with scenes from the fall of Granada. It is hard to sit and take tea with your head leaning against a carving of the tearful Moorish king Boabdil and his stern mother, while my cousin Sonsoles sits under a column portraying Isabel la Católica in the encampment of Santa Fe, about to have a last swing at the infidel. —Will the gentleman take a little tea? the silly little thing asks.

I say yes with my most, well, *gentlemanly* smile. She serves me the tea. It doesn't steam. I take a sip and spit it out involuntarily. It's cider, a lukewarm apple drink, unexpected, repugnant. She looks at me with her hazel eyes very round, not sure whether to smile or take offense. I didn't know what to say. I saw her there with the teapot in her hand, spilling out of her Hollywood vamp costume, bending over to expose her breasts while she pours the tea: the freckled, deceitful, heavily powdered breasts of my cousin Sonsoles, who looks at me with a question on her face, asking if I don't want to play with her. But I only see a pale face, long and narrow, without artifice, almost unpainted, nunlike, protected from the sun and air for five hundred years— since the fall of Granada!—and now showing up, like a pale conventual ghost, in the century of the swimsuit, tennis, and suntan lotion.

—A little tea, sir?

She probably has a dollhouse in her bedroom. Then Aunt Fernandita arrives, what a surprise, stay for dinner, spend the night, Bernardito, Feliciano had to go to Veracruz to fill out the papers on some imported goods, he won't be back until Thursday, stay with us, boy, come on, why not, it's what your mother would want.

Toño

Bernardo hasn't come back. I think of him; I hadn't imagined that his absence would bother me so much. I miss him. I ask myself why, what is it that binds us? I look at her sleeping, her eyes always open but languid. There is no other mannequin like her; who can have given her this singular expression?

Since childhood, our literary vocation has earned us nothing but scorn. Or disapproval. Or pity. I don't know what he is going to write. Nor what I am going to write. But our friendship derives from others' saying: They're crazy, they want to be writers. How can it be? Here, in this country that's now wide open, anything you want, easy money, easy power, anyone can make it to the top . . . What binds us is that Lázaro Cárdenas is president and he brings a moment of moral seriousness to politics. We feel that Cárdenas values power and money less than justice and work. He wants to get things done, and when I see his Indian face in the newspaper, I sense that's his one great anxiety: so little time! Then the crooks, the bullies, the murderers will be back. It's inevitable. It's wonderful, Bernardo, that we grew up under the power of a serious man, a decent man. If power can be ethical, then why can't two young men be writers, if that's what they want?

(They're crazy: they hear music without instruments, the music of time, bands in the night. They feed the woman soup. She drinks it, mute and grateful. How can Bernardo be so sensitive in everything and so brutal to a sick woman who only needs a little care, attention, tenderness?)

Bernardo

I ran into Arturo Ogarrio in the hall at school and he thanked me for the other night's dinner. He asked if he could go with me, where was I headed? That morning I had gotten a check from my mother, who lives in Guadalajara, at Aunt Fernandita's house, where I'm staying until the tempest with Toño passes over.

I intend to blow it on books. Ogarrio takes my arm, stopping me; he asks me to take a moment to admire the symmetry of the colonial patio, the arches, the porticoes of the old school of San Ildefonso; he complains about Orozco's murals, those violent caricatures that disrupt the harmony of the cloister with their parade of oligarchs, their beggars, their Liberty in chains, their deformed prostitutes, and their cross-eyed Pancreator. I ask him if he prefers the hideous stained-glass window in the stairway, a hopeful salute to progress: salvation through Industry and Commerce, in full color. He says that is not the problem, the problem is that the building represents harmony and Orozco's violent fresco represents discord. That's what I like, that Orozco doesn't go along with the consensus, that he tells the priests and politicians and ideologues that things are not going to turn out well— just the opposite of Diego Rivera, who keeps on saying that this time, yes, things will turn out all right for us. No.

We ventured into the Porrúa Brothers Bookstore. The employees, walled in behind glass counters, their arms crossed, block the path of the presumed client and reader. Their brown jackets, their black ties, their false black elbow-length sleeves make a single statement: *They shall not pass.*

—Surely it was easier to acquire that mannequin in a shop— said Arturo quietly—than it is to acquire a book here.

I placed my check on the counter and on top of the check my student ID. I asked for the *Romancero Gitano* of Lorca, Andreyev's *Sashka Yegulev*, Ortega's *Revolt of the Masses*, and the review *Letras de México*, where I had published, hidden toward the back, a little poem.

—Unless, as Ventura says, you ran the risk of stealing her . . .

—She's flesh and blood. The other night she wasn't feeling well. That's all. Look—I said quickly—I'll give you this Ortega book; you know it?

—No, you can't, said the clerk. You have to cash the check in a bank and pay in cash; checks are not accepted here, or money orders, or anything of the sort, said the employee with the black sleeves and coffee-colored jacket, assiduously reclaiming the books one by one:

—Above all, young man, we do not extend credit.

—Toño has been looking for the Andreyev novel for a long time. He wanted to give it to her. It's the story of a young rebel. And an anarchist, besides. I turned to face him. —She is flesh and blood.

—I know—said Ogarrio with his usual seriousness. —Come with me.

Toño

I think she's feeling better, thanks to my care. Bernardo has stayed away for several nights and hasn't helped me. I spend hours watching over her, ministering to her complaints, to her needs. I understand her: in her condition, she needs all sorts of attention. It's Bernardo's fault she feels bad: he should have been here, helping me, instead of hiding in the tower of his resentment. Thank God, she's better. I look at her face, so thin and sweet.

. . . I feel an overwhelming fatigue in the morning, as I've never felt before.

I dream that I'm talking with her. But she only talks to herself. When I talk, she doesn't listen. She talks over my head, or around me, to some other person who is above or behind me, someone I can't see. It makes me sick with grief. I believe in someone who doesn't exist. Then she caresses me. She does believe in me.

I wake up with a big scratch on my face. I raise my hand to my wounded cheek, I see the blood on my fingers. I look at her, awake, sitting in bed, motionless, looking at me. Does she smile? I take her left hand, roughly: it lacks the ring finger.

Bernardo

He said that I shouldn't be wasting my time with virginal fiancées or with whores. Much less with mannequins! He laughed, undressing.

I knew it as soon as I entered the room on the Plaza Miravalle, full of Chinese screens and mirrors in gilded frames, divans heaped with soft cushions and Persian carpets, smelling of lost churches and distant cities; nothing in Mexico City smelled like this apartment where she appeared from behind some curtains, identical to him, but with a woman's body, pale and slim, almost without breasts but with luxuriant pubic hair, as if the dark profundity of her sex made up for the plainness of her adolescent body: from afar she smelled of almonds and unknown soaps. She

walked toward me, her long hair hanging loose, her heavy eyes
ringed with dark circles, her lips painted deep red to disguise
their thinness: her mouth was two red lines, just like his. Naked
except for black stockings that she held up, poor thing, with her
hands, with difficulty, practically scratching her thighs.

—Arturo, please . . .

She could have been his twin. He smiled and said no, they
were not brother and sister, they had searched for a long time
before finding each other. The penumbra she brought with her.
He had asked his father: Don't throw out the old furniture, what
you don't sell give to me. Without the furniture, perhaps, the
room would not be what I see now: an enchanted cave in the
middle of Plaza Miravalle, near the Salamanca ice-cream parlor,
where we used to go for delicious lemon ices . . .

—Perhaps all this attracts her: the curtains, the rug, the furniture . . .

—The penumbra—I said.

—Yes, the penumbra, too. It's not easy to produce this exact
light. It's not easy to conjure up another person who not only
resembles you physically but wants *to be* like you, even wants to
be *you*. Frankly, I wouldn't want to be *like* her, but I would like
to be her, do you understand? That's why we've been searching
until we found each other. By force of attraction, but also by
force of repulsion.

—Arturo, please, my garters. You promised.

—Poor thing!

He told me that she made love with someone else only if he
was present, if he participated. He was taking off his dark gray
jacket, his black tie, his stiff collar. He dropped the collar button
into a black lacquer box. She looked at him fascinated, forgetting
about her garters. She let her stockings fall to her ankles. Then
she looked at me and laughed.

—Arturo, this fellow loves another. She laughed, taking my
hand in hers, sweaty, an unexpectedly nervous hand for that
woman the color of a waning moon, carrier no doubt of the

infirmity of the romantic century: she looked like one of Ruelas's tubercular sketches, and I thought of La Desdichada and a line from the *Romancero* of Lorca that I hadn't been able to buy this morning, which describes the Andalusian dancer as *paralyzed by the moon*: —Arturo, look at him, he's afraid, he's one of those who love only one woman, I know them, I know them! They're looking for that one woman and that gives them license to sleep with them all, the swine, because they're looking for just that one. See: he's a decent boy!

She laughed. The piercing wail of a baby interrupted her. She cursed and rushed off, with her stockings slipping, to hide behind a screen. I heard her soothing the infant. "Poor little one, poor little one, my baby, go to sleep now, it's all right . . ." while Arturo Ogarrio threw himself, naked, mouth open, onto the divan piled with cushions covered in arabesques and pillows patterned in cashmere.

—I shouldn't kid myself. She always preferred him to me, from the beginning, that head leaned against his shoulder, those little glances, those escapades in the bathroom, the whore!

Toño

When Bernardo mistreated her, I didn't say anything. But at night she reproached me. —Are you going to defend me or not? Are you going to defend me . . . ? she asked several times.

Bernardo

My mother writes from Guadalajara just to tell me: she has taken the tunic, the pants, the belt off the bed. She has taken the boots off the floor. She's put them all away, shined his boots and put everything in a trunk. They're not needed anymore. She has seen my father. An engineer who had taken pictures of the political events and public ceremonies of recent years invited her and other members of families that had supported Don Venustiano Carranza to see a film in his house. A silent film, of course. From the dances of the turn of the century to the murder of Don Venustiano and the ascent to power of those horrible characters from Sonora and Sinaloa. No, that was not important. That didn't interest her. But there, in a congressional ceremony in Donceles Street, behind President Carranza, was your father, Bernardo my son, your father was standing there, very serious, very handsome, very formal, protecting the president, in the very uniform that I have taken such zealous care of, your father, my son, moving, dressed up for me, my son, for me, Bernardo, he looked at me. I have seen him. You can come home.

How can I explain to my mother that I cannot compensate for the death of my father with the mobile simulacrum of the film; rather, my way of keeping him alive is to imagine him at my side always, invisible, a voice more than a presence, answering my questions, but silent in the face of those actions of mine that do not conform to his counsel, that kill him over again, with as much violence as the bullets themselves? I need a father close by me to authorize my words. The voice of my father is a secret endorsement of my own voice. But I know that with my words, even though he inspires them, I deny my father's authority, I instill rebellion, at the same time that I try to impose obedience on my own children.

Does La Desdichada save me from family obligations? The immobile dummy could free me from the responsibilities of sex, parenthood, matrimony, releasing me to literature. Could literature be my sex, my body, my posterity? Could literature provide friendship itself? Is that why I hate Toño, who gives himself purely to life?

Toño

I hear Bernardo's step on the stairs. He is returning; I recognize him. How can I tell him what has happened? It is my duty. Is it also my duty to tell him that she's dangerous, at least at times, that we must be on guard? The bed is wet with urine. She doesn't recognize me. She cowers in the corners, rejecting me. What does this woman want of me? How can I know, if she keeps so stubborn a silence? I have to tell Bernardo: I've tried everything. The bed is wet. She doesn't recognize me, doesn't recognize her Toño, her tony Toño, she called me like a child. She has wet the bed, she doesn't recognize me. I have to prepare her pabulum, dress her, undress her, clean her, tuck her in at night, sing her lullabies . . . I held her, I soothed her, now you belong to me, child, now you're mine, I said, little baby, the boogeyman . . . Desperately I push her away, far from me. She falls to the floor with a horrible crash of wood against wood. I rush to pick her up, to embrace her. For God's sake, what do you want, Desdichada, unhappy one, why don't you tell me what you want, why don't you hold me, why don't you let me loosen your dressing gown a little, lift up your skirts, see if what I feel, what you want is true, why not let me kiss your nipples, doll, embrace me, you can hurt me, but not him, he has to do things, you understand, Desdichada? He has to write, you mustn't hurt him, you can't scratch him, infect him, destroy his confidence, or wound him with your polymorphous perversity, I know your secret, doll, you're in love with all shapes, doll, that's your perversion, but he is pure, he is the young poet, and you and I have had the privilege of witnessing his youth, the birth of his genius, the nativity of the poet.

My brother, my friend.

Since I have known you I have realized the importance of forming an image of oneself at the moment when youth and talent meet: the sign of that meeting can manifest itself as a spark of ingenuity—and sometimes as a flash of genius. That is something you find out later (do you understand me, Desdichada, wretched one?). What the image of the young artist (you, Bernardo, coming up the stairs) tells the rest of us is that we can recapture that moment: the image reveals a vocation; if we falter, it can return to reawaken us. You remember, Bernardo? I cut out a print of the self-portrait of the young Dürer and stuck it into a corner of the mirror: to my friend, the young poet, who is going to write what I will never be able to write. Perhaps you understood. You didn't say anything. Like you, I write, but I am afraid of my potential to call forth darkness. If creation is absolute, it will reveal good, but also evil. That must be the price of creation: if we are free, we are free both to create and to destroy. If we don't want to be responsible to God for what we are and do, we must make ourselves responsible, don't you agree, Bernardo? Don't you agree, unhappy woman, Desdichada?

You believe that she has the right to impose herself between us, to destroy our friendship, bewitch you, turn you from your vocation, deliver you unto evil, frustrate your monogamous romanticism, initiate you in her voracious, perverse love of all shapes? I don't know what you think. I have seen her up close. I have observed her changes of mood, of time, of taste, of age; she is tender one minute and violent the next; she comes to life at certain hours, she seems near death at others; she is enamored of metamorphosis, not of the inalterable form of a statue or a poem. Bernardo, my friend, my poet: let her go, your fascination with her is unhealthy for you, you must fix your words in a form to transmit them to others: *they* must return them to flux, instability, uncertainty; you can't be expected to give form to loose and common words and then reanimate them as well: that is my responsibility as your reader, not yours, my creator.

She wants you to believe the opposite: nothing should ever be fixed, everything must always be in flux, that is pleasure, liberty, diversion, art, life. Have you heard her moaning at night? Have you felt her nails on your face? Have you seen her sitting on the toilet? Have you had to clean her filth from the bed? Have you ever soothed her to sleep? Have you ever prepared her pap? Do you know what it's like to live every day with a woman with no voice, no language? Pardon me, Bernardo: do you know what it's like to open your hand and find there that . . .

Sometimes I see myself behind him in the glass, when we are

in a hurry and must both shave at once. The mirror is like an abyss. It doesn't matter that I fall in it. Not everything happens only in the mind, as you seem to think, Bernardo.

Bernardo and Toño

She whispered in my ear, with a breath of dust: How would you like to die? Can you picture yourself crucified? Can you imagine yourself with a crown of thorns? Tell me if you would like to die like Him. Would you dare, you wretch? Would you ask for a death like His? Don't cover your ears, poor devil! You want to possess me and you aren't capable of thinking of a death that would make me adore you? Then I will tell you what I'll do with you, Toño, my little tony Toño, I'll make you die of sickness, young or old, murdered like your friend Bernardo's father, in a street accident, in a nightclub quarrel, fighting over a whore, gunned down, die however you die, tony Toño, I'll dig up your body, gnaw your skeleton until you are sand, and I'll put you in an hourglass, to mark the passing time: I'll turn you into the sand in an hourglass, my little one, and I'll turn you over every half hour, that will keep me busy until I die, turning you on your head every thirty minutes, how do you like my idea, how do you like it?

Bernardo

I know: I am coming back to take care of her. I enter our apartment without a sound. I open the door carefully. I'm sure that even before I'm inside I can hear her voice, very low, very far off, saying: I believe in you, I'm not sick, I do believe in you. I slam the door and the voice stops. I hate hearing words not meant for me. Can one be a poet in that case? I believe so, deeply: the words that I must hear are not necessarily directed toward me, they are not words only for me, but they are never words I shouldn't be hearing. I've thought that love is an abyss; language

too, and the words of another's confidences, intrigues, and secrets—words of friends, politicians, insincere lovers—they are
not mine.

The poet is not a Peeping Tom—that may be the novelist's
role, I don't know. The poet doesn't seek, he receives; the poet
doesn't look through keyholes, he closes his eyes in order to see.

She stopped talking. I went in and found Toño lying in my
bed, his arms crossed over his face. I heard the clear glug-glug
of the *enchanted water*. Slowly I entered the bath, parting the
beaded curtain with its Malaysian sound.

There she was, at the bottom of a tub full of steaming-hot
water, her paint peeling, with barely a trace of eyebrows, of lips,
of her languid eyes, already peeling away, blistering from the
hot water, submerged in a glassy death, her final display window,
her long black hair free at last, floating like algae, clean at last,
no longer matted down, my woman was sleeping, in the window
where no one would ever see her or admire her or desire her:
never again imagine her, unhappy one, Desdichada . . .

And yet I had to take her out and hold her one more time,
comfort her, now cling to me, only me, go to sleep, my soul . . .
How would it have been—I say to Toño—if one afternoon I had
listened to you and taken La Desdichada to have tea at Aunt
Fernandita's house, and cousin Sonsoles had served us an insipid
tea that was really an apple drink, and then the silly girl had
invited us up to her dollhouse, to stay there, the three of us?
Then what—I asked Toño—then what? Take this handkerchief,
these panties, these stockings. They're just things I've been gathering for her, here and there.

Toño

Throughout the wake, Bernardo didn't look at her. He only
looked at me. It doesn't matter; I accept his reproaches. He
doesn't say a word to me. I don't respond to his silent question.

I could tell him—though it isn't true: "You know why: because she refused to love me."

I went to buy her casket from the funeral home on the corner.

Teófilo Sánchez and Ventura del Castillo came over. Ventura brought a sprig of fragrant spikenard. Arturo Ogarrio arrived with two tall tapers, he placed them at the head of the coffin and lit them.

I went out to eat a sandwich nearby, watchful and sad. Bernardo left after me. He paused in the patio. He looked at the bottom of the dry fountain. It began to rain: the warm round drops of the month of July in the Mexican plateau. The sky-high tropics. The cats of the neighborhood slunk across the roofs and eaves of the house.

When I came running back, protecting myself from the torrential rain with a copy of the *Ultimas Notícias de Excélsior*, with my lapels turned up, brushing the water off my shoulders and stomping hard, the coffin was empty and none of the four—Ventura, Teófilo, Arturo, Bernardo—was there.

I laid out the wet paper on the sofa. I hadn't read it. Besides, we saved the papers to light the water heater. I read the news of July 17, 1936: four generals had taken up arms in the Grand Canary Island against the Spanish Republic. Francisco Franco flew from Las Palmas to Tetuán in a plane called the *Rapid Dragon*.

Bernardo
(i)

Some months later my loneliness led me back to the Waikiki. My Aunt Fernanda had let me stay at her house. All right, I will be frank: my poverty was great, but not as great as my wretchedness. I will go further. I needed the warmth of a home, I admit it, and the evocations of the Andalusian sun of my ancestors gave it to me, notwithstanding even the flirtations of that fake *maja*, cousin Sonsoles. On the other hand, I found it more difficult every day to put up with Uncle Feliciano, a Franco supporter to the bone; his trips to Veracruz provided the only relief, before I realized that he went to the port to organize the Spanish merchants against the red republic of Madrid, as he liked to call it.

I began to spend a lot of time at the nightclub, stupidly blowing my mother's check on dolls and drink. This was Toño's world, not mine; perhaps my secret desire was that I'd run into him there, we'd make up, forget La Desdichada, and resume our comfortable life together, which permitted us to share expenses that we really couldn't afford if we each lived alone.

There is something else (I must add): the visits to the nightclub reconciled me to the mystery of my city. The Waikiki was a public hiding place, as well as a private agora. In it, one felt oneself surrounded by the vast enigma of the oldest city of the New World, a city that one can travel to by train, plane, and highway, stay in a hotel, eat in restaurants, visit museums, and still never see.

The unwary visitor doesn't understand that the true Mexico City is not there. It must be imagined, it can't be seen directly. It demands words to bring it to life, like the Baroque statue that can be fully seen only if one moves around it; like the poem that makes one condition to be ours: Speak me. Syllables, words, images, metaphors: a lyrical sentence is completed only when it goes beyond metaphor and becomes epiphany. The intangible crown on this web of encounters is, finally, amazement: the epiphany is wonderful because the poem now is written but cannot be seen; it is *said* (it *said-duces*).

There must be a place for the final encounter of the poet and his reader: a port of sail.

I see my city like this poem of invisible architecture, successfully concluded only to begin again, perpetually. The conclusion is the condition of the new beginning. And to start anew is to be led to the epiphany to come: I evoke names and places, Argentina and Donceles Streets, Reforma and Madero Avenues, the Churches of Santa Veracruz and San Hipólito, the *pirul* and the ahuehuete trees, calla lilies, a skeleton on a bicycle and a wasp stinging my forehead, Orozco and Tolsá, Porrúa Brothers Bookstore and Tacuba Café, the Cine Iris, sunstone and stone sun, zarzuelas at the Arbeu Theater, *ahuautles* and *huitlacoche*, pineapple and coriander, jicama and cactus with white cheese; Los Leones desert, Ajusco Mountain and Colonia Roma, gooey popcorn and morning sweet rolls, the Salamanca ice-cream shop, the Waikiki and Rio Rosa cabarets, wet season and dry season: Mexico, D.F. In the renewed mystery of the city, starting from any of its streets, eating a taco, entering a movie house, I could meet my dear friend Toño again and tell him it's all right, it's all over, shake hands, man, buddies again, brothers forever, come on, Toñito . . .

I released myself from the woman who was rubbing my knee, and set my glass on the table. The comic uproar in the middle of the nightclub's raised runway, the unexpected Spanish dancing, the mood of a bullfight victory celebration, the play of warm red and blue lights, and the unmistakable figure of Teófilo Sánchez, his short jacket, his miner's boots, his hair like a new recruit's (shaved with the aid of a bowl), dancing to the exuberant music with a woman dressed in a wedding gown, moving back and forth, lifting her in the air, the arms of the popular poet showing her, on high, to all, clasping her tightly to his chest like a prize he'd been coveting, head to toe, that light, stiff, unpainted creature; again they crossed the stage, now spinning, her rigid arms raised as for a chant of hallucinated snakes, turning in circles, the music swelling double-time, and now Teófilo Sánchez threw his companion dressed as a bride into the air, her collar buttoned to her ears, her face covered by a wedding veil, hiding the signs of age, destruction, water, fire, pockmarks . . . the intensely sad eyes of the mannequin.

I went to jump up on the runway to put an end to the horrible spectacle. It wasn't necessary. Other small disturbances succeeded the first, like an earthquake followed by an aftershock, a new shaking that makes us forget the first, which seems remote, though it's only a few seconds old. A commotion on the runway, an angry scream, confused movement, injured bodies, shouted curses.

Then the lights dimmed. The scene cooled down. The darkness surrounded us. A single ray of icy light, a silver light in a world of black velvet, shone like a lunar spotlight on the runway, and the band began the slowest *danzón*. A young man dressed all in dark gray, pale and sunken-eyed, with his lips pressed tight and his black hair slicked back, took the woman dressed as a bride in his arms and held her in the slowest *danzón*, moving, yes, over the space of a single tile, practically a postage stamp, almost without moving his feet, without moving his hips or his arms, the two held each other in aquarian silence. Arturo Ogarrio and the rescued woman, slow, ceremonious as a Spanish Infanta, her face hidden behind a cascade of veils, but finally free, I realized with sudden relief, finally her own mistress in the arms of this young man who did the *danzón* so slowly, tenderly, respectfully, passionately, while I watched the figures of the dancers moving farther and farther away in the silver light, leaving more and more space, for me, for my life and my poetry, giving up a meeting with Toño, writing a farewell to Mexico in this night the color of smoke, in exchange for a meeting with literature . . .

(ii)

The words of a poem only return to *life*, imperfect or not, when they flow anew; that is, when they are *said*. Better said (read) than dead! The poem I'm translating is called *El Desdichado*— Nerval's French did not offer the verbal phantasm of the Spanish words, in which what is said (*dicho*) defeats what is sad (*des-dicha*), and what is unsaid (*des-dicho*), and what's unsound(ed) (*des-dicho*) is rent by the sword of words. Silence is the unsaid; it is sadness, whereas a word is award. The wordless are worldless, for silence is shapeless, hapless. It's voice versus vice—so voice verses!

But she, La Desdichada, does not speak, she does not speak . . .

I think this and surprise myself. Emotion floods over me, I translate it as she *who doesn't speak*: Love, be who you may, named as you're named (name, flame: benighted, be lighted—to name is to bring to life, to flame is to inflame), speak through me, Desdichada, unhappy, unsaid one, trust in the poet, let me be your voice, your word/world. I will make you sound. Speak to me, through me, for me, and in exchange for your voice I swear I will always be true, always true to you. That is my desire, Desdichada, the world is slow to give me what I want, one woman who is mine alone, and I only hers.

Let me draw near your wooden ear, while I'm still under twenty, and tell you: I don't know if the world will ever bring me that one woman, or if so, when. Perhaps to find her I would have to change my ways (my virtue), perhaps I would have to love many women before discovering *this is it*, the one and only, the here and now. And even if I find her, what will become of me then, having loved so many to find that one, telling her that it was all for her and her alone—will she believe me when I tell her that I am a man meant for only one woman?

How can I be believed? How can I prove my sincerity? And if she doesn't believe me, how can I believe in her? It's okay for a nineteen-year-old writer to say these things; perhaps confidence is, after all, the most important thing. But my fear is something known best in adolescence, though never completely forgotten, even if concealed: love is an abyss.

I choose henceforth to put my trust in one woman: will La Desdichada be my abyss, the first, best, and most faithful lover of my life? Toño would laugh. It's easy to count on the fidelity of a wooden doll. No, it's hard, I tell him, for a wooden doll to rely on the fidelity of a man of flesh and blood.

(iii)

Twenty-five years later, I returned from all the cities of the world. I wrote. I loved. I did things that pleased me. I tried to turn them into literature. But the things that pleased me were sufficient unto themselves. They didn't want to be words. Likes and dislikes, tastes and distastes fought among themselves. With luck, they became poetry. The poetry of the changing city reflected my own tensions.

I knew the old Waikiki was closing, so I went there one night. The last night it was open. I saw Toño sitting a little ways from me. He had gotten fatter and had an impressive mustache. There was no need to greet each other. What would he think of me, after a quarter of a century? We walked between the tables, the dancing couples, to shake hands and sit down together. All this without speaking a word, while the band played the anthem of all slow dances, *Nereidas*. Then we laughed. We had forgotten the ceremony, the rite that affirmed our public friendship. We stood up. We embraced. We slapped each other on the back, on the waist, Toño, Bernardo, how are you?

We didn't want to reminisce. We didn't want to slip into an easy nostalgia. The Waikiki was taking care of that. We started talking as if no time had gone by. But the end of an era was being celebrated all around us; the city would never be the same, the Expressionist carnival was ending, from now on everything would be much too vast, distant, ground down; tonight marked the end of the theatrics that everyone could share, the witticisms that everyone could repeat, the celebrities that we could celebrate without risk of foreign comparisons: our village, rose-colored, blue, vivid, was going away, it was whirling around us, inviting us to a carnival that was a funeral, the footlights pointed toward the edges of the nightclub full of smoke and sadness so that we were all mixed together: show, audience, whores, johns, band, masters, servants, slaves: out of this crowd that moved like a sick serpent, two extraordinary figures emerged: a Pierrot and a Columbine in perfect costume: they both wore whiteface, his forehead was black, her tragic smile was painted on with lipstick; he had the black gorget, the shiny white suit of a clown, the black buttons, the satin slippers; Columbine had the white wig, the tiny fairy cap, the white gorget, the white mesh stockings, the ballet slippers; their moonlike faces were both masked.

They came over to us, said our names. Bernardo, welcome to Mexico! Toño, we knew you'd be here! Come on! Today marks the end of the Mexico City we knew, today one city dies and another is born, come with us!

Laughing, we asked their names.

—Ambar.

—Estrella.

—Come with us.

We took taxi after taxi, the four of us squeezed in together, breathing the intense perfume of those strange creatures. It was the last night of the city we had known. The ball at San Carlos, where they took us that night (the perfumed couple, Pierrot and Columbine), was the annual saturnalia of the university students, who cast aside the medieval prohibitions of the Royal, Holy University of Mexico amid the Neoclassicism of the eighteenth-century palace's stone staircases and columns: disguises, drinks, abandon, the always threatening movement of the crowd carried away by the dance, the drunkenness, the sensuality on display, the lights like waves; who was going to dance with Ambar, who with Estrella: which was the man, which was the woman, what would our hands tell us when we danced first with Columbine, then with Pierrot? And how easily the two were able to avoid our touch so that we were left without sex, with only perfume and movement. We were drunk. But we justified intoxication with a thousand excuses: seeing each other after so many years, the night, the dance, the company of this couple, the city celebrating its death, the suspicion I formed in the taxi, when we all climbed in and Estrella ordered: "Let's have one for the road at Las Veladoras"—an outdoor bar lit by votive lamps: could it be Arturo Ogarrio and his girlfriend, his double? I asked Toño. No, he answered, they're too young, the best thing would be to pull off their masks, find out for sure. So we tried, and they both shrieked in androgynous voices, screamed horribly, squealed as pigs would if we took their hind legs and castrated them, and they cried for the taxi driver to stop, they're killing us, and the flustered driver came to a stop, they got out, we were in front of the cathedral, Ambar and Estrella ran past the iron gate into the churchyard and on into the splendid cave of carved stone.

We followed them inside, but our search was futile. Pierrot and Columbine had disappeared into the bowels of the cathedral. Something told me that Toño and I had not come here to find them. Sacred, profane, cathedral, cabaret, school, Orozco's mural, the carnival of San Carlos, the agony of Mexico; I felt dizzy, I grasped a gilded screen in front of a dark side altar. I tried to catch Toño's eye. He didn't look at me. Toño was holding on to the screen with both hands and gazing intently at the altar behind it. It was dawn and some religious women who had been there for four centuries knelt down one more time, wrapped in black shawls as always, with skins like yellow onions. Toño didn't look at them. The incense made me nauseated, the smell of rotting spikenard. Toño stared fixedly at the altar.

The Virgin, with her cowl, her gown of ivory and gold, and her velvet cape, was weeping as she gazed at her dead Son lying cradled in her arms. The Christ of Mexico, wounded like a bullfighter, cut to pieces in a great, never-ending *corrida*, bathed in blood, gored: His wounds would never heal, that's why His Mother cried; although He came back to life, He was wounded, caught by the bull. She rested her feet on the horns of a bull, and she wept. Down her cheeks rolled huge black tears, like the ones on the Pierrot who wouldn't let me take off his mask. He never stopped bleeding, she never stopped crying.

Now I joined in the contemplation of the Virgin. Her sculptor had given her a face of classic features, a straight nose and nicely

spaced eyes, languid, half open, and a tiny, tight mouth painted
to look like a ribbon. Her chin was a little prognathous, like the
Infantas of Velázquez. She also had a long neck, perfect for her
gorget, which was like Columbine's. At last she had found her
niche. At last the cause, the background of her misery, her *des-
dicha*, became clear. She opens her arms to ask mercy for her
Son, and her praying hands, open, don't quite touch the object
of her passion. The ring finger of her left hand is missing. Her
long eyelids, like a lizard's, look at us half-closed, look at Toño
and me as if we are lifeless wooden dolls. Her eyes are infinitely
sad. As if they had witnessed a great unhappiness *in another time.*

Toño

*. . . The air became so filthy, the city so sprawling and remote, our
destinies were fulfilled, accomplished—we were what we were, writers, journalists, bureaucrats, editors, politicians, businessmen, no
longer "will be," but "were," back in those years, when the air was
so . . .*

*Vineyard Haven,
Massachusetts
Summer 1986*

The
Prisoner of
Las Lomas

To Valerio Adami, for a Sicilian story

1

As incredible as this story is, I might as well begin at the beginning and continue straight on to the end. Easy to say. The
minute I get set to begin, I realize I begin with an enigma. It
follows that difficulties ensue. Oh, fuck! It can't be helped: the
story begins with a mystery; my hope, I swear, is that by the
end you'll understand everything. That you will understand me.
You'll see: I leave out nothing. But the truth is that when I
entered the sickroom of Brigadier General Prisciliano Nieves on
February 23, 1960, in the British hospital then located in the
Avenida Mariano Escobedo (present site of the Camino Real
Hotel, to orient my younger listeners), I myself had to believe
in the enigma, or what I was planning would not succeed. I want
to be understood. The mystery was true. (The truth was the
mystery.) But if I was not myself convinced of it, I would not
convince the old and astute Brigadier Nieves, not even on his
sickbed.

He was, as I said, a general. You know that already. I was a
young lawyer who had recently received my degree—news for
you and for me. I knew everything about him. He, nothing about
me. So when I found the door to his private room in the hospital
ajar and pushed it open, he didn't recognize me, but neither did
he draw back. Lax as security is in Mexican hospitals, there was
no reason for the brigadier to be alarmed. I saw him lying there
in one of those beds that are like the throne of death, a white
throne, as if cleanliness were the compensation that dying offers
us. His name *Nieves* means *snow*, but lying in all that bleached
linen he was like a fly in milk. The brigadier was very dark, his
head was shaved, his mouth a long, sourish crack, his eyes masked
by two thick, livid veils. But why describe him, when he was
so soon gone? You can look up his photo in the Casasola Archives.

Who knows why he was dying? I went by his house and they said to me:

—The general's bad.

—It's just he's so old.

I scarcely noticed them. The one who spoke first seemed a cook, the second a young girl servant. I made out a sort of majordomo inside the house, and there was a gardener tending the roses outside. You see: only of the gardener was I able to say definitely, that man is a gardener. The others were just one thing or another. They didn't exist for me.

But the brigadier did. Propped up in his hospital bed, surrounded by a parapet of cushions, he looked at me as he must have looked at his troops the day he singlehandedly saved the honor of his regiment, of the Northeast Corps, almost of the very Revolution, and maybe even of the country itself—why not?—in the encounter of La Zapotera, when the wild Colonel Andrés Solomillo, who confused extermination with justice, occupied the Santa Eulalia sugar mill and lined both masters and workers against its wall to face the firing squad, saying the servants were as bad as those they served.

—The one who holds the cow is as bad as the one who slaughters it.

So said Solomillo, helping himself to the possessions of the Escalona family, masters of the hacienda: quickly grabbing all the gold coins he'd found in the library, behind the complete works of Auguste Comte, he proposed to Prisciliano: —Take these, my captain, so that for once those who are as hungry as you and I may be invited to the banquet of life.

Prisciliano Nieves—the legend goes—not only refused the gold his superior offered him but, when it came time for the execution, he placed himself between the firing squad and the condemned and said to Colonel Andrés Solomillo: —The soldiers of the Revolution are neither murderers nor thieves. These poor people are guilty of nothing. Separate the poor from the rich, please.

What happened then—so the story goes—was this: the colonel,

furious, told Prisciliano that if he didn't shut up he would be the second feature in the morning's firing; Prisciliano shouted to the troops not to kill other poor people; the squad hesitated; Solomillo gave the order to fire at Prisciliano; Prisciliano gave the order to fire at the colonel; and in the end the squad obeyed Prisciliano:

—Mexican soldiers do not murder the people, because they are the people, said Prisciliano beside the body of Solomillo, and the soldiers cheered him and felt satisfied.

This phrase, associated ever since with the fame, the life, and the virtues of the instantly Colonel and soon-to-be Brigadier General Don Prisciliano Nieves, surely would be engraved on the base of his monument: THE HERO OF SANTA EULALIA.

And now here I come, forty-five years later, to put a damper on the final glory of General Prisciliano Nieves.

—General Nieves, listen carefully. I know the truth of what happened that morning in Santa Eulalia.

The maraca that sounded in the throat of my brigadier Prisciliano Nieves was not his death rattle, not yet. In the dim light of the hospital, my middle-class lawyer's young breath smelling of Sen-Sen mixed with Don Prisciliano's ancient respiration, a drumroll scented of chloroform and *chile chipotle*. No, my general, don't die without signing here. For your honor, my general: worry no more about your honor, and rest in peace.

2

My house in Las Lomas de Chapultepec has one outstanding virtue: it shows the advantages of immortality. I don't know how people felt about it when it was constructed, when the forties were dawning. The Second World War brought Mexico a lot of money. We exported raw materials at high prices and the farmworkers entered the churches on their knees, praying for the war to go on. Cotton, hemp, vegetables, strategic minerals; it all went out in every direction. I don't know how many cows had to die in Sonora for this great house to be erected in Las Lomas, or how many black-market deals lay behind its stone and mortar. You have seen such houses along the Paseo de la Reforma and the Boulevard de los Virreyes and in the Polanco neighborhood: they are architectural follies of pseudo-colonial inspiration, resembling the interior of the Alameda movie house, which in turn mimics the Plateresque of Taxco with its cupolas, towers, and portals. Not to mention that movie house's artificial ceiling, dappled with hundred-watt stars and adorned with scudding little clouds. My house in Boulevard de los Virreyes stopped short of that.

Surely the Churrigueresque delirium of the house I have lived in for more than twenty years was an object of derision. I imagine two or three caricatures by Abel Quezada making fun of the cathedral-like portal, the wrought-iron balconies, the nightmare ornamentation of decorations, reliefs, curves, angels, madonnas, cornucopias, fluted plaster columns, and stained-glass windows. Inside, things don't get any better, believe me. *Inside* reproduces *outside*: once again, in a hall that rises two stories, we encounter the blue-tile stairs, the iron railing and balconies overlooking the hall from the bedrooms, the iron candelabra with its artificial candles dripping fake wax of petrified plastic, the floor of Talavera tile, the uncomfortable wood-and-leather furniture, straight and stiff as if for receiving a sentence from the Holy Inquisition. What a production . . . !

But the extraordinary thing, as I was saying, is that this white elephant, this symbol of vulgar pretension and the new money of the entrepreneurs who made a profit off the war, has been converted, with time, into a relic of a better era. Today, when things are fast going downhill, we fondly recall a time when things were looking up. Better vulgar and satisfied than miserable but refined. You don't need me to tell you that. Bathed in the glow of nostalgia, unique and remote in a new world of skyscrapers, glass, and concrete, my grotesque quasimodel home (my Quasimodo abode, my friends, ha ha! it might be hunch-backed, but it's mine, all mine!) has now become a museum piece. It's enough to say that first the neighbors and then the authorities came to me, imploring:

—Never, sir, sell your house or let it be demolished. There aren't many examples left of the Neocolonial architecture of the forties. Don't even think of sacrificing it to the crane or (heaven protect us!) (we would never imagine such a thing of you!) to vile pecuniary interests.

I had a strange friend once, named Federico Silva, whom his friends called the Mandarin and who lived in another kind of house, an elegant villa dating from the adolescent decade of the century (1915? 1920?), squeezed and dwarfed by the looming skyscrapers lining the Calle de Córdoba. He wouldn't let it go on principle: he would not cave in to the modernization of the city. Obviously, nostalgia makes demands on me. But if I don't let go of my house, it's not because of my neighbors' pleas, or because I have an inflated sense of its value as an architectural curiosity, or anything like that. I remain in my house because I have lived like a king in it for twenty-five years: from the time I was twenty-five until I turned fifty, what do you think of that? An entire life!

Nicolás Sarmiento, be honest with those who are good enough to hear you out, pipes up the little inner voice of my Jiminy Cricket. Tell them the truth. You don't leave this house for the simple reason that it belonged to Brigadier General Prisciliano Nieves.

3

An entire life: I was about to tell you that when I took over this meringue of a house I was a miserable little lawyer, only the day before a clerk in an insignificant law office on the Avenida Cinco de Mayo. My world, on my word of honor, went no farther than the Celaya candy store; I would look through the windows of my office and imagine being rewarded with mountains of toffees, rock candy, candy kisses, and *morelianas*. Maybe the world was

a great candied orange, I said to my beloved fiancée, Miss Buenaventura del Rey, from one of the best families of the Narvarte
district. Bah, if I had stayed with her I would have been turned
into a candied orange, a lemon drop. No: the world was the
sugared orange, I would take one bite and then, with disdain
and the air of a conquistador, I would throw it over my shoulder.
Give me a hug, sweetheart!

Buenaventura, on the other hand, wanted to eat the orange
down to the last seed, because who knows if tomorrow will bring
another. When I walked into the house in Las Lomas for the
first time, I knew that there was no room in it for Miss Buenaventura del Rey. Shall I confess something to you? My sainted
fiancée seemed to me less fine, less interesting than the servants
that my general had in his service. Adieu, Buenaventura, and
give your papa my warmest thanks for having given away to me,
without even realizing it, the secret of Prisciliano Nieves. But
goodbye also, worthy cook, lovely girl servant, stupid waiter,
and stooped gardener of the Hero of Santa Eulalia. Let no one
remain here who served or knew Prisciliano Nieves when he was
alive. Let them all be gone!

The women tied their bundles and went proudly off. The
waiter, on the other hand, half argued and half whined that it
wasn't his fault the general died, that nobody ever thought of
them, what would become of them now, would they die of hunger, or would they have to steal? I would like to have been more
generous with them. I couldn't afford it; no doubt, I was not the
first heir that couldn't use the battalion of servants installed in
the house he inherited. The gardener returned now and again
to look at his roses from a distance. I asked myself if it wouldn't
be a good idea to have him come back and take care of them.
But I didn't succumb: I subscribed to the motto *Nothing from
the past!* From that moment, I started a new life: new girlfriend,
new servants, new house. Nobody who might know anything
about the battle of La Zapotera, the hacienda of Santa Eulalia,
or the life of Brigadier Prisciliano Nieves. Poor little Buena-

ventura; she shed a lot of tears and even made a fool of herself calling me up and getting the brush-off from my servants. The poor thing never found out that our engagement was the source of my fortune; her father, an old army accountant, cross-eyed from constantly making an ass of himself, had been in Santa Eulalia and knew the truth, but for him it was just a funny story, it had no importance, it was a bit of table talk; he didn't act on the precious information he possessed, whereas I did, and at that moment I realized that information is the source of power, but the crucial thing is to know how to use it or, if the situation demands, not use it: silence, too, can be power.

New life, new house, new girlfriend, new servants. Now I'm reborn: Nicolás Sarmiento, at your service.

I was reborn, yes, gentlemen: an entire life. Who knew better than anyone that there was a device called the telephone with which a very foxy lawyer could communicate better than anyone with the world, that great sugared orange? You are listening to him now. Who knew better than anyone that there is a seamless power called information? Who knows knows—so the saying goes. But I amended it: who knows can do, who can do knows— power is knowledge. Who subscribed to every gringo review available on technology, sports, fashion, communications, interior decoration, architecture, domestic appliances, shows, whatever you need and desire? Who? Why, you're listening to him, he's talking to you: the lawyer Nicolás Sarmiento, who joined information to telephone: as soon as I found out about a product that was unknown in Mexico, I would use the telephone and in a flash obtain the license to exploit it here.

All by telephone: patents for Dishwasher A and Microcomputer B, for telephone answering machines and electromagnetic recorders, rights to Parisian *prêt-à-porter* and jogging shoes, licenses for drills and marine platforms, for photocopiers and vitamins, for betablockers for cardiacs and small aircraft for magnates: what didn't I patent for Mexico and Central America in those twenty-five years, sirs, finding the financial dimension for every service, tying my Mexican sub-licenses in with the fortunes of the manufacturing company in Wall Street, the Bourse, and the City? And all, I tell you, without stirring from the house of my Brigadier Prisciliano Nieves, who to do his business had, as they say, to shunt cattle all around the ranch. Whereas, with telephone raised, I almost singlehandedly brought Mexico into the modern era. Without anybody realizing. In the place of honor in my library were the telephone directories of Manhattan, Los Angeles, Houston . . . St. Louis, Missouri: home of the McDonnell Douglas airplane factory and Ralston cereals; Topeka, Kansas: home of Wishwashy detergent; and Dearborn, Michigan, of the auto factory in the birthplace of Henry Ford; not to mention nacho manufacturing in Amarillo, Texas, and the high-tech conglomerates on Route 128 in Massachusetts.

The directory, my friends, the phone book, the area code followed by seven numbers: an invisible operation, and, if not quite silent, at least as modulated as a murmur of love. Listen well: in my office at Las Lomas I have a console of some fifty-seven direct telephone lines. Everything I need is at my fingertips: notaries, patent experts, and sympathetic bureaucrats.

In view of what has happened, I'm speaking to you, as they say, with all my cards on the table and nothing up my sleeve. But you still don't have to believe me. I'm a bit more refined than in those long-ago days of my visit to the British hospital and my abandonment of Miss Buenaventura del Rey. I'm half chameleon, you can't tell me from any middle-class Mexican who has become polished by taking advantage of trips, conversations, lectures, films, and good music available to . . . well, get rich, everyone has a chance, there's a field marshal's baton in every knapsack. I read Emil Ludwig in a pocket edition and learned that Napoleon has been the universal supermodel of ascent by merit, in Europe and in the so-called Third World. The gringos, so dull in their references, speak of self-made men like Horatio Alger and Henry Ford. We, of Napoleon or nothing: Come, my Josephine, here is your very own Corsican, St. Helena is far away, the pyramids are watching us, even if they are in Teoti-huacán, and from here to Waterloo is a country mile. We're half Napoleon, half Don Juan, we can't help it, and I tell you, my terror of falling back to where I'd come from was as great as my ambition: you see, I hold nothing back. But the women, the women I desired, the anti-Buenaventuras, I desired them as they desired me, refined, cosmopolitan, sure, it cost me a little some-thing, but self-confident, at times imperious, I made them un-derstand (and it was true) that there was no commitment between us: grand passion today, fading memory tomorrow . . . That was another story, although they soon learned to count on my dis-cretion and they forgave my failings. Women and servants. From my colonial watchtower of Las Lomas, armed with telephones that passed through all the styles, country black, Hollywood white, October crisis red, bright green Technicolor, golden Bar-bie Doll, detached speaker, hand-dialed, to telephones like the one I am using at present, pure you-talk-to-me-when-I-press-the-button, to my little black Giorgio Armani number with TV screen, which I use only for my conquests.

Women: in the sixties there were still some foreign castaways from the forties, a little weather-beaten now but eager to acquire a young lover and a large house where they could throw parties and dazzle the Aztecs; it was through them that I burst on the scene and went on to charm the second wave of women, that is, girls who wanted to marry a young lawyer on the way up who had already had as lover the Princess of Salm-Salm or the heiress of the Fresno, California, cardboard-recycling factory. Such is this business of love. I used those young girls to tell the world I was on the make. I seduced all I could, the rest went running to confide to their coreligionists that the spirits that flowed here were strong but fleeting: Nicolás Sarmiento isn't going to lead you to the altar, dearie. I made myself interesting, because the sixties demanded it. I tried to seduce the two Elenas, mother and daughter, though without success. They still kept their par-ticular domestic arrangements. But after them came a generation of desperate Mexican women who believed that to be interesting was to be melancholy, miserable, and a reader of Proust. As soon as they satisfied me they would try to commit suicide in my bathroom, with such frequency that I turned, in reaction, to the working class. Secretaries, manicurists, shop clerks who wanted to hook a husband the same as the Mexican princesses, but whom I sidetracked with sweet talk, educating them, teaching them how to walk, dress themselves, and use a finger bowl after eating shrimp (things the women of my first generation had taught me). They coaxed me into educating them, instead of being educated, as I had been by the three preceding generations. So where was my golden mean? The fifth generation left me at a loss. Now they wanted neither to teach me nor to learn from me, only to vie and divide. Sure of themselves, they acted like men and told me that was what it meant to be women. Can that be true? But the philosophy of the good Don Juan is simply this: check out the chicks and chalk them up. And although, when I talk about it, this all sounds quite orderly, the truth is that in my bed, ladies and gentlemen listeners, a great chaos reigned, because there was always an Austro-Hungarian of generation number one who had left a prescription in the medicine cabinet ten years before and returned to reclaim it (in the hope of fanning old flames) and who, seated under said cabinet in a compromising position, would find a potential Galatea throwing up an unknown (to her) kir and, in the bathtub, smothered in soapsuds scented of German woods, a potential Maria Vetsera from the Faculty of Letters and, knocking at the front door, an ex-girlfriend, now married and with five children, with a mind to show me all of them, lined up like marimba keys, simply to make me see what I had lost! I won't even mention the girls (most amusing!) who, during the eighties, began to appear at my house unexpectedly, on pogo sticks, leaping fences behind the Churrigueresque mansions of Virreyes, hopping here and there, from house to house, demonstrating thereby that:

—Private property is okay, pal, but only if it's shared!

They passed like wisps in the breeze, on their pogo sticks, so nubile, ah, as I, turning fifty, saw them bound by as if in a dream, all of them under twenty, assuming the right to enter all the houses, rich or poor, and to talk, to talk, nothing else, with everyone, saying: Get with it, get with what's happening, now!

If you're still listening to me, you might conclude that my destiny was to end up with a woman who would combine the qualities (and the defects, there's no way around it!) of the five generations of ladies I had seduced. You see: the essence of Don Juan is to move, to travel, to scoff at boundaries, whether between countries, gardens, balconies, or beds. For Don Juan there are no doors, or, rather, there is always an unforeseen door for his escape. Now my merry bands of girls on pogo sticks were the Doña Juanitas (damned if they don't smell of pot!) and I, as you know by now, tied to the phone, doing everything by phone, meetings, business deals, love affairs . . .

And servants. I needed them, and very good ones, to throw my famous parties, to receive equally a woman in intimate and attentive circumstances and a crowd of five hundred guests for an epochal bash—the frosting on my house of meringue! But eventually they went out of style, those offensive shows of extravagance, as the richest politicians in Mexico called them, and although I never made a public display of crying over the poverty of my countrymen, at least I always tried to give them honest work. Honest but temporary: what I never could stand was a servant staying with me too long. He would gain power from my past. He would remember the previous women. He couldn't help making comparisons. He would treat the new ones the way he treated the old ones, as if he were trying to serve me well and perform satisfactorily, when the sly fellow would know perfectly well that he was performing poorly and making me look bad: Here's your hot-water bottle, madam, the way you like it. Listen, dog, who are you confusing me with? The diuretic morning grapefruit for the pudgy lady who prefers cheese and tortillas. The confusion becomes an allusion, and no Mexican woman was ever born who can't see, smell, and catch those subtle little in-nuendos. (Except one from Chiapas who was so out of it that I had to clap like crazy to wake her up when she fell asleep in the middle of the action, and then the cunt would pop up and start doing her regional dance. It must be something in the genes. Send them all back to Guatemala!)

Besides denying them the power that cumulative memory gave them over me, I refused to retain my servants, to keep them from intriguing with each other. A servant who stayed more than two years would end up conspiring with other servants against me. The first year, they idolize me and compete with each other; the second, they hate the one they see as my favorite; the third, they join together to throw me out on my ear. All right, then! Here no one passes more than two Christmases in a row. Before the Wise Men make their third trip through the desert on their camels, let the Star of Bethlehem be put out: my butcher and baker and candlestick maker, hey diddle diddle, out on your asses! Cook, upstairs maid, boy, gardener, and a chauffeur who only runs errands because, tied to my telephones and computers, I hardly ever leave my colonial house. That's all I need.

Since I inherited the house, I've kept an exact list of lovers and servants. The first is already rather long, though not like Don Juan's; besides, it's pretty personalized. The servants' list, on the other hand, I try to do seriously, with statistics. Into the computer I put their birthplace, previous occupation. In that way, I have on hand a most interesting sort of sociological profile, since the regions that provide me servants have come down, over the years, to Querétaro, Puebla, the state of Mexico, and Morelos. Next, within each of these, come the cities (Toluca wins by a long shot), the towns, the villages, the old haciendas. Thanks to the relative speed with which I change servants, I think I'll end up covering every square inch of those four federal states. It will be highly entertaining to see what sorts of coincidences, excep-tions, and convergences, among them and in relation to my own life, the detailed memories of my computers will provide. How many instances will there be of servants coming from Zacatlán de las Manzanas, state of Puebla? Or, how many members of the same family will end up in my service? How many will know each other and will gossip about me and my house? The possible combinations of their employment and my accounting are obvious: both are infinite, but the calculation of probabilities is, by definition, finite—repetition is not dispersion but, finally, unity. We all end up looking at ourselves in the mirror of the world and seeing our own foolish faces and nothing more.

The world comes to me and the proof is that here you are, listening to me and hanging on my wise and statistical words. Ahem, as they say in the funnies, and also: How fickle is fate, and how often it manages to give a kick in the pants to the best-laid plans!

The present revolving odalisque was, in a certain sense, my ideal lover. We met by telephone. Tell me if there could be a more perfect *class action*, as we Mexican legal types say; or *serendipity* (what a word!), as the gringo yuppies, who keep on looking for it, say; or *birds of a feather flocking together*, as the prole Indian types around here whom we call *nacos* say. (*Naco* hero on a train: Nacozari. Jealous *naco* in an inn: Nacothello. Corsican *naco* imprisoned on a remote island: Nacoleon. Anarchist *nacos* executed in the electric chair: Naco and Vanzetti.)

—Nacolás Sarmiento.

So she addressed me, mocking me, my last conquest, my latest love, my last girlfriend, how could she fail to conquer me if she entered my game list in this way? Nacolás Sarmiento, she called me, putting me down and tickling me at the same time; her name was Lala and she possessed characteristics of each of the generations that preceded her. She was polyglot like my first round of women (although I suspect that Lala didn't learn languages in an ancestral castle surrounded by governesses, but by the Berlitz method here in the Avenida Chapultepec, or serving meals to the gringo tourists in Ixtapa–Zihuatanejo). Her melancholy was the genuine article, not put in her skull by a decadent prof of philosophy and letters; she didn't know Proust, not even by the book covers—her melancholy was more in the style of the mariachi singer José Alfredo Jiménez:

> *And if they want to know about my past,*
> *I'll have to tell them another lie,*
> *I'll tell them I came from a different world . . .*

I mean that she was pretty mysterious, too good to be true, and when she sang that hold-me-tight, I'd rush to bury myself in her arms and whisper sweet nothings in my tenderest manner . . . Ah, Lala, how I adored you, love, how I adored your tight little ass, my sweet, your savage howling and biting each time I entered your divine zoology, my love, so wild and so refined, so submissive and so mad at the same time, so full of unforgettable details: Lala, you who left me flowers drawn with shaving cream on the bathroom mirror; you who filled champagne bottles with soil; you who highlighted in yellow your favorite names in my telephone books; you who always slept face-down, with your hair disheveled and your mouth half-open, solitary and defenseless, with your hands pressed against your tummy; you who never cut your toenails in my presence, who brushed your teeth with baking soda or ground tortilla, Lala, is it true that I surprised you praying one night, kneeling, and you laughed nervously and showed me a sore knee as excuse, and I said, Let Daddy kiss it and make it better? Lala, you existed only for me, in my bed, in my house, I never saw you outside my vast Churrigueresque prison, but you never felt yourself a prisoner, isn't that so? I never wanted to know about you; as I've said: in all this, the truth is the mystery. Light streaks ran through your hair; you drank carbonated *Tehuacán* before sleeping; you paid the price for a ravenous appetite; you knew how to walk barefoot.

But let's take things in order: of the fourth generation, Lala had a certain lack of breeding that I was going to refine—and to which she submitted willingly, which was the part of her makeup she got from the fifth generation of young little Mexicans, sure of themselves, open to education, experience, professional responsibility. Women, ladies and gentlemen, are like computers: they have passed from the simplest operations, such as adding, subtracting, carrying sums and totaling columns of figures, successively, to the simultaneous operations of the fifth generation: instead of turning each tortilla in turn, we'll turn them all at once. I know this because I've brought to Mexico all the innovations of computation, from the first to the fourth, and now I wait for the fifth and know that the country that discovers it is going to dominate the twenty-first century, which is now approaching, as the old song says, in the murk of night, like an unknown soul, through streets ever winding this way and that, passing like an old-time lover, cloaked in a trailing cape . . . and then the surprise: who'd known all along? Why, who else but Nicolás Sarmiento, the same son of a bitch who subscribes to the gringo magazines and does business by phone and has a new squeeze, dark and silky, called Lala, a true guava of a girl, in his house in Las Lomas.

Who lacked a past. And yet it didn't matter that I learned nothing, I sensed that part of my conquest of Lala consisted in not asking her anything, that what was new about these new Mexicans was that they had no past, or if they had one it was from another time, another incarnation. If that was the case, it only increased Lala's mysterious spell. If her origins were unknown, her present was not: soft, small, burning in all her recesses, dark, always half open and mistress of a pair of eyes that never closed because they never opened; the deliberation of her movements restraining an impetuousness that she and I shared; it was the fear that once exhausted it would not return. No, Lala, always slow, long nights, endless hope, patient flesh, and the soul, my love, always quicker than the body: closer to decadence and death, Lala.

Now I must reveal a fact to you. I don't know if it's ridiculous or painful. Maybe it's simply what I've just said: a fact. I need to have servants because physically I'm a complete idiot. In business I'm a genius, as I've established. But I can't manage practical things. Cooking, for example: zilch. Even for a couple of eggs, I have to get someone to fix them for me. I don't know how to drive; I need a chauffeur. I don't know how to tie my tie or untie my shoes. The result: nothing but these monkey ties with clips that stick in your shirt collars; nothing but slip-ons, never shoes with laces. To women, this all seems sort of endearing and they become maternal with me. They see me so useless in this, such a shark in everything else; they're moved, and they love me that much more. It's true.

But nobody but Lala has known how to kneel before me, with such tenderness, with such devotion, just as if praying, and what's more, with such efficiency: what more perfect way to tie a shoe, leaving the loop expansive as a butterfly ready to fly, yet bound like a link yoked to its twin; and the shoe itself, secure, exact, comfortable, neither too tight nor too loose, a shoe kind to my body, neither constricting nor loose. Lala was perfection, I tell you: *purr-fec-tion*. Neither more nor less. And I say so myself, I who classify my servants by provinces on my computer, but my girls by neighborhoods.

What else should I tell you before I tell you what happened? You suspect already, or maybe not. I had a vasectomy when I was about thirty to avoid having children and so no one can show up in these parts with a brat in her arms, weeping: "Your baby, Nicolás! Aren't you going to acknowledge it? Bastard!" I arranged everything by telephone; it was my business weapon, and although I traveled from time to time, each time I stayed shut up longer in Las Lomas de Chapultepec afterwards. The women came to me and I used my parties to take new ones. I replaced my servants so they wouldn't get the idea that here in Don Nico we've found our gold mine. I never cared, as other Mexican politicians and magnates do, to employ procurers for my women. I make my conquests by myself. As long as I always have someone around to drive my car, cook my beans, and tie my shoes.

All this came to a head one night in July 1982, when the

economic crisis was upon us and I was getting nervous, pondering the significance of a declaration of national bankruptcy, the interplanetary travels of Silva Herzog, the debt, Paul Volcker, and my patents and licenses business, in the middle of all this turmoil. Better to throw a big party to forget the crisis, and I ordered a bar and buffet by the pool. The waiter was new, I didn't know his name; my relationship with Lala had lasted two months now and the lady was growing on me, I was liking her more and more, she made me, I confess, hot and bothered, if the truth be told. She arrived late, when I was already mingling with a hundred revelers, calling on my waiters and the guests alike to sample the Taittinger; who knew when we would see it again, much less taste it!

Lala appeared, and her Saint Laurent strapless gown, of black silk, with a red wrap, would likewise not be seen again *pour longtemps*—believe me, who had arranged for her to wear it. How she glowed, my beautiful love, how all eyes followed her, each and every one, you hear me? to the edge of the pool, where the waiter offered her a glass of champagne; she stood for a long time looking at the *naco* dressed in a white cotton jacket, black pants shiny from so much use by previous boys in my service, bow tie—it was impossible to tell him from the others who had had the same position, the same clothes, the same manner. Manner? The servant lifted his head, she emptied the glass into his face, he dropped the tray in the pool, grabbed Lala's arm violently, she drew away, said something, he answered, everyone watched, I moved forward calmly, took her arm (I saw where his fingers had pressed my lady's soft skin), I told him (I didn't know his name) to go inside, we would talk later. I noticed he seemed confused, a wild uncertainty in his black eyes, his dark jaw quivering. He arranged his glossy hair, parted in the middle, and walked away with his shoulders slumped. I thought he was going to fall into the pool. It's nothing, I told the guests, and everything seemed fine, ladies and gentlemen who are listening to me. I laughed: Remember, the pretexts for parties like this are going fast. Everyone laughed with me and I said nothing to Lala. But she went up to bed and waited for me there. She was asleep when the party ended and I got in. I stepped on a champagne glass as I entered the room. I left it on the floor; and in bed, Lala was sleeping in her elegant Saint Laurent dress. I took off her shoes. I studied her. We were tired. I slept. The next day, I got up around six, with that faint sense of absence that takes shape as we wake—and *she* wasn't there. The tracks of her bare feet, on the other hand, were. Bloody tracks; Lala had cut her feet because of my carelessness in not cleaning up the broken glass. I went out the rococo balcony to the pool. There she was, floating face-down, dressed, barefoot, her feet cut, as if she had gone all night without huaraches, walking on thorns, surrounded by a sea of blood. When I turned her over, there was a gaping wound in her belly; the dagger had been withdrawn. They took my servant Dimas Palmero to the Reclusorio Norte, where he was held, awaiting the slow march of Mexican justice, accused of murder. And I was given the same sentence, though in the Churrigueresque palace of Las Lomas de Chapultepec, once the residence of Brigadier General Prisciliano Nieves, who died one morning in 1960 in the old British hospital on the Avenida Mariano Escobedo.

4

The morning of the tragedy, I had only four servants in the big colonial house of Las Lomas, apart from the said Dimas Palmero: a cook, a maid, a chauffeur, and a gardener. I confess that I can barely recall their features or their names. That is perhaps because, as I work in my house, I have rendered them invisible. If I went out every day to an office, I would notice them, by contrast, on my return. But they stayed out of sight so as not to disturb me. I don't know their names, or what they are like. My secretary, Sarita Palazuelos, dealt with them; I was busy with my work in the house, I'm not married, the servants are invisible. They don't exist, as they say.

I think I'm alone in my house. I hear a voice, I ask:

—Who's there?

—Nobody, sir, answers the maid's little voice.

They prefer to be invisible. But there must be someone.

—Take this gift, girl.

—Oh, sir, you shouldn't. I'm nobody to get presents from you, oh, no!

—Happy birthday, I insist.

—Oh, but you shouldn't be thinking of me, sir.

They return to being invisible.

—Oh! Excuse me!

—Please excuse my boldness, sir.

—I won't bother you for even a moment, sir. I'm just going to dust the furniture.

Now one of them had a name: Dimas Palmero.

I couldn't bear to see him. Hate kept me from sleeping; I hugged the pillow that held the scent, each day fainter, of Lala my love, and I cried in despair. Then, to torture myself, I racked my mind with her memory and imagined the worst: Lala with that boy; Lala in the arms of Dimas Palmero; Lala with a past. Then I realized that I couldn't recall the face of the young murderer. Young: I said that and began to remember. I began to draw him out from the original anonymity with which I regarded him that fatal night. Uniformed as a waiter, white cotton jacket, shiny pants, bow tie, identical to all, same as none. I began to wonder how Lala might have regarded him. Young, I said; was he handsome as well? But, besides being young and handsome, was he interesting? and was he interesting because he held some secret? I induced and deduced like mad those first days of my solitude, and from his secret I passed to his interest, from his interest to his youth, and from there to his good looks. Dimas Palmero, in my strange fiftyish pseudo-widowhood, was the Lucifer who warned me: For the first time in your life, you have lost a woman, cuckold Nicolás, not because you left her, or chased her out, not even because *she* left you, but because I took her away from you and I took her forever. Dimas had to be handsome, and he had to have a secret. No other way a cheap *naco* could have defeated me. It couldn't be. It would have to take a youth who was handsome, at least, and who held a secret, to defeat me.

I had to see him. One night it became an obsession: to see Dimas Palmero, speak with him, convince myself that at least I deserved my grief and my defeat.

They had been bringing me trays of food. I barely touched them. I never saw who brought the tray three times a day, or who took it away. Miss Palazuelos sent a note that she was waiting for my instructions, but what instructions could I give, drowned as I was in melancholy? I told her to take a vacation while I got over my broken heart. I noticed the eyes of the boy who took the message. I didn't know him. Surely Miss Palazuelos had substituted a new boy for Dimas Palmero. But I was obsessed: I saw in this new servant a double, almost, of the incarcerated Dimas. How I wanted to confront my rival!

I was obsessed, and my obsession was to go to the Reclusorio and speak with Dimas, to see him face to face. For the first time in ten days, I showered, I shaved, I put on a decent suit, and I left my bedroom, I went down the stairs of gargoyled ironwork to the colonial hall surrounded by little balconies, with a glazed-tile fountain in the corner, burbling water. I reached the front door and tried, with a natural gesture, to open it. It was locked. Such security! The help had turned cautious, indeed, after the crime. Skittish and, as I've said, invisible. Where were the damned bastards? How did I call them? What did I call them?? Boy, girl! Ah, my good woman, my good man! . . . Fuck it!

Nobody answered. I looked out the stained-glass windows of the hall, parting the curtains. They were there in the gardens. Settled in. Sprawled over the grass, trampling it, smoking cigarettes and crushing the butts in the rose mulch; squatting, pulling from their food bags steaming pigs' feet in green mole and steaming sweet and hot tamales, strewing the ground with the burnt maize leaves; the women coquettishly clipping my roses, sticking them in their shiny black hair, while the kids pricked their hands on the thorns and the piglets crackled over the flame . . . I ran to one of the side windows: they were playing marbles and ball-and-cup, they had set some suspicious, leaking casks by the side of the garage. I ran to the right wing of the mansion: a man was urinating in the narrow, shady part of the garden, a man in a lacquered straw hat was pissing against the wall between my house and . . .

I was surrounded.

A smell of purslane came from the kitchen. I entered. I had never seen the new cook, a fat woman, square as a die, with jet-black hair and a face aged by skepticism.

—I am Lupe, the new cook—she told me—and this is Don Zacarías, the new chauffeur.

Said chauffeur did not even rise from the table where he was eating purslane tacos. I looked at him with astonishment. He was the image of the ex-president Don Adolfo Ruiz Cortines, who in turn was identified, in popular wit, with the actor Boris Karloff: bushy eyebrows, deep eyes, huge bags under the eyes, wrinkles deeper than the Grand Canyon, high forehead, high cheekbones, compressed skull, graying hair brushed to the back.

—Pleased, I said, like a perfect idiot.

I returned to the bedroom and, almost instinctively, I decided to put on some of the few shoes with laces that I have. I looked at myself there, seated on the unmade bed, by the pillow that held her scent, with my shoelaces untied and hanging loose like inert but hungry earthworms. I pulled the bell cord by the headboard, to see who would answer my call.

A few minutes passed. Then knuckles rapped.

He entered, the young man who resembled (according to my fancy) the incarcerated Dimas Palmero. I decided, nonetheless, to tell them apart, to separate them, not to allow any confusion. The murderer was locked away. This was someone else.

—What is your name?

—Marco Aurelio.

You'll notice he didn't say "At your service, sir," or "What may I do for you, *patrón*." Nor did he look at me sideways, eyes hooded, head lowered.

—Tie my shoes.

He looked at me a moment.

—Right now, I said. He continued to look at me, and then knelt before me. He tied the laces.

—Tell the chauffeur I'm going out after eating. And tell the cook to come up so I can plan some menus. And another thing, Marco Aurelio . . .

Now back on his feet, he looked at me fixedly.

—Clear all the intruders out of my garden. If they're not gone within half an hour, I'll call the police. You may go, Marco Aurelio. That's all, you hear?

I dressed, ostentatiously and ostensibly, to go out, I who had gone out so seldom. I decided to try for the first time—almost— a beige gabardine double-breasted suit, blue shirt, stupid yellow clip tie, and, sticking out of my breast pocket, a Liberty handkerchief an Englishwoman had given me.

Real sharp, real shark: I spoke my name and, stomping loudly, I went downstairs. But there it was the same story. Locked door, people surrounding the house. A full-fledged party, and a piñata in the garage. The children squealing happily. A child making a hubbub, trapped in a strange metal crib, all barred in up to the top, like a furnace grate.

—Marco Aurelio!

I sat down in the hall of stained-glass windows. Marco Aurelio solicitously undid my shoes, and, solicitously, offered me my most comfortable slippers. Would I like my pipe? Did I want a brandy? I would lack nothing. The chauffeur would go out and get me any videotape I wanted: new pictures or old, sports, sex, music . . . The family has told me to tell you not to worry. You know, Don Nico, in this country (he was saying as he knelt before me, taking off my shoes, this horrendous *naco*) we survive the worst calamities because we take care of each other, you'll see, I was in Los Angeles as an illegal and the American families there are scattered all around, they live far apart from each other, parents without children, the old ones abandoned, the young ones looking to break away, but here it's just the opposite, Don Nico, how can you have forgotten that? you're so solitary, God help you, not us—if you don't have a job, the family will feed you, it will put a roof over your head, if the cops are after you, or you want to escape the army, the family will hide you, send you back from Las Lomas to Morelos and from there to Los Angeles and back into circulation: the family knows how to move by night, the family is almost always invisible, but what the fuck, Don Nico, it can make its presence felt, how it can make its presence felt! You'll see. So you're going to call the police if we don't go? Then I assure you that the police will not find us here when they arrive, although they will find you, quite stiff, floating in the pool, just like Eduardita, whom God has taken onto . . . But listen, Don Nico, there's no need to look like you've seen a ghost, our message is real simple: you'll lead your usual life, phone all you like, manage your business, throw parties, receive your pals and their dolls, and we'll take care of you, the only thing is, you'll never leave this place as long as our brother Dimas is in the pen: the day that Dimas leaves jail, you leave your house, Don Nico, not a minute before, not a minute later, unless you don't play straight with us, and then you'll leave here first—but they'll carry you out, that much I swear.

He pressed together his thumb and index finger and kissed them noisily as I buried myself in the pillow of Eduardita—my Lala!

5

So began my new life, and the first thing that will strike you, my listeners, is the same thought that occurred to me, in my own house in Las Lomas: Well, really my life hasn't changed; indeed, now I'm more protected than ever; they let me throw my parties, manage my business affairs by telephone, receive the girls who console me for the death of Lala (my cup runneth over: I'm a tragic lover, howboutthat!), and to the cops who showed up to ask why all these people have surrounded my house, packed in the garden, frying quesadillas by the rosebushes, urinating in the garage, they explained: Because this gentleman is very generous, every day he brings us the leftovers from his parties—*every day*! I confirmed this personally to the police, but they looked at me with a mournful smirk (Mexican officials are expert at looking at you with a sardonic grimace) and I understood: So be it. From then on, I would have to pay them their weekly bribe. I recorded it in my expense books, and I had to fire Miss Palazuelos, so that she wouldn't suspect anything. She herself hadn't an inkling why she was fired. I was famous for what I've mentioned: nobody lasted very long with me, not secretary or chauffeur or lover. I'm my own boss, and that's the end of it! You will note that this whole fantastic situation was simply an echo of my normal situation, so there was no reason for anyone to be alarmed: neither the exterior world that kept on doing business with me nor the interior world (I, my servants, my lovers, the same as ever . . .).

The difference, of course, is that this fantastic situation (masquerading as my usual situation) contained one element of abnormality that was both profound and intolerable: it was not the work of my own free will.

There was that one little thing; this situation did not respond to my whim; I responded to it. And it was up to me to end it; if Dimas Palmero went free, I would be freed as well.

But how was I going to arrange for said Dimas to get off? Although I was the one who called the police to have him arrested, he was now charged with murder by the District Attorney's office.

I decided to put on shoes with laces; it was a pretext for asking the valet Marco Aurelio to come up to help me, chat with me, inform me: Were all those people in the garden really the family of the jailed Dimas Palmero? Yes, answered Marco Aurelio, a fine, very extended Mexican family, we all help each other out, as they say. And what else? I insisted, and he laughed at that: We're all Catholic, never the pill, never a condom, the children that God sends . . . Where were they from? From the state of Morelos, all *campesinos*, workers in the cane fields; no, the fields were not abandoned, didn't they tell you, Don Nico? this is hardly the full contingent, ha ha, this is no more than a delegation, we're good in Morelos at organizing delegations and sending them to the capital to demand justice, surely you remember General Emiliano Zapata; well, now you can see that we've learned something. Now we don't ask for justice. Now we make justice. But I am innocent, I said to Marco Aurelio kneeling before me, I lost Lala, I am . . . He lifted his face, black and yellow as the flag of an invisible, hostile nation: —Dimas Palmero is our brother.

Beyond that, I couldn't make him budge. These people are tight-lipped. Our brother: did he mean it literally, or by solidarity? (Stubborn sons of that fucking Zapata!) A lawyer knows that everything in the world (words, the law, love . . .) can be interpreted in the *strict* sense or in the *loose* sense. Was the brotherhood of Marco Aurelio, my extraordinary servant, and Dimas, my incarcerated servant, of blood, or was it figurative? Narrow, or broad? I would have to know to understand my situation. Marco Aurelio, I said one day, even if I withdraw the charges against your brother, as you call him (poker-faced, bilious silence), the prosecutor will try him because too many people witnessed the scene by the pool between Lala and your brother, it doesn't depend on me, they will proceed ex officio, understand? it's not a question of avenging Lala's death . . .

—Our sister . . . But not a whore, no way.

He was kneeling in front of me, tying my shoelaces, and on hearing him say this, I gave him a kick in the face. I assure you it wasn't intentional; it was a brutal reflex responding to a brutal assertion. I gave him a brutal kick in the jaw, I knocked him good, he fell on his back, and I followed my blind instinct, left reason aside (left it sound asleep), and ran down the stairs to the hall just as an unfamiliar maid was sweeping the entrance, and the open door invited me to go out into the morning of Las Lomas, the air sharp with pollution, the distant whoosh of a balloon and the flight of the red, blue, yellow spheres, liberated, far from the empty barranca that surrounded us, its high euca- lyptuses with their peeling bark fighting the smell of shit from the bluff's recesses: globes of colors greeted me as I went out and breathed poison and rubbed my eyes.

My garden was the site of a pilgrimage. The scent of fried food mixed with the odor of shit and eucalyptus: smoke from cookstoves, squeals of children, the strumming of guitars, click of marbles, two policemen flirting with the girls in braids and aprons on the other side of the gargoyled grillwork of my man- sion, an old, toothless, graying man in patched pants and hua- raches, his lacquered straw hat in his hand and an invitation— he came over to me: Please try something, sir, there are good tacos, sir. I looked at the policemen, who didn't look at me but laughed wickedly with the country girls and I thought the stupid cunts were practically pregnant already, who said they weren't whores, giving birth in the open fields to the bastard kids of these bastard cops, their children adding to the family of, of, of this old patriarch who offered me tacos instead of protecting the two girls being seduced by this pair of sinister uniformed bandits, smiling, indifferent to my presence on the steps of my house. Was he going to protect them the way he protected Lala? I got up. I studied him, trying to understand.

What could I do? I thanked him and sat down with him in my own garden and a woman offered us hot tortillas in a willow basket. The old man asked me to take the first bite and I repeated the atavistic gesture of taking the moistened bread of the gods out from under the damp colored napkin, as if the earth itself had opened up to offer me the Proustian madeleine of the Mex- ican: the warm tortilla. (You who are listening to me will re- member that I had plied a whole generation of young readers with Marcel Proust, and he who reads Proust, said a staunch nationalistic friend of mine, Proustitutes himself!) Awful! The truth is that, sitting there with the old patriarch eating hot salted tortillas, I felt so transported, so back in my mama's arms again or something like that, that I was already telling myself, forget it, let's have the tortillas, let's have those casks of *pulque* that I saw going into the garage the other day; they brought us brimming glasses of thick liquor, tasting of pineapple, and Marco Aurelio must have had a pretty good knock, because there wasn't a trace of him to be seen. I sat with my legs crossed on my own lawn, the old man feeding me, I questioning him: How long are you going to be here? Don't worry, we don't have to return to Morelos, this could go on for years, do you realize that, señor? He looked at me with his ageless face, the old goat, and told me that they were taking turns, hadn't I caught on? They came and went, they were never the same twice, every day some went home and others arrived, because it's a question of making a sacrifice for Dimas Palmero and for Eduardita, poor child, too, hadn't I realized? Did I think it was always the same folk outside here? He laughed a little, tapping his gummy mouth: the truth was that I had never really noticed them, to me they had, indeed, all appeared the same . . .

But each one is different, the old man said quickly, with a dark seriousness that filled me with fear, each one comes into the world to aid his people, and although most die in infancy, those who have the good fortune to grow, those, señor, are a treasure for an old man like me, they are going to inherit the earth, they are going to go to work there in the North with the gringos, they are going to come to the capital to serve you; and they won't send money to the old folks, you can't argue with that, señor (he resumed his usual cordiality), if the old folks don't know who each of their children are, their names, what they do, what they look like, if we depend on them to keep from dying of hunger when we grow old? Just one condition, he said, pausing:

—Poor, señor, but proud.

He looked over my shoulder, waved. I followed his look. Marco Aurelio in his white shirt and his black pants was rubbing his chin, resting against the door of the house. I got up, thanked the old man, brushed the dirt from my rear, and walked toward Marco Aurelio. I knew that, from then on, it would be nothing but loafers for me.

6

That night I had a terrifying dream that those people would stay here forever, renewing themselves again and again, generation after generation, without concern for any one individual destiny, least of all that of a little half-elegant lawyer: the canny dandy of Las Lomas de Chapultepec. They could hold out until I died. But I still couldn't understand how my death would avenge that of Dimas Palmero, who languished in preventive custody, waiting for the Mexican judicial tortoise to summon him to justice. Listen close. I said tortoise, not torture. That could take years, didn't I know it. If they observed the law limiting the amount of time a man can be detained before being tried, Mexico would stop being what it always has been: a reign of influence, whim, and injustice. So I tell you, and you, like it or not, you have to listen. If I'm the prisoner of Las Lomas, you're the prisoners of my telephones—you listen to me.

Don't imagine I haven't thought of all the ways I could make this my link to the outside, my Ariadne's thread, my vox humana. I have a videotape I often watch, given the circumstances: poor Barbara Stanwyck lying paralyzed in bed, listening to the footsteps of the murderer climbing the stairs to kill her and take control of her millions (will it be her husband? suspense!), and she is trying to call the police and the telephone is out of order, a voice answering, sorry, wrong number . . . What a thriller! — *La voix humaine*, a French girlfriend told me . . . But this was not a Universal picture, only a modest Huaraches Films production, or some such totally asshole thing. All right, I know that I speak to you to take my mind off things for a while; don't think, however, that I have ever stopped plotting my escape. It would be so easy, I tell myself, to go on strike, stop using my phones to make money, neglect my bank accounts, stop talking to you, to my public auditors, my stockbrokers . . . My immediate conclusion: these people wouldn't give a fuck about my poverty. They are not here to take my cash. If I didn't feed them, they would feed me. I suspect that this Morelos operation functions as efficiently as a Japanese assembly line. If I became poor, they would come to my assistance!

You are free as I was once, and you will understand when I say that, come what may, one doesn't easily resign oneself to giving up one's liberty just like that. Very well: they have sworn to kill me if I denounce them. But what if I managed to escape, hide, set the authorities on them from afar? Don't try it, Don Nico, said my recovered jailer, Marco Aurelio, we are many, we will find you; he laughed: there are branches of the family in Los Angeles, in Texas, in Chicago, even in Paris and London, where rich Mexican señoras take their Agripinas, their Rudecindas, and their Dalmacias to work abroad . . . It wouldn't surprise me to see some guy in a big sombrero get off a jumbo jet at Charles de Gaulle Airport and chop me to bits in the middle of Paris, laughing wickedly, brandishing the machete that dangles eternally from him like a spare penis. How I hated Marco Aurelio! How dare one of these cheap *nacos* talk so familiarly about General de Gaulle! That's instant communications for you!

They knew my intentions. I took advantage of one of my parties to put on the overcoat and hat of a friend, without his noticing, and while everyone was drinking the last bottle of Taittinger (the pretext for the party) and eating exquisite canapés prepared by the block-shaped fat woman of the kitchen, Doña Lupe (a genius, that woman!), with the hat pulled down over my ears and my lapels turned up, I slipped through the door, which was open that night (and every night: you must realize that my jailers no longer imagined that I would escape, what for? if my life was the same as ever!—me inside with my parties and my telephones; they outside, invisible: as always!). As I say, they no longer locked the door. But I disguised myself and slipped through the door because I didn't want to accept a sentence of confinement imposed by others. I did so without caring about success or failure. The door, freedom, the street, the jumbo to Paris, even if I was met there by Rudecinda, the cousin of Marco Aurelio, rolling pin in hand . . .

—You forgot to tie your shoes, Don Nico, said Marco Aurelio, holding high a tray heaped with canapés, looking at my feet, and blocking the way to the front door.

I laughed, sighed, took off the overcoat and the hat, returned to my guests.

I tried it several times, I wouldn't give up, to keep my self-respect. But one time I couldn't get beyond the garden, because the children, instinctively, surrounded me, forming a circle, and sang a play song to me. Another time, escaping at night by the balcony, I was hanging by my fingernails when I heard a group at my feet serenading me: it was my birthday and I had forgotten! Many happy returns, Don Nico, these are the years of your life that . . . ! I was in despair: fifty springtimes in these circumstances! In desperation I resorted to Montecristo's strategy: I feigned death, lying very stiff in my bed; not to give up, as I say, to touch all the bases. Marco Aurelio poured a bucket of cold water on me and I cried out, and he just stood there, saying: Don Nico, when you die on me, I'll be the first to let you know, you can be sure. Will you cry for me, Marco Aurelio, you bastard? I was incensed! I thought first of poisoning my immediate jailers, the valet Marco Aurelio, the cubic cook, the Karloff car man; but not only did I suspect that others would rush in to replace them, I also feared (inconsistent of me!) that while the lawsuit against the miserable Dimas Palmero dragged on indefinitely, an action against me for poisoning my servants would be thunderous, scandalous, trumpeted in the press: Heartless Millionaire

Poisons Faithful Servants! From time to time, a few fat morsels must be cast to the (nearly starved) sharks of justice . . . Besides, when I entered the kitchen, Doña Lupe was so kind to me: Do sit down, Don Nico, do you know what I'm fixing today? Can you smell it? Don't you like your cheese and squash? Or would you rather have what we're fixing ourselves, *chilaquilitos* in green sauce? This made my mouth water and made life seem bearable. The chauffeur and the boy sat down to eat with Doña Lupe and me, they told me stories, they were quite amusing, they made me remember, remember her . . .

So why didn't I explain my situation to the girls who passed through my parties and my bed? What would they think of such a thing? Can you imagine the ridicule, the incredulity? So just leave when you want to, Nicolás, who's going to stop you? But they'll kill me, baby. Then I'm going to save you, I'm going to inform the police. Then they'll kill you along with me, my love. Or would you rather live on the run, afraid for your life? Of course I never told them a thing, nor did they suspect anything. I was famous as a recluse. And they came to console me for the death of Lala. Into my arms, goddesses, for life is short, but the night is long.

7

I saw her. I tell you I saw her yesterday, in the garden.

8

I called a friend of mine, an influential man in the District Attorney's office: What do you know about the case of my servant, Dimas Palmero? My friend stopped laughing and said: Whatever you want, Nicolás, is how we'll handle it. You understand: if you like, we'll keep him locked up without a trial until Judgment Day; if you prefer, we'll move up the court date and try him tomorrow; if what you want is to see him free, that can be arranged, and, look, Nicolás, why play dumb, there are people who disappear, who just simply disappear. Whatever you like, I repeat.

Whatever I liked. I was on the point of saying no, this Dimas or Dimass or Dimwit or whatever he's called isn't the real problem, I'm the prisoner, listen, call my lawyer, have the house surrounded, make a big fuss, kill these bastards . . .

I thanked my friend for his offer and hung up without indicating a preference. What for? I buried my head in my pillow. There is nothing left of Lala, not even the aroma. I racked my brains thinking: What should I do? What solution have I overlooked? What possibilities have I left in the inkwell? I had an inspiration; I decided to speed things up. I went down to the kitchen. It was the hour when Marco Aurelio, Doña Lupe, and the chauffeur with the face of the former president ate. The smell of pork in purslane came up the rococo stairway, stronger than the scent, ever fainter, of Lala—Eduardita, as they called her. I went down berating myself furiously: What was I thinking? Why this terrible helplessness? Why did I think only of myself, not of her, who was the victim, after all? I deserved what had happened to me; I was the prisoner of Las Lomas even before all this happened, I was imprisoned by my own habits, my comfortable life, my easy business deals, my even easier loves. But also—I said when my bare feet touched the cold tile of the living room— I was bound by a sort of devotion and respect for my lovers: I didn't ask questions, I didn't check out their stories: —I have no past, Nico, my life commenced the moment we met, and I might whistle a tune as my only comment, but that was all.

The three were sitting comfortably eating their lunch.

—May I? I inquired cordially.

Doña Lupe got up to prepare something for me. The two men didn't budge, although Marco Aurelio waved for me to sit down. The presidential double merely looked at me, without blinking, from the imperturbable depths of his baggy eyes.

—Thank you. I came down just to ask a question. It occurred

to me that what is important to you is not to keep me imprisoned here but to free Dimas. That's right, isn't it?

The cook served me an aromatic dish of pork with purslane, and I began to eat, looking at them. I had said the same thing that they had always said to me: You leave here the day our brother Dimas Palmero gets out of jail. Why now these little looks exchanged between them, this air of uncertainty, if I had only repeated what we all knew: the unwritten rule of our covenant? Give me statutory law; down with *common law*, which is subject to all sorts of interpretations and depends too much on the ethics and good sense of the people. But these peasants from Morelos must be, like me, inheritors of Roman law, where all that counts is what is written, not what is done or not done, even if it violates the letter of the law. The law, sirs, is august, and supersedes all exceptions. These people's lands always had depended on a statute, a royal decree; and now I felt that my life also was going to depend on a written contract. I looked at the looks of my jailers as they looked at each other.

—Tell me if you are willing to put this in writing: The day that Dimas Palmero gets out of the pen, Nicolás Sarmiento goes free from Las Lomas. Agreed?

I began to lose confidence; they didn't answer; they looked at each other, suspicious, tight-lipped, let me tell you, the faces of all three marked with a feline wariness; but hadn't I merely asked them to confirm in writing what they had always said! Why this unforeseen suspicion all of a sudden?

—We've been thinking, Don Nico, said Marco Aurelio finally, and we have reached the conclusion that you could quickly arrange for our brother Dimas Palmero to be freed; then we let you go; but you could still play us a trick and have the law spread its net over Dimas again. —And over us, too, said the cook, not even sighing.

—That game has been played on us plenty, said the pale, baggy-eyed chauffeur gloomily, arranging his hair with his five-fingered comb.

—Come on, come on, the cook emphatically exhorted the electric stove, atavistically airing it with her hands and lips, as if it were a charcoal brazier. The old idiot!

—So what we're willing to write down, Don Nico, is that you'll be freed when you confess to the murder of Eduardita, so that our brother cannot be judged for a crime committed by another.

I won't give them the pleasure of spitting out the pork (anyway, it's quite tasty), or of spilling my glass of fermented pineapple juice, which, quite complacently, the cook has just set in front of my nose. I'm going to give them a lesson in cool, even though my head is spinning like a carousel.

—That was not our original agreement. We've been shut up together here more than three months. Our accord is now binding, as they say.

—Nobody ever respected any agreement with us, the cook quickly replied, waving her hands furiously, as though they were straw fans, in front of the electric burner.

—Nobody, said the chauffeur sepulchrally. All they do is send us to hell.

And I was going to pay for all the centuries of injustice toward the people of Morelos? I didn't know whether to laugh or cry. The simple truth was, I didn't know what to say. I was too busy taking in my new situation. I pushed my plate aside and left the kitchen without saying a word. I climbed the stairs with the sensation that my body was a sick friend I was following with great difficulty. I sat down in the bathroom and there I remained, sleeping. But even my dreams betrayed me. I dreamed that they were right. Damn! They were right.

9

And it is you who wake me, with a furious ringing, a buzz of alarm, calling me on the phone, questioning me urgently, sympathizing with me: Why don't I ask them about her? About whom? I say, playing the fool. About Lala, la Eduarda, la Eduardita, as they called her, la Lala, la . . . Why? She's the key to the whole business! You're completely in the dark: what was behind that scene between Lala and Dimas by the pool? Who was Lala? Have all these people besieged you because of her, or him, or both of them? Why not find out? Fool!

Both of them. I laughed, fell back to sleep, sitting on the toilet in the bathroom, with my pajama bottoms rolled down around my ankles, in a stupor: both of them, you said, without realizing that I can't bear to imagine, much less to pursue the thought, of her with another—she with another, that thought I cannot bear, and you laugh at me, I hear your laughter on the telephone line, you say goodbye, you accuse me, you ask when I got so delicate and sentimental? You, Nicolás Sarmiento, who have had dozens of women just as dozens of women have had you, both you and they members of a city and a society that abandoned all that colonialcatholiccantabrian hypocrisy a few generations ago and cheerfully dedicated themselves to fucking anyone, you who know perfectly well that your dames come to you from others and go from you to others, just as they know that you weren't a monk before you knew them, nor will you become one after leaving them: you, Nicolás Sarmiento, the Don Juan of venture capital, are going to tell us now that you can't bear the thought of your Lala in the arms of Dimas Palmero? Why? It turns your stomach to think that she slept with a servant? Could it be that your horror is more social than sexual? Tell us! Wake up!

I tell you I saw her in the garden.

I got up slowly from the bathroom, I pulled up my pajamas, I didn't have to tie them, they closed with a snap, thank God, I'm hopeless for daily life, I'm only good at making money and making love; does that justify a life?

I look at the garden from the window of my bedroom.

Tell me if you don't see her, standing, with her long braids, a knee slightly bent, looking toward the barranca, surprised to be caught between the city and nature, unable to tell where one begins and the other ends, or which imitates the other: the barranca doesn't smell of the mountains, it smells of the buried city and the city no longer smells of city but of infirm nature: she longs for the country, looking toward the barranca, now Doña Lupe goes out for air, approaches the girl, puts a hand on her shoulder, and says: Don't be sad, you mustn't, you're in the city now and the city can be ugly and hard, but so can the country, the country is at least as violent as the city, I could tell you stories, Eduarda . . .

I'll say it straight out. There is only one redeeming thing in my life and that is the respect I've shown my women. You can condemn me as egotistical, or frivolous, or condescending, or manipulating, or unable to tie my shoes. The one thing you can't accuse me of is sticking my nose where it doesn't belong. I think that's all that has saved me. I think that's why women have loved me: I don't ask for explanations, I don't check out their pasts. No one can check the past of anyone in a society as fluid as ours. Where are you from? What do you do? Who were your mama and papa? Each of our questions can be a wound that doesn't heal. A wound that keeps us from loving or being loved. Everything betrays us: the body sends us one signal and an expression reveals another, words turn against themselves, the mind cons us, death deceives death . . . Beware!

10

I saw Lala that afternoon in the garden, when she was nobody, when she was someone else, when she looked dreamily over a barranca, when she was still a virgin. I saw her and realized that she had a past and that I loved her. These, then, were her people. This, then, was all that remained of her, her family, her people, her land, her nostalgia. Dimas Palmero, was he her lover or her brother, either one longing for revenge? Marco Aurelio, was he really the brother of Dimas or, perhaps, of Eduardita? What was her relationship to the cook Doña Lupe, the baggy-eyed chauffeur, the shabby old patriarch?

I dressed. I went down to the living room. I went out to the garden. There was no longer any reason to bar my way. We all knew the rules, the contract. One day we would sit down to write it out and formalize it. I walked among the running children, took a piece of jerky without asking permission, a plump red-cheeked woman smiled at me, I waved cordially to the old man, the old man looked up and caught my eye, he put out his hand for me to help him up, he looked at me with an incredible intensity, as if only he could see that second body of mine, my sleepy companion struggling behind me through life.

I helped the old man up and he took my arm with a grip as firm as his gaze, and said: "I will grow old but never die. You understand." He led me to the edge of the property. The girl was still standing there, and Doña Lupe put her arms around her, enveloping her shoulders in her huge embrace. We went over to her, and Marco Aurelio, too, half whistling, half smoking. We were a curious quintet, that night in Las Lomas de Chapultepec, far from their land, Morelos, the country, the cane fields, the rice fields, the blue sculpted mountains cut off at the top, secret, where it is said the immortal guerrilla Zapata still rides his white horse . . .

I approached them. Or, rather, the old patriarch who had also decided to be immortal came to me, and the old man almost forced me to join them, to embrace them. I looked at the pretty girl, dark, ripe as those sweet oranges, oranges with an exciting navel and juices slowly evaporating in the sun. I took her dark arm and thought of Lala. Only this girl didn't smell of perfume, she smelled of soap. These, then, were her people, I repeated. This, then, was all that remained of her, of her feline grace, her fantastic capacity for learning conventions and mimicking fashions, speaking languages, being independent, loving herself and loving me, letting go her beautiful body with its rhythmic hips, shaking her small sweet breasts, looking at me orgasmically, as

if a tropical river suddenly flowed through her eyes at the moment
she desired me, oh my adored Lala, only this remains of you:
your rebel land, your peasant forebears and fellows, your province
as a genetic pool, bloody as the pool where you died, Lala, your
land as an immense liquid pool of cheap arms for cutting cane
and tending the moist rows of rice, your land as the ever-flowing
fountain of workers for industry and servants for Las Lomas
residences and secretary-typists for ministries and clerks in de-
partment stores and salesgirls in markets and garbage collectors
and chorus girls in the Margo Theater and starlets in the national
cinema and assembly-line workers in the border factories and
counter help in Texas Taco Huts and servants in mansions like
mine in Beverly Hills and young housewives in Chicago and
young lawyers like me in Detroit and young journalists in New
York: all swept in a dark flow from Morelos, Oaxaca, Guana-
juanto, Michoacán, and Potosí, all tossed about the world in
currents of revolution, war, liberation, the glory of some, the
poverty of others, the audacity of a few, the contempt of many
. . . liberty and crime.

Lala, after all, had a past. But I had not imagined it.

11

It wasn't necessary to formalize our agreement. It all started long
ago, when the father of my sainted fiancée, Buenaventura del
Rey, gave me the key to blackmail General Prisciliano Nieves
in his hospital bed and force him to bequeath me his large house
in Las Lomas in exchange for his honor as hero of Santa Eulalia.
Like me, you have probably asked yourselves: Why didn't Buenaventura's father use that same information? And you know the
answer as well as I. In our modern world, things come only to
those who know how to use information. That's the recipe for
power now, and those who let information slip through their
fingers will fail miserably. On one side, weak-knees like the papa
of Buenaventura del Rey. On the other side, sharks like Nicolás
Sarmiento your servant. And in between, these poor, decent

people who don't have any information, who have only memory, a memory that brings them suffering.

Sometimes, audaciously, I cast pebbles into that genetic pool, just to study the ripples. Santa Eulalia? La Zapotera? General Nieves, whose old house in Las Lomas we all inhabit, they unaware and me well informed, naturally? What did they know? In my computer were entered the names and birthplaces of this sea of people who served me, most from the state of Morelos, which is, after all, the size of Switzerland. What information did Dimas Palmero possess?

(So you come from La Zapotera in Morelos. Yes, Don Nico. Then you know the hacienda of Santa Eulalia? Of course, Don Nico, but to call it a hacienda . . . you know, there's only a burnt-out shell. It's what they called a sugar mill. Ah yes, you probably played in it as a child, Dimas. That's right, señor. And you heard stories about it? Yes, of course. The wall where the Escalona family was lined up in front of a firing squad must still be there? Yes, my grandfather was one of those who was going to be shot. But your grandfather was not a landowner. No, but the colonel said he was going to wipe out both the owners and those who served them. And then what happened? Then another commander said no, Mexican soldiers don't murder the people, because they are the people. And then, Dimas? Then they say that the first officer gave the order to fire on the masters and the servants, but the second officer gave a counterorder. Then the soldiers shot the first officer, and then the Escalona family. They didn't fire at the servants. And then? Then they say the soldiers and the servants embraced and cheered, señor. But you don't remember the names of those officers, Dimas? No, even the old ones no longer remember. But if you like I can try to find out, Don Nico. Thank you, Dimas. At your service, sir.)

12

Yes, I imagine that Dimas Palmero had some information, who knows—but I'm sure that his relatives, crammed into my garden, kept the memory alive.

I approached them. Or, rather, I approached the old patriarch
and he practically forced me to join them, to greet the others. I
looked at the pretty, dark girl. I touched her dark arm. I thought
of Lala. Doña Lupe had her arm around the girl. The bluish-
haired grandfather, that old man as wrinkled as an old piece of
silk, supported by the solid body of the cook, playing with the
braids of the red-cheeked girl, all looking together toward the
barranca of Las Lomas de Chapultepec: I was anxious to find
out if they had a collective memory, however faint, of their own
land, the same land about which I had information exclusively
for my advantage; I asked them if someone had told them the
names, did the old men remember the names? Nieves? Does that
name mean anything to you—Nieves? Solomillo? Do you remember these old names? I asked, smiling, in an offhand manner,
to see if the laws of probability projected by my computer would
hold: the officers, the death of the Escalona family, Santa Eulalia,
the Zapotera . . . One of those you mention said he was going
to free us from servitude, the old man said very evenly, but when
the other one put all of us, masters and servants, in front of a
wall, Prisciliano, yes, Prisciliano, now I remember, said, "Mexican soldiers don't murder the people, because they are the people," and the other officer gave the order to fire, Prisciliano gave
the counterorder, and the soldiers fired first at Prisciliano, then
at the landowners, and finally at the second officer.

—Solomillo? Andrés Solomillo.

—No, Papa, you're getting mixed up. First they shot the landowners, then the revolutionary leaders began to shoot each other.

—Anyway, they all died, said the old survivor with something
like resigned sadness.

—Oh, it was a long time ago, Papa.

—And you, what happened to you?

—The soldiers shouted hurray and threw their caps in the air,
we tossed our sombreros in the air too, we all embraced, and I
swear, sir, no one who was present that morning in Santa Eulalia
will ever forget that famous line, "The soldiers are the peo-

ple . . ." Well, the important thing, really, was that we'd gotten rid of the landowners first and the generals after.

He paused a moment, looking at the barranca, and said: *And it didn't do us a bit of good.*

The old man shrugged, his memory was beginning to fail him, surely; besides, they told so many different stories about what happened at Santa Eulalia, you could just about believe them all; it was the only way not to lie, and the old man laughed.

—But in the midst of so much death, there's no way to know who survived and who didn't.

—No, Papa, if you don't remember, who is going to?

—You are, said the old man. That is why I tell you. That is how it has always been. The children remember for you.

—Does Dimas know this story? I ventured to ask, immediately biting my tongue for my audacity, my haste, my . . . The old man showed no reaction.

—It all happened a long time ago. I was a child then and the soldier just told us: You're free, there's no more hacienda, or landowners, or bosses, nothing but freedom, our chains were removed, *patrón*, we were free as air. And now see how we end up, serving still, or in jail.

—Long live our chains! Marco Aurelio gave a laugh, a cross between sorrow and cynicism, as he passed by, hoisting a Dos Equis, and I watched him, thinking of Eduarda as a child, how she must have struggled to reach my arms, and I thought of Dimas Palmero in prison and of how he would stay there, with his memory, not realizing that memory was information, Dimas in his cell knowing the same story as everyone, conforming to the memory of the world and not the memory of his people— Prisciliano Nieves was the hero of Santa Eulalia—while the old man knew what Dimas forgot, didn't know, or rejected: Prisciliano Nieves had died in Santa Eulalia; but neither of them knew how to convert his memory into information, and my life depended on their doing nothing, on their memory, accurate or not, remaining frozen forever, an imprisoned memory, you understand, my accomplices? Memory their prisoner, information my prisoner, and both of us here, not moving from the house, both of us immobile, both prisoners, and everyone happy, so I immediately said to Marco Aurelio: Listen, when you visit your brother, tell him he'll lack for nothing, you hear me? Tell him that they'll take good care of him, I promise, he can get married, have conjugal visits, you know: I've heard it said in the house that he likes this red-cheeked girl with the bare arms, well, he can marry her, she's not going to run off with one of these bandits, you've seen what they're like, Marco Aurelio, but tell Dimas not to worry, he can count on me, I'll pay for the wedding and give the girl a dowry, tell him I'm taking him, and all of you, into my care, you will all be well cared for, I'll see to it that you'll never lack for anything, neither you here nor Dimas in the pen, he won't have to work, or you either, I'll look after the family, resigned to the fact that the real criminal will never be found: Who killed Eduarda? We'll never know, I swear, when a girl like that comes to the city and becomes independent, neither you nor I, nobody, is guilty of anything . . .

That was my decision. I preferred to remain with them and leave Dimas in jail rather than declare myself guilty or pin the crime on someone else. They understood. I thought of Dimas Palmero locked up and also of the day I presented myself to Brigadier Prisciliano Nieves in his hospital room.

—Sign here, my general. I promise to take care of your servants and your honor. You can rest in peace. Your reputation is in my hands. I wouldn't want it to be lost, believe me. I will be as silent as the grave; I will be your heir.

The dying Brigadier Prisciliano Nieves looked at me with enormous brazenness. I knew then that his possessions no longer mattered to him, that he wouldn't bat an eyelash.

—Do you have any heirs, other than your servants, I asked, and the old man surely had not expected that question, which I put to him as I took a hand mirror from the table next to the bed and held it in front of the sick face of the general, in this way registering his surprise.

Who knows what the false Prisciliano saw there.

—No, I have no one.

Well informed, I already knew that. The old man ceased to look at his death's face and looked instead at mine, young, alert, perhaps resembling his own anonymous youthful look.

—My general, you are not you. Sign here, please, and die in peace.

To each his own memory. To each his own information. The world believed that Prisciliano Nieves killed Andrés Solomillo at Santa Eulalia. The old patriarch installed in my house knew that they had all killed each other. My first sweetheart Buenaventura del Rey's papa, paymaster of the constitutionalist army, knew that as well. Between the two memories lay my twenty-five years of prosperity. But Dimas Palmero, in jail, believed like everyone else that Prisciliano Nieves was the hero of Santa Eulalia, its survivor and its enforcer of justice. His information *was* the world's. The old men, by contrast, *held* the world's information, which isn't the same. Prisciliano Nieves died, along with Andrés Solomillo, at Santa Eulalia, when the former said that the soldiers, being the people, would not kill the people, and the latter proved the contrary right there, and barely had Prisciliano fallen when Solomillo, too, was cut down by the troops. Who usurped the legend of Prisciliano Nieves? What had been that man's name? Who profited from the slaughter of the leaders? No doubt, someone just as anonymous as those who had invaded my garden and surrounded my house. That was the man I visited one morning in the hospital and blackmailed. I converted memory to information. Buenaventura's papa and the ragged old man residing in my garden retained memory but lacked information. Only I had both, but as yet I could do nothing with them except to ensure that everything would go on the same as always, that nothing would be questioned, that it would never occur to Dimas Palmero to translate the memory of his clan into information, that neither the information nor the memory would ever do anyone any good anymore, except for me. But the price of that deadlock was that I would remain forever in my house

in Las Lomas, Dimas Palmero in jail, and his family in my
garden.

In the final analysis, was it I who won, he who lost? That I
leave for you to decide. Over my telephone lines, you have heard
all I've said. I've been completely honest with you. I've put all
my cards on the table. If there are loose ends in my story, you
can gather them up and tie them in a bow yourselves. My memory
and my information are now yours. You have the right to criticize,
to finish the story, to reverse the tapestry and change the weave,
to point out the lapses of logic, to imagine you have resolved all
the mysteries that I, the narrator crushed under the press of
reality, have let escape through the net of my telephones, which
is the net of my words.

And still I'll bet you won't know what to do with what you
know. Didn't I say so from the beginning? My story is hard to
believe.

Now I no longer had to take risks and struggle. Now I had
my place in the world, my house, my servants, and my secrets.
I no longer had the guts to go see Dimas Palmero in prison and
ask him what he knew about Prisciliano Nieves or what he knew
about Lala: Why did you kill her? On your own? Because the
old man ordered you to? For the honor of the family? Or for your
own?

—Lala, I sighed, my Lala . . .

Then through the gardens of Virreyes came the girls on pogo
sticks, hopping like nubile kangaroos, wearing sweatshirts with
the names of Yankee universities on them and acid-washed jeans
with Walkmans hooked between blue jean and belt and the fantastic look of Martians, radio operators, telephone operators, avia-
tors all rolled into one, with their black earphones over their
ears, hopping on their springy pogo sticks over the hedges that
separate the properties of Las Lomas—spectacular, Olympic
leaps—waving to me, inviting me to follow them, to find myself
through others, to join the party, to take a chance with them:
Let's all crash the parties, they say, that's more fun, hopping by

like hares, like fairies, like Amazons, like Furies, making private property moot, seizing their right to happiness, community, entertainment, and God knows what . . . Free, they would never make any demands on me, ask for marriage, dig into my affairs, discover my secrets, the way the alert Lala did . . . Oh, Lala, why were you so ambitious?

I wave to them from a distance, surrounded by servants, goodbye, goodbye, I toss them kisses and they smile at me, free, carefree, dazzling, dazzled, inviting me to follow them, to abandon my prison, and I wave and would like to tell them no, I am not the prisoner of Las Lomas, no, they are my prisoners, an entire people . . .

I enter the house and disconnect my bank of telephones. The fifty-seven lines on which you're listening to me. I have nothing else to tell you. Soon there will be no one to repeat these fictions, and they will all be true. I thank you for listening.

Merton House
Cambridge
May 1987

Viva Mi Fama

Muera yo, pero viva mi fama
Let me die, but let my fame endure
    Guillén de Castro, *The Youth of El Cid*

For Soledad Becerril and Rafael Atienza, ex toto corde

Sunday

What he would particularly remember about that Sunday was the quiet tedium. Lying on the sofa in T-shirt and briefs to beat the unbearable heat, but wearing his socks out of a sense of decorum even he could not explain, he leaned his head against his raised arms and clenched fists, watching the frozen, repeating image of the black bull in an Osborne brandy ad on the television screen: why should that seductive yet bestial image linger there, inviting us to consume an alcoholic drink, perhaps threatening us—will we be killed, gored by that mercantile bull, if we reject his command: Drink me? Rubén Oliva was about to pose that question to his wife when the voice of the announcer praising the bull's brandy became smothered by the smells of other, louder voices wafting in from the street, from neighboring balconies and from distant open windows. He heard them as smells because those voices—bits of soap-opera dialogue, commercials like the one he was watching, children's squeals, domestic squabbles—reached him with the same mixture of faintness and force, immediate yet immediately dissipated, as the kitchen smells that circulated through that lower-class neighborhood. He shook his head; he didn't distinguish between a newborn's wail and a whiff of stew. He put his hands back over his eyes and rubbed them, as if his hands could scour out the shadows under his intense green eyes, lost in cavernous depths of dark skin. Surely those eyes shone more brightly because they were ringed by such darkness. They were lively but serene eyes, resigned, always alert, though without illusions that anything could be done with the day's news. To wake, to sleep, to wake again. He looked back at the television screen, the figure of the bull at once dark and clear, heavy and light, a pasteboard bull that was also flesh and blood, ready to attack if he, Rubén Oliva, didn't obey the command: Drink!

He got up with a wince, but easily; he wasn't heavy, he never had to make an effort to stay slim. A doctor had said to him: —It's heredity, Rubén, you can thank your metabolism. —Centuries of hunger, you mean, he had answered.

He worried sometimes about turning forty within the year, developing a paunch; but no, skinny he was born and skinny he would die. He smiled and, smelling beans cooking in oil, went to the balcony to watch the kids running along Calle Jesús Fucar, like him dressed in T-shirt, shorts, and sandals with socks, repeating until everyone was sick of it the tired old comic ditty about the days of the week: "Monday one, Tuesday two, Wednesday three, Thursday four, Friday five, Saturday six," they sang all together, and then a single voice, "and Sunday seven!" The others laughed and they began another round of the week, ending with another lone voice crying out the "Sunday seven!" business, and the others laughing again. But Sunday would come in turn to each, muttered Rubén Oliva from his balcony, his elbows resting on the iron balustrade, the taunts and the jests divided equally, and then he stopped talking, because talking to yourself was the mania of a deaf man or a madman and he wasn't even alone, which would have been a third excuse for such a monologue.

The voices, the various emissions, were silenced then by a sudden wind, a summer gust that picked up worn-out dust and discarded papers, whirling and swirling them along the narrow, boxed-in street, forcing Oliva to close the window and the voice from the kitchen to scream at him: —What are you doing? Can't you help me in the kitchen? Don't you know it isn't good to fix a meal when you're menstruating? Are you going to help me, or would you rather have poisoned soup?

Rubén Oliva had forgotten she was there.

—You can fix dinner, Rubén called back, what you can't do is water the plants. That *is* true, you could kill the plants if you water them when you are unwell. That is true, Rocío, yes.

He lay back down on the sofa, raising his arms and resting his

head on the joined fingers of his open hands. He closed his eyes
as he had closed the window, but in such intense heat the sweat
dripped from his forehead, neck, and armpits. The heat from the
kitchen added to that of the living room, but Rubén Oliva remained there, with his eyes shut, incapable of getting up and
reopening the window that let in the little noises and fading
smells of a Sunday afternoon in Madrid, when the unexpected
breeze died away and they were shut inside the little four-room
flat—living room, bedroom, bath, and kitchen—he and his wife,
Rocío, who was menstruating and fixing supper.

And yelling from the kitchen, always complaining, why was
he so shiftless, idling there instead of going out to work, others
worked on Sunday, he always used to, things were getting so
bad for them now that he wasn't working on Sundays, she could
see she was going to have to support the household soon if they
didn't want to live like beggars, just look at them stuck in this
pigsty, and in the middle of August, when everyone else had
gone to the beach, can you tell me why, listen to me, if you go
on this way I'm going to look for work myself, and the way
things are, with all the nudity these days, I'll probably end up
posing naked for some magazine, that's the kind of thing I'll have
to do, why don't you answer me, you don't even show me that
basic courtesy anymore; yes, said Rubén Oliva, his eyes closed
and his mouth shut, like a deaf man or a madman, not even that,
just to imagine myself sleeping, imagine myself dreaming, imagine myself dead, or, best of all, as a dead man who is dreaming
that he's alive. That would be perfect, instead of having to listen
to Rocío's complaints from the kitchen; she seemed to read his
mind, cutting him with her recriminations: why didn't he go
out, do something, she laughed bitterly, Sundays used to be
festive days, unforgettable days, what had happened to him, why
was he afraid now, why didn't he go out and kill, show his
courage, yelled Rocío, invisible in the kitchen, almost inaudible
as she poured the sputtering oil out of the frying pan, why don't
you fight anymore, why don't you go out and follow someone,

why don't you pursue glory, fame? So she argued, just so she, by God and His most Holy Mother, could leave Madrid and spend the summer by the sea.

She gave a cry of pain, but he didn't stop to ask what had happened and she didn't come into the living room but contented herself with screaming at him that she had cut a finger opening a tin of sardines, she took more risk, taunted Rocío, opening a tin than he, forever lying on the sofa, in his shorts—with the paper open on his belly and a black bull looking at him from the little screen, recriminating him for his idleness—such a sluggard she had married, and nearly forty, things would only get worse, since, as her grandfather used to say, from forty on, no man should get his belly wet, and she had loved him because he was brave, handsome, and young, because he was courageous, and he killed, and . . .

Rubén no longer heard her. He smelled her and felt like killing her, but how can you kill the moon, for that was what she was for him, not the sun of his life but, yes, a familiar moon that appeared every night without fail; and although its light was cool, its appearance excited him; and although its sands were sterile, they seemed fertile since its hypnotic movements moved the tides, marked the dates, governed the calendar, and drained the garbage from the world . . .

He got up suddenly, put on his shirt and pants and shoes, while she kept on talking from the kitchen, and the children kept repeating over and over the ditty about "Sunday seven!" and as he dressed he only wanted the day to end, the slow and tedious day with its bits of soap operas and scraps of kitchen chatter, snatches of childish rounds and bits of old newspapers, traces of dust and traces of blood; he looked out the window— the waning moon appeared suddenly in the night sky, the moon was always a woman, always a goddess, never a god, unless it was a Spanish saint: San Lunes, Saint Monday, tomorrow, the day of leisure, of old men as lazy as he was (as Rocío would be going on without letup, invisible, bleeding, cut by the open tin, in the kitchen), and Rubén Oliva decided that he would let her go on talking forever, he didn't even grab a bag or anything, he would leave quickly, before the night ended, when Sunday had passed, he would leave Madrid at the first tolling of San Lunes, go far away from the immortal tedium of Rocío, the filthy moon who was his wife, and the black bull, forever immobile, frozen on the television screen, watching him.

Monday

He hurried down Calle Ave María to Atocha and turned back to lose himself in the side streets of Los Desamparados, quickly passing the markets and taverns and tobacco shops, fleeing that confinement, walking down the middle of the street in the August heat, until he came to the fountain of Neptune, source of the invisible waters of La Castellana, and everyone was there, and freedom was there too, and Rubén Oliva—skinny and slick, with his white shirt and black pants, his green eyes and the dark shadows under his eyes—joined the endless summer nighttime stroll, the human river that runs from the Prado to the Columbus monument; Rubén Oliva lost himself for a moment in that sea of people moving without haste but without hesitation, from terrace to terrace, seldom stopping, choosing to see or be seen, beneath neon lights or other times under a single dangling bulb, the crowd lingering on elegant decks with chrome-and-steel furniture or stopping at movable stands covered with circus-like tents: seeing or being seen, the ones sitting in folding chairs watching and being watched by the passing multitude, which in turn observed those who watched and were watched by them; Rubén Oliva had the sudden feeling that he had returned to the Andalusian towns where he had grown up, where the night life of summer took place in the streets, in front of the houses, yet close to the doors, as if everyone were ready to run inside and hide as soon as the first thunderclap or gunshot broke up the peaceful nocturnal gathering of villagers sitting on seats of straw;

then the memory of the people and their poverty was driven away
by the present scene: Rubén Oliva, surrounded this August night
by thousands of people, by boys and girls fifteen to twenty-five,
young Madrid men and women who were thin like him, but not
from generations of hunger or the disasters of war, no, they were
thin by choice, from aerobics, strict diets, even anorexia; there
was no other place in Spain—said the deaf man, the madman,
the solitary man—where you could see such fine boys' and girls'
faces, such willowy figures and such graceful walks, such fash-
ionable summer clothes, such studied haughtiness, such pene-
trating gazes, such tantalizing flirtations, and yet Rubén Oliva
kept scanning these faces for something he could recognize from
places completely foreign to these Spanish youths of August—
from poor hamlets, miserable towns, villages where boys first
fought bulls in the dust by the stables, boys not unlike the stray
dogs, the calves, or the roosters they imitated; brushing against
these golden youths on that San Lunes dawn, Rubén Oliva saw
in new guises the same poses of honor, the tremulous cool, and
the disdain of death that is born of the conviction that in Spain,
the country of delay, not even death is punctual; all this he saw
where it shouldn't have been, in the half-open lips of a girl
bronzed by the sun, her peach skin contrasting with the brightness of her eyes; in the matador look of a tight-assed boy who
held the waist of a bare-shouldered girl with silver specks between her braless, bouncing breasts; in the bare, smooth, lazily
crossed legs of a girl sitting before an iced coffee or in the infinitely
absent look of a boy on whose face a full beard had sprouted at
fifteen, abruptly killing off the cherub who still survived in his
eyes: it was a way they had of holding a glass, of lighting a
cigarette, of crossing their legs, of placing their hands on their
sides, of seeing without looking or being seen, becoming invisible
to those who looked at them, and saying: I may not live long
but I am immortal; or, rather, I'm never going to die, but don't
expect to see me again after tonight; or See in me only what I
show you tonight because I don't give you permission to see

anything more; so said the moving bodies, the restless eyes, the laughter of some and the silence of others, prolonging the night before returning to their elegant middle-class homes and standing before their fathers, the doctors, the lawyers, the engineers, the bankers, the notaries, the real estate agents, the tour directors, the hotelkeepers . . . to ask for money for the next night, money for shopping at Serrano, treating themselves to the indispensable blouse, trying out the shoes without which . . . It was the village gathering, only now with Benetton and Saint Laurent logos; it was the romantic stroll through the plazas of past years, the boys in one direction, the girls in the other, measuring each other for engagement, marriage, procreation, and death the way a mortician measures the bodies of the clients who one day, inevitably, will visit him and occupy his deluxe coffins. Luxury, lust of death that robs us of the past; but in this Madrid stroll the boys and the girls were not going in opposite directions—they couldn't, because it was hard to tell them apart; Rubén Oliva, thirty-nine years old, unemployed (for the moment), fed up with his wife, victim of a tedious Sunday, was glad that, even though it was still night, San Lunes had arrived; he was not so different, physically, from the golden youths of Madrid: like them, like almost all Spanish gallants, he had an androgynous quality; but now the good-looking girls had that quality, too—they had more of the moon ways of Mondays than of the mercurial ways of Wednesdays; they were Tuesday's martial Amazons, yet Friday remained their Venus day—*lunes, miércoles, martes, viernes*: they were still celestial goddesses, but in a new way for a new day, a way different from the tradition set by their stout, pallid, veiled, doughy, thick-ankled, heavy-hipped predecessors; Rubén Oliva amused himself, as he studied the slow nocturnal stroll, by picking out the boys who appeared to be girls, the women who resembled men, and he felt a sudden vertigo; the march of pleasure and extravagance and ostentation of a rich, European, progressive Spain, where everyone, however grudgingly, paid his taxes and could go to the beach in August, not wanting to be judged, not anymore, or classified so simply by gender, masculine/feminine, no, not now, now even sex was as fluctuating as the sea, which came closer to Madrid in August, because there was nothing the city denied itself, not even the sea, which it brought there through the secret power of the moon, converting Madrid, at daybreak on Monday, San Lunes's day, into a summer beach of seas and undercurrents and daily menstruations, sewers, and purified water.

—Madrid denies itself nothing, said the woman who paused beside him, watching the spectacle, and only her voice told Rubén Oliva that she was a woman, not one of these girls who resembled Tuesday's warriors more than they did the mercurial girls of Wednesdays; Rubén could not make her out very well because there was a bank of Osborne brandy lights in the terrace where they were standing, and the black bull and the fluorescent glow blinded him and also her, the woman who first appeared as a blaze of light, blind or blinding, seen or seeing, who could tell which . . .

—I think we're the only ones here over thirty. The woman smiled, blinded by the light, by the bull, by Rubén Oliva's own invisibility in that crowd: he could see the sign of the bull more clearly than he could see the woman who was talking to him.

—I can't see you very well, said Rubén Oliva, lightly touching the woman's shoulder, as if to move her into the light so that he could see her better, though he realized that this invisible light, this dazzling darkness, was the best light for . . .

—It doesn't matter how I look, or what my name is. Don't take the mystery out of our meeting.

He said she was right, but could she see him?

—Of course—the woman laughed—how do you think you and I have met in the middle of this youthful throng; they used to say never trust anyone over thirty; here, that's still true.

—Maybe it always will be, for the young. At fifteen, would you trust an old man of forty . . . well, of thirty-nine? The man laughed.

—I'm willing to imagine that on this entire avenue there are only two people, a man and a woman, over thirty. She smiled.

Rubén Oliva said it seemed a marriage made in heaven, and she replied, in a country where for centuries people had no choice about their own marriages, where they had to obey their fathers' arrangements, that one could experience the chance, the adventure, the excitement of a casual encounter, and decide to prolong it voluntarily, to decide, man, to decide, that was truly a blessing, a wonderful thing indeed . . .

He couldn't get a look at her. Each movement, hers, his, hers responding to his, his leg moving forward as if by chance to change her direction, as if making her accept the bullfighter's will, joined the play of lights—dangling bulbs, neon constellations, errant cars like caravans in the desert, lights of the sea of Madrid, electric sunflowers of night, moonflowers of the city's eternal undercurrent—Rubén Oliva felt unable to direct, to curb the turns of the woman, to make her yield, to snatch her image from the perpetual flight: what was she like? and she, had she seen him, did she know what he was like?

Hours later, at daybreak, in a loft on Calle Juanelo, their arms around each other in her bed, she asked him if he had not been afraid of her sexual aggression, that she was a prostitute or carried the new plagues of the dying century, and he answered no, she should realize that a man like him took life as it came; true, there were diseases less than deadly, but the only true disease, after all, was death and who could avoid that? and if nobody avoided it, then it was better to face it over and over, by choice. He explained that right away, so she would understand with whom she lay, that the worst thing the world could do to him was no worse than what he could do to himself; for example, if she gave him a fatal disease he could hasten his death, not in the cowardice of suicide, nothing like that, but by giving himself fully to his art, to a profession that justified death at any moment, welcomed and honored it: to die with honor he simply had to do his daily work, and you couldn't say that about the lawyers, doctors, and businessmen who were the young people's parents, and whom the young people would inevitably turn into someday—no longer slender, no longer luminous, no longer hermaphroditic, definitively fathers or mothers, potbellied and gray, for sure!

—And you weren't curious, you never wanted to look at me before sleeping with me?

He shrugged and replied as before, it's like looking the bull in the face, that's the most important thing in the ring, never to lose sight of the bull's face, but at the same time not to lose sight of the public, your cuadrilla, your rivals who are watching you, in fact, not to lose sight even of the water boy, like Gallito did once in Seville—he had to quiet the water boy when he realized his cries were distracting the bull: you have to be aware of everything, sweetheart, can I call you that? Call me what you like, call me whore, actress, consumptive, performer, call me whatever you want, but show me again what you've got.

He did, and distractedly registered the spare furniture in the room, almost nothing but a bed, a chest of drawers by its side, cool candles on it, cold tile floor, fresh curtains blocking out the daylight, an old-fashioned washbasin, a chamber pot his fingers touched under the bed, and dominating everything a great ornate armoire, the only luxury in the room—he looked in vain for an electric light, an outlet, a telephone; he was mixed up, then he thought he understood: he had confused luxury with novelty, with modern comfort, but was it really the same thing? Nothing was modern in this room, and the armoire with its two doors was adorned with a crest of vines, cherubs, and broken columns.

Before sleeping again in each other's arms, he wanted to tell her what he had thought, separated from Rocío in the apartment they shared, something that Rocío didn't understand perhaps, and perhaps not this woman either, but with her it was worth it, worth the risk of not being understood: when we die, we lose the past, that's what we lose, not the future, as he told her . . .

At midday Monday, on waking again, Rubén Oliva and his lover abandoned themselves to the day, convinced that the day belonged to them, without interruption, rejoicing in their chance encounter on the nocturnal terraces of Madrid. (How many of the young people consummated a marriage of the night as they had, how many only celebrated the nuptials of the spectacle: to show oneself, see, be seen, not touch . . . ?) They confessed that they could hardly see each other in the shifting light of the terraces, she felt the attraction, perhaps because it was Monday, moon day, day of tides, decisive dates, violent currents, overpowering attractions and impulses, she was drawn to him as though magnetized, and he couldn't see her clearly in the whirlwind of artificial light and shade, and that is how it had to be, because she had to tell him that, now that she had seen him, he was . . .

He covered her mouth gently with his hand, put his lips to her ear, told the woman lying there that it didn't matter, he confessed it wouldn't matter to him if she was a boy, a transvestite, a whore, diseased, dying, nothing mattered to him, because what she had given him, how she had given herself to him, excited him, attracted him, made him feel that every time was the first time, that every repeated act was the beginning of a night of love, so that each time he felt as if he hadn't done it for a year, all of that was what . . .

Now she covered his mouth with a hand and said: —But I did know you. I picked you because of who you were, not because you were unknown to me.

The words were hardly out of the woman's mouth when the doors of the armoire opened with a heart-stopping thump and two powerful hands, stained, dripping colors from the fingers, threw apart the panels, and a waistcoated, frock-coated body emerged, in a linen shirt and short pants, white silk stockings and country-style shoes, clogs maybe, smeared with mud and cow dung, and this creature jumped onto the bed of love, smeared the sheets with shit and mud, wrapped its hands around the woman's face, and, without paying the slightest attention to Rubén Oliva, smeared the face of his lover with its fingers as it had just smeared the soiled sheets, and Rubén Oliva, paralyzed with astonishment, his head planted on a pillow, unable to move, never knew if those agile, irreverent fingers erased or created, composed or disfigured, while with equal speed and art, and with incredible fury, they traced on the woman's featureless face the deformed arc of a diabolic brow or the semblance of a smile, or if they emptied out her eye sockets, turned the fine nose that Rubén had caressed into a misshapen cabbage and erased the lips that had kissed his, that had told him, I did know you, I chose you because of who you were . . .

The giant—or perhaps it only appeared so because it was standing on the bed, doubling its size to destroy or create the woman's face with its colors—panted, exhausted, and Rubén Oliva contemplated the woman, her face besmeared, made and unmade, covered by the two floods of flowing tears and a veil of hair; and watching the raging terror that had escaped from the armoire, he finally realized what he had known from the moment he had seen it appear—but what he couldn't believe until, little by little, sweating, he began to overcome his panic: this man, atop his body and clothes and shoes and stooped shoulders, had no head.

Tuesday
1

Imagine three spaces, said the headless giant then, three perfect circles that must never touch, three orbs, each circulating in its independent trajectory, with its own reason for being and its own court of satellites: three incomparable and self-sufficient worlds. So, perhaps, are the worlds of the gods. Ours, shamefully, are imperfect. The spheres meet, repel one another, penetrate each other, fertilize, vie against, and kill each other. The circle is not perfect because it is pierced by the tangent or the chord. But imagine only those three spaces: each in its own way is a dressing room, and in the first, a theatrical dressing room, a naked woman

is being dressed slowly by her maids, though she isn't talking
to the servants but to her dancing monkey, with white necktie
and blue-painted genitals, that swings among the mannequins,
and those cloth breasts are the anticipation of the body of his
mistress, who addresses her words to the monkey and to whom
the monkey, as his day's prize, addresses itself: its reward will
be to jump onto the shoulder of the woman and leave with her
for the stage first, to the dinners afterwards, on Sundays to a
stroll on San Isidro, and at night, if he behaves well, to the foot
of the bed of his mistress and her lover, to disconcert her venereal
companions and amuse Elisia Rodríguez, called "La Privada,"
queen of the Madrid stage, who can keep her acting glory alive
in only one way: each night, before going onstage, she talks to
the ape, who is dressed up and secretly bedaubed (for the spectators' laughter, the families' scandal, and her lovers' discomfort:
the blue prop noticeable only on certain occasions), and tells him
who she is, where she came from, in order to appreciate her own
success all the more for having risen from below, as she had,
from so godforsaken a town that more than once the princes of
the royal house had gone there to marry, because the law decreed
that the place where the princes contracted matrimony would
remain exempt from paying taxes forever, so they had to go to
a place as dirt-poor as that, so its release from taxation would
not matter to the Crown—though it did to the princes forced to
marry in the ruined church, with crows flying past constantly,
and bats too, except when it was daytime and they were asleep,
hanging from the corners like shards of sleeping shit, like the
shit of the unpaved streets, into which the finest shoes and the
shiniest boots sink, where the wagons get stuck, at the mercy of
the shoulders of the local studs who, to demonstrate their man-
hood, would rescue them, at times with their giddy duchesses,
rocking amid the smell of sweat, onions, and excrement, and the
processions were trailed and swelled by stray dogs and clouds of
flies, and flanked by phalanxes of cockroaches in the corners of
rude eateries (first let me see myself naked in the mirror, ape,

and admit you've never seen anything more perfect than this hourglass of silky white skin whose uniformity—you have to season the dish—is barely interrupted by what is revealed at the tip of the tits, the navel, below the arms if I choose to raise them, and between the legs if I don't care to close them), and if that was how the weddings of the princes were, then women like me had betrothals that were long and unbroken: no girl had the right, you hear me, ape? to have a second suitor: you married your first and only one, chosen by your parents, after waiting five years, to make sure of the good intentions and the chastity of all.

—What are you laughing at, you old farts, Elisia Rodríguez, La Privada, said then, slapping the shoulders of her maids with feigned annoyance—one, two, three, four—with the end of her fan, although the servants, all of them Mexican, were of stoic cast and were neither frightened nor insulted by their whimsical mistress. If La Privada said to Rufina from Veracruz or Guadalupe from Orizaba, see how high a girl from a town exempted from taxes can climb, the servants, who perhaps were descended from Totonac and Olmec princes, were grateful to have arrived there to lace up the most celebrated performer in Spain, instead of being branded like cattle or lashed like dogs in the colonial haciendas.

If they felt any sorrow (Rufina from Veracruz and Guadalupe from Orizaba, already mentioned, plus Lupe Segunda from Puebla and Petra from Tlaxcala), Elisia Rodríguez did not, as she looked at herself, first naked, then with a single ornament, the fan in her hand, and now they were going to put on her rings—naked, fan, rings, she grew excited on seeing herself in the mirror—and still talking to the ape, never to the Mexicans, who pretended not to hear, she told how she was seduced after the royal wedding by a young Jesuit traveling with the court to chronicle the events, and how the lettered youth, to gain absolution for his sins, concupiscence, and the pregnancy announced by Elisia, had taken her to Barcelona, promised to teach her to read works of theater and poetry, and married her to his uncle, an importer of Cuban goods, an old man undaunted by the institution of *chichisveo*, which authorized the ménage à trois with the consent of the old husband, who showed off his young wife in public but privately freed her from sexual obligations, granting them to the young man, though with certain conditions, such as his right to watch them, Elisia and the nephew, making love, secretly, naturally, the old man wanted to behave decently, and if they knew he was watching them without their seeing him, perhaps that would excite them even more.

It happened, however, related Elisia, that in a little while the husband began to be annoyed that the beneficiary of the institution was his nephew, and he began to add to his complaints that it didn't bother him so much that he was his nephew as that he was a priest. Elisia, hearing these retractions, began to believe that her husband desired her, and even began to wonder if he could satisfy her female desires. What made her decide to follow the advice of her husband—"Be mine and mine alone, Elisia"— is that she was annoyed by the contrast between the Jesuit's flattery of the powerful and his contempt for the weak, which he showed so often that she considered it the true norm of conduct not only of her lover but of the entire Company of Jesus, whereas rich and poor, powerful and weak were treated alike by her husband, a good, honest man. Elisia's husband said simply that in business one saw the rise and fall of fortunes: the poor of today could be the rich of tomorrow, and vice versa. But then the old man would quickly repeat his formal argument that he was dissolving the agreement of *chichisveo* because the young man was a priest, not because he was his nephew: nothing demanded respect but religion, he again advised Elisia.

—Religion and, he added quickly, commerce.

And the theater? Elisia, after a few months of his amorous admonishments, decided that there was a lover more varied, neither too permanent nor too fleeting, less faithful perhaps but also less demanding than any individual, momentarily more in-

tense if temporally less enduring. In other words, Elisia wanted
the public for her lover, not a naïve seminarian; she wanted the
spectators as her beloved, not the writers of plays, and her husband consented to these thousands of lovers, relieved that his
precious Elisia, from that forsaken, flea-ridden town that paid
no taxes, preferred this form of *chichisveo* to the other, more
traditional kind.

He got her singing teachers and dance masters, he got her
speech and voice instructors, he got her as much work as he
could find, from religious roles to profane comedies, but Elisia's
wisdom surpassed their teachings (her maids covered her charms
with a bodice and for a minute Elisia was dissatisfied, but then
she remembered that there were men who had loved her more
for her bodice than for her body, she had even discovered one
of them kneeling before the actress's nightstand, kissing her intimate apparel, more excited there than in bed, he wanted to sing
a hymn to the inventor of underclothing, but her earthy and
practical side simply concluded that everything has its use in this
world, where love is king. So her enthusiasm returned, and *olé*:
the pregnancy that frightened the Jesuit was as much a deceit
as the bustle the Mexican maids were now pinning on her). Elisia
had a bloodhound's instinct in her butterfly body, and she had
arrived in Barcelona when all Spain had but two passions: the
theater and the bulls, actresses and bullfighters, and the passion
of passions, the rivalry among actresses, or among matadors, the
disputes of one group and another, this one bedding that one
(quick, it's getting late, the white stockings, the garters, the
sashes for the waist), and her husband doing his Pygmayonnaise
number, and you, my Galantine, or something like that, as she
said, showing off her learning before her teachers and the Jesuit
nephew (the nephew-Jesuit), who gave her lessons in the dramatic arts and in the refinement of diction through recitation of
verses, but she felt something different, her heart told her that
the theater was the theater, not a repetition of words that nobody
understood, but the occasion to display herself before an audience

and make them feel that they were part of her, of her life, that they were her friends—and what is more, to reveal her greatest intimacies from the stage; and if her husband, who preferred the footlights to the *chichisveo* but now showed dangerous inclinations toward the conjugal bed instead of the theatrical boards, didn't understand that, the members of the court who came to Barcelona to see Elisia did, including Princess M——, who had gotten married in Elisia's town to spare that poor village from taxes and who imperiously demanded the presence of the entertainer, and Elisia said to tell her she wasn't an entertainer but a tragedienne.

—Haven't you seen the Empire styles with which Mam'selle George is dazzling Paris? And the princess said yes, she had seen them, and she wanted Elisia to wear them in Madrid, where she was urged, by royal decree, to present herself, with or without her husband, for he insisted that the best clothing was sold in the shop, and if she went so far from the Catalán port and his business in tobacco, sugar, fruit, rare woods, and all the riches of Havana, who was going to pay for his wife's singing classes and her stiff silk bows?

In other words: her husband forbade Elisia to travel to Madrid; theaters and actresses, although his wife was one of them, were for passing the time, not for making fortunes; but Elisia went anyway, laughing at the old man, and he locked up her costumes and told her, Now show yourself naked on the stage, and she said, I am quite capable of doing so, and she went to Madrid, where the princess who had gotten married in her village presented her with a wardrobe the likes of which had never been seen before in the court at Madrid or anywhere else, for the princess raided the oldest wardrobes in the palace and found in them the forgotten Chinese garments brought to Europe by Marco Polo and the feathered Indian capes that Captain Cortés presented to the Crown after the fall of Mexico, and although Elisia said she wasn't going to dress like a savage, the princess called her both beggar and chooser, Havanera and despot, but

Elisia took the Chinese fabrics and the feathered Aztec capes and made them into Empire fantasies, until the Duchess of O——, rival of Princess M——, had copies made of all of Rodríguez's outfits to give to her own favorite actress, Pepa de Hungría, and Elisia gave her outfits to her chambermaids so they would be dressed the same as Pepa, in rags, as Elisia announced in a song, and now no one wanted to compete with her, not La Cartuja, or La Caramba, or La Tirana, or any of the other great stage sirens (quick, the gold brocade skirt, the white muslin, the taffeta and rose silk cloak), no orator or singer or dancer, just Elisia Rodríguez, ape, who was all that and more, who was the first to say to hell with written texts, who said what interests people is me, not someone embalmed two hundred years ago, and improvising texts and songs, she resolved to speak of herself, her most intimate affairs, her evolving loves, urgent as her need to feed her legend before the footlights, and while she invented something here and there, she began to feel an increasingly pressing need for real adventures, stories that the people could share, it's true, she lay with that one, you know, ape, you were a witness, your mistress doesn't lie, she spent the night in his palace, we saw her leaving at daybreak, she appeared at the windows, she greeted the doorkeepers, who knew her well, who all loved her because she greeted them all with a smile, and Elisia consolidated her fame singing only of her own loves, her own desires, her own struggles and adventures: that is what the public craved and that is what she gave them, and all she lacked was a special name, which is the symbol of fame, so:

—A name is not enough, one needs a nickname.

And they began, secretly and laughingly, to call Elisia "La Privada," the private one, and at first everyone thought it was a joke to designate so public a woman that way; and even if its significance was extended later to God's having deprived her of children, other nicknames failed to stick. Not simply Elisia, not La Rodríguez, not the Havanera, not the Barren One: even the seminarian could not effect that amazing conception; the woman was barren. This convinced no one, and although Elisia's fame kept growing, it was fame without a name, which is fame without fame, until the truth became known and shone like the sun and filled everyone with the warmth, feeling, jealousy, the divided emotions that constitute fame itself: Elisia Rodríguez, whispered the growing legion of her lovers, fainted at the climax of love-making: she came and she went!

—La Privada! The deprived! The unconscious one! The fainter!

(All she lacked now was the cape, that's it, and the satin shoes too, and the hairpiece, the great bow of rose silk on her head, ah, and the disguised mustache on her upper lip, bah, she had to be a woman with hair, and that scent of garlic, caramba, if I don't eat I die, what do they want, a corpse?, and her eyes were dead beneath her heavy eyebrows, and her eyes were dead, and her eyes—were dead.)

2

Pedro Romero was stark naked in his dressing room and didn't need to look at himself in the mirror to know that his caramel skin didn't show a single scar, not the wound of a single horn. His dark, long, delicate, firm hand had killed 5,582 bulls, but not one had touched him, even though Romero had redefined the art of bullfighting; it was one of the oldest arts in the world, but it was the newest for the public that filled the plazas of Spain to admire—Romero realized—not only their favorite personalities but also themselves, for bullfighters were neither more nor less than the people's triumph, the people doing what they had always done—daring, defying death, surviving—and now being applauded for it, recognized, lavished with fame and fortune for surviving, for lasting another month, when what everyone hoped was that the bull of life would rip you open and send you off to rot once and for all.

And yet, naked in that cool, dark dressing room, Pedro Ro-

mero felt the fiction of his own body and the virtual sensation of
having previously inhabited that body, which so many had
loved—he looked down, gauged the bulk of his testicles, as the
sword handler would do in a minute to adjust his breeches—but
which was, in the end, in a more profound sense, a virgin body,
a body that had never been penetrated. He smiled at the thought
that all men who aren't queer are virgins because they always
penetrate, they're never penetrated by the woman; but the bullfighter knew that he had to be penetrated by the bull to lose his
macho virginity, and that had never happened to him.

He considered himself, naked, at forty still possessing a nearly
perfect figure, a muscular harmony revealed by the soft caramel
color of his skin, which accentuated his body's classic Mediterranean forms, the medium height, strong shoulders, long upper
arms, compact chest, flat belly, narrow hips, sensual buttocks
over well-formed but short legs, and small feet: a body of bodies,
a soft-assed English lover had told him, jealous not just of his
tight ass but of the blood beneath his skin, his skin and body
molded like almond paste by Phoenician and Greek hands,
washed like Holland sheets by waves of Carthaginians and Celts,
stormed like a merlon by Roman phalanxes and Visigoth hordes,
caressed like ivory by Arab hands, and kissed like crosses by
Jewish lips.

It was a body of bodies, too, because more than five thousand
pairs of bulls' horns had failed to wound it; his body had never
bled, suppurated, scabbed; it was a good body, at peace with the
soul that inhabited it, but also a bad body, bad because it was
provocative. It continually exceeded its moral constraint, its suf-
ficiency as the container of Pedro Romero's soul, exhibiting itself
before others, exciting them, saying to them: Look, more than
five thousand bulls and not a single wound.

And bad, too, because the body of the bullfighter had the right
to do what others could not: to parade itself in public, exposing
itself on every side, in the midst of applause, parading its sexual
attributes, its tight little ass, its testicles straining beneath the

silk, the penis that at times was plainly revealed through the breeches that were the perfect mirror for the torero's sex.

—Dress me, quickly . . .

—Come on, *Figura*, you know I can't do that in less than forty-five minutes, you know that . . .

—I'm sorry, Sparky. I'm nervous this afternoon.

—That's not good, *Figura*. Think of your fame. You may call me Spark, but it's you who's the light, the Great Figure of the Ring.

Let me die but let my fame endure—Pedro Romero smiled and let the attendant dress him, slowly: first the long white underpants, then the rose stockings with garters below the knees, next the hairpiece with the pigtail at the nape of the neck; his breeches, which this afternoon were silver and blue, and Sparky matched up the three hooks and eyes on the legs; the shirt that was a wash of white, the suspenders caressing his chest, the yellow cummerbund wrapped around his waist, or rather, it was the man himself wrapped in that mother of clothing, its symbol, its origin, a long ribbon of yellow silk, the cradle of the body, its maternal embrace, its umbilical projection, or so Pedro Romero felt that afternoon, as Sparky tied his narrow necktie, adjusted his majestic vest, his silver caparison, not as strong a shield as the bullfighter's own armor, which is his heart, and his own natural mane, still silky, even though, like this afternoon's suit, it was now silver; and finally the black shoes, the laces tied as only Sparky knew how, like two perfect rabbit's ears.

Are there many people? Ah, a great crowd, *Figura*, you know, when you're fighting, everyone shows up, rich and poor, men and women, everyone loves you, they would sell their beds to see you, and how they prepare for the fiesta, how many hours they spend to shine elegantly before you, elegantly *as* you, *Figura*, you, the King of the Ring, and then the hours they talk about you, commenting on the fight, looking forward to the next one: there's a whole world that lives only for you, for your fame . . .

—Sparky, I'm going to confess something to you. This is my

last fight. If the bull kills me, it will be for that reason. If I kill it, I will retire without a single wound.

—You care so much about your body, *Figura*? What about your fame?

—Don't insult me. I haven't yet taken as my motto: Let me endure, even if my fame dies.

—No, *Figura*, none of that. Look, you are going to fight in the oldest and most beautiful arena in Spain, here in Ronda, and if you die, at least you will be looking upon something beautiful before you close your eyes.

My town: a gash, a deep wound such as I never had, my town like a body with a scab that will not heal, contemplating its own wound from a perpetual watchtower of houses that are white-washed every year to keep them from dissolving in the sun. Ronda, the most beautiful, because it opens the white wings of death and forces us to see it as our unexpected companion in the mirror of an abyss. Ronda, where our vision soars higher than the eagle.

3

Naked he was not, although those who remembered him young, with his wide-brimmed hat and his cape of braided cloth, or even younger, as he had first arrived in Madrid, in a low-crowned hat and a suit with fringed trousers, would not recognize him in his old age, disheveled, carelessly dressed, unshod, his pants stained (grease? urine?), his shirt sweaty, loose-fitting, hanging open, showing his gray chest, and crowning it all his great giant's head, unkempt, gray, with sideburns, but not as fierce as the grimace on his thick lips, the eyes veiled by what they had seen, the eyebrows mussed by where they had been, and in spite of that, the high, impertinent, innocent nose, the stubborn, childish nose of an Aragón waif, constantly belying all the rest, belying all the godforsaken waifs, wretched as the river that gave birth to them, shit-assed kids of the Manzanares who wrote on the walls of his estate: *Here lives the deaf man.*

He didn't hear the shouting of those or other jerks. Stone-deaf, shut inside his bare workroom, naked—comparatively—as a savage, he who shaped and helped invent a society of unabashed pomp and ostentation, he who gave the ears to every torero, the award to every actress, the medals at every festival, the prizes to every potter, every weaver, every witch, every pimp, every soldier, and every penitent, making them all *protagonists*, endowing rich and poor with the fame and form they had never had before: *now* he felt as naked as they who acquired an image at his hands, the hands full of the suns and shades of Francisco de Goya y Luz, lucid, loose, Lucifer, lost cipher, lust for light—Francisco de Goya y Lucientes: even the nobles who had always been painted—they alone, the kings, the aristocracy—now had to see themselves for the first time, full body, just as they were, not as they wished to be seen, and when they did (this was the painter's miracle, his mystery, perhaps his defeat) they were not threatened, they accepted it: Carlos IV and his degenerate, concupiscent, disloyal, ignorant court, that collective phantasm with eyes frozen by abulia, with mugs lewdly drooling, with powdered wigs instead of brains, and with moles screwing their concave foreheads, Fernando VII and his image of self-satisfied cretinism, active, reckless cretinism, in contrast to that of the bewitched wretch Carlos II, that Goya before Goya, foolishly compassionate, dreaming of a better world, that is, a comprehensible one, that is, one as crazy as he was: they all accepted the painter's reality, they clung to it, celebrated it, and didn't realize that they were being seen for the first time, just like the actress, the swordsman, the circus performer, and the peasant, who had never been favored by the court painter's brush before . . .

Now, naked and deaf, with no court but the mocking kids painting insults on his fences, without Mexican maids or Andalusian cuadrilla, he felt his abandonment and nakedness reflected in the unsilvered mirrors, the two canvases that for some

reason reminded him of a boy's pants, a rustic skirt: blind canvases, there was nothing on them, everything was in the painter's
head; so-onto the imagined canvas he placed the actress, his last
desire as an old man: he had loved and been loved and also
abandoned by the most beautiful and the cruelest women of his
time, and now he went down to Madrid to see this woman on
the stage and she never looked at him, she saw only herself,
reflected in the public eye, and now he wanted to capture her in
this rectangle; he began to outline her entire body with charcoal,
there he would put her and from there she would never escape;
he quickly drew the naked form, standing, of the coveted
woman—this woman was not going to fly off on a broom; this
woman was not going to be stolen by death, because he was
much older than she (and yet . . .); this woman was not going
to run away with a soldier, an aristocrat, or (who knows?) a
bullfighter—he advanced slowly, yet every movement of the deaf
old man was like a seismic shock that was felt by the unruly
children outside, and they left their own brushes beside the wall
and ran away, as if they knew that inside the workroom the other
brush, the Great Brush, was outdoing theirs and would not admit
of any rival; and now, on the second canvas, he began, in a high-
minded spirit, with a restraint that surprised the painter himself,
so given to satire, caricature, and the strictures of realism, he
began to sketch the torso of a man, without any indication of a
head, because the head would naturally be the crown of that
grave body, full of dignity and repose; he sketched long, delicate,
strong hands, and put in the cape, which he pictured a dark pink
velvet, then the jacket, which he saw dark blue, and the waistcoat,
which he knew had to be gray, colorless, to give the linen of the
front and the neck of the shirt an exceptional whiteness, if only
because of the contrast with those serene colors, and then he
returned to the first canvas (and, outside, the walnut trees quiv-
ered) and he surprised the woman, who was pure silhouette,
without features or details, on the point of escaping from the
canvas, and the old man laughed (and the walnut trees, terrified,
clung to one another), and he said to the woman:

—You can't leave. There you are and there you will stay forever. And although she tried to hide, to take refuge in the darkest
corner of the canvas, in the shadows, as if she divined the painter's
repugnance, he knew, although he would never say so, that it
was an empty threat, because when the canvas left his studio and
was seen by other eyes, those eyes would free Elisia Rodríguez,
La Privada, whom he had captured, from the canvas, and they
would give her liberty, releasing her from the prison of the canvas
to imprison them, to sleep with those who avidly eyed her, fainting *à son plaisir*, wrapped in the arms of one after another, never
directing even a smile toward her true creator, the painter who
held his brush suspended in the air, who looked at the actress's
empty face and decided not to add features, to leave it in suspense,
in ellipsis, and in the actress's stylized hand, raised in a gesture
of exiting a stage, he quickly drew a chain, and at the end of the
chain he attached a hideous ape with human eyes and a shaved
rump, masturbating merrily.

Turning back to the second canvas, he really wanted to stick
his brush like a banderilla in the bullfighter's heart, but an unwanted feeling of respect again possessed him (deaf man, deaf
man, the waifs cried at him from the wall, as if he could hear
them, or they, fools, imagined that they could be heard) and he
began to fill in the face with Pedro Romero's noble features, the
firm jaw, the elegant, taut cheeks, the small pressed mouth with
its slight irregularity, the virile emerging beard, the perfectly
straight nose, the fine, separated eyebrows, worthy physical base
of a forehead as clear as an Andalusian sky, barely ruffled by a
hint of *widow's peak*, as Wellington's elegant officers called the
point formed by the hair in the middle of the forehead, which
was besieged by the first gray hairs of his fourth decade. Don
Francisco was about to give the bullfighter some of his own, all
the way down his forehead, and call the painting *The Man with
Streaked Hair*, something like that, but that would have meant
sacrificing the center of his particular orbit of beauty, the famous
eyes, full of competence, serenity, and tenderness, which were
the source of Pedro Romero's humanity, and that was sacred,

the artist could not joke about it, and all his rancor, his jealousy, his resentment, his malice, even his cleverness (which he was always forgiven) was subjected to a sentiment, weakly traced by the restless brush, not a banderilla, barely a quill, a full caress, a complete embrace that told the model: You are not just what I would like to see in you, to admire or injure you, to portray or caricature you, you are more than I saw in you, and my canvas will be a great canvas, Romero, only if I explore the one thing I'm sure of, which is that you are more than my compassion or judgment of you at this moment; I see you as you are now but I know what you were before and you will continue to be, I see only one side of you, not all four sides, because painting is the art of a single moment's frontal perspective, not a discursive and lineal art, and I lack your genius, Romero, for peril, I can't paint your face and your body, Romero, as you fight a bull, in three dimensions, from four sides, subsuming every one of the angles of both you and the bull, and all the lights in which they are bathed. And as I can't and don't dare do that, I give you this image of your nobility, which is the only one that shows that you are more than the figure painted by your humble and invidious servant Lucifer lusts for lights, Lucientes, Francisco de Goya y.

She huddled on the canvas, naked, faceless, with a horrid chained ape. He hastily painted a butterfly covering her sex, like the ribbons that adorned her hair.

Outside, the urchins cried, *Deaf man, deaf man, deaf man.*

And in the whirlwind of sudden nightfall, hundreds of other women, laughing at the artist, preparing their revenge through the pain of the man seduced and abandoned—and what about them? When had they been treated with truth and care? They who dealt to sinners their just deserts—and as he sleeps, his head planted amid the papers and brushes on his worktable, they, the women of the night, fly about his sleeping head, dragging with them other papers with notices so new that they seem old, *There is plenty to suck*, reads one, and *Until death*, says another, and *Of what illness will he die*, asks a third, and all together, *God forgive you*, swathed in their veils, harnessed by mothers preparing to sell them, fanning themselves, rubbing themselves with oil, embalming themselves alive with unguents and powders, straddling brooms, rising in flight, hanging like bats in the corners of churches, carried on winds of dust and garbage, fanning, flying, uncovering tombs, looking for you, Francisco, and casting a final cackle at your face, dreaming and dead, both dead and dreaming.

—But I am the only one who can show the bullfighter and the actress in their true garb. Only I can give them heads. Afterwards, do with me what you will.

—May God forgive you!

4

—Never marry or begin a journey on Tuesday, an old woman sitting in a corner of the main square told Rubén Oliva as he passed, so discomposed and hurried that only a witch like her—shrouded in a newspaper but with a coquettish little hat made from the front page of *El País* on her grotesque head, to protect her from the midday August sun—could know that the man was going far away, even though it was Tuesday, the dangerous day, the day of naked war, hidden war, war of the soul, on the stage, in the rings, in the shops: *Martes*, Mars' day, the god of war's day, the day of dying, vying, plying, and crying, said a bitch half buried under the garbage in the plaza.

Wednesday

Rubén Oliva raised the open envelope to his lips and was about to lick the gummed border when he was halted by two hardly surprising occurrences. The desk clerk watched him preparing the envelope, writing the name and address, as if Rubén Oliva hadn't the right to such whims, which only added, he seemed to be thinking, to the staff's work load; doesn't the guest, who is as rude as he is foolish, realize that his epistolary follies could not possibly interest anyone and, besides that, interrupted other activities, activities that are truly indispensable to the smooth operation of the hotel: for example, his lively phone conversations with his sweetheart, which required the lines for two hours at a time, or the games he played on that same telephone, refusing to give his name, or giving the concierge's name instead of his own as head desk clerk, or using the slightest pretext to interrupt the examination of accounts and urgent papers, while the telephones rang and the guests waited patiently before the counter, letters pressed to their tongues.

Rubén Oliva didn't have time to insist on his rights before— the second occurrence—an English gentleman with tight lips, watery eyes, and hair like sand, his ruddy nose trembling, paralyzed all circumstantial activity with one slap of his hand on the reception counter, followed by this question of surpassing importance: Why is there no soap in my bath? The desk clerk considered this question for a moment with feigned interest before haughtily responding: Because there is no soap in any of the bathrooms (don't imagine yourself an exception, please!). But the obstinate Englishman insisted: Very well, then, why isn't there soap in any of the baths? And the desk clerk said with marked scorn, seeking approval from the onlookers: Because in Spain we let everyone smell just as he likes.

—I have to go out and buy my own soap?

—No, Mr. Newton. We would be delighted to send the bellboy out for it. Oh, Manuelito, this gentleman is going to tell you what kind of soap he prefers.

—Don't be so pleased with yourself—said Newton—reception desks are the very image of purgatory, not only here, but all over the world.

He invited Rubén Oliva to join him for a glass in the bar to settle his nerves and because, as he said, drinking alone is like masturbating in the bath. A bath, he added, without soap, that is. Rubén Oliva sat with the Englishman, whose manner was peevish, nervous, and ill at ease, but who concentrated on not showing any emotion, through the supernatural control of his stiff upper lip. And not only that, he said, searching unsuccessfully for something in the pockets of his beige poplin suit, which was wrinkled and loose, commodious, yet failing to yield what Mr. Newton searched for so assiduously, while Rubén Oliva watched him with a smile and waited to drink a toast with him, his glass of Jerez slightly raised in cordial expectation, while Newton desperately groped, without saying what he was looking for—mirror, pipe, cigarettes, ballpoint pen?—all the while condemning the age, cold, and dampness of this hotel, which seemed unreal in a country where it was impossible to escape the sun and heat, even in the shadows, whereas in his country, where one strove for light and warmth, you had to endure . . . He got lost in an endless round of complaints, groping nervously, his upper lip as stiff as ever, and Rubén Oliva stopped waiting for him and drank a sip and thought of repeating to the old, out-of-sorts Englishman what he had just written to Rocío in the unsealed letter he carried in the pocket of his white shirt: it was true, you were right, love, returning to the village is returning to an endless sleep, a long siesta, an eternal midday that he refused to escape on his return, not seeking refuge from the sun at its zenith, as was the custom.

He remembered that as a child, right here in the towns of Andalusia, he knew one thing, which was that in the heat of the day the towns were emptied of people; Rubén, the town is yours, the people hide in the cool shadows and sleep while you, Rubén, walk along the narrow streets that are your only defense against the sun, seeing how they protect you from the blaze, and you dream of returning to them someday, at two in the afternoon, with a beautiful foreigner, teaching her how to use the labyrinth of shadows to avoid the sun; Rubén, don't hide from it, acknowledge it and defy it and even adore it, because you have a holy trinity in your soul where God the father is the sun, his crucified son is the shadow, and the holy spirit is the night, dissolving the troubles and joys of the past day and mounting forces for the next: today is Wednesday, said the Englishman, who had finally found a harmonica in the back pocket of his pants and, holding the instrument in his hands, got ready to raise it to his lips, and after announcing that Wednesday was Woden's day, a day of commerce and robbery, so that it was not surprising that he found himself in this den of thieves, he began to play the old ballad of "Narcissus come kiss us," while Rubén Oliva regarded him with an understanding smile and would have liked to tell him that his complaints didn't matter, he accepted them with good humor, but the Englishman must know that he, Rubén Oliva, was revisiting his hometown, or a town like his, which was much the same, and for him—whether it was Tuesday, day of war, or Wednesday, day of commerce, or Friday, Venus's day— all the days, except one, were waiting days, holy days because, like the Mass, they repeated an eternal rhythm—the same morning, noon, and night, winter, spring, and summer, as certain as the continuity of life, and the stages of that daily ceremony were repeated also in Rubén Oliva's soul, as he would have liked to explain to the Englishman who resisted the pain of Spain with a harmonica and a barroom tune: they were identical yet distinct rhythms; as if Rubén, in some mysterious way that he hardly dared attempt to put into words, were always the exception that could arrest and express the forces of nature that surrounded him at birth and would continue to surround him one day when he would die but the world would not.

Therefore, he returned to his village when things had turned sour for him, when things became incomprehensible, exhausting, or nebulously dangerous; he returned as if to reassure himself that it was all still there, in its place, and consequently that the world was at peace; and he always arrived at daybreak, not to miss a single testimony of the land: Rubén Oliva returned to Andalusia, as today, traveling in the middle of the fleeing night, anxious to come near, to see from the windows of the blazing train the first glimmers of dawn, when the Andalusian fields became a blue sea under the starry morning sky, a blue field of light, a field of azure that appeared on waking, first and fleetingly, as an illusion of ocean depths and only gradually, in the growing light of day, acquired a third and unfolding dimension, always still, yet ever changing in the light that woke it to increasingly beautiful and variable forms.

First, from his village's hillside, Rubén Oliva would discover that geometry of graceful inclination formed by the distant ridge and the valley that lay between: all day the ridge would remain hazy, spectral, as if it held for all the world, like a treasure, the blue of night, which elsewhere was freed by the dawn from its gauzy veil; the ridge remained a veiled night, the valley an open abyss, terrible as the claws of a devouring Saturn, and between the hills and the gorge unfolded a rolling geometry, always gradual, never precipitous; each decline, offering its accompanying curve of ascent to the light, had its own pattern of silvery olives and patches of sunflowers gathered like yellow flocks. At the height of day the sun would blank it all out, but the afternoon, Rubén knew, would restore all the variety of light, reflecting first the sunflowers, which were a group of captured planets; then the silver of the olives like threads being spun for Holy Week; and finally a spectacular bath of mustard, ocher, and sepia, depending on the afternoon light, while the white town fought to maintain an eternal midday in the face of their colors. Rubén Oliva had wanted to tell the Englishman that the whiteness of the walls was a necessity, not a vanity: it was because of the age of these towns, through which all races had passed, forcing them to whitewash the walls every year or die away: only the lime preserved those bones worn out by the battles of time.

Rubén Oliva had wanted to explain something else to the Englishman, that his love for his land's setting and for the landscape of the town itself brought both joy and sadness: joy because they grew along with him, sadness because someday they would remain there without him, he would not see them anymore. For Rubén, this sentiment was the most important, the most insistent of all, present in him, in his body and mind, whenever he observed the landscape or loved a woman, or, loving the world and a woman, wasn't sure whether keeping them alive or killing them would gain him victory. Would that be a crime or a tribute? Who best to kill, the woman or the bull, he or death itself? *What's that? What are you talking about? Why do you always mutter everything between your teeth, you want me to believe I'm going deaf? Ah, now look, I've cut myself opening this can! Stop distracting me, Rubén, or you won't get dinner!*

It was morning in the fields. Rubén went closer and then paused, studying everything he could see, touching everything he could touch, examining as closely as he could everything of which one day his fingers would miss the touch. Touching, seeing, the rows of bent poplars, seemingly paired like a corps de ballet or a troop of toy soldiers, trees that had witnessed merciless winds, leaning but not fallen, bent by winter storms; opening all his senses to the white flower and dry fruit of lemon mint, to the smell of squeezed lemons and sliced oranges, to the black purple of wild plum and the faint scent of quince, lemon mint, lily, and verbena: he had lain among their shoots since childhood, the trees and flowers of Andalusia were the visible memory of his childhood; now he expected them to wash away all his ills and closed his eyes in an act of thanks because he knew that when he opened them he would be compensated for his dream by the sight of almonds, diamonds caught in a web of sky, and by the scent of muscadine.

But above the vast geometry of the landscape, duplicating the curves and arcs of the Andalusian horizon in its flight, a restless bird with a scythe-like body reminded him of what his Godmother Madreselva, his false, his substitute mother, the childless progenitor, the protector of Rubén's adolescence and that of the other orphan children like him, had told him long ago: Rubén, study the flight of the swallow, which never tires, feeds in flight, sleeps in flight, makes love in flight; watch its long wings like sharp lances of death. If you want to be an apprentice in the ring, you must be like the swallow, cast away your land and adopt no other, though many may welcome you, nomad bird, bird of the steppes—so his Godmother Madreselva had whispered in the boy's ear.

And she had warned him against the basic dangers: beware the thorny contact of the thistle, don't be seduced by its blue leaves, never drink the narcotic and purgative sap of those prickly leaves. Bitter cress, sawtooth nettles, yellow basil, and green pear, they all beckoned to him—to love, use, contemplate, smell, touch, partake of them—and he, in his youth, never felt that he abused what he shared, whether it was the pleasure of contemplation or the equally blessed pleasure of touching, uprooting, trampling, eating, cutting the fruits and flowers, of carrying them to his mama, or, after she died, to his Godmother Madreselva, who gathered together all the children in the town of Aranda, or, when she died, to his sweetheart, and if she died, why, he'd carry them to the Virgin, because even when all our women have died, the Virgin always remains.

—See that the holy thistle doesn't purge you, Rubén.

Instead, he sought the tracks of winters past.

He sought the snows of January as he sought the memory of his childhood in the village, for when he became a man he always compared his childhood with snow. This had never impressed Rocío, or, indeed, anyone else. These were things that were his, only his, that nobody else understood. Andalusia was his intimacy. And this was the ardent summer, without the memory of the winds of January.

He had spent the morning walking through the fields and composing in his mind a song to the wormwood and the swallows, but his poetic flight was interrupted by practical observations; he was surprised, for example, to see the cows lying down, as though forecasting rain, creating their own dry space, warning the unwary pilgrim that the morning, which had begun so blue and fresh a few hours ago, was turning threatening, turning into a day of accumulating clouds and heavy heat . . .

He raised his eyes and met the image of the black bull of Osborne brandy, waiting for him at the entrance to his village.

A breeze blew from the Levant, and the clouds disappeared.

He arrived at the hotel and smelled wax candles, lacquer, dishrags, and soap, a different soap, not the soap that is never put in the hotel baths.

He had written to Rocío, trying to make sense of their situation, to return to the first days of their love: was that really impossible, as he felt in his heart? and he had tried to explain—would this, too, be futile?—what returning home meant to him, touching and smelling and cutting and eating its fruits and flowers—would she understand?—and he summoned his courage and put his tongue to the gummed flap of the envelope, and the Englishman, who suddenly, out of breath, stopped playing his music-hall ditties and began to ask, sitting with him in the bar, where it was shady at the hottest hour of the day, if he had looked in the shop windows of these little towns where everything was old, none of it was attractive, it was all covered with dust, the signs were from another era, as if the world hadn't undergone a revolution in advertising, he knew because he had worked his whole life in publicity, now he was retired, nothing to do but take care of his garden and his dog, but before . . . He accompanied his commentary with a commercial jingle played on his harmonica, his eyes bright—and he let out a laugh, wasn't he right, these people live in the past, the sweets in the shops seemed to have been there for twenty years, the clothes in the store windows were out of style, the mannequins were ancient, their wigs were full of lice, and had he noticed the mustaches painted on the male dummies, and how moth-eaten the stuffed female breasts and mannequins were, and the cult of miracles, the saints, the images, papist idolatry everywhere . . . ?

Now he played a Protestant hymn on his harmonica and Rubén Oliva was going to tell him that it was true, nothing had changed, not the sweets, the hats, the mannequins, or the holy images in the shops, why should it, when everyone knew exactly what was sold in the shops, and . . .

Mr. Newton interrupted him: —Do you know that nobody here will marry a woman who isn't a virgin?

—Well . . .

—Do you know that nobody shaves after dinner for fear of ruining his digestion, and nobody invites anyone to dine the way they should, in their houses at civilized hours, but instead they go out for coffee after dining, at one in the morning?

—Well . . .

—Look, in a palace in Seville I measured the quantity of spit on the floor, which has turned into crusts of stone over the years, centuries of phlegm, marble oysters, sir, revealing the arrogance of those who always depended on legions of slaves to clean up their filth; where would this country be without servants? And another thing . . .

Without a word Rubén got up and left; the Englishman was still talking to himself. Rubén walked off without paying his part of the tab, as gentlemen ought, just so the Englishman could add to his criticism: freeloaders, ill-mannered brutes.

The town was waking from its siesta.

The heat had not let up, and Rubén followed his own counsel, walking the back streets, sheltered in the shade, rediscovering what he had known since childhood, that all the narrow lanes of this town communicated with one another, feeding into a single narrow entryway. Two- and three-story houses, of varying sizes, beaten down by time, cured with lime like mummies wrapped in white bandages, watched over each route and prevented anyone from leaving. Some were shut up with wooden shutters; others had open balconies of yellowing plaster. Narrow passages with tile roofs and clumps of wild fig trees rising above the buildings, crowns of weeds appearing through all the cracks in the plaza. Clothes hung out to dry. Television antennas. More windows, tightly shuttered. The first denizens of the night began to appear from the upper stories, old village women, cloaked, curious, craning to see him, the outsider, the prodigal son no one knew—was there no one left who had known him as a child? he thought, and almost said, talking to himself like a deaf man.

He watched the first children chasing the pigeons in the dusty square. The whole plaza was sand. The balconies, the upper stories, the shuttered windows and the open windows, all eyes faced the enclosed sand of the plaza: there was only one entrance, fewer than in a bullring; it had only one gate to let the bulls in safely—although it was not safe to guess in what state they would leave. It was a plaza where people turned their backs to their doors. The women came out carrying their cane chairs, locked their doors, and sat in a circle to shell almonds and gossip. The smell of cooking and of urine got stronger. Other women crocheted in silence, and men sat down cautiously with their backs turned. Some young people formed another circle, boys and girls together, and began to clap and sing loud, sorrowful songs, in a rough and halting performance. A beautiful woman with heavy eyebrows, her hair in a bun, sat in a rocking chair as if presiding over the evening; she bared her breast, brought to it a bundle and uncovered the head of a black boy, and offered her breast to him; the boy took it eagerly, her breast's white blood dripping down his purple lips.

The young men were taunting and teasing a gnarled old man with side-whiskers, gray kinky hair, a turned-up nose, and thick lips, who went over to a broken-down wagon, set his jaw, dribbling spittle as though his mouth were watering for a banquet, tucked up the sleeves of his soiled, loose white shirt, got under the wagon, and hoisted it over his shoulders, while the young men looked on, excited and provoked.

A girl sat in a corner of the plaza with her skirts raised high up her legs to catch the dying rays of sun.

It was the twilight hour and Rubén Oliva was in the center of the plaza, surrounded by all this life.

This was his village, which he had left to live as he had to live, but to save himself, to die in peace, he had to return.

Andalusia was his love, not despite his having left, but because he had left. There was nothing true on this earth, not even solitude, that wasn't me/us/the other.

But this afternoon the gods (pickpockets, quick, winged Mercurys, snoops, merchants, restless thieves) denied Rubén Oliva, back among his people, even that: pausing in the center of the plaza of sand where the darting kids and the startled pigeons and the restless heels of the group of singers raised swirls of dirt, Rubén Oliva felt that his town had become no more than a vague memory, incapable of dominating a space that was beginning to be governed by inexplicable laws, all of them—Rubén scanned the sky in vain for an escape: he discovered the swallow—preventing escape from the closed-in plaza.

The hoary, robust old man dropped the wagon and raised his hands to his ears, covering his side-whiskers, crying that his ears hurt, that the effort had burst his eardrums, that the young men and women should sing louder, he couldn't hear a thing.

> *For songs, as you well know, are only grief:*
> *If you don't hear one, you don't hear the other,*
> *Oh, child of witchcraft, until you die.*

He dropped the wagon and at that dusty impact the ground of the plaza suddenly sprouted moist flowers, and Rubén didn't know if they had arisen from the arid crash of that wagon or if they had rained down from the sky in tribute to the singers, and there were cress and myrtle and lilies and impatiens and morning glories.

Then the night seemed to catch fire inside the houses and the women shelling almonds looked for open doors and ran in to save their possessions from the sudden blaze, but the beautiful woman on the rocker had none, and she was not alarmed, she laughed easily and let the black child go on nursing, and then, when she raised him up for all to see, he was a white boy, just look, look, as white as my milk, white because of my milk, I have transformed him!

The youths, frightened by the cries from the houses, turned away from the deaf old man, shouting to him that he had got what he deserved, trying to prove at his age that he was just as strong as they, but they were stopped in their tracks by the stampede of a herd of neighing horses that suddenly rushed into the square, trampling the flowers, halting the youths.

The old women closed the shutters on the upper floors.

The women who watched from the yellow balconies went inside, shaking their heads sadly.

But others came into the arena, into the confusion, surrounding Rubén Oliva, all of them in the midst of the wild chestnut horses, all of them within the suddenly deep blue night: sumptuously dressed women completely indifferent to the fires and the neighing, came through the single narrow lane and entered the square; they were wrapped in capes of raw silk, trailing pear- and orange-colored taffeta, carrying trays bearing teeth, eyes, and tits, so that Rubén was forced to examine the mouths, the empty eye sockets, the mutilated breasts of the women slowly walking in procession, led by a woman more opulent than the others, a woman whose face, wrapped in a cowl, was like a moon girded with emeralds, whose head was crowned by a dead sun with razor-sharp rays, whose bosom sported artificial roses, and from her shoulders to her feet there hung a great triangular cape contrived with elaborate ornamentations of ivory and precious stones, medallions shaped like roses and coiled like metal snakes.

But the woman's hands, though covered with rings, were empty. Her marked face, her moonlike face, was furrowed by tears, cruel drops, and she didn't stop crying until her three attendants approached the beautiful woman with the heavy eyebrows and the hair in a bun and struggled with her, and touched the dead eyes to her face, and covered with the severed ones the breasts that had nursed the black boy, and forced open her mouth to fill it with those bloodless teeth; they left her teeth and her eyes and her breasts but they snatched away her child and placed him in the hands of the Lady, and the despoiled woman cried, her eyes full of blood, her mouth full of teeth, her four breasts sticking to her like a bitch's, but now the Lady stopped crying and smiled, and the procession began again: first, the bejeweled attendants dressed in rich shades of lemon and fig; then the herd of chestnut horses, now tame; behind them, a rebirth of myrtle, four-o'clock, honeysuckle, and morning glory, sweet perfume, the earth transformed into a garden; they led her to the narrow lane and there began a slow ascent to the throne that awaited her, motionless, but which now, as she approached with the white child who had been black, began to sway and rose on a wooden platform lifted by bearers hidden beneath its draperies; the deaf old man pulled Rubén Oliva under it and said: Quick, there's no other way out, and he made him stand behind the draperies, under the throne that was now beginning to move, snaking off, carried by the bearers, including the hoary old man, who had as much trouble lifting the float as before he had had lifting the cart, paying dearly for his effort, perhaps seeking to demonstrate something to the world and to himself, and by his side was Rubén Oliva, watching the deaf old man with thick lips half open, winking his sleepy eye at Rubén: Don't be a loafer, hey, pull your weight, we have to hoist up the Virgin and carry her through town, through the night, the old man told him, the day is done and the night deals out deception, didn't he know? It mocks the florid fragrances and sweet caresses of daytime, when you think you are in love with nature and she with you, not realizing that love—the old man almost spit out the words—is impossible between her and ourselves. He asked Rubén to tread firmly, don't fall, don't give up, trample the flowers, hard, hard—for we have to kill her to survive, and she demands a final accounting. The old man gave Rubén Oliva a sharp elbow in the ribs, and Rubén realized that he was one among many, one more bearer in the brotherhood that was carrying the Virgin in a nocturnal procession. And if for the average person the night produces monsters, the old man continued, for you they appear by day, for you the day is mad, unreal, and chimeric. What do you do at night, Rubén? Do you dream when you sleep, exhausted by the chimeras of your day? What are you left with? Then welcome to the sleep of reason, now lift, walk, and believe with me that it's better to live with illusions than to die disabused of them, now lift, heave, haul, you idler, you loafer . . .

Rubén Oliva licked the gummed edge of the envelope and cut his tongue.

Thursday

1

The deaf old man recalled how as a boy, when he came from Fuendetodos to Zaragoza to watch the procession, he had wanted to be under the throne, alongside the porters, hidden by the corduroy curtains of the float, peering through them to spy the legs of the women on the balconies, especially when the procession would stop for some reason, and the tolling of the bells was like a holy dispensation to listen more closely to the rustle of petticoats and the rubbing of legs and the wagging of hips and the tapping of heels, and he imagined couples embracing in the streets, loving . . .

But in Seville, said the deaf man, when a pause is imposed by the street song, *la saeta*, it's like a cry for help in the desert, everyone disappears, and only the Virgin and the person who is singing to her remain. Seville becomes invisible then, and of all the invisible ones the most invisible of all are those who carry the throne of the Virgin, as he is doing now, the ones who can feel themselves alone with the Virgin, carrying her like Atlas bearing the world on his shoulders, along with the symbols of Holy Mary, palm and cypress and olive, mirrors and stairs, fountains, doors, enclosed gardens, the evening star, the entire universe, and, above all, the tower, the tower of David, the ivory tower, the Giralda, which he glimpsed, looking for legs and finding legs, looking through the panting line of porters and finding, if not the erotic life that he had imagined, at least the popular life that was once again the material sustenance of life itself. In Seville, as in Madrid, in this year of grace 1806, on the brink of all the disasters of war, the past century's libertine dream was capriciously prolonged—its festive and egalitarian customs, the people and the nobility all mixed together—for the nobility had taken to imitating the people, going to popular fandangos, thronging into bullrings and theaters, adulating bullfighters and actresses, the dukes dressing up like banderilleros, the duchesses like *chulaponas*, and in the center of this whirlwind, before history claimed its due and festival turned to warfare and warfare to guerrilla struggle and guerrilla struggle to revolution and revolution, ah, revolution to government and constitution and law, and law to despotism, before all that, it was he, it was Don Francisco de Goya y Lost Senses, who showed the people to the aristocracy, and what is more, who showed the people to themselves.

He left Madrid amid the waving washerwomen, the peddlers, the jugglers, the chestnut venders whom he had endowed with faces and true dignity for the first time, and now in Seville he was welcomed with waves and cheered through the streets by guilds of dyers and silk mercers, weavers of linen and dealers in gold thread, all those who labored in the making of the cloaks and mantles, skirts and hoods, veils and tunics of all that divine seraglio: La Virgin del Rocío, La Señora de los Reyes, La Macarena, and La Trianera; in the old deaf man passing among them wearing a crowned hat and a gray frock coat the workers recognized one of themselves, the son of a gilder from Fuendetodos, the artisan who was who he was because he had done what he had done: canvases, engravings, murals, independent of any explanation, felt rather than revealed: he has presented us to the world, and, more important, to ourselves, who lived like blind people, not recognizing ourselves, not recognizing our strength . . .

But he, Don Francisco de Goya y Light Sensors, didn't want to hear about recognition this Maundy Thursday night in Seville; all he wanted was to take off his hat and his frock coat, to be again what he wanted to be, a worker, a gilder, an artisan, a member of the guild, in his shirtsleeves, his shirt open at the neck, unkempt and sweaty, barefoot, carrying the tower that was the Virgin alongside the porters, hidden from those who applauded him because they recognized themselves in him, when he secretly wanted them to recognize something else, the way he had exposed the excitements of perversion and imaginative sexual intimacy. He introduced the most obscure people to themselves, but especially he introduced man and woman in darkness, he put them beneath this float and this procession, wrapped them in sheets as if in sacred robes and sighs, and showed them, as he was doing now, carrying the weight of the world, wrapped in the sheets as the porters scrambled beneath the skirts of the Virgin and as the whole town mingled in the narrow lanes of Seville.

He felt alone and soiled and tired. He had to prove that he was still strong. Strong not just as an artist but also as a man. He bore the throne of the Virgin and panted among the panters, protected by the billowing skirts of the Virgin, the virgins of Seville: he saw nothing. And then he remembered that he was the king of the keyhole, the most lucid and cruel spy ever. As a reward, he was allowed to look through locks, to glimpse flesh drained of color, clenched in carnal embrace by the side of the sepulcher, to expose in black and white what that flesh could do in its mad effort to hold back time, to drive away death and consecrate life.

2

This, many years later, is what the old man saw through the keyhole of his canvas. A fresh, bare one, though already populated in his mind by a jumbled confusion of sheets and flesh clamoring to emerge, and again he paused before the empty canvas like a village gossip in front of the lovers' door at the hour when a nocturnal wind from the Levant silenced the rest of the world, and the lovers too, and the old man hesitated: Should he allow them to appear or not? Should he let them inhabit his canvas?

And he looked at them through that keyhole—at her, coated
with a lubricating oil like a second skin over her totally naked
body, with the exception of her sex, which was covered by a
butterfly, inviting her masculine companion to bring close his
own sex, a scythe of flesh, or rather a swallow, a black swooping
bird that never rested, that never ceased its flight, that ate and
fornicated in the air, to bring that bird to the butterfly, as if she,
the woman of thick eyebrows and tight lips, bathed in oil, could
gore him: dragonfly against dragonfly, wing against wing, you
will find I am not defenseless, you will find I am not as before,
an unshielded, lubricated hole; now the scythe of your sex must
first defeat my butterfly, and my butterfly bites, be careful, and
soars, and pricks, and punctures, I warn you, never again will
you find me defenseless, and then he takes her by the waist and
turns her over with a single motion, places her face-down with
a single stroke, exposing to the lover and the watcher her avid
buttocks, lubricated, easy to penetrate, and he enters her from
behind, not in the anus but in the sweet vagina, proffered, half
open, oiled, shaved, reduced to the impalpable and invisible down
of puberty, the shaved mons veneris covered by the butterfly,
which now flew away to keep from being crushed, revealing the
woman's pubic mound, already darkened, despite the morning
shave, by a heavy, quick rebirth of stubble, member and mem-
brane rejoined; you also have a hole: as if obeying its mistress,
the butterfly alighted between the man's small, raised buttocks
and tickled him there, and he came and came again, praising
her, thanking her for his victory, Elisia, Elisia, you can transport
me with nothing but a look, how can you give me more than
this, for which I can never repay you; yes, Romero, do me as
you would a bull, stick me, Romero, as you would like to stick
the bull but don't dare, macho bullfighter, because you don't
want to admit that the bull is your stud and you are two lost
fags, except the bull wants to impale you and you don't want to
be impaled, now stick me as you would stick the bull, make me
come as you would make that impossible couple, the butterfly

and the bull, come together, Romero, the unchanging sun and the moon that waxes and wanes to become a claw, rend me, Romero, your claw, love me, your whore, only a claw, lover, and then again to swell, to grow, aren't you jealous, sun, constant one, immutable, in your suit of eternal lights, while the universe whirls in circles around your waist, and although your rays scorch them all you cannot reach them with your shaft of fire, for the night renders you impotent?

—The shame, the shame . . .

—I gave you everything, and you, nothing.

—The shame, the shame.

—Make me dance naked for you, murmured La Privada, and at the very moment of orgasm she fainted in the arms of Pedro Romero.

The painter, watching the scene through the white view hole of his canvas, felt a twinge of sadness and envy, it was proper that there should be so much envy in Spain, where there was so much to be coveted, but nothing as much as this, the desirable body of the bullfighter embracing the waist of the inanimate, desirable body of the actress, who appeared dead, giving the matador this supreme trophy, the reenactment of the agony in each act of love, because that is what Goya most feared and most envied: that this serious woman of joined brows and downy upper lip, Elisia Rodríguez, La Privada, fainted every time they made love.

Who could stop adoring her after knowing that?

Men would leave her but they would neither forget her nor stop loving her passionately, never, never.

—No man has ever left me. I have sacrificed all my best lovers so as to be the first to break away. Everything comes to an end . . .

Pedro Romero and Elisia Rodríguez, La Privada, remained asleep, naked, arms around each other, barely covered by a heavily starched sheet that seemed to have a life of its own, bodies and clothes soiled by a bath of oil that was like the blood of the two of them, their bodies joined by a pleasure that separated them, all the secrets of the bodies slipping away in a perpetual flight that the old painter paused to contemplate as one contemplates a Muslim patio where the stone is constantly turning to water, returning to stone, and in water and stone finds no face or object other than the word of God . . .

This he saw, his heart steeled, faithful witness to the love-making of the matador Pedro Romero and the actress Elisia Rodríguez, his eyes coldly watching, but his heart bitter and his gut wrenched with fire.

This he saw. What he rapidly rendered on his canvas was black-and-white, drained of color, a double-washed sky, dark gray and impure white, the black stone of a cemetery in place of the starched bed, and the bodies dressed, standing, but the man dead, dressed in white frock coat and tie, and white shoes, stockings, and pants, as if for his First Communion, but the occasion was death, the corpse of the man with his eyes closed and his mouth open in agony, without grace, without butterflies, without adornment, held by the unkempt woman, close-browed, emaciated, grasping the head and the waist of the dead man. He, fainted forever, dead in Goya's engraving, not she, awake in her sorrow.

For once she had been abandoned.

He signed it in the corner and titled it *Love and Death*.

He looked at the drawing, the drawing looked at him. The dead man opened his eyes and looked at him. The woman turned her head and looked at him. There was no need for words. They had appeared, they were going to appear, with or without him. They had defeated him. They needed him only to form the triangle that would make the act more exciting: the old man watched the act only to excite the young lovers. With or without him, they were going to appear. In 1806, when all this happened, or in 1821, when Goya painted it in his Quinta del Sordo, or even today, when all this *is* happening.

3

Don Francisco Goya y Lost Census bought a pistachio ice cream in the sweet shop on the Plaza del Salvador, turned down Villegas, and entered the small plaza of Jesús de la Pasión, where the famous actress Elisia Rodríguez, La Privada, was performing this Holy Saturday of the Resurrection. Out of the corner of his eye the old painter, licking his green ice, saw the bridal shops that were the dominant businesses in the square, which was called the Plaza del Pan when Cervantes wrote there, and he mockingly compared the organdy and tulle outfits with the hoods and long skirts of the Virgins carried in procession through Seville. Of course, the skirts that draped the Virgin from waist to ground, like those on the mannequins in the shops, only served to cover a taper, the underlying wooden structure of the image, which has features carved only on its face and hands.

La Privada, Elisia Rodríguez, in contrast, was dressed as a Maja, with low-cut Empire gown and shoes of silver silk, her splendid body not reduced to hands and face. Had he seen her? Of course he had, he had even painted her. But it would be truer to say that, because he had painted her, he had seen her. But now the painter was crossing a patio rimmed with orange trees whose dropped fruit lay rotting on the cobblestones, coming to see the model, to ask her to pose nude for him.

She received him out of curiosity. Is he famous? she asked her lover, Pedro Romero, and the bullfighter said he was, he was a famous son of Aragón, a peasant, but also a painter of the court and all that; they said he was a genius.

Is he amusing? At times, answered Romero, when he paints attractive things, festivals, parasols, kids playing, girls running, bulls in the plaza, all that. He paints kings—very ugly he paints them, but if they like it, what can you do? And then he paints dreadful, awful things, women with monkey faces, women selling their daughters, witches, old women fucking, horrible things.

And you, has he painted you? Once, from a distance, awaiting
the charge in the ring, and another time, killing. He's told me
he wants to do a canvas that will make me immortal. Well, my
immortality is no more than two passes of the cape and a flourish
over the head of the bull. The rest, Elisia, I will never see, nor
you either. Come on, dance naked just for me.

He took off his high hat. He wasn't going to hide his years.
His hoary crest sprang out, freed from its high, narrow prison.
They exchanged banalities, sweets, drinks, thanks, compliments,
praises, candied egg yolks, and then he repeated that he wanted
to paint her. And she said she already knew that, through Romero. And he said that Romero neither knew nor, perhaps, approved of what he wanted. And what was that? Then the old
deaf painter, looking at her in a way that seemed to say "I have
eyes, all the rest has failed me, but I have eyes, and my blood
throbs," said simply that actresses die. She knew that; he ate an
egg yolk as if to seal the comment. They die, he continued, and
if they get lucky they die young and beautiful, but if their luck
fails them they lose their youth and beauty: then they are nothing.
I know that, replied La Privada, that's why I live for today, and
that is my message every time I love or sing or dance or eat:
there is nothing better waiting for me, this is today and tomorrow;
and only today is real for me—only today. No, but there is a way
of surviving, continued the old man. I know, she said, a painting.
Yes, but nude, señora.

—You're asking for yourself? she asked him, suddenly switch-
ing to the familiar form of address.

—Yes, and for your lover, too. Someday, one of you will die.
The two bodies that are so drawn to each other will be separated.
Not by choice, not in anger, not at all, but by something that
cruelly crushes our will and our whim. We are born separate,
we meet, and in the end, death will separate us again. That is
intolerable.

—For you, perhaps. I, truthfully . . .

—No. Elisia . . . I may call you Elisia? . . . For your lover and, yes, for me, too, it would be so, it would be intolerable to cease to love only because death intervened.

—So you like me?

—I desire you.

—Then you may have me, Paco, you may take all of me for yourself, in fact and not in a painting, but on one condition, sweetie . . .

Sitting there, a little stooped over, his high hat in his gnarled, agile hands, the serious hands of an artist and a teamster, the deaf man felt stripped. The actress ran to an ornate Tabasco wooden chest she had gotten from her servant Guadalupe, knelt down, opened it, poked among the clothes, releasing an intense smell of musk, and she extracted something that was wrapped in lace shawls, and from inside that, a green velvet case, and, with sensual urgency mixed with religious respect, with the delicacy of her long, loving, digging fingers, which could be claws when she wished, feathers if she pleased, the actress finally pulled from the case a portrait, which she showed to the painter. His eyesight already faded, he held it in front of his nose, smelling, more than anything, the whiff of sulfur that clung to the portrait, an odor that even a heretic like Don Francisco de Goya y Lucifers associated with the Malignant One, Asmodeus, Beelzebub, Satan, and was this his portrait, the portrait of the devil himself? Why not? Intense green eyes set in dark sockets dominated his fine features, giving them a kind of resignation that Goya associated with his own demons, and looking from the portrait to the woman who offered him that diabolic image, Goya leapt from painting to grammar, only the non-possessive pronoun defined this otherwise ordinary and unusual man, who had been captured in a portrait of repulsive fidelity.

Nobody had ever painted such dark skin, such a white shirt, the Adam's apple in his throat, all so offensively exact. The weary gaze of the painter was led over all the realistic details of the painting, the cracks in the lips, the stubble of the beard, the deep blue of the background. Nothing is artificial, exclaimed the artist, nothing is artistic here, this is devilry, not its representation, this is the devil because this is pure reality, without art, he cried, possessed now by the terror that surely she and her repulsive lover, the subject of the portrait, wanted to instill in him. There is no art in this, Elisia, this is reality, this portrait is the man himself, reduced to this immobile and trapped condition, transformed into a pygmy by the art of witchcraft. This is not a painting, Elisia, what is it? the painter asked in anguish, reduced to one of her possessions, exactly as she had wanted him to be, as he read the living but motionless eyes, without art, of the man-portrait, disabused, disillusioned, despairing, disturbed, deconstructed, destroyed . . .

—If you paint me like this, I will let you see me naked . . .

—But this isn't painting, it's witchcraft.

—I know, silly, a witch friend gave it to me, and she told me, Elisia, you come from a flea-bitten town where the princes married to avoid losing taxes, and you will never understand what this is that I'm giving you, you must find a painter or a poet to put a name to this painting that I'm giving you because you are my most loyal pupil . . .

God forgive you, said the painter, imagining the horror in the triangular union of the aged witch, the young Elisia, and this man who was the devil himself in a portrait.

—But the witch said to me: Elisia, although this man is very handsome and well endowed, I warn you of one thing . . .

—Good advice.

—This man is not yet born, this is the portrait of someone who does not yet exist, and if you want him you are going to have to wait many years . . .

—Until your death!

—Then, Paco, you must make me a painting the same as this, so that my portrait and that of this man who has not yet been born can meet someday, and we can love each other, together at last, he and I.

4

He gave up the thought of painting her as he would have wanted but he wanted her as he couldn't paint her. She was free with her favors and this famous old man amused her, he told her things she didn't understand, he was held as much by the sexual pleasure that she knew how to give him as by the challenge that he couldn't accept: to paint her a companion portrait to the one she had shown him and then returned to its place in her chest.

Of course, she didn't stop seeing Romero in Seville, she returned with him to Madrid, and Goya, who in any case, had to return to "the city and court" (as Madrid is known), followed them. That was the humiliating thing. He had to return anyway, but now it appeared that he was following them. He longed for what he didn't dare request. Something more than the careless love she gave him and the passionate love—he watched them through a keyhole—she gave the bullfighter. He was an old man, famous but old, deaf, a little blind, over seventy; his own lovers had all died or he had broken with them, or sometimes they had broken with him. But passion's ring of flames still blazed, and in its center was a man, Francisco de Goya y Lightning, luminance, lucidity. But now he was only Paco Goya y Lucinderella.

He watched the lovers through the keyholes of his canvases. Once he even tried to sneak into the apartment of La Privada, but he could get no farther than a closed balcony where he almost fell down to Calle Redondilla and cracked his skull. Yet he managed to see something, though he couldn't hear a thing, and they suspected nothing. But he could distinguish once again, so exalted was it, so commanding an act, the orgasmic climax of Elisia's fainting. But not with him, with him that never happened, for him she never fainted as she was doing now, stiffening and trembling one moment and collapsing in the bullfighter's arms the next.

Was it only with Pedro Romero that La Privada fainted? Or

would people say: —Everyone made her faint with pleasure, except Francisco de Goya y Lost Sensations?

Spying on them, he would have liked to join them through a generous, possible act of communication. He imagined that it would be like carrying the Virgin in the procession. He was unable to see, under that throne, but his feet and his sense of direction told him that all the streets and lanes of Seville communicated with each other, from the Cinco Llagas Hospital to the Casa de las Dueñas to the Patio de Banderas and Huerta del Pilar and, through the tunnel beneath the Guadalquivir, to the glories of Triana. That was the law of water, universally communicating, springs with gorges and rivulets, and those with rivers, and rivers with lakes, and those with waterfalls, and the falls with the deltas and those with the ocean and the vastness of the sea with the darkness of the depths. Why should the beds of the world be any different, why shouldn't they all communicate with one another, not a single door shut, not a single padlock or clasp, not a single obstacle to desire, to the text, the tact, the satisfaction of the bed?

He wanted the two of them—Elisia and Romero—to invite him to be part of the final, shared lust; what did it matter to them, if he was going to die before them? Romero would retire from the ring, Goya would paint the bullfighter his immortal canvas, more immortal than his immortal manner of awaiting the bull stock-still; she might die before the two men, but that would be an aberration: it would be natural that he, the painter, would die before the others and leave the painted canvas of the loves of Goya and Elisia, of Elisia and Romero, of the three together, a canvas more immortal than that fraud she showed one afternoon in Seville, between servings of cakes and candied egg yolks, which he accepted, still stuffed with ice cream, his belly swelling, about to reply to the world with a sonorous and catastrophic belch. What did it matter to them, if he was going to die before they did? Then he realized, horrified, that the portrait she showed him in Seville was an intolerable thing. A brutal reality, an incomprehensible portrait made by no one, a canvas without an artist. How could it be! Could any canvas surpass that brutal realistic fidelity that La Privada revealed to Goya, saying:

—Paco, make me a portrait like this one?

Death was going to cast the three of them to the four winds before love united them. That thought was killing Goya. He was an old man and he didn't dare ask for what he wanted. He couldn't endure the scorn, the mockery, the simple denial. He didn't know what Elisia whispered in Romero's ear:

—He's an old tightwad. He never brings me anything. He doesn't bring me what you do, sweet things, honey and bread . . .

—I've never brought you rich things. Who are you confusing me with?

—With no one, Romero: you bring me sweet things, not sweets but sweetness, because you know I'm endearing . . .

—You're a flirt, Elisia . . .

—But him: nothing. A tightwad, a miser. No woman can love that sort of man. He lacks those attentions. He may be a genius, but he doesn't know anything about women. Whereas you, my treasure . . .

—I bring you almonds, Elisia, bitter pears and olives in oil, so you are forced to draw sweetness out of my body.

—Lover, how you talk, how you flatter, stop talking now and come here.

—Here I am, all of me, Elisia.

—I'm waiting. I'm not impatient, Romero.

—That's what I've always said, you have to wait for the bull to get to you, that's how it discovers death.

The painter didn't hear them but he didn't dare tell them what his heart desired.

—But if only I could watch, only watch . . . I have never wanted anything else . . .

Did they think of him as they fornicated? At least to this extent: they thought of him when they wanted what a painter could not refuse: a witness.

But he had to be honest with himself. She denied him something else. With Romero, she fainted when she came. With him, she did not. She denied him the fainting.

Then, shut within his estate, with the children shouting insults that he didn't hear and scrawling on his wall, he rapidly sketched and painted three works, and in the first the three of them were lying in a bed of rumpled sheets, Romero, Elisia, and Goya, but she had two faces on the same pillow, and one of her faces was gazing passionately at Pedro Romero while she embraced him feverishly, and Pedro Romero also had two faces, one for the pleasure of Elisia, the other for the friendship with the painter, just as she, too, had a second face for the painter, and she winked at him while he kissed her, and at the same time she looked ardently at the bullfighter, and there were frogs and snakes and jesters with fingers at their lips surrounding them, not a triangle now but a sextet of deceptions and betrayals, a gray hole of corruption.

In the second painting she ascended skyward in her actress costume, her bun, and her flat shoes, but with her naked body, defeated, aged, straddling a broom, impaled by death's own member, and accompanying her in her flight were the blind bats, the ever-vigilant owl, the swallows as tireless as eternal entreaties, and the preying vultures, eaters of filth, bearing the actress up to the false sky that was the paradise of the theater, the cupola of laughter, obscenities, and belches, the snap of whips, the farts, and the hissing that no clamor of paid applauders could silence: La Privada ascended to receive her final face, which Goya gave her, not warning her this time, as he had before (You will die alone, with me and without your lover); but using her as a warning, making her a witch, an empty hide, as her rival La Pepa de Hungría had once described her; he was the final arbiter of the face of the actress who had once asked him to portray her for eternity, as she was, in reality, without art. And that was what the artist could not give her, even though it cost him the supreme sexual gift of the despot: fainting at the moment of climax.

He also finished the third painting, that of Pedro Romero. He accentuated, if possible, the nobility, the beauty of that forty-year-old face, the calmness of the hand that had killed 5,892 bulls. But the spirit of the artist was not generous. —Take my head, he said to the painting of the bullfighter, and give me your body.

He opened a window to let in a little fresh air. And then the actress, the despot, the witch that he himself had imprisoned in the painting, mounted her broom and flew away cackling, chortling, laughing at her creator, spitting saliva and obscenities onto his gray head, saving herself like a swallow on the nocturnal breeze of Madrid.

5

Old and barefoot, his thick lips open and cracked, begging for water and air like a true penitent, he carried the Virgin of Seville on his shoulders.

—Actresses die, but Virgins do not.

That was when he remembered that, as covered as she was, this Most Holy Virgin whose throne he carried was no more modest than Elisia Rodríguez, when La Privada, naked, told him: You never give me anything, so I won't give you anything either, and she pulled forward her fantastic black hair and covered her entire body with it, like a skirt, looking at Goya through the curtain of hair and saying vulgarly:

—Come on, don't look so shocked, where there's hair there is pleasure.

Friday
1

She asked the boys to test themselves alone first, to find out their capacities and then return and tell her their experiences, while she spent her days between cooking chick-peas and running to the henhouse, stopping from time to time to stand with her arms crossed by the wattle fence that separated her house from the immense cattle pastures.

The house should have been very large to hold all those boys, mostly orphans, some still of school age, others already masons, bakers, and café waiters, but all unhappy with their work, their poverty, their short, all too recent childhood, their rapid, hopeless aging. Their useless lives.

But the house was not large; there was little more than a corral, the kitchen, two bare rooms where the boys slept on sacks, and the señora's bedroom, where she kept her relics, which were just some mementos of other kids, before the present group, and nothing from before that. It was known she had no husband. Or children. But if someone flung that in her face, she would answer that she had more children than if she had been married a hundred times. Parents, brothers, or sisters, who really knew? She had simply shown up at the village, appearing one fine day from among some rocks covered with prickly pear along a chestnut-lined path. Alone, hard, resolute, and sad, so skinny and dry that it wasn't clear if she was a woman or a man, with a wide hat and a patched cape on her shoulder, a cigar between her teeth, she inspired many nicknames: Dry-Bone, Hammerhead, Boldface, No Fruit, Crow's Foot, Cigar.

It was easy and even amusing to give her nicknames, once everyone realized that her severe appearance did not imply malice but simply a kind of sober distance. But who could say if those nicknames really fit her. She gave shelter to orphan boys, and when the village was scandalized and demanded that the dry, tall, thin woman give up that perverse practice, nobody else was inclined to take them in, so, through sheer indifference, by default, they let her continue, although from time to time a suspicious (and perhaps envious) spinster would ask:

—And why doesn't she take in orphan girls?

But there was always some other old lady, even more suspicious and imaginative, who would ask if they wanted to give the impression that they had a whorehouse of young girls in their village.

And there the matter ended.

So they let her continue her solitary labors, taking care of the boys. She stayed alone every night, watching them go off as soon as Venus, the evening star, rose; early in the morning, after her rest, she reappeared at the wattle fence, when Venus was the last light to retire from the sky and the boys returned from their nocturnal roamings. The woman and the star had the same schedule.

So, in a sense, for her every day was Friday, the day of the goddess of love, a day governed by the appearance and disappearance of Venus, the evening star, which in the sky's great game was also the morning star, as if the firmament itself were the best teacher of a long, eternal pass, like the passes Juan Belmonte made in bullfights she saw when she was a girl. Despite all that, nobody in the town thought of calling her Venus. With her cape and her broad hat, her multiple skirts, and her leather boots, she held on to a single beauty trick, they said—she, as unpainted as an Andalusian midday, with her face cracked by early aging, her eyes buried deep in their sockets, her rabbit's teeth!—and that was to put two cucumber slices on her temples, which was a well-known protection against wrinkles; but the apothecary said no, it's a cure for fainting, she thinks that will drive away migraines and faints, she has no faith in my science, she is an ignorant countrywoman. Poor kids.

And although the apothecary added another nickname—Cucumbers—the boys called her Mother, Madre, and when she told them not to and said they should call her Madrina, Godmother, they called her Madreselva, Honeysuckle, by instinct, seeing her as that spreading plant, flowering and aromatic, that was the only adornment of her poor house and was there, like her, for everyone, naturally, like the landscape that spread before the boys' eyes, from the oaks to the hills to the windswept pass, embracing everything, gardens, houses, and fields, and ending in the prickly-pear-covered rocks through which Madreselva had entered this town to take charge of the unfortunate but ambitious boys.

2

Rubén Oliva waited impatiently for the night. He had the gift of seeing the night during the day, beyond the spreading fields of sunflowers that were the day's escutcheon, vegetable planets that drew the sun to the earth, sky magnets on the earth, ambassadors of the heavens, flourishing in July and dead in August, scorched by the very sun they mimicked. His land taught Rubén that the sun that gives the day can also take it away; his Andalusian land was a world of sun and shade, where even the saints belonged to one or the other, so that he felt excited but also guilty to realize that his pleasures, his intoxications, were of the night; was it Madreselva's fault, the children wondered, as they waited for the last candles of the sun to be extinguished before going out to test themselves, when sunflowers became moonflowers, they slipped through the hedges, leapt the wattle fences, and danced past the barbs in the grazing range, stripped by the bank of the river, its water deep and cold even in the summer, felt the first chilling thrill of the caressing nocturnal water flowing through their legs, and floated along the banks, grasping the corkwood branches, feeling their bodies cooled and refreshed by the liquid breath of the river, and then suddenly they would feel the slap of dung that told them they were nearing what they sought, blindly, gropingly, in the darkest hour of the night, the hour when Madreselva urged them to go out, blind, in search of the beast: groping through the unlit corral, the boys' bodies brushing those of the calves, which they imagined black, only black, nobody wanted any other color, fighting body to body, bull and matador-child locked in their private dance, bound to each other, if I let the body of the bull elude me, the bull will kill me, I have to cling to that body, Madreselva, remembering the cool water between my legs and on my chest, where now I feel the animal's throbbing hide, his breath, his mouth by mine, the black sweat of his skin brushing my breast, my belly, my nascent male down joined to the sweaty bristles of the calf's hide, hair to hair, my penis and testicles lacquered, caressed, threatened, painted by the enemy love of the beast that I have to keep pressed against my fifteen-year-old body, not just to feel, Mamaserva, Motherserf, but to survive: that is why you send us here, night after night, to learn to fight without fear, otherwise one cannot be a matador, there must be pleasure bound to that enormous danger, Ma, and I, your newest liege, am only happy fighting bulls by night, thrusting blindly in the dark, with nobody watching, acquiring a pleasure and a vice that will be bound together all my life, Honeysuckle, the pleasure of fighting bulls without an audience, without giving pleasure to anyone except myself and the bull, and letting the bull make the thrusts, letting him seek me, fight me, attack me, so that I feel the thrill of being attacked, immobile, without ever feinting, deceiving my dangerous companion on those nights, my first nights as a man.

At times, the ranch guards detected those nocturnal intrusions and ran after us, shouting, brandishing sticks if there were any at hand, firing into the air, but without any real ill will, because even the cattleman knew that sooner or later these kids would be what kept his business from failing. But when the guards set dogs on the boys, even the watchmen questioned the goodwill of the cattleman.

When she heard about that, Madreselva made an agreement with the cattleman that, once their nocturnal apprenticeship was completed, the boys could continue their lessons in the ring at the hacienda, with her as the teacher, and she told the cattleman that, if he liked, the older boys could handle the preparations, but once it was time for the lesson, she would be in charge, she would throw off her hat and cape, her wide lock of hair blinding her and she puffing it away from her face to be able to see; she would be dressed in a short Andalusian outfit with leather leg coverings, she would teach the kids, and especially Rubén Oliva, because in that child's dark eyes, and in the shadows under his eyes, she saw a longing for the night, she would tell them the three cardinal commands, *parar*, keep the feet still, *templar*, move the cloth slowly, *mandar*, make the bull obey the cloth, those three verbs are the watchwords of the bullfighter, they are more your mothers than the ones you have lost, and that means you must lead the bull where you want him to be, not where he wants to be . . .

—Don't worry, said Madreselva, looking at Rubén more than at the others, at the end it will be just you and the bull, face to face, seeing yourself and seeing death in the face of the other. Only one of you is going to come out alive: you or the bull. And the art of bullfighting lies in reaching that point legitimately, with skill. You will see.

Then Madreselva gave the first lesson, how to stop a calf that had newly emerged from the cow as though from the belly of a mythological mother, fully armed, already in possession of all its powers, watch, Rubén, don't get distracted, don't make faces, the bull appears before you as a force of nature, and if you don't want to turn that into a force of art, you might as well become a baker: measure yourself against those horns, cross yourself with them, Rubén, place yourself before the horns, and go, boy, go to the opposite horn, or the bull is going to kill you. Here is the bull galloping toward you. Poor thing, what will you do?

Then Madreselva gave her second lesson, how to *cargar la suerte*, to move the cloth to turn the bull away, not let the attacking bull do what nature tells it, but instead what it is told by the bullfighter, who is there for that purpose, not at the mercy of fortune but controlling it with his cape, never relinquishing the beauty and magic of the pass, boys; put your leg forward, so, making the bull change direction and go into the field of battle— put your leg forward, Rubén, bend at the hip, don't break the pass, summon the bull, Rubén, the bull moves, why don't you! You're not listening to me, boy, why do you stand there like a statue, letting the bull do whatever it wants? If you don't take charge now, make it obey, the bull will be fighting you, and not you the bull, the way it should be . . .

But, after that, nobody was going to move Rubén Oliva.

The bull took charge; the bullfighter was rooted in place.

Rubén was rooted in place.

What did Madreselva say, gritting her rabbit's teeth, puffing from her lower lip to blow the ashen tuft from her forehead?

—You have to break the bull's charge, Rubén.

—I won't take the advantage, Ma.

—It's not advantage, cunt, it's leading the bull where it doesn't want to go, so you can fight it better. That is what Domingo Ortega said—you know more than the maestro, I suppose?

—I don't move, Ma. Let the bull take control.

—What do you want from bullfighting, boy! said Madreselva then, expressing her annoyance, which she knew was reprehensible but necessary.

—That everyone's heart should stop when they see me fight the bull, Ma.

—That's good, boy. That is art.

—That they should all feel like a thousand cowards in face of a brave man.

—That's bad, boy, very bad, what you said. That's vanity.

—Then let my fame endure.

She taught them—always quoting Domingo Ortega, for in her opinion there had never been a bullfighter more intelligent and more in control and aware of his every move—that there is nothing more difficult for the bullfighter than to think when facing the bull. She asked them to think of bullfighting as a battle not just between two bodies but between two faces: the bull looks at us, she taught them, and what we must do is reveal its death to it: the bull must see its death in the cape, which is the bullfighter's face in the ring. And we must see our death in the face of the bull. Between those two deaths lies the art of bullfighting. Remember: two deaths. Someday you will know that the bullfighter is mortal, that it is the bull who does not die.

So taught the insatiable madwoman, whose mother and father could have been a bull and a cow, or perhaps a calf and a bull-fighter, who could tell, seeing her there, an image of dust, the statue of a brown and barren sun, a star as cracked as the lips and hands of this woman teacher, who showed them how to feint, to be slow to kill, to take advantage of the bull's speed, for the bull is a rough beast that must be smoothed, posed and disposed by the bullfighter's art, thus, thus, thus, and Madreselva made the slowest, the longest, the most elegant passes that pack of forsaken, deceived boys had ever seen, recognizing in the woman's long, decisive passes a power that they wanted for themselves; Madreselva not only taught them to be bullfighters in the feverish September mornings that succeeded the fiery death of the sunflowers, she also taught them to be men, to have self-respect, to command with elegant, long, and . . .

—Deceitful passes, said the rebellious Rubén, what you call feinting is only deceit, Ma . . .

—And what would you do, maestro? Madreselva crossed her arms.

The proud, imperious boy told her then to play the bull, form its horns with her fists and rush straight at him, neither of them dodging, neither she nor he, neither the false bull nor the incipient torero, and she became for that moment the captive cow, and she appraised the proud, gaunt figure of this Rubén Oliva, puffed up with puerile but impassioned honor, and she, mother-bull, did what he asked: against her judgment as his teacher, she charged full-out at Rubén, and he did not guide her with his cape as she had shown them, he remained as motionless as a statue, combining the passes as she wanted, but without any of the feints she called for, instinctively he fought her face, beautifully, moving her though not moving himself, dominating the bull without commanding it, showing it its death as she wanted, as she had done.

And then Rubén Oliva spoiled it all, after he ended the series of passes, unable to resist the temptation to make a triumphal flourish, saluting, acknowledging, freezing his hips, and flashing his black eyes as though to outshine the sun, while she, the teacher, the mistress, called Dry-Bone in the village and Madreselva, Ma, Maresca by her disciples, each according to his own stone-deaf Spanish, language of the country of the deaf and therefore of the brave, of those who can't hear good advice or the voice of danger, while she shouted with fury, Beggar! Sponge! Don't ask for an ovation you don't deserve—if you deserve it, they will give it to you without your making a fool of yourself, but what other chance did he have, he answered softly, wrapping his arms around Madreselva, asking her forgiveness, though she knew he was not repentant: the boy was going to be that kind of bullfighter, daring, stiff, and stubborn, demanding that the public admire his triumphal pass, his courage, his consummate manliness, the exhibition of his masculinity before the multitudes, which was permitted, encouraged, which the bullring authorized and which Rubén Oliva was not going to forgo, sacrificing instead the art which he considered deceit—breaking the savage force of the bull. They would always applaud his statue-like pose, his refusal to *cargar la suerte*, to direct the bull, the way Manolete won his acclaim. —This one doesn't dodge, they said, he exposes himself to death right in front of us. He welcomes the thrust of the horns. Just like Manolete!

And she was resigned yet determined, and she asked them to time the passes they made at the calves; resting now, a light between her rabbit's teeth, more mannish than ever, Dry-Mother, Sea-of-Sand, Junglemother, what should they call her?, she made them track each bull's speed, to encapsulate that speed within the matador's own rhythm, because otherwise the bull would trap theirs in his, boys, slowly, listen to the metronome, each time, slower, slower, longer, until it's more than the bull can do to rend cape or body.

Or body. That was the sensual longing that possessed Rubén Oliva: naked, at night, pressed against the body of the bull that he had to hold to keep from being stuck, divining the body of the enemy in a mortal embrace, all wet, emerging out of the cold river into that heated contact with the beast.

3

When Madreselva felt she had no more to teach them, she told those eleven, as she had told others on other graduation days, to prepare their bundles, get their hats, and go out into the bull-fighting villages together to try their fortunes. She liked the number 11 because she was superstitious sometimes and like a witch she believed that when a 1 turns on another, the world becomes a mirror, in itself it sees itself and there it stops: beyond, it leads too far, to transgression, to crime. The witch was there to warn, not to entice. She was an exorcist, not a temptress.

Besides, she thought eleven generations of boys with a passion for the ring were not only sufficient but even significant, and signifying; she imagined them on the roads of Spain, reproducing themselves, eleven thousand matadors, the perfect reply to its eleven thousand virgins; and perhaps the two bands—matadors and virgins—would meet, and then Troy would blaze again. For they would meet in freedom, not by force.

She had her rules, and everyone accepted them, except Rubén Oliva. Who but he would have the cheek to go and wake her, a comic hat perched jauntily on his black hair, tieless though his shirt was buttoned to the neck, in a threadbare vest, peasant pants, with leather boots and empty hands: he had borrowed an old cape to throw over his shoulder to announce that he was a bullfighter.

No, she was enraged because Rubén Oliva entered without knocking and surprised her with her skirts up, rolling a cigarette on her thigh, which was fat and fine, in contrast with the rest of her body: no, she was enraged, dropping her skirts and hastily putting her breeches back on, as if magically to revert to her role of female bullfighter, you are not even an apprentice yet, don't affect a guise you have not attained, don't be impatient, don't imagine the world is yours for the picking—the world is not your oyster, believe me, your wretched youth is stamped all over your rags and bags, and if that's not enough, it's plain to see in the hunger etched on your face, Rubén, which neither I nor anyone else will ever erase, because from now on your only thought will be where to sleep, what to eat, who to hump, and even if you get rich, even if you're a millionaire, someone like you will still have a rogue's mentality, you'll just want to make it through the day and wake up alive the next and have a plate of lentils, even if they are cold.

She laced the legs of her trousers and added: You will never be an aristocrat, my Rubén, mornings will always torment you.

But we are all going together, we'll help each other, said Rubén, still so much of a child.

No, there are only ten of you now, said Madreselva, taking his hand, forgetting her leather breeches and her tobacco: his Mareseca whom he longed to kiss and embrace.

Pepe is staying here, she said, anxiously.

With you, Ma?

No, he will return to the bakery.

What will become of him?

He will never leave here. But you will, said Madreselva, the rest of you will escape, you won't be caught in a poor town, in a bad job, boring, the same thing over and over, like a long night in hell, you'll be far from the bricks and ovens and kitchens and nails, far from the noise of cowbells that turns you deaf and the smell of cowshit and the threat of the white hounds, you will be far from here . . .

He hugged her and he felt no breasts—his own adolescent chest was rounder, it retained the lingering fullness of childhood; he was a cherub with a sword, an angel whose eyes were cruelly ringed, but whose cheeks remained soft.

All he did was repeat that the eleven of them, no, the ten, would go together and help one another.

Ha, laughed Madreselva, surprised by his embrace but not rejecting it, you will go together and sleep together and walk together and fight together and keep each other warm, first you were eleven, now you are ten, one day you will be five, and in the end one man will be left, alone, with the bull.

No, that's not what we want, we're going to be different, Ma.

Sure, boy, that's right. But when you're alone, remember me. Remember what I tell you: on Sundays you are going to see yourself face to face with the bull, then you'll be saved from your solitude.

She pulled away from the boy and finished dressing, telling him: You are stubbornness itself, you will let the bull kill you to keep from wielding your cape, from luring the bull away from you.

When a matador dies of old age, in bed, does he die in peace? Rubén watched her put on her jacket.

Who knows?

I will remember you, Ma. But what is going to become of you?

I am ready to leave this town. I am going, too.

Where did you come from, Ma?

Look, said the dry, cracked woman with cucumbers on her temples, with her unruly hair hanging over her brow and a black cigarette between her yellow fingers, look, she said after a while, let's just go without asking questions; things may be bad someplace else, but they've got to be better than here. I took care of you, boy, I gave you a profession; now just leave. Don't ask me any more questions.

You talk as if you saved me from something, Ma.

Here you have no choice—he looked into her eyes, the eyes of his false mother—here you have to obey, there are too many people with nothing here, serving too few people with much, there are too many people here, and so they are used like cattle; you cannot be chaste that way, Rubén, when you're one of that abundant, docile herd, when they call you and tell you to do this or that, you do it or you are punished or you are driven out, there's no alternative. What they call sexual liberty really exists only in the fields, only in poor, lonely regions full of servants and cows. You obey. You must. There is no one to turn to. You are a servant, you are used, you are meat, you become part of a lie. The masters do whatever they want with you, for you are their servant, always, but especially when there are no other servants around to see what the masters do with you.

She smiled and gave Rubén a pat on the rump. It was the most intimate and loving gesture of her life. As far as he traveled, Rubén still would feel that hard and loving hand on his backside, far from the burnt sunflowers and the goatbells sounded by the wind of the Levant, leaving behind the superb firs and horses of Andalusia, which are white at birth but which Rubén Oliva found to be black on his return. Now he was going far away, to the salt flats and estuaries, the landscapes of electric towers and the mountains of garbage.

Saturday

—Don Francisco de Goya y Lucientes!

—What are you doing in Cádiz?

—Looking for my head, friend.

—Why, what happened?

—Are you blind? Can't you see it's missing?

—I did think something was odd.

—But don't dodge the question, what happened?

—I don't know. Who knows what becomes of your body after you're dead?

—So how do you know you don't have a head?

—I died in Bordeaux in April of 1826.

—So far away!

—So sad!

—You couldn't know. Those were dangerous times. The absolutists came to Madrid and persecuted every liberal they saw. They called themselves the Hundred Thousand Sons of San Luis. I only called myself Francisco de Goya . . .

—Y Lost Census . . .

—The kids stopped writing "deaf man" on the wall of my estate—instead, the absolutists wrote "Francophile." So I fled to

France. I was seventy-eight years old when I was exiled to Bordeaux.

—So far from Spain.

—Why did you have to paint the French, Paco.

—Why did you have to paint guerrillas, Francisco.

—Why did you have to paint for the court, Lost Senses.

—But what happened to your head, son, lopped off that way?

—I don't remember.

—So where did they bury you, Paco?

—First in Bordeaux, where I died at age eighty-two. Then I was exhumed; they were going to send me back to Spain in 1899, but when the Spanish consul opened the coffin, he saw my skeleton didn't have a head. He sent a wind message to the Spanish government . . .

—It's called a telegraph, Paco, a telegraph . . .

—We didn't have those in my day. Anyway, the message read: SKELETON GOYA NO HEAD: AWAIT INSTRUCTIONS.

—And what did the government say? Come on, Paco, don't leave us hanging, you always were such a . . .

—SEND GOYA, HEAD OR NO HEAD. I was exhumed five times, friends, from Bordeaux to Madrid and from San Isidro, where I painted the festivals, to San Antonio de la Florida, where I painted frescoes, five burials, and the boxes they put me in kept getting smaller every time, every time I had fewer bones and they were more brittle, every time I left more dust behind, so that now I'm about to disappear completely. My head foretold my destiny: it just disappeared a little before the rest.

—Who knows, my friend? France was filthy with mad phrenologists, crazy for science. Who knows, maybe you ended up a measure of genius—what a joke!—like a barometer or a shoehorn.

—Or maybe an inkwell for some other genius.

—Who knows? That was a century in love with death, the romantic nineteenth. The next century, yours, consummated that desire. I'd rather go headless than have to witness your time, the age of death.

—What are you saying, Paco? We're lolling in the lap of luxury here.

—Don't interrupt, Uncle Corujo.

—Hey, aren't we all part of the gang here, Aunt Mezuca? What's wrong with a little gossip?

—And who said anything about being part of the gang, you stunted old fool?

—It's okay, part of the gang, old wives' tales, old men's chatter, call it anything you like, what are you going to do here in Cádiz, where the streets are so narrow, and hotter than in Ecija, and lovers can touch fingers from one window to the next . . .

—And have to listen to the chatter of gossipmongers like you, Uncle Soleche . . .

—Shut your mouth, you old hen . . .

—Don Francisco was saying . . .

—Thanks for the respect, son. A lot of times we dead ones don't even get that. I just wanted to say that my case is not unique. Science takes absolute liberties with death. Maybe scientists are the last animists. The soul has gone, to heaven or hell, and the remains are just vile matter. That's how the French phrenologists must have seen me. I don't know whether I prefer the sacred fetishism of Spain or the soulless, anemic Cartesianism of France.

—The eyes of St. Lucy.

—The tits of St. Agatha.

—The teeth of St. Apollonia.

—The arm of St. Theresa in Tormes.

—And that of Alvaro Obregón in San Angel.

—And where is the leg of Santa Anna?

—The blood of San Pantaleón in Madrid, which dries up in bad times.

—Yes, in England, my skull might have been the inkwell of some romantic poet.

—Did what happened to you, Paco, happen to anyone else?

—Of course. Speaking of England, poor Laurence Sterne, with

whom I often chat, because his books are something like written premonitions of my *Caprichos*, though less biting, and . . .

—You're digressing, Paco . . .

—Sorry. My friend Sterne says that digression is the sun of life. Digression is the root of his writing, because it attacks the authority of the center, he says, it rebels against the tyranny of form, and . . .

—Paco, Paco, you're straying, man! What *happened* to your friend Sterne?

—Oh, nothing, except when he died in London in 1768 his corpse disappeared from its tomb a few days after his burial.

—Like your head, Paco . . .

—No, Larry was luckier. His body was stolen by some students from Cambridge, knockabouts and idlers the way they all are, who were celebrating the rites of May in June, whiling away their white nights, using him for their anatomy experiments. Laurence says nobody needed to dissect him because he was more dried up and full of parasites than mistletoe, but since he had written so brilliantly of prenatal life, he approved of someone prolonging his postmortal life, if you can call it that. They returned it—the corpse, I mean—to its tomb, a little the worse for wear.

—Then your case is unique.

—Not at all. Where are the heads of Louis XVI and Marie-Antoinette, of Sydney Carton and of the Princesse de Lamballe?

—Oh, crime, how many liberties are committed in your name!

—And the wheel keeps on rolling, Roland!

—You bet. But Byron, who's my neighbor these days—though not a sociable one—had his brains stolen when it was discovered that they were the biggest in recorded history. And that's nothing. There's a guy who's more sullen than anyone in my parts, he looks like a Ronda highwayman, a masher and slasher for sure. Dillinger he's called, John Dillinger, and I always think Dildo-ger, because when they cut him down leaving a theater . . .

—It was a movie house, Paco.

—In my day we didn't have those. A theater, I say, and when they did the autopsy they found he had a bigger dick than Emperor Charles V had titles, so they lopped it right off and stuck it in a jar of disinfectant, and there is the outlaw's John Thomas to this very day, in case anyone wants to compare sizes, and die of envy.

—Did you envy Pedro Romero, Paco?

—I wanted to live to be a hundred, like Titian. I died at eighty-two, and I don't know if I had already lost my head.

—Romero died at eighty.

—I didn't know that. He doesn't reside in our district.

—He retired from the ring at forty.

—Hold on, I know that story better than anyone.

—That's enough, old woman, you'll fall clean out the window, you'd better get yourself off to bed.

—Oh, I know all about it.

—Come on, don't be childish.

—Oh, let me tell Don Paco the whole story, before I die of frustration . . .

—Who do you think you are, Aunt Mezuca, the morning paper?

—Listen here: Pedro Romero was the greatest bullfighter of his day. He killed 5,588 fierce bulls. But he was never touched by a single horn. When he was buried at eighty, his body didn't have a single scar, see, not even a little scratch this big.

—It was a perfect body, a nearly perfect figure, with a muscular harmony revealed in the soft caramel color of his skin, which accentuated his body's classic Mediterranean forms, the medium height, strong shoulders, long upper arms, compact chest, flat belly, narrow hips, sensual buttocks over well-formed but short legs, and small feet: a body of bodies, crowned by a noble head, firm jaw, elegant, taut cheeks, virile emerging beard, perfectly straight nose, fine, separated eyebrows, clear forehead, widow's peak, serene, dark eyes . . .

—And how you know that, Don Francisco?

—I painted him.

—All of him?

—No, only the face and a hand. The rest was just his cape. But to fight bulls, Pedro Romero, who stood to receive the bull as no one had ever done before, and who froze for the kill as nobody had ever done either, and who, between stops and commands, bequeathed us the luxury of the most beautiful, uninterrupted series of passes that had ever been seen . . .

—And olé . . .

—And recontraolé . . .

—Well, to fight bulls that way, Pedro Romero had only his eyes, those were his weapons—he looked at the bull and thought as he faced the beast.

—Just his eyes!

—No, also a way of fighting bulls by making them see their death in the cape. He invented the encounter, the only one permitted, my Cádiz friends, between the nature that we kill to survive and the nature that for once excuses us for our crime . . . only in the bullring.

—And in war, too, Paco, if you consider how we excuse our crimes here in Cádiz.

—No, old man, a man never has to kill another man to survive; to kill your brother is unpardonable. If we don't kill nature, we don't live, but we can live without killing other people. We would like to receive nature's pardon for killing her, but she denies us that, she turns her back on us, and instead condemns us to see ourselves in history. I assure you, my Cádiz friends, that it's in our loss of nature and our meeting with history that we create art. Painting, I . . .

—And the bullfight, Romero . . .

—And love, La Privada . . .

—I invented both of them.

—They existed without you, Goya.

—All that remains of Romero is a single painting and two engravings. Mine. Of Elisia there remain a painting and twenty engravings. All mine.

—Simply lines, Paquirri, just lines, but not life, not that.

—Where do we find lines in nature? I see only light and dark bodies, advancing and receding planes, reliefs and concavities . . .

—And what about those bodies that approach, Don Paco, and the ones that recede, what about them?

—Where's the body of Elisia Rodríguez?

—She died young. She was thirty.

—And what did you give her, Goya?

—What she didn't have: age. I painted her wrinkled, toothless, wasted, absurdly persisting in using unguents, vapors, pomades, and powders to rejuvenate herself.

—Until death!

—Surrounded by monkeys and lapdogs and gossips and ridiculous fops; the final few spectators of her faded glory . . .

—Wait till you've been anointed!

—But La Privada escaped from me, she died young . . .

—Her final fainting, Paco.

—La Privada who denied you the pleasure of seeing her dazed in your arms when you made love . . .

—Oh, listen, listen to this, everyone, window to window: Elisia Rodríguez never fainted with Don Paco de Goya, with everyone else, yes . . .

—Shut up, damn it . . .

—Hey, Don Paco, don't get worked up, here in Cádiz we laugh at everything . . .

—Nothing between us . . .

—I gave you everythin', but you, nothin'.

—And that's the way it was!

—No, the reason La Privada didn't faint for me was that she had to stay wide awake to tell me things about our people, she wanted me to know them; listen, her fainting was just a pretext so she could sleep anyway, and not be bothered, once she had got what she . . .

—And did they let her sleep in peace?

—Except for a few dense fellows who would shake her by the neck trying to wake her . . .

—Poor La Privada: how many times was she doused with cold water to wake her from her trance!

—How many pinches on the arm!

—How many slaps on the rear!

—How many times did she get her feet tickled!

—But not with me. With me she always stayed awake to tell me things. She told me about a little dog she loved that fell in a well where no one could get it, he couldn't grab the ropes they lowered, bulls have horns but dogs have only the eyes of sad and defenseless men, which call to us, and ask our help, and we can't give it . . .

—Elisia Rodríguez told you that?

—As if to a deaf man, shouting in my ear, that's the way she told me her stories. How was she going to faint with me, if I was her immortality!

—And the witches' Sabbath, Goya . . .

—And the starving beggars, cold soup dribbling down their lips, the infinite bitterness of being old, deaf, impotent, mortal . . .

—Keep going . . .

—She told me how the people in her town amused themselves by burying the young men up to their thighs in sand and giving them clubs to fight to the death, and how that torture became a regular custom and then, without anyone forcing it on them, the men took it up as a way of resolving disputes of honor—buried, clubbing each other, killing each other . . .

—What didn't La Privada know . . . ?

—Daughter of those flea-bitten towns where the princes went to marry to spare the most miserable districts from taxes . . .

—Stop shouting, you old fool . . . !

—Daughter of centuries of hunger . . .

—You'll never escape!

—She was a child of misery, misery was her true homeland, her dowry, but she had such intelligence, such strength, such will, that she broke through the circle of poverty, escaped with

a Jesuit, married a trader, reached the highest heights, was celebrated, loved, and she exercised her blessed will . . .

—All fall down!

—They all fall, and if she didn't give me her fainting, Elisia
gave me something better: her memories, which were the same
as her vision, both bright and bitter, realistic, of the world . . .

—You have a golden beak, Paquirri!

—Because I might have had that black vision, since I was old
and deaf and disabused, but that she, young, celebrated, desired,
that she possessed it, and not only that, that she, at twenty, knew
the cynicism and corruption of the world more clearly than I
with all my art, that brought more to my art than all the years
of my long life: she saw first, and clearly, what my broad pallet
brushes then tried to reproduce in the deaf man's estate. I think
La Privada had to know everything about the world because she
knew she was going to leave it soon.

—Of what illness did she die?

—What everyone died of then: obstructed bowels, the miserable colic.

—It's called cancer, Paco.

—There was no such thing in my time.

—Why was she so sensitive?

—She had no choice, if she wanted to be what all the generations of her race had not been. She existed in the name of the
past of her village and her family. She refused to say to that past:
You are dead, I am alive, you can go on rotting. Instead, she
told them: Come with me, sustain me with your memories, with
your experience, let's even the accounts, no one will ever make
us lower our eyes again while they take the bread from our hands.
Never again.

—Nobody knows himself!

—She did. She was my secret sorceress, and I didn't deny her
that image: I painted her as a goddess and as a witch, I painted
her younger than she ever was, and I painted her older than she
would ever be. A sorceress, friends, is an esoteric being, and that

curious word means: I cause to enter, I introduce. She introduced me, flesh in flesh, sleep in sleep, and reason in reason, for each of our thoughts, each of our desires and our bodies, has a double of its own insufficiency and its own dissatisfaction. She knew it: you think that a thing is yours alone, she told me between bites of cookies (she was very fond of sweets), but soon you discover that only what belongs to everyone belongs to you. You think the world exists only in your head, and she sighed, sticking a candied yolk in her mouth, but you soon learn that you exist only in the head of the world.

—Oh, you're making me hungry.

—I see Elisia on the stage, and I see her and feel her in bed. I see her strip off her clothes in her bath and at the same time I see her carried in a litter so that the people of Madrid, who can't afford the theater admission, can render her homage. I see her alive and I see her dead. I see her dead and I see her alive. And it's not that she gave me more than she gave others; she just gave me everything more intensely.

—You mean, as they say these days, in a more representative manner?

—Exactly. Cayetana de Alba came down with her charms to the people. Elisia Rodríguez *ascended* with her charms, thanks to the people, because she was one of them. She didn't hide her disillusionment, bitterness, and misery from the people when, despite her fame and fortune, she was plagued with them. I was witness to that encounter: the popular, famous actress and the anonymous people from whence she came. That's why I follow her, even though I'm headless, I can't leave her alone, I interrupt her lovemaking, I frighten her new lovers, I trail her in her nocturnal affairs through our cities, so different from before, but secretly so faithful to themselves . . .

—And you, Goya, who came from Fuendetodos in Aragón . . .

—A town that makes you shudder just to look at it!

—Yes, I follow her in her nocturnal affairs, in search of love, in the free time this hell where we live grants us to leave and roam outside. She doesn't want to lose the source, she returns, and that keeps her alive. I keep my sanity to surprise her when she's with someone else and plaster her face with pigment, to disfigure her and frighten the poor unwitting stud she's picked up for the night, huddled under the sheets.

—Two of a kind!

—Don Francisco and Doña Elisia!

—The painter and the actress!

—May they never rest in holy ground!

—May they always want something!

—May they always have to leave their graves at night to find what they're missing!

—The third party.

—The other.

—The lover.

—Pedro Romero.

—He got away from them.

—He lived eighty years.

—A bullfighter who died in bed.

—Not a scar on his body.

—Him they did bury in consecrated ground, even though he was, in his way, both artist and actor.

—Lie: nobody escapes from hell.

—Sooner or later, they all fall.

—Death merely confirms the laws of gravity.

—But we ascend, too.

—We all have a double of our own dissatisfaction.

—Don Francisco Goya y Lost Scents.

—You think that you put the world in your canvases and you created the world in your art and nothing remained of that mud except this dust. What do we know except what you taught us!

—This dust!

—I didn't invent anything, Christ! I only showed those who showed themselves. I made known the unknown who wanted to be known. Come high, come low: see yourselves. Ladies, gentlemen: see yourselves, see yourselves.

—Here comes the bogeyman.

—They dug you up five times, Paco, to see if your head had reappeared.

—Nothin'.

—But Romero, nobody was curious to see if his skeleton was all there or if his bones had invisible cuts.

—Nothin'.

—And she?

—She, yes, everyone wanted to know if she, who had been so beautiful and had died so young, was going to outlive death. What would her remains be like? To ask that was secretly to ask: What would her ghost be like?

—Goya and Romero agreed to bury her secretly, so that the curious could not find her. Isn't that true, Don Paco?

—Not only true but sad.

—Look, Goya, only in death did you complete your *ménage à trois*.

—No, we didn't want others to see her, and we didn't want to see her either. But some years later, when nostalgia erased the sins of La Privada, her miserable natal town, which, although exempt from taxes, remained impoverished, tried to benefit from the enduring fame of the actress. The village leaders said they were sure Elisia Rodríguez had left something in her will for the town of her birth. She was faithful to her origins, you know that. But nobody found any such paper. Had she been buried with the will in her hands? Exhumation was requested. All the curious came to see if the beauty of the famous entertainer—or tragédienne, as she preferred to be called—had overcome death. Romero betrayed the secret of her grave; he said he was always ready to aid the authorities. He was old, established, respected, the founder of a dynasty of bullfighters.

—Did you go along with him, Don Francisco?

—No. I said no, and I began a painting, a picture of angels, moreover, in the poor, secret corner of the church where she was now so private, Elisia. The mobs stepped over my paint jars, making a rainbow to death and an obscene gesture at me.

—And then?

—They exhumed her right then and there.

—And then?

—When they opened the coffin, they saw that nothing remained of the body of the beautiful Elisia.

—She had risen!

—Pray for her!

—Nothing was left but the worm-eaten bun crowning the actress's skull. La Privada was bone and dust.

—Caramba!

—But then from that dust a butterfly flew out and I laughed, I stopped painting, put on my cape and hat, and left, laughing like crazy.

—Her bun by her buns.

—The butterfly in her cunt!

—Who would believe it!

—Until death!

—What did you do, Don Francisco!

—I followed the butterfly.

—Touch my fingers, sweetie, my balcony faces yours and I'm so cold, in the middle of August.

—Our streets are so narrow!

—Our sea is so vast!

—Cádiz, little silver teacup.

—Cádiz, the balcony of Spain facing America.

—Cádiz, the double: American shores, Andalusian lanes.

—Reach out your window to touch my hand.

—You, nothin'.

—I gave you everythin', and you, nothin'.

—Nobody marries a woman who is not a virgin.

—Don't shave after eating.

—The noble Spaniard and his dog tremble with cold after dining.

—Let death find me in Spain, so it will be late in coming.

—Titian: one hundred years.

—Elisia Rodríguez: thirty.

—Pedro Romero: eighty.

—Francisco de Goya y Lucientes: eighty-two.

—Rubén Oliva, Rubén Oliva, Rubén Oliva.

—Six bulls, six.

—When?

—Tomorrow, Sunday, at exactly 6 p.m.

—Where?

—In the royal grounds at Ronda.

—Are you going to go?

—I always go to see Oliva.

—Why? He's a disaster.

—You just never saw him when he wasn't.

—When?

—Sixteen years ago, at least.

—Where?

—Also in Ronda.

—And what happened?

—Nothing, except nobody alive has seen a performance that could compare, except Manuel Rodríguez. There was never anything like it, since Manolete. That fellow stood in the center of the plaza like a statue, without moving, violating all the rules of the fight. Letting the horned beast do what it wanted with him. Exposing himself to death every minute. Not raising a hand to the bull. Refusing to fight, exposing himself to death. As if he wanted to embrace the bull. Closing his eyes when it came near, almost enticing it: Oh, bull, don't leave me, let's perform the ceremony together. And that's how the fight went: with love for the bull, Rubén Oliva inviting it to his domain as he had always entered the bull's, refusing to *cargar la suerte*, to control the bull with his cape, refusing to trade the steel for the aluminum blade, fighting with steel the whole time. That first bull of Rubén Oliva's did not have time, gentlemen, to orient itself, to back off, to find a middle ground, to paw the ground. Rubén Oliva didn't let it, and when the bull asked for death, Rubén Oliva gave it to it. It was madness.

—But he never repeated the deed.

—Correction: he hasn't repeated it yet.

—You're still waiting, eh?

—Maestro, when you've seen the best fight of your life, you can die in peace. The bad thing is that this bullfighter neither retires nor dies.

—It seems to me that this Rubén Oliva has conned you all and lives on the fame of his first fight, knowing he'll never repeat it.

—May his fame endure!

—Well, if the fellow wants to live on that . . .

—Look: this is what makes bullfighting bad: a bullfighter keeps coming back for years and years even though he's terrible, because, from one fight to the next, hope is reborn, and the final disillusionment is sometimes years in coming. Rubén Oliva is a scoundrel, he was good only once. We'll see if he can ever repeat that day.

—Twenty years, for Rubén Oliva.

—And you're going to Ronda to see him fight.

—Yes, who knows, maybe tomorrow he'll surprise us.

—Tomorrow Rubén Oliva will be forty.

—The same age as Pedro Romero when he retired from the ring.

—Well, let's wish him luck.

—That he won't get pelted with pillows!

—Poor Rubén Oliva!

—You know him, Paco?

—Nobody knows him.

—Look, Paco. Here's his photo in *Diario 16*.

—But this can't be the man you've been talking about!

—This isn't Rubén Oliva? Well then, even his own mother was mistaken, but you, Don Francisco, you dare to . . . ?

—This is not Rubén Oliva . . .

—Who is it, then?

—This is the portrait without an artist that Elisia Rodríguez showed me one day, saying: If you paint me, I'll let you see me naked, I'll faint in your arms, I'll . . .

—You told me, Paco: a witch gave it to her and told her, Elisia, find a painter who can put a name to this portrait . . .

—Which is not a portrait but a photograph . . .

—In my time, we didn't have those . . .

—Rubén Oliva.

—It's not a portrait, it's the man himself, reduced to this frozen, imprisoned condition . . .

—It's the man-portrait.

—Rubén Oliva . . .

—I followed the butterfly through the night, I found it in the arms of this man, fainting. I took La Privada's face, painted it and unpainted it, made it and destroyed it, that is my power, but this man, this man I couldn't touch, because he's identical to his portrait, there's nothing to paint, there's nothing to add, it drove me crazy!

—Nobody knows him.

—Don Francisco.

—Headless.

—Y Lost Sentiments.

—Try to sleep, Auntie Mezuca.

—Boys, in this heat you can't even talk.

—Silver teacup.

—Balcony of Andalusia.

—Vast sea.

—Narrow streets.

—Touch hands from window to window.

—Nobody knows himself.

Sunday

It seemed that the afternoon darkened.
   —García Lorca, *Mariana Pineda*

1

He was dressed in the Palace of Salvatierra, by Sparky, his sword handler, watched gravely by an old friend, Perico of Ronda, who had served him fifteen years before. His suit was on a chair waiting for him when he entered the large stone-and-stucco room whose balcony faced the steep gorge dividing the city.

The clothes set out on the chair were the ghost of fame. Rubén Oliva stripped and looked out at the city of Ronda, trying to define it, to explain it. Swallows, those birds that never rested, flew overhead, and with the fluidity of an unforgettable song they seemed to recall some distant words to Rubén's ear, which until then had been as naked as the rest of him. My village. A deep wound. A body like an open scar. Contemplating its own wound from a watchtower of whitewashed houses: Ronda, where our vision soars higher than the eagle.

Sparky helped him put on his long white underpants, and although Perico was watching them, Rubén Oliva felt that he was alone. The sense of absence persisted while he was helped into the stockings held up by garters under the knee. Sparky fastened the three symmetrical hooks and eyes on the legs as Rubén looked for something he failed to find outside the balcony. The attendant helped him put on his shirt, his braces, his cummerbund, and his tie. Perico went out to see if the car was ready, and Sparky began to help Rubén put on his vest and one-piece coat. But he didn't want any more help. Sparky discreetly withdrew and the bullfighter fastened his vest and adjusted its fit.

He was barefoot. Now Sparky knelt before him, helping him put on his black shoes, and the eyes of the bullfighter met those of the sword handler as they followed the swift, soaring flight of the swallows, their eyes blinded by the afternoon summer sun that moved so slowly and was so distant from his own agony.

—What time is it?

—Five-twenty.

—Let's go to the plaza.

He arrived in an apple-green suit of lights, and gazed up at the high iron balcony, the pediment facing the Royal Display Grounds, as if expecting to see someone there waiting for him. Time had been shattered into isolated moments, separated from each other by the absence of memory. He tried to remember the events just prior to his dressing. How had he gotten here? Who had hired him? What was the date? He knew the day: it was Sunday, Sunday seven, that's what the boys outside the bullring sang, Saturday six and Sunday seven, but time was still fragmented, discontinuous, and all he could remember was that Perico of Ronda had told him that some very important people were coming from Cádiz, and from Seville, Jerez, and Antequera, too; but it was the people from Cádiz who had come to the house to warn him: —Tell the *Figura* we're going to be out there, see if he'll give us the great fight he owes us this time.

The words were almost a threat, and that was what Rubén Oliva found disconcerting and bitter. But no, he was sure it was just well-wishing. He made a great effort to concentrate, to tie it all together, everything that had been happening, acts, thoughts, memories, desires, the ebb and flow of the day, a succession of distinct moments, yet linked to each other, like the passes he would string together this afternoon, if he was favored by luck and was able to overcome the strange state that held his will; in it, time seemed to have been ruptured, as though many distinct moments, from different times, had taken residence in the house of time that was his soul. He had always been a man of the present. That was what his profession demanded, that he banish memory; in the ring, memory is no more than a longing for the sweetest, the most peaceful times: it is, in the ring, the presentiment of death.

To live in the moment, but a moment tied to all other moments, like a stupendous series of passes, that's how to drive away nostalgia and fear, the past that is lost to us and the future that awaits us when we die. He thought of all that, kneeling before a wide-skirted, rosy Virgin, with her Child on her knees, in the chapel on the plaza. The angels flying above her were the true crown on that queen, but Rubén Oliva found them unsettling: they were angels with incense burners, and on their faces were mocking smiles, almost grimaces, which distanced them from ironic complicity, setting them apart from the central figure of the Virgin? the Mother? Their smiles made him wonder what they had been perfuming. He thought they gave off a miasma of perspiration and the dark humors of long, tiring, penitent pilgrimages.

And there was something else he wished he knew: what had happened between his prayer imploring the Virgin for protection (he couldn't remember it, but that's what it *had* to have been) so that he would come safely out of the ring he had not yet entered, and his arrival just now at the entrance, where, alone with his cuadrilla, he was getting ready for the bullfight, suddenly realizing that this was a cattleman's contest, that he, Rubén Oliva, would fight six bulls in the next three hours. He would have the opportunity—six opportunities—to prove that his previous fight, which was so renowned, had not been a fluke after all. Now, with luck, he could show that he was capable of defeating fear, not once but six times.

—I'm not afraid this time—he said, loud enough for the sword handler to hear when he hung the bullfighter's cape over Rubén's left shoulder.

—*Figura* . . . If I may . . . said Sparky, embarrassed, not meeting the bullfighter's eyes, arranging the cape over Rubén's left hand, and leaving his right hand free to hold the hat, which Rubén Oliva dropped and the swordhandler picked up, alarmed, putting it back in Rubén's hand without a word, just as the music announcing the beginning of the fight was heard.

Then Rubén entered the arena, and he experienced the unexpected, and it was simply fear, simple fear, the perfectly banal horror of dying right in the middle of his debate with himself, before he could answer the questions: am I a good artist, am I a true bullfighter, can I give a good performance today, or is that no longer possible, and will I die, will I live to see forty, or is it too late? Those questions had always been provisional (which was natural, Rubén Oliva told himself), because all the while he was fighting the interminable fight, there was a public in front of him and around him that was going to give or withhold their applause, their sympathy, the trophies of the fight. But not this time: this time, the public did not exist for him.

Nervously, breaking an almost sacred tradition, he looked behind him, but his cuadrilla showed no surprise, they seemed to see a normality that he was denied: the two stories, the hundred thirty-six columns, the sixty-eight arches, the four sections of the plaza of Ronda full of people turned toward Rubén Oliva, anxious to see if he would fulfill his promise this time. The picadors looked at the crowd, the banderilleros looked at the crowd, but Rubén Oliva did not.

He walked into the glory of the arena, perspiring not from the familiar burden of the suit of lights which he wore, or from the secondary fear that its weight would plant him motionless in this beach of blood. He was not afraid of that, even when Sparky gave him the look he knew so well, the one that said you've forgotten something, Rubén, you're not doing it right. What, what have I forgotten, Sparky?

—You forgot to salute the president's box, *Figura*, the sword handler murmured as he removed the display cape and gave him the one he would use in the bullfight.

Rubén Oliva assumed his position, the heavy cape, starched and stiff, held between his spread-out legs. The eighteen pounds of thick fabric seemed to rest on the flimsy pedestal of his dancer's shoes. It was a ballet of sun and shade, the matador thought, standing there waiting for the first bull, an instinctive decision, waiting in the ring rather than watching the bull from the entrance to assess its color, its temperament, its speed, which might differ from the bullfighter's expectations.

He moved forward and halted, presenting his cape like a shield to the bull, which came tearing out of the pen to its encounter with Rubén Oliva, who was without fear that afternoon because he couldn't see anyone in the seats; he looked first at the sun and the shade and then adjusted himself to meet the bull, halting him with a feint of the cape, making a long pass, as timeless as the two singular presences Rubén Oliva recognized at that moment: not the bull, not the public, but the sun and the moon; that was what he thought during the eternal first pass that he made at the wild animal, black as the night of the moon in its half of the arena, raging against the sun that occupied the other half, which was Rubén, blazing in the ring, a luminous puppet, a golden apple, the matador.

It was the longest pass of his life because he didn't make it, it was made by the sun he had become, the sun he had envisioned in his endless agony, Rubén Oliva, prisoner of the sky, pierced through by the rays of the sun that was himself, Rubén Oliva, who held the fighting cape over the sand, not ceding his place in the center of the sky to the picadors, who were impatient, alarmed, satisfied, envious, astonished, afraid perhaps that this time Rubén would offer what he was offering—what the public, invisible to the bullfighter, acknowledged with a growing roar: the *olés* that rained down on him from the sky, broad and round as pieces of gold, fading in the shadows, as if the promised victory were a fruit of Tantalus, and the moon, residing in the shadowed stands, said to the bullfighter, not yet, everything requires a period of gestation, life's beginning, rest, so pause now, feint now, give us a display of art that will never be forgotten: your slowness was such, Rubén (the shadows told him, the moon told him), that the bull didn't even graze your cape, now show us something more than your adolescent valor, when you clung to the dark bulls and rubbed your sex against their skin; now show us the courage of distance, of domination, of the possibility that the bull will cease to obey, will pierce you, transforming you from an artist into a hero.

He heard the voice of Madreselva in his ear: —Their hearts should stop beating when they watch you fight a bull.

—Yes, Mother, said the matador, the good people will doze off if they see a bullfighter who is in no danger, who is indolent, slow, untouched. Let me be brave.

—Be careful, said the woman with the unruly forelock and the cucumbers on her temples, this is a fierce bull, fed on grasses, broad beans, and chick-peas. Don't rub his horn!

Which is just what Rubén Oliva did, and the five thousand spectators that he couldn't see cried out in shock at the bullfighter of the night, the swordsman of the moon, who seemed to be returning to his first adventures, crossing the river naked to fight the forbidden beasts in the darkness, intimate in the closeness it imposed in those first fights, sensing the warm proximity, the humid breath, the quick invisibility of the bull, blind as his master.

The public he couldn't see screamed, the cuadrilla cried out, but on that afternoon of bulls in Ronda, Rubén Oliva did not release the animal, would not yield despite the second admonition: he had violated the rules, he knew it, he would receive nothing, neither the ear nor the tail, no matter how excellent his fight, because he had defied authority.

He had violated the ceremony of the sun and the moon, of the solar Prometheus condemned if he used his freedom but also damned if he didn't use it, of a Diana who waxed and waned, changeable yet regular in her tides, washing over the plaza, draining it away from the bullfighter. Now, as it grew late, the public of the shadows, the only audience that remained for him, left him stranded, alone in the arena's pool of light.

—Leave me alone, leave me alone, that was all Rubén Oliva asked that afternoon, and let's see who will dare to stop him, to oppose him, when he throws off his fighting cape and stands still for a moment ("They think I'm mad, the emptiness of the

plaza stares me in the face, accusing me: he's gone mad"), and
Sparky, with tears in his eyes, ran to give him the discolored red
muleta, the cloth wrapped around the shining steel, as if urging
him, end it, *Figura*, do what you have to do, but kill this first bull,
and then see if you can kill the five that are waiting, if the authorities don't expel you from the Royal Display Grounds of Ronda,
this afternoon and forever. It's madness, Rubencillo! Worse than
madness! It's a crime what you did, a transgression of authority.
The bull was dangerous and brave; it was of good breeding, it
hadn't backed off, nor was there reason for it to do so: it had not
shed a drop of blood, it raised its head and looked at Rubén Oliva,
the madman of the ring, who beckoned it again, immobile, refusing to *cargar la suerte*, to manipulate the cape, defying his teacher
Madreselva, stopping the hearts of the audience, ignoring the
looks telling him to do what he was supposed to do.

The bull charged and Rubén Oliva stood motionless, resolved
not to feint with the cape but to let the bull do what he wanted;
his head high, his gaze defiant, not even looking at the bull,
seeing instead, for the first time—although he knew that they
had been watching him from the moment he had dazedly entered
the ring, forgetting the rules, neglecting to salute the president's
box—two pairs of eyes concentrated entirely on him, on him
alone.

Now he saw them and he knew that if he had not been able
to see anyone in the stands, only the sun and the moon, it was
because the sun and the moon were the only ones who had seen
him. The big-headed man, with his high hat and unruly white
side-whiskers, his turned-up nose and his thick-lipped, sarcastic
mouth, looked at him with the eloquent look of one who has
seen everything and knows that nothing can be done.

—Now is the time.

The woman with heavy eyebrows that met over her nose, with
hair on her upper lip, with the high, curled hairstyle of another
age crowned by a pink silk topknot, exposed her breast, offering
it to a black child so he could nurse, and fixed Rubén with a
pitying but peremptory look that commanded him:

—To the death, Rubén.

—You won't escape this time, Pedro.

—There it goes, Rubén.

—*Bravísimo*, Pedro.

—What a sacrifice, Rubén!

—Of what illness will you die, Pedro?

—In bed?

—In the ring?

—Old?

—Young?

—Neither more nor less.

—Rubén Oliva.

—Pedro Romero.

He wanted to fight the bull face-on, to kill from the receiving end, using the ploy of the wrist. But the bull never lowered his head. The bull looked at him the way the woman with the bows and the man in the top hat had looked at him, demanding: One of us is going to die. How can you imagine you can kill me, when I am immortal?

And if he could have spoken, Rubén Oliva would have answered: Come to me, attack me, and discover your death. You are right. The bullfighter is mortal, the bull is not, that is nature.

And if Madreselva had been there, she would have cried: No, look at the bull, you don't have the right to choose, boy, take the muleta in your left hand, so, and the sword in your right, so, at least show that you have chosen the *volapié*, the "flying while running" technique, keep the sword low, see if this virgin bull lowers its head a little and discovers its death instead of yours, boy: Do what I tell you, son (like a tide, like a drain, like a sewer, the dry, smoke-choked voice of the woman coursed through the shells of Rubén Oliva's ears), now bury your sword in the cross of this virgin bull, where the shoulders meet the spine of this defiant female male, this cunt, this prick, obey me, I only want to save your life!

—No, Madreselva, let the bull come to me and discover its death that way . . .

—Oh, my son, oh, Rubén Oliva, was all the bullfighter's god-mother could say when at that moment and eternally he was gored by the virgin bull and began to die for the first time that summer afternoon in Ronda.

—Oh, my men, oh, Pedro, and oh, Rubén, who made you be so much alike? said Elisia Rodríguez, La Privada, from her seat of that moment, when Rubén Oliva and Pedro Romero began to die together that summer afternoon in Ronda.

—Oh, my rival, oh, Pedro Romero, how could you imagine that you were going to exist outside my portrait, said Don Francisco de Goya y So Sorry from his seat beside La Privada's, at that moment, when Pedro Romero began to die in a bullring for the first time, the very one where he had killed his first bull.

But while Elisia Rodríguez felt the loss of the pleasure that only they, her lovers, had given her and that her toreros now had withdrawn, Goya looked at the dead body and said to the torero that he would have painted him for eternity, immortal, truly identical to how he was in life, but in the canvas that he painted . . .

More than five thousand bulls killed and not a single gore, Pedro Romero, who had retired at forty, who had died at eighty without a single wound on his body: how could he imagine, and Don Francisco de Goya y Lucifer laughed, that he could escape the destiny my picture gave him? How could he imagine that he could reappear in a different picture that wasn't by Don Paco de Goya y Losthishead, a natural portrait, without art, with no space for the imagination, a reproduction indistinguishable from what Romero was in life, as though he were sufficient unto himself . . .

—*Without my painting* . . . Oh, Pedro Romero, forgive me for killing you this time in the fine ring of Ronda, but I cannot allow you to return to life and go around competing with my portrait of you, I cannot permit that; I cannot allow Elisia to go looking for you among the street stands and the bullrings, outside the destiny I gave you when I painted you together . . .

No, certainly not: he could not allow what she told him, before, can't you see, the witch showed him to me in that magic portrait, and now here he is, throbbing and pale, throbbing and impaled, and you, headless, you dirty old fool! No, certainly not, repeated the old man with the high silk hat and the crooked mouth, surrounded by women as dark and tremulous as the afternoon, as death.

Between being gored and dying, the torero raised his eyes to the sky, and, as the plaza of Ronda is not very high, he felt that he was in the middle of a field, or a mountain, or the very sky that the bloody eyes of Rubén Oliva were contemplating. The plaza of Ronda is part of the nature that surrounds it, and, who knows, perhaps that is why Rubén Oliva, that Sunday, fixed his eyes on an audience of flowers and birds and trees, everything he knew and loved in childhood, and throughout his life, seeing the arches of the plaza covered with jasmine and four-o'clocks, and decking the spandrels with blackthorn, basil, and verbena, and spewing impatiens and balm gentle over the rosettes of the cornice, twin streams flowing over the roof tiles, where cranes nest and robins flutter. He heard the mocking voice of the kite, directing his attention to the sky where it was tracing its graceful curves. Rubén Oliva, through the blood of his eyelids, looked for one final time at the sun and the moon, and at last he saw that the light of the most recent, the nighttime star reached him forty years late, while the light of the sun that he was seeing now for the last time was only eight minutes old.

Rubén Oliva looked into space and knew, finally, that he had spent his whole life watching the passage of time.

And then he felt that nature had abandoned the land forever.

First he closed his own eyes to die for the first time.

Then he closed the eyes of the bullfighter Pedro Romero, who had just died, gored, at forty, as he was retiring from the bullring in the Royal Display Grounds of Ronda, beside Rubén, inside Rubén.

He no longer heard the voice that said: My land, Ronda, the

most beautiful because it opens the white wings of death and makes us see it as our inseparable companion in the mirror of the abyss.

He no longer heard the actress's cry of terror, or the nursing boy's wail, or the cackle of the old painter in his silk hat.

2

Rocío, the wife of Rubén Oliva, put aside her kitchen affairs for a moment, and out of the corner of her eye she saw the black bull of Osborne brandy on the television screen, and, attracted by the young group in the street singing that childish round about Sunday seven, she looked out from the balcony and said with amazed delight, Rubén, Rubén, come and look, the sea has come to Madrid.

Ronda
July 31, 1988

Reasonable
People

There are three partners at every birth:
the father, the mother, and God.

Talmud

To Gabriella van Zuylen

I. CONSTRUCTIONS

1

Again last night the glow appeared.

2

We invited our old teacher, the architect Santiago Ferguson, to join us for lunch at the Lincoln Restaurant. It was a long-standing custom: we'd gone there regularly, every month or so, since 1970. Eighteen years later, our teacher sitting there between us, we felt both sorrow and relief: he was getting old, but he had kept his vigor and, perhaps more important, his manias.

One of them was eating in this restaurant, which was always very busy but still managed to seem a secret. One of the best restaurants in the city, it's called the Lincoln only because it's annexed to the hotel of that name. The Great Emancipator never saw anything like the food it serves: brain quesadillas, basted red snapper, the best marrow soup in the world . . .

The restaurant is divided into several long, narrow sections, with the staff lined up on either side. The waiters look as if they've been there since 1940, at least. They greet our teacher by name, and he responds in kind. We're like a family, and we'd prefer to go on being one even when our teacher is gone.

When we mention that possibility—the teacher's death—our thoughts immediately turn to his daughter, Catarina, the girl of our twenty-year-old dreams. She was older than we were; we met her through her father, and we were desperately in love with her. Catarina, of course, never even gave us a glance. She treated us like a couple of kids. Her father was aware of our youthful passion and may even have encouraged it. He was a widower and proud of his stately daughter; she was quite tall and she held herself very straight; she had the longest neck seen outside a Modigliani painting, dark eyes, and an uncommon style—she wore her hair pulled back in a bun. You had to be as attractive as Catarina to dare defy fashion and wear a hairstyle associated, and with good reason, with do-gooders, old maids, nuns, school-marms, and such.

—So you're both in love with the Salvation Army gal! said a waggish fellow student in a University City classroom, but he didn't say any more because we knocked him out with a classic one-two punch. From then on, everyone knew that Professor Ferguson's daughter had two gallant, though unrequited, ad-mirers: us, the Vélez brothers, José María and Carlos María.

Our teacher knew it as well; Catarina never gave us any en-couragement. We were never sure if the professor himself had arranged the one thing we got out of it. What happened was that one afternoon he scheduled an appointment with us in his office in Colonia Roma. We went up to the third floor, knocked, the door was open, the secretary was out and so was our teacher, so we ventured into the architect's elegant office, an Art Nouveau whimsy—serpentine woodwork, stained-glass windows, and lamps like drops of molten bronze—complete with kitchen, toilet, and bath. We saw smoke pouring out of the bathroom, we were alarmed, but when we got a little closer we calmed down, seeing that it was steam, the hot water in the shower turned on full blast.

It was easy to make out white tiles decorated with a floral pattern and a white bathtub with inlaid porcelain frogs. It was harder to distinguish the clothes hanging over the shower pole, and even harder to see the naked body of Catarina, unaware of our presence, facing us, her eyes closed, holding a man with his back toward us, the two of them naked, making love amid the clouds of steam and the Art Nouveau frogs, in the bathroom of her father the architect.

Catarina, her eyes closed, her legs wrapped around her lover's waist, had her arms clasped behind the head of a man who held her suspended in the air.

We said we would never know if that was to be our reward: a single glimpse of Catarina, naked, making love. Two months later, our teacher told us that Catarina was getting married to Joaquín Mercado, a thirty-five-year-old politician, for whom we immediately conceived a blind hatred.

3

The approach to the Lincoln had become an obstacle course, thanks to the never-ending construction on Revillagigedo, Luis Moya, Marroquí, and Artículo 123, the streets around it. The Federal Attorney's Office, the site of the old Naval Ministry, several popular movie houses, and a real jungle of businesses, garages, hardware stores, and used-car lots made that part of the city look like a metallic mountain range: twisted, tortured, rough, rusty; several stages in the life of steel were exposed there, like the entrails of an iron-age animal—literal, emblematic—they were bursting out, exposing themselves and revealing their age, the age of the beast, the geology of the city. The deterioration of the iron and concrete amazed us: only a short time ago they were the very latest and most modern. Today, Bauhaus sounds like a cry or a sneeze.

Professor Ferguson loved to discuss these things over lunch. Tall, balding, white as the tablecloth where we set our beers, Santiago Ferguson spent the meal railing vainly against the destruction of the oldest city in the New World. Not the oldest dead city (Machu Picchu, Teotihuacan, Tula), but a city that's still alive, and has been since 1325—Mexico.

It's alive, you know, says Don Santiago, in spite of itself and in spite of its inhabitants: we have each, every one of us, tried to kill it.

Seen from the air, it's a valley seven thousand feet above sea level, surrounded by lofty mountains that trap the exhaust vomited from cars and factories under a layer of frozen air, and we've added a new mountain range, surrounding ourselves with smoldering piles of garbage. And on this early afternoon in a typically rainy August we leap across holes as big as canyons, open sewers, protruding steel reinforcing rods, broken pavement, and huge puddles, amid the excavations and the shattered glass between San Juan de Letrán and Azueta, remembering something Professor Ferguson said:

—Mexico has ruins. The United States has garbage.

Then, we said, we're growing more alike every day. But he replied that we must lose no time in freeing ourselves from garbage, cement, glass boxes, architecture that is not our own.

What we must do, immediately—he said—is see the modern as a ruin. That's what it would take to make it perfect, like Monte Albán or Uxmal. The ruin is architecture's eternity—he went on, this excitable, fast-talking, opinionated, wildly imaginative, affectionate, genial son of the open hearts and open arms of Glasgow. He said this between his last bite of red snapper stuffed with olives and his first taste of a rum-soaked cake: Professor Ferguson, the restorer, for us, of the wall as the fundamental principle of architecture.

He said that if Indians used the wall to separate the sacred from the profane, Spanish conquistadors to separate the conqueror from the conquered, and modern citizens the rich from the poor, the Mexican of the future should use the wall again (opposing it to glass, concrete, and artificial verticality) as an invitation to move freely about, leave and enter, flow along its horizontal lines. Arches, porticoes, patios, open spaces, extended by walls of blue, red, and yellow; a fountain, a canal, an aqueduct; a return to the shelter of the convent, to the solitude that is as indispensable to art as it is to knowledge itself; a return to the water we obliterated in what used to be a city of lakes, the Venice of the New World.

His voice and gestures grew more impassioned and we all were silent and listened, gratefully, respectfully. We Mexicans love utopias, which, like chivalric love, can never be consummated, so they are all the more intense and enduring. Ferguson's vision of horizontal spaces—walls and water, arcades and patios—had only been achieved in a few houses in certain outlying districts, which he had wanted to keep pristine, private, but which were ultimately absorbed by the vast, spreading urban gangrene.

Sometimes, resigning himself, he could admit that eventually the walls would grow tired, so that even the air could pass through them.

But that's all right—he would add, regaining his momentum—because it means that architecture will have fulfilled its original function, which was to serve as refuge.

Even though its pretext might be religious? (He spoke, but we also spoke about him; he was a teacher who became the subject of the students he taught.)

There has never been a civilization that hasn't needed to establish a sacred center, a point of orientation, a place of refuge, from the pyramids of Malinalco to Rockefeller Center, replied Santiago Ferguson; for him, what was important was to distinguish a structure that was not visible at first (to the naked eye), a structure whose spirit would signify to him the unity of architecture, the building of buildings.

His thought (we students said) was part of his incessant search, his effort to find the point at which a single architectonic space, even if it doesn't contain every space, symbolizes them all. But this ideal, because it was unattainable, at least led us toward its approximation. And that was the essence of the art.

We discussed this among ourselves and decided that perhaps the ideal of the architect was to affirm as far as possible our right to live in the spaces that most resemble our dreams, but also to recognize the impossibility of achieving that. Perhaps our teacher was telling us that in art a project and its realization, a blueprint and the construction itself, can never correspond perfectly; the lesson we learned from him was that there is no perfection, only approximation, and that's the way it should be, because the day a project and its realization coincide exactly, point by point, it will no longer be possible to design anything: at the sight of perfection—we said to him, he said to us—art dies, exhausted by its victory. There has to be a minimal separation, an indispensable divorce between idea and action, between word and thing, between blueprint and building, so that art can continue to attempt the impossible, the absolute unattainable aesthetic.

So—our teacher smiles—always remember the story of the Chinese architect who, when the Emperor scolded him, disappeared through the door he'd drawn on his blueprint.

We caught Ferguson's determination from him and we shared his dreams, all of us, his former students, now almost forty years old, gathered around him in this restaurant, with its gleaming wood and copper, spicy with the sharp smells of garlic, oil, and fresh greens, but for us those dreams took a path that nobody else, not even the professor himself, knew: at the end of his porticoes, patios, passages, and monastic walls lay the secret source of water, not vaulted but serpentine, where the moisture surging from the earth and the moisture falling from the sky join the fluids of the human body and together are reduced to steam. Catarina Ferguson in the arms of a man who had his back to us while she, her eyes shut in pleasure, raised her rapt face to her two youthful admirers, confused, cautious, and, finally, discreet.

We carried that dream with us always; we believed it was our teacher's compensation for the melancholy burden of the imperfection of things, which, no matter how beautiful they might be, are created to be used up, to grow old, to die; but a few weeks later Ferguson said to us:

—Catarina is getting married two months from now. Why not do me a favor, boys? Go shopping with her. I know her, she won't be able to carry everything. You have a van. Don't let her get too carried away, keep an eye on her, take care of her for me, all right, boys?

4

Ferguson knew our father, an architect like us, and he told us that as time went by, we would look more and more like "the old man," until we couldn't anymore, since he had died at fifty-two. But that was enough of a life, said our teacher, to establish comparisons between father and sons. The Vélezes, he said, would all end up looking alike, the same high forehead, dark complexion, thick lips, narrow nose, deep furrows running down the cheeks, glossy black hair, which later turned gray, so much so that our father, with his skin as dark as a Moor's and his snow-white hair, got the nickname "The Negative." But, and we laughed, we didn't yet deserve such a nickname.

—And that restless, darting Adam's apple that bounced like a bobber, like a bobbing ball—the professor laughed—like the virile hook from which your own restless bodies hang, bodies almost as metallic as the twisted rack of rusty iron that is our city, wired bodies, hanging and, well, hung, Adamic and Eden-ic—joked the professor—strung-out bodies that rise up like kites and soar like comets, like Giacomettis, yes, heavenly bodies at high velocity, the velocitous, preposterous, felicitous Vélezes! He laughed again.

—Architecture's destiny is ruin, he repeated. The walls will crumble and anything will be able to pass through them, the air, a look, a dog . . . or the velocitous Vélezes.

As for us, sitting in the Lincoln having lunch with Santiago Ferguson, we saw a more subtle resemblance, our resemblance to Ferguson, our teacher; it wasn't a physical similarity—he was fair, we were dark, he was balding, we had thick hair—it was more that we imitated him. We are formed not merely by our ancestors but by our contemporaries, especially our teachers, who are studied, admired, and respected by us. Our Indian blood was obvious in our dark complexions, while Ferguson was but a third-generation Mexican. His ancestors were part of that small wave of Scottish, Irish, and English immigrants who came to Mexico at the turn of the century, armed with surveyor's tools, blueprints, and cases of whiskey, to build our bridges and railroads. They easily adapted to their new lives, married Mexican women; they stopped feeling homesick as soon as they found out that, among us, Galicians had a monopoly on bagpipes; they never switched from whiskey to cider, but they did change their baptismal names—James became Santiago: a militant Apostle, a soldier, a Moor-slayer instead of a tender young Apostle, the companion of Jesus, Santiago the Lesser—and nobody wore kilts anymore (except for a doll Catarina played with as a child; the Scottish skirt persisted, but they put it on a girl). Santiago Ferguson, who could have been James, from a family of engineers, studied in Britain, but while he was there he had a revelation: what impressed him was not the iron of bridges and trains but the gilded stone of the cathedrals.

—English cathedrals are the best-kept secret of Europe, he often said during the course of our lunches, sometimes almost obsessively wrinkling his forehead and squinting his restless little brown eyes. —No one goes to see them because England is no longer Catholic; for the Catholic tourist, going to Salisbury or York is like entering a den of heretics; and this prejudice has spread since the Middle Ages became the monopoly of Rome. We forget that English architecture still has a primeval quality, it's like returning to our origins, it inspires awe in a way that Bruges or Rheims never can, because they are the product of a strictly formal Catholicism. The English cathedral is entirely different: it asks us to dare to go back to being Catholic, to rebel toward the sacred, to abandon the dreadful secular life that was supposed to bring us happiness but only brought us horror.

And then he would say, in a serious voice:

—I like the religious secret of my old islands. I would like to be buried in an English cathedral. I would go back there in rebellion, in affirmation of the sacred, the incomprehensible.

Gradually, we began to adopt his mannerisms—the way he

arranged his napkin in his lap, for example; his movements—the self-conscious way he bent his head to clinch an argument, conveying an element of doubt, a horror of dogma, even the rejection of the very conclusion he was asserting; his irony, the feigned shock, the exaggerated open mouth, when someone proposed a belated discovery of the Mediterranean; his humor, his taste for the practical joke in the British style (what the Spanish call *broma pesada*): he would pretend a classmate was getting married, invite us to the wedding; when we got there, amid the laughter, there would be a celebration going on all right, but not of an alarming marriage, rather of our same old comfortable friendship; the fraternity of celibates that could be our camaraderie, in which we shared the discipline of the lecture hall, the apprenticeship, the examination, the imagination. Another of his jokes was always to refer to his enemies in the past tense, as dead and gone ("the late critic X; the architect Y, who in his lifetime perpetrated such-and-such an atrocity; the celebrated architect Z, whose work, unfortunately, is ugly, but, fortunately, is destined to perish . . ."). He had no patience, basically—with pretentiousness, with lack of discipline and of punctuality, with the worship of money or its opposite, the cryptogenteel pretense of scorn for it: any lack of authenticity was anathema to him. But he didn't confuse sincerity with the absence of mystery. We ate with him and he told us that our ancestors could be our ghosts but that we are the ghosts of our teachers, the same way the reader, in a certain sense, is the ghost of the author who is being read: I, ghost of Machen; you, ghost of Onions; he, ghost of Cortázar; we, ghosts of . . .

There are no empty houses, he said on one occasion, remember that . . . He sometimes imagined ghosts that were jokers, a lot like him, the professor, often so playful. He had invited us to so many weddings that when he told us about his daughter Catarina's, we thought it would be one more joke, a cruel one, but still a joke. Deep down inside, we were convinced that he had kept her from us, that was why he had perversely agreed to meet us in his office that afternoon, knowingly (or not?), the afternoon of the steam and the tiles, and the frogs, of the girl enjoying herself. Perhaps he knew this would excite us even more. But now here we were, just like Professor Ferguson and, by extension, his daughter, tall, dark, and proud, holding her head as high as ever as she walked toward the nave of the Church of the Holy Family on the arm of her father the architect, dressed in a white gown that we had helped her choose in an old seamstress's shop downtown, where they still make those old marvels, a Swiss-organdy dress with English embroidery—as the seamstress said, as modest as she was expensive, a gossamer veil that would have floated away if it hadn't been weighted down with jewels and beads, and a full, heavy skirt that dragged on the ground, that we would have carried with pleasure, two mere attendants to our putative, unattainable bride, so much like us— dark, with flashing eyes and hair pulled back—who was approaching the altar to be joined to that chubby little lawyer, half freckled, half tan, who shook his little coffee-colored head with the satisfaction of a eunuch who's been made to think he's a stud.

That's how we saw her, so different from her father (except that they were both tall), and we thought of the dead mother of our impossible lover; we looked at her and it struck us that there had never been a single photograph of the late Mrs. Ferguson in the professor's house in the Pedregal, and, on top of that, he never mentioned her in conversation. Perhaps the combination of these things allowed us to give our imagination free rein. Catarina's mother, who was not present at her daughter's wedding, was dark like her, but dead, we decided. Catarina's mother: unmentionable, clamorously mute. What would she, that gaping void, have thought of her son-in-law, Joaquín Mercado, the orange-complexioned groom? It was enough to make us want to speak for her, saying:

—Carlos María, you know, that speckled piece of shit isn't the man we saw Catarina screwing in the bathroom.

—Don't get excited, José María. Better think about the little porcelain frogs.

—As the professor says: Well, what can you do?
—I don't think Catarina is ever going to be ours, brother.

5

We appreciated the fact that the place where we met for lunch
with the professor turned out to be close to the place we worked,
the busy area just south of the old, crowded avenue of San Juan
de Letrán (which is now called Eje Lázaro Cárdenas), where
several construction projects were going on at the same time: the
metro was being expanded, the buildings damaged in the 1985
earthquake were being torn down, new green spaces were being
created, historic buildings preserved, and a parking garage big
enough for three hundred cars was being built—an urban smor-
gasbord that had turned those twenty-odd blocks in the center
of the city into a combat zone.

In fact, all you had to do was close your eyes to imagine you
were in the thick of a World War I battlefield: trenches, gas,
bayonets that weren't entirely imaginary; and all this beneath the
summer rain that we should have been used to, God knows, it's
nothing new; but we acted as if it were: we can't seem to give
up on our toxic city's promise of eternal spring—beneath a layer
of industrial smoke and exhaust fumes; it's another of our utopias.
Even though we know that from May to September it's going
to rain hard all afternoon and a good part of the evening, we
don't carry umbrellas and we don't wear raincoats. If the Virgin
of Guadalupe could give us roses in December, perhaps one day
her Son will give us summers without rain (without smog, without pollution).

Until then, this is a city of people (us included) who run
through the rain with newspapers over their heads.

When he got to the door of the Lincoln, our teacher laughed
and, more or less, put on his mackintosh—a Scottish architect
with the same surname as the inventor of the raincoat, which
could well be our professor's ghost, a ghost that makes its appearance now with the peculiar sound of a black umbrella snap-

ping open at a single touch: the umbrella is the ghost; it leaves with our teacher, whose giant strides carry him away from us, down Calle Revillagigedo, in the rain.

We were wet when we got to the center of the construction site on San Juan de Letrán, as we, traditionalists to the death, insisted on calling it.

The excavation had kept on growing until six or seven municipal projects converged on a point from which radiated, on one side, the tubes for a grand new subway station; on another, black bundles of telephone lines; a little farther, the earthquake-proof foundation of a twenty-story building that its owners wanted to save at all costs; and, nearby, the spot where we were going to put our rather Babylonian project, a garden, still completely imaginary, sunk in the mud, which was supposed to act as the "lungs of the city"—at least, that's how it was euphemistically described.

We took the job at the urging of Professor Ferguson, who insisted that, come hell or high water, fine old buildings should be saved from the wrecking ball. They had told him that there were no such buildings there. Typically, he replied that that remained to be seen; behind a lunchstand, under a filling station, there could be a marvelous Neoclassical building from the eighteenth century, or a stairway to a forgotten colonial cemetery, who knows? It's like Rome, Ferguson told the authorities. Mexico City has an almost geological layering of architectural styles.

Ferguson's arguments won over the municipal bureaucracy (no doubt, they wanted to be rid of this tall, ungainly, and stubborn professor who came into the federal offices like a fjord cutting into the coastline: cold, violent, sure of his right to be there, and even more sure of the beauty of his rightness), and he even won over the two of us, his old disciples, when he also convinced the bureaucracy that we, the Vélez brothers, were the ideal architects for the project.

—But what are we supposed to do?

Our position (we consulted with each other) was none too clear.

—Someone has to preserve the historic buildings.

—But there aren't any here.

—You two know as well as I do that these things can appear unexpectedly.

—But we need something more concrete to do.

—Think of our dignity, maestro. We have to keep up a front. People already think architects are a bunch of designing loafers.

He laughed and said that we hadn't lost our student humor, adding that our job, officially, would be to create the garden, the green space—and that our contribution to the campaign against the urban emphysema wouldn't be just hot air, certainly—but we would also be rescuing from bureaucratic and commercial pillory a vestige of the crystalline city Mexico used to be.

—And don't tell me that neither you nor the gross municipal bureaucracy can find any building worth saving in this project; don't give up the architect's vision so easily, he said, furrowing his brow so his bald head looked like a white lake stirred up by a sudden storm, his head wrinkled from eyebrows to crown (quite a spectacle: we exchanged glances). That excuse won't work, Professor Ferguson said seriously, quietly, because the architect must look at chaos—including a chaos that seems as irredeemable as this project—intently, as an artist would, and organize that chaos, knowing that if you can't find the work of art in the midst of material confusion, the fault is yours, entirely yours, the architect's, the artist's.

—All architecture becomes distant; it occurred a thousand years ago, or will occur a thousand years from now. *Ab ovum.*

—But we are here today, we see the gray disorder of the everyday, and we don't know how to see what has occurred and what will occur, without realizing—he opened his eyes and looked at us very seriously, without theatrics—that it is all occurring at all times.

He shook his head a little and looked at us, first at Carlos María, then at José María: us, the Vélez brothers.

—Okay, it's all approximation, I've said it before, it's nothing but approximation. But it's the architect's job, you know, to

locate the space between the demands of the style and the response of the artist. We all want to consummate symbolic
unions—for example, between change and the unchanging, or
between the permitted and the prohibited. But another part of
us wants to confront the product of these weddings with their
probable divorce. I urge you, boys, my friends, to go out into
the world denying what you yourselves do or see. Submit your
vision to the negative that emerges from within yourselves. The
perfect union of self and other, of reason and nature, is the most
dangerous thing in the world. Art exists to keep desire alive, not
to satisfy it. For example, if you could already see some likely
architectural jewel in the middle of the mess in the construction
zone, you would be identical with your desire, which is to con-
serve architecture. But since no one can see it, not you, not me,
not anyone, at least so far, we are separated from our desire and
therefore we are artists. And therefore we are sensual beings,
searchers for the other. Or of the other . . .

He was silent for a while, and then he repeated: —Approxi-
mate, keep your eyes open, there is always a point in space where
architecture organizes the sense of things, if only temporarily.

For the moment, however, the only thing we want is to set
the scene for an experience that began that same August afternoon, in the rain, after we had brain quesadillas with Professor
Ferguson, and to say here what we learned from the quesadilla
wit of the cultivated architect. And isn't that what Mexican architects are known for, since we are students, you know: we are
the most elegant, the most handsome, the most sociable (professional deformation, virtue born of necessity, as you like), and
surely the most cultivated.

Only a step separates us from the artist, the professor is right,
but, unfortunately, another step, more inevitable, and we resemble a construction worker; and this afternoon, in the rain, stuck
at the foot of the abyss that was the heart of all the muddy
excavations in the center of the city, we noticed a tranquillity,
an absence of the usual noises, which seemed supernatural. A

group of engineers in white hard hats were talking to a group of workers in black hard hats. We got close to guessing the reason for the dispute; it wasn't the first. They were always fighting about holidays. We had to observe the official holidays (the birthday of Juárez, the nationalization of petroleum), they wanted to observe the saints' days (Maundy Thursday, the Cruz de Mayo—the masons' feast day—the Ascension), and we were continually making a compromise between the two calendars, the civil and the religious, so as not to add to the infinite number of holidays, long weekends, and vacation time that kept paralyzing construction work in the city.

We tried to be reasonable when we talked with them. What they said to us was not.

6

As the word "miracle" bounced like a pinball from mouth to mouth (from hard hat to hard hat), we assumed it was another question of adjusting the calendar so that some vital holiday could be observed. We were amused by this recurring spectacle of the Catholic proletariat wrangling with atheist capitalism. It's not easy to identify capitalism with the Catholic religion; but in Mexico the problem is not "being a Catholic" or "being an atheist" (or the variants: an obscurantist, a progressive). The problem is whether or not to believe in the sacred.

Right away, the miracle the group of construction workers at the San Juan site was discussing, with a mixture of reverence and fear, smelled to us more like blood than like incense, which is the difference (when it comes to miracles) between representation and execution.

Blood, because one of the foremen, a man named Rudecindo Alvarado, not known for his piety, showed us an injured hand and a blind eye, and when he touched his hand to his eye, it was covered with blood, and he began his self-reproach: it was punishment from heaven, because he was a heretic and an unbeliever,

that's what the dark-skinned, pimply Rudecindo, with his thinning hair and mustache, was yammering. All the other comments
we managed to overhear were in the same vein: our sins . . . a
warning . . . give up drinking . . . a vision. Rudecindo tried to
catch it, and look what happened to him: he got it good!

We asked one of the engineers to give us the lay version of the
excitement that had interrupted the whole project, with serious
conse . . .

He interrupted us, shaking his head: How could you even talk
about anything serious with this bunch of superstitious half-wits?
They saw some lights last night hovering over the works and
decided it was some sort of sign.

—It didn't occur to them to think of flying saucers?

—One of them says he saw an image; it's a boy or a girl, or
all of a sudden it's a ghost, or a dwarf, or an I-don't-know-what,
I just don't know, continued the engineer, as condescending and
uncomfortable as usual, in front of us. —I don't know if architects
can make out what is veiled to the rest of us, but if you'd like to
spend the night, maybe the Vélezes will spot what the Pérezes
cannot, and the miserable little engineer laughed, his talent for
silly rhymes making us curse his wit.

We laughed disdainfully and went to work: the garden. This
was a work of public health and culture, we could easily concentrate on it and not worry anymore about the tangle of engineers, construction workers, metro stations, skyscrapers, and
telephone cables.

Everybody else had little shelters against the rain. We, the
Vélezes, just like the British Army in the Great War we've already mentioned, had them build us a clean little office that
smelled of pine, with a bathroom added, and a grill to warm the
kettle. It wasn't for nothing that we were disciples of Santiago
Ferguson and his exquisite sense of style. In any case, why work
in a dump when we could have beauty and elegance?

From there we watched the rain pour down the mouths of the
different projects, the open mouths, ready to swallow up the mud

excreted by the soft, loose entrails of the city, which we sometimes pictured as a grotesque sausage shop, its sky a ceiling hung with ham, baloney, pork sausage, and especially tripe infested with rats, snakes, and toads: from the small window of our temporary office, we saw a slice of the old city of Mexico, as Professor Santiago said, an almost geologic slice, exposing the depths of time, ever-deeper circles reaching to an inviolate center, a foundation that dates from pre-history.

We are architects, we can read the circles of this excavation, we can name the styles, Mexican Bauhaus, Neocolonial, Art Nouveau, Neo-Aztec, the imperious style of the turn of the century (when the Fergusons arrived from Scotland) with its boulevards and neo-mansard roofs, the Neoclassical style of the eighteenth century, then Churrigueresque, Plateresque, Baroque, the Indian city, finally . . . Far below what we facetiously call the dominant profile, the Bauhausmann, much deeper, we imagined the city beneath the city, the original lake, the symbol of all that Mexico would once again be, surviving only in ruins, not in garbage, as Ferguson said. But we didn't see any of this then: none of the styles just mentioned emerged from the wretched magma of this construction zone. The ripples of memory didn't go much further than: garage, lunchstand, hardware store, filling station . . .

We stood staring for a long time, imagining the probable center of this excavation, and that's where we first saw it, that afternoon, although initially we thought it was just that we'd been almost hypnotized by concentrating too hard: we saw the glow dancing in the rain.

We shut our eyes and then opened them.

We laughed together.

Saint Elmo's fire, an electrical illusion caused by the rainstorm.

We were a bit tired, we thought we'd have a cup of Earl Grey, and everything would still have been the same if that distant light, the glow moving along the edge of the site, over the restorations, the earthquake hazards, and the devastated gardens, had not been accompanied by the most mournful sound that anyone has ever heard: a groan unmistakably bound to the two extremes of existence.

We looked at each other as brothers, recognizing each other at last. We had been born together.

And the glow became a single point before our eyes and vanished into space.

7

The next day there was even more commotion at the project. A lot of the workers wanted to bypass the civil authorities and go right to the heads of the Church. Even so, the growing number of people who wanted to see a divine miracle (how many human miracles are there?) in the phenomenon of the glow never shed their suspicion, after yesterday afternoon's cry, that it might all be a trick of the devil. Thirty thousand years of magic and only five hundred of Christianity had taught the Mexican people at least not to be blinded by appearances. Enigma, enigma: Is the devil using the image of God to deceive us, or God the tricks of the devil to test us? Divine that, diviner.

While this was under discussion, we maintained our personal façade of serene rationality, and although we had heard yesterday afternoon's horrible howl, we neither admitted it nor elaborated on it. We had an implicit agreement: to be born or to die was nothing out of the ordinary; and that's what the famous cry sounded like, one of those two verbs. So the engineers and the workers turned to their superstitions, sacred or profane. We stayed firmly ensconced in our tower of secular skepticism. We were reasonable people.

But it was not God or the devil, a construction worker or an engineer, who changed our minds; it was a dog. A dog soaked to the skin, its hair so damp it looked as if it were rotting, falling in clumps from its poor skin, arrived whimpering at the door of our office, which faced the excavations. It made a tremendous racket, so we were forced to open the door.

It was carrying a broken object in its mouth, a piece of something. It dropped the object, opening its sticky drooling mouth, shook its spotted mangy hide, and turned away, showing us its wounded rump. At our feet was part of a frog, a piece of porcelain, a green frog in a sinuous style, part of a decoration that we knew and remembered only too well, that we longed for too much . . . We picked it up. The dog disappeared, running toward the same point where the glow had disappeared the afternoon before.

We looked at each other and in no more time than it took for the water in the teapot to come to a boil and for us to be intoxicated by the bergamot perfume, we had reached an ironic conclusion, laughing: if God or the devil wanted to get us in his clutches, he certainly knew our weakness.

The workers could be enticed by a miracle; for us, the lure was architecture, decoration, the art object, above all—were we still smiling?—those things coming together in a green porcelain frog that we saw for the first time in the bathroom of Catarina Ferguson, our unattainable love. Our banter, our self-absorbed thoughts while we drank our tea in silence, our emotional desire (every kind of desire) were all interrupted by new shouting in the construction zone, by the workers flying toward us like a flock of birds, advancing on our private belvedere, since we, the architects (artists? the grains or the brains? the glorified bricklayers?), were also the arbiters, and the dispute was this: the mother of one of the night workers, the watchman, in fact, whom we needed to keep an eye out for accidents, mud slides, thieves, the thousands of things that can happen at a project like this, anyway, she was bringing her son his dinner of lentil soup—the workers are very precise about their meals—with chicken, rice, and soft white cheese, and as she was making her way to the hut where her son spent the night, she ran into a little kid, maybe twelve years old, barefoot, sort of blond, she said, a cute little rascal, wearing just a short skirt, but the señora insisted it wasn't a girl, it was a boy, she could tell, and she, the mother of fourteen, knew the difference: a luminous child, said the mother, if you could have seen it, a child who glowed, and if that doesn't prove what is happening here, what more proof do they want, the heretics and unbelievers?

—The Child Jesus has appeared. It's a miracle, I tell you it's a miracle.

—Just a minute, madam. You say that you know it was a boy, and not a girl.

—It stuck out. It raised his skirt.

Deliver us from temptation. From our heights, we were not going to fall for a miracle. With Cervantesque irony, we could readily accept Don Quixote's celebrated explanation of miracles to Sancho: "They are simply things that seldom occur . . ." Otherwise, they would be the norm, not the exception. Blessed Quixote, who has saved your children from the pangs of contradiction, you're a little like Lenin for the Communists that way.

The fact is, without offending the popular faith of the workers who wanted the miracle, or the agnostic faith of the engineers who denied it, we would have to be the arbiters that both parties wanted.

To the workers we said: The engineers are unbelievers; let us investigate this, we promise we'll be perfectly honest about it.

To the engineers, we explained with a wink (the ploy of con-men, for which we beg pardon) that if we didn't decide in favor of belief, belief, as always, was going to decide against us. If word of this got out—the Child Jesus appearing in the construction site on Calle José María Marroquí, between this subway station and that pile of boulders—in less than twenty-four hours, just picture it, there'd be television crews, cameras, newsmen, reporters, opposition representatives hooked on religion and official representatives hooked on the secular rule of the Constitution but afraid of offending the simple faith of the people, et cetera, and all of them followed by crowds of the faithful, vigil lights, stalls, relics, balloons, lottery tickets, sweatshirts with the Sacred

Heart, even a ferris wheel and Coca-Cola venders and pinwheels: is that what they wanted? It would cost them their jobs. Leave it to us.

—Ah, these architects. Always so nice and tactful! said the wisecracking engineer who had made the rhyme on Vélez and Pérez and who, but for a stroke of luck and a mistake in scholarship awards, would still be washing dishes in a tamale parlor.

We laughed at him, but not at ourselves. We spoke to the group of workers. You trust us? Grudgingly, they said yes; we were the most important-looking people on the job; reasonable people, they could see in us what, in the end, they always needed: masters they could respect—the bosses. Yes, yes, we trust you. Then, we trust you, too. It was hard, but we asked them to be silent about what the mother of one of them had seen.

—Doña Heredad Mateos, mother of our buddy Jerónimo Mateos, who is night watchman here.

—That's okay, boys. And, Jerónimo, listen.

—Go ahead, sirs. Tell me.

—Say to your mother: If you tell anyone about this, Mama, the Child Jesus will never appear to you again.

Their faces said, are you kidding? yet they took us seriously; but we couldn't help picturing the mamacita, Doña Heredad, getting back to her neighborhood, scattering the information from patio to patio, upstairs, downstairs, as you scatter seed for the birds.

Has your mama gone back home? No, boss, she was too excited, I got her to lie down on my cot. Well, leave her there, please, Jerónimo. But she can't stay there all night, she'll freeze to death. Why? There's no glass in the window of the night watchman's hut. Then we'll put some in, so that the señora will be comfortable. But she mustn't go back to her neighborhood. My mamacita has to work to live, was Jerónimo Mateos's answer, and it sounded like a reproach. Then she can go on working, we told him, she can do it here, at the construction site. Really? She can? So, what does she do? Bridal gowns, boss. She repairs

old bridal gowns. The rich women sell them when the dresses
get old, and she mends them and sells them to poor brides.

—Then she can bring some outfits here to mend—we said, a
little impatient at all the complications—but tell her not to accept
any more work.

—Oh, each outfit takes her a month, at least. My mamacita is
a very careful worker.

—And, above all, make sure nobody comes to visit her here.

—Only the Child Jesus, said her silly son Jerónimo Mateos,
adding with a sigh, "This is what I get for being an unbeliever."

We laughed at his parting shot and returned to our own work,
satisfied that we'd smoothed things over on a project that had
really gotten beyond us. The projects we worked on were precise;
we worked on small areas, at an extremely slow pace (like Doña
Heredad and her bridal outfits); our projects were adapted more
to permanency than to haste. But word of the miracle forced us
to move faster; we would have liked more calm, but that was a
luxury we couldn't afford if we wanted to avoid the damage a
rumor can do, the eventual paralysis of the project; none of us
can resist the temptation of a religious celebration; it's our moment of respite in the middle of so many calamities.

8

Everything seemed pretty much back to normal when the engineers came to consult us about where to put the traffic signals,
as their contract required them to do.

They looked at us with more animosity than usual, as if to say
what the hell do these architects know about the best place to
put a traffic signal in streets as congested as these, but we had
insisted (we were throwing our weight around, it's true) on a
clause giving us a voice in all matters concerning the aesthetics
of the work. A traffic signal, we maintained, is like a pimple on
the face of a goddess; we couldn't allow the constant blinking of
tricolor lights to ruin the total effect.

We have to be practical, said the engineers. We have to consider beauty, we replied. Traffic will be even more congested, they said, exasperated. There were no automobiles in the eighteenth century, we said, half smug, half pedantic.

The engineers had done more than make up their minds, they had planted the first traffic light at the entrance to the project. We had no choice, they insisted. If the drivers don't see this perpetual red light from a distance, they could make a mistake and drive into the project. Then we'd have to ask them to leave, it'd be a waste of time. You could put up a sign saying DO NOT ENTER, we said with a certain irony. Most of them are illiterate, said the poor engineers; better to rely on their reflex reaction to a red light. We were amused by these byzantine arguments. How many angels fit on the head of a pin? How many semi-literate drivers depend on an innate Pavlovian reflex?

They were giving up. This was getting ridiculous. We just liked to get their goat, we repeat.

Then our dispute was interrupted by an ancient woman who came out of the watchman's hut at the entrance to the project. Shhh, she said, with a finger pressed to her toothless lips, shhh, don't disturb the child; all the shouting upsets him.

We dropped the argument; but the old woman was carrying a wedding gown, white and filmy, that contrasted with the black severity of her own attire. It had to be her, the mother of the watchman; for God's sake, what was the name?

—Him? Jerónimo Mateos.

—No, his mother.

—Heredad Mateos, at your service. Don't make any noise. It makes him very nervous.

A scream. The sound of a pitiful scream came from inside the hut. We ran to see what had happened; the engineers, some of them, made a gesture of indifference; others, the sign that some-one is a little crazy, a finger moving in circles near the temple. We ran; we were excited, anticipating a sign, without even know-ing it, that would take us beyond our innocent complacency.

Then everything happened at once: we went into the shack where
Señora Heredad Mateos was living, a room full of filmy tulles,
brocade bodices, and jeweled veils. Oh, my pet, what happened?
she asked, and we were looking at a little boy about twelve years
old, dressed as if for a costume ball or a pastoral, a very fair child,
with wavy blond hair, false eyelashes, and a dreamy look, who
had just pricked his finger on the seamstress's needle: blood oozed
out and one of us took the stained veil from him, the Swiss-
organdy dress with English embroidery, it forced us to look at
it and recognize it, but the child ran off, and we watched him
go. We followed, running after him, but he disappeared with the
speed of light; he glowed for a moment and then disappeared,
where? We didn't know how to express the fact that he hadn't
simply vanished, he had gone into the construction site, and at
the same time somewhere else, into a space we had never seen
before . . .

We returned to the watchman's hut, converted to a seamstress
shop by Doña Heredad Mateos, who was sequestered there to
prevent gossip in the neighborhood. Now the old lady was shaking her gray head with a mixture of disapproval and resignation,
and we turned back together, clasped hands, and in our free
hands we held the veil, the dress, stained with the blood of the
child.

—It can't be. You must be wrong.

—You've forgotten already? It can't be.

—Then I'm right.

—No, I mean that it's the same dress. It's unforgettable.

—I haven't forgotten it either. But it can't be.

—We'd better go ask her.

But we didn't dare, as if both of us—Carlos María, José
María—were afraid that if the mystery were lost, our souls would
be, too.

The old lady shakes her head, picks up the needle the child
dropped, puts it in a pincushion, goes back to her work, singing
a wordless song.

—I tell you it's Catarina's dress.

Perhaps we both think that although the mysterious can never be obvious, we had at hand a way to get closer to it. It's true: we were now near the place where we worked, the garden that we had to restore in the midst of the hopelessly twisted ugliness of the city's premature ruins.

We looked at the construction zone. We said it was a web of contorted materials torn from the earth and abandoned there. All the metallic elements seemed revived by a final, fiery cold meeting; this late afternoon's sickly capricious light played over all the angles of the remnants of foundations, of buildings, of columns and spiral staircases, of balconies, of cars and hardware, all mixed together, tangled up, forged with a glimmer of living copper here, of dying gold there, with the opacity of lead sucked dry by a great transparent exhalation of silver, until something new forms in this excavation in the center of Mexico City, which we're seeing anew this afternoon, a hole stretching from Balderas to Calle Azueta, past Revillagigedo, Luis Moya, and, farther, to San Juan de Letrán and even, if we follow the line, to the walls of the old convent of the Vizcainas.

We looked at the construction zone.

We looked at each other.

Were we seeing the same thing? Were we looking at the invisible that had become visible, its separate elements organized little by little in our heads, through concentration or nostalgia, as Ferguson the architect had wanted?

—Do you see, José María?

We had worked on this project more than six months.

—Do you see? It all fits together, our teacher was right, we weren't concentrating, brother, we hadn't managed to see it, what our teacher told us, the point where architecture appears as the only unity possible in a fragmented world . . .

—You're too worried about unity. Better to respect diversity. It's more human. More diabolic.

—You know how I feel, José María? Like a traveler who

reaches the mountain highlands for the first time and his need for oxygen gives him a marvelous sensation of happiness and exaltation . . .

—Careful. Exhaustion will follow, and death.

—José María, don't you see?

—No.

—It's the entrance. We're looking at the entrance.

—I don't see anything.

—Come with me.

—No.

—Then I'll go alone.

—Don't forget the little frog.

—What?

—Take the little porcelain frog, will you?

—The dog only brought half, remember?

—And you and I must also separate for a while.

—You think that's necessary?

—We are going to tell two separate stories, brother.

—But I hope they become a single true story in the end.

9

When I was young I made a trip to Scotland, my grandparents' country, Santiago Ferguson told his daughter, Catarina. *For me, that visit was both an inspiration and a reproach. In Glasgow, I encountered the past.*

Let me tell you how in 1906 the architect Charles Rennie Mackintosh bought a house in a suburb of Glasgow and moved there with his wife, Margaret, and their two little children. Mackintosh retained the Victorian façade but converted the four floors into a modern habitation where his creative imagination could be exercised daily. He replaced doors, fireplaces, and ornamentation; he tore down walls; he installed new windows, new lights, and in that new space he laid out the invisible spaces and the visible details of a new art, an art of rebellion, of purgation, the style of art that, in Barcelona, is associated with Gaudí's treelike cathedrals and cathedral-like gardens, in Paris with Guimard's métro entrances, and in Chihuahua with the mansion abandoned by the Gameros family, who, before they ever lived there, fled the excesses of Pancho Villa's revolution: in Scotland there is only the modest residence of the Mackintoshes, the architect and his family: a spectacular succession of absences, a black-and-white entryway, like an ideal division between light and shade, life and death, outside and inside (*rest, Catarina*), a dining room of high beams and walls covered in gray wallpaper, a study full of white light (*close your eyes, Catarina*), but the white and the dark always equally artful, the unexpected blaze of the lamp, pearl, bronze . . .

Mackintosh was not a success, he was not understood (*the professor told his daughter, who was lying with her head on his shoulder, as he told us, his students, walking down the street, or in class, or at dinner*), he and his family left their ideal house, it passed from hand to hand. I was there in the fifties and I saw what was left of it, desecrated and diminished; in 1963 the house was demolished, but its decorative elements were collected in an art museum, some of the architectonic sequences and the furniture were saved and others were reconstructed and hidden inside a shell of cement. There are photos of the architect and his wife. They do not look Scottish, but that may be because, like everyone in 1900, they tried to look old, dark, sober, serious, and respectable, even though his art was dedicated to a scandalous light. Both Charles and Margaret Mackintosh—he with his thick mustache, his black silk cravat, his funereal attire, and his thick mane, she with her high dark hair parted in the middle, wearing a severe dress that went down over her feet and half her hands and covered her entire throat, up to a black choker—seemed thirty years older than they were, and thirty meridians south. But their children were fair and dressed in sugar-candy colors, clear colors, like the bedrooms of the house, wonderfully displayed in the heart of their cloister, like the green bath decorated with porcelain frogs. Those who saw how they lived there say that although the ornamentation and the entire architectural conception were revolutionary, the couple lived in a world of look-but-don't-touch. Everything was always in its place: immobile, perfect, clean, perhaps unused.

One day, already ill, Santiago exclaimed: —To think that so beautiful a conception, one of the heights of Art Nouveau, has to be shut away, preserved and enshrined, as fragile as a cathedral of cards, as protected as a sand castle, ephemeral as an ice palace, within the walls of a concrete jail. It was one of the most detestable triumphs of Le Corbusier—he said dejectedly, always mixing his most intimate feelings with his professional judgments—and of Gropius: architects whom Professor Ferguson spoke of as his personal enemies. But Ferguson did not exempt the Mackintoshes from his criticism—perhaps they deserve to live on in that concrete tomb, since while they were alive they themselves treated their creation with conventional middle-class respect— look-but-don't-touch, as if it didn't deserve to live, as if it were destined, from the beginning, to serve only as an example.

—Bah, if that was the case, the Mackintoshes deserve their tomb, their frigid museum, he exclaimed, before reversing himself and praising them again.

Perhaps that was what was most characteristic of him: Santiago Ferguson was able to rekindle his love, and when he told his daughter, Catarina, lying there with him, the story of his return to Scotland, he insisted, *let our homes be places that are really lived in, not museums but houses where love can be shared, again and again.*

And when you die?

I fear that like the achievements of the magnificent Charles Rennie Mackintosh—sighed the professor, who was ill, confined to his bed—my poor accomplishments will end up encased in some museum.

No, we aren't thinking of your work, but of its death, your death (*we said, Catarina and us, the Vélez brothers, the daughter and the disciples): Had he chosen where he wanted to be buried: his final refuge?*

The father and the daughter are embracing each other and he is telling her stories about houses the way other fathers tell stories about ogres, sleeping beauties, and children lost in the woods; Santiago Ferguson extrapolates a single element from all the legends—the dwelling, because he believes that we can learn to love only from what we have constructed; nature, *he murmurs to his daughter*, is too destructive and too often we must destroy it in order to survive; architecture, on the other hand, can only be a work of love, and love requires a haven; Mackintosh and his family, in Glasgow, didn't understand that they made their refuge into a museum, *you and I, Catarina*, we keep on searching, we keep on identifying with the place that rescues us, if only for a moment, from the dilemma plaguing us from the moment we are born, exiled from the belly that gave us life, condemned to the exile that is our punishment, *daughter*, but is also the condition of our life, *yes, Santiago, I understand, Santiago: Catarina*, inside or outside, that's the entire problem, inside you live, but if you don't leave, you die; outside you live, but if you don't find a refuge, you also die; entombed inside, exposed outside, ever condemned, you search for your exact place, an outside/inside that nurtures you, *daughter*, and protects you, *father*; now we are in Thomas Jefferson's Monticello, where he is telling his daughter, the architect is saying to his daughter, come to me, my house is a belvedere, and it has mountains, woods, rocks, and rivers extending from it: the house is suspended over nature, it neither ruins it nor is ruined by it, so I call our house *monte*, the mount, of the *cielo*, the sky, *daughter*, an ark against the storms, a tower that enables us to look endlessly into the workshop of nature: spread before us, *daughter*, are the clouds, snow, hail, rain, and storms; we watch them being made: nature does not surround us, does not threaten us any longer, *daughter*, we are united, *you and I, Santiago*, in this perfect viewpoint, the refuge that contains all refuges; the world constructs itself at our feet, and when the sun appears, it seems to be born from the water, and when it reaches the top of the mountains, it gives life equally to you, to me, and to nature.

—Open the door. The boys want to come inside.

—No. They have separated. Only one of them wants to enter here.

—Where is the other one?

—Pardon me. He is also seeking entry.

—Open the door, I say. Don't abandon anyone, daughter.

—I'm not your daughter, Santiago. It's your lover you have invited to Monticello. The mount of heaven, the mount of Venus, he murmured, lost in love, intoxicated with sexuality, Santiago Ferguson, Monticello, Venusberg, sweet mound of love, soft slope of goddesses.

II. MIRACLES

1

He went back slowly to the elevated portion of the project. His desire to return immediately to the watchman's shack where Heredad Mateos was stitching the bridal gown was weakened by a sense of propriety, or perhaps the weakening really came from being alone: without me.

So he stopped in our belvedere, as we sometimes called it, calmly fixed himself a cup of tea, and sat down to sip it, staring out at the project, something we had often done together, but I don't know if he saw what I had discovered miraculously, or if everything had returned to its original state—twisted iron, broken glass, corroded structures worn away by the city's toxins.

I want to think that, separated from me, my brother José María lost the vision that we might have been able to share, the magic vision that two people can sometimes achieve, like spotting a fleeting film image, seeing what is rarely seen though it is always there.

2

I turned away from you and walked toward the hut where the old woman was mending the bride's gown. I took the porcelain frog that we had seen in Catarina Ferguson's bath. You headed toward the project, into the center of the maze, remembering what Professor Santiago Ferguson had said when we parted after lunch: "You have to accept the fact that we architects want to save what can be saved, but to do that, we must know how to see, we must learn to see anew."

—Everything conspires to keep us from seeing. Remember Poe's story "The Purloined Letter"? Nobody can find the letter because it's right out in the open, not hidden but in plain sight, where anyone can see it. The same thing happens to some of the most beautiful architecture in our ancient city of palaces.

You head toward something you've finally managed to see, in the middle of this mountain range of twisted metal; before, we looked at it without really seeing it, we saw it as one of the many constructions of our anarchic city, we saw only what concerned us: the problem of designing the public garden, caught between the practical constraints imposed by the engineers and our own indecision about what the garden should look like, what we, the Vélez brothers, José María and Carlos María, should do with the beautiful space that was entrusted to us: the space, as Professor Ferguson taught us, between what style demands and what the artist contributes.

You walk toward something you've finally found, an entrance, a door in a Neoclassical building, shrouded in gray stone, a severe style, but one that forces you to appreciate the nobility of the columns on either side of the main entrance, the triangular lintels over the windows without balconies, which have been covered over with gray bricks.

You ask yourself if you alone could see it, if I could not, or if I could see it, too, but let you go alone, seeing what you saw, desiring what you desired.

The windows are bricked up, the balconies closed off, and so you are afraid that the inside door will block your entrance. But your excited touch meets no resistance, nothing stops the impetus that is an extension of your will: an ardent will, as if in preparation for the cloistered fervor that you imagine in this house of zealously guarded entrances. You push the eighteenth-century entry door that appeared to you in the middle of the ruins in the heart of Mexico City. You fear what seems forbidden. You desire an image of a hospitality as warm as the welcome your teacher Ferguson always associates with Glasgow, the city of his ancestors, where a brilliant building, novel and revolutionary, by the architect Charles Rennie Mackintosh met the scandalized disapproval of Victorian society and ended up, hypocritically, entombed inside the walls of a museum.

You push open the door, you take a step inside. Then you remember your teacher's lesson: Mexican houses are all blind on the outside; the blank walls around their entrances tell us only that these houses look inward, to the patios, the gardens, the fountains, the porticoes that are their true face.

You push the door, you take a step inside.

3

Then I put down my cup of tea and walked toward the hut. The sounds of the project were the same as always: engines, riveters, excavators, and cranes, their bases buried in muck, overhead the midday sun masked by clouds. The gathering storm accompanied me, swelling up out of the high plateau, practically without warning, bringing on an early darkness.

I rapped my knuckles on the door of the hut. Nobody answered. When I tried to look through the little window, I saw that our promise to Jerónimo Mateos the watchman had been fulfilled: a pane of glass had been put in the window, to protect his mama from the wind and the rain. I rapped again, this time on the glass, and was blinded by the sudden reflection of a red light. I cursed instinctively—against all our entreaties, they had installed the traffic light. Never had they gotten work done so promptly. But once it became a matter of crossing the architects, even the vice of slowness could seem a sin, and they could be efficient for a change. But Heredad Mateos, it seemed, was not about to make any exceptions to our great national sluggishness.

I was tempted to go in, to force the entrance, I always had the excuse of being the architect. The light flashed on the glass again and I heard a groan—aged, this time, and brief, but of an ecstatic intensity—and I knocked on the window again, and then on the door, more loudly, more insistently . . .

—I'm coming, I'm coming, take it easy . . .

The old woman opened the door for me and her tortilla face—pocked with cornmeal moles, mealy as a stack of corn cakes, surrounded by cornhusk hairs, lit only by a pair of eyes like hot chiles in the dried, burnt surface of her skin—looked at me curiously, though with no sign of surprise. The candles burned, like the orange eyes of a cat, behind the old woman. She said nothing, but gave me a questioning look that seemed to be echoed by other looks behind her: the lights of the votive candles.

—May I come in?

—What do you want?

She was a small woman, and I am a rather tall man. I tried to see, over the aged woman's cornhusk head, below the votive lights, the image of the Virgin of Guadalupe illuminated by the burning tapers, the cot . . . Señora Heredad seemed to rise up on her toes to block my passage and my view. Embarrassed, uninvited, rude, I found it impossible to say, Señora, you are repairing a bridal gown, I think I recognize it, that is, my brother and I, we both recognized it, and we would like . . .

—What do you want, señor? Doña Heredad said to me, firmly enough to convey a suggestion of irritation.

—Nothing, señora. I am the architect. I wanted to see if everything was in order, if there was anything you needed.

—Nothing, sir. My son takes care of that. But if I don't work,
I'll die of sorrow. Good afternoon.

4

You were alone for some time, getting used to your surprise.
You asked me if I saw the same thing you did, or if only you
saw it; you asked me if what you saw is true if I saw it and false
if I did not share your vision. You ask this constantly now that
you are inside the house and you are alone.

You find yourself in a hall that does not match the severe style
of the entrance, which you leave behind when the eighteenth-
century exterior door closes behind you and becomes an Art
Nouveau door through which the luminous child and the dog
and even the frog that you hold in your hand had, perhaps,
entered: you are blinded by the serpentine plaster roses, the silver
fans, the embedded crowns of pearl, glass, and ivory; you move
along a gallery that contains nervous peacocks, crystal nests,
silver confessionals, zinc washbasins, perfumed by a heavy fragrance of spent flowers, and into a long, narrow passage entirely
bare except for a lead umbrella stand—you touch it, as if it were
an anchor in the emptiness of the salon. It holds several parasols,
some black, others multicolored, and almost a dozen umbrellas,
carelessly dumped, still damp, in the lead receptacle—you touch
them and you have the feeling that solitude and silence would
be complete here if the passage were not illuminated by four
lamps, one in each corner, all of them—you touch them, too—
made of copper, and the copper painted silver, and with glass
drops around the center of the febrile carbon filaments, like the
antennas of the first insect that saw the light of the newly created
universe.

This illumination seems fainter because it contrasts with a

torrent of white light that comes through a half-open door, a light as sharp and steely as the blade of a knife.

You walk to the half-open door and enter, covering your eyes with your hand, pausing to get used to the dining room's unfamiliar glow, its high, narrow chairs, mahogany table, walls covered with elegant beige wallpaper, and only gradually do you realize that numerous objects are strewn over the floor where you can trip on them, instead of on the table: on the floor are cornhusks, and vases of water, and flowers—the yellow dianthuses of All Souls' Day, spikenards and calla lilies, gardenias: the heavy odor of dead flowers or, what is the same, flowers for the dead—on the floor are hampers full of fabric, baskets holding thimbles, colored thread, yarn, knitting needles, pins. There is a basket of eggs. There is a chamber pot.

You look up. You search for something else in this dining room, so cleanly conceived but so full of the wrong things, as if the present inhabitants of the place were totally foreign, or were almost enemies of the work of the decorator and the architect, depreciating it, consciously or not. That's what you would like to think, anyway: the inhabitants of this house must hate it, or at least hate its maker and the style he wanted to give it. What most shocks you, more than the objects strewn over the floor, the eggs, or the chamber pot that almost makes you want to smile, are the rustic chairs of woven straw, low to the ground, which seem to defy, even insult, the narrow, high-backed chairs: those chairs like Giacometti statues (Giacometrics) are insulted by the terrestrial, agrarian abundance of everything else in the room (everything else: you sensed a silent conflict in this room between an exclusive, elegant refinement and a gross inclusiveness, an affirmation of the abundance of poverty, as if a chicken coop had been set in the middle of Versailles).

A woman is sitting on one of the low chairs, sewing. The child sitting with her has just pricked his finger with a needle, he sucks it, the woman looks at him sadly, the blood stains the basket of eggs at the woman's feet. A dog enters, barks, and goes out again.

5

For the first time in my life, I stayed and slept in the little office on the construction site: I was wakened by a whistling that I took to be the teapot signaling that the water had come to a boil. It found me asleep in one of our pair of director's chairs; as a joke, we'd had VELEZ ONE and VELEZ TWO stenciled on their canvas backs, identifying ourselves the way English schools distinguish brothers with the same surnames.

I was sleeping with my legs stretched out and when I woke up I felt a dull but persistent pain in my ankles.

The whistling was coming from the construction area, and from the office I could see a crowd of people running every which way, but converging on the project's entrance, on the watchman's shack. I ran out of the office, not even closing the door behind me—I was upset, afraid I was going to lose what I sought. I might already have lost it. I imagined ways of obtaining that object, of getting hold of it somehow or other.

I made my way through the chill morning mist, through the crowd, people with wool jackets slung over their shoulders, with mufflers around their necks, their hands joined amid the hustle, barring the way to the hut. I am Vélez the architect, it's urgent, let me through, let me through. I couldn't get anywhere and I heard a noise that I found unendurable, almost unspeakable. If I closed my eyes, everything disappeared except that intolerable murmur of the unspeakable: I wanted to identify it, and I pushed my way toward the door of the hut. Sighs. Moans. Wails. A solemn hum came from the watchman's shack, but that high-pitched sadness disguised a celebration. Dressed in black, clasping her hands in prayer one moment, making the Sign of the Cross the next, tears rolling down her cheeks like oil on a burnt tortilla, Doña Heredad Mateos was kneeling before the window of the shack, hissing through her wrinkled lips:

—A miracle, a miracle, a miracle!

Behind her, on the cot, I saw Catarina Ferguson's wedding dress, lying inert, held together with pins, ready to pass into new hands, to dress a young bride, ignorant of the marvelous woman who had filled it once and then forgot it, who, perhaps, gave it to a friend, the friend to a poor relative, she to her servant. And next to Señora Mateos, I could make out a form in the glass that had recently been put into the window; it was as fuzzy as an out-of-focus photograph, vague but three-dimensional, like a holograph, and, obsessed with the bride's gown on the cot, I could not really say what it was; but she, Doña Heredad, proclaimed it:

—The Virgin and the Child! Reunited at last! Praise be to God! A miracle, a miracle, a miracle!

6

You wanted to speak to them and you stepped forward to say something, to call out, to ask them . . . The bells rang and the woman and child hurried on, without looking at you. The child smoothed his curly hair and white tunic, the woman threw a heavy cloak over her shoulders and with nervous, awkward fingers arranged a white cowl on her head, leaving the ends loose under her chin.

The child took the woman's hand and held it as the sound of the bells swelled. They opened a door and went into a colonial patio, another negation—you notice at once—of the previous styles, Neoclassical, Art Nouveau. Now the colonnades supported four arched porticoes, and chest-high screens that allowed—allowed *you*—to observe the woman's anxious arrival, holding the child's hand, at the center of the bare patio—it had neither garden nor fountain, only implacably naked stones—and to see the pair join the women who were walking there, together in the rain, protected by their umbrellas, walking in circles, Indian-file, one behind the other, one of them lightly touching the shoulder of the woman in front of her from time to time: but the woman with the child, not protected by an umbrella, seemed to be looking for something, as the ends of her cowl whipped against her cheeks, and the child, who was holding her hand, let the rain wet his face and mat down his blond curls, his eyes closed, wearing a grimace that was half gleeful and half perverse.

They all walk like that—the nine women and the child—in circles, in the rain, for more than an hour, not acknowledging your presence, but not asking you to leave, as you feared they might at first—one of the women, in a straw hat and pink brocade dress, even approaches you and touches your hand, though without looking at you—and the others, also without looking at you, make a huge clamor as soon as she touches you. You try to distinguish between their laughter, exclamations, bawls, groans, sobs, complaints, moans, exultations, but, unable to, you turn your attention to what those figures in the rain are looking at and what each is carrying in the hand that doesn't hold an umbrella. They give you an oppressive sensation of dynamic abulia, a paradox, but it seems to describe them because they don't take a single step that isn't slow and solemn, and there isn't a single one of their gestures that isn't deliberate. In one hand, each holds an umbrella; in the other, they carry various objects, shielding them from the rain. The first a basket and the second a shepherd's staff. The third a bag full of teeth and the fourth a tray holding bread that's been sliced in two. The fifth wears bells on her fingers and the sixth has a chameleon clasped in her fist. The seventh holds a guitar and the eighth a sprig of flowers. Only the ninth woman does not hold an object—instead, she holds the hand of the drenched child with his eyes closed.

They all wear cloaks draped over their shoulders like shadows.

Suddenly, unexpectedly, the woman with the shepherd's staff raises it and dashes it against your hands; you cry out; they, too, cry, and you drop the frog that you had been holding in your fist. They laugh, flee, the patio is a confusion of umbrellas and water splashing, and the bread falls, and the teeth roll in the puddles, chattering madly, and the dog with the wounded rump, which had been watching them silently, now lets loose a howl, takes the frog in its muzzle and runs toward the convent.

7

They said they couldn't see anything from the outside, it was just an old lady's craziness, seamstresses get too wrapped up in themselves, they're alone too much, with nothing but their thoughts, pretty soon they end up needing glasses, why should anybody believe her? And she answers that they should go in one by one, or two together, and then they will see what *she* saw on the windowpane in her bedroom. He saw what he had been afraid of, just what he had been trying to avoid, publicity, idle gossip—and the worst thing was that the people who were gathered around the shack wanted to believe, they were hoping that this would turn out to be a true miracle, that they would be the witnesses who would tell everybody else about it, since the worst thing about miracles was the way, after you saw them, you had to tell somebody else about them for them to be believed, and it was the same thing here at the shack of Doña Heredad Mateos, mother of Jerónimo the watchman of the same last name, where from outside you couldn't see anything, and if you went into the little space you could see the señora was telling the truth. When you looked at the glass, the figures stood out clearly, so close together they were like one, the Virgin with the Child in her arms, a recognizable silhouette, the Madonna and the Child who was conceived without sin, with halos around them as white as snow: it's splendid, if a little blurry, but you can't see it from outside, you understand? only from in here. You have to go in one at a time, or by twos, that would be better, by twos so there won't be malicious talk, you can see it only in here, in the shack where, as luck would have it, Señora Heredad Mateos was staying, the one who set out the orange votive lights and the images of the Virgin in the back, the one who brought all these precious bridal gowns, which, if it's proper to think such a thing, are the dresses of the wife of heaven, Holy Mary full of grace, who conceived without sin.

—They're going to ruin the dresses, he said to her.

—We never know how the Lady will choose to come to us.

—It's dangerous, let me take care of them . . .

—Here they stay. Otherwise, what will the Virgin wear, tell me that . . . ?

—I swear that as soon as this is over you'll get them back.

—Praised be the Lord, who sent His wife and His Son here, where they could receive lodging and even clothing, a thousand times praise the Lord!

Doña Heredad Mateos gave me (José María Vélez) a look with her eyes of hot chile, her tortilla face marked by pocks of corn.

—And you know, the Son of God is a most venerable Child.

—By all you hold dearest, señora, do not give that dress to anyone!

8

The nine women are gathered around the wooden table, sitting in the high-backed Art Nouveau chairs. At last you can see them clearly, although the child, sitting next to you, constantly tugs at your sleeve and tells you stories—wicked tales, slanders—about the women in the refectory. They pour cups of chocolate from a steaming pitcher and pass the sweet rolls hot from the oven, and the fair child, whose hair is limp from the rain, picks up a corner of the tablecloth to rub it dry, with an impudent laugh at the women, who continue eating impassively, without even glancing in his direction. He will talk only to you, the stranger, but his remarks are intended for the women, who are now revealed in all their splendor—they've taken off their rain capes and are dressed in silks, brocades, multicolored shawls; their collective beauty is enhanced by the brilliance of pink and green, orange and pale yellow. The table is heaped with flowers and fruits and they extend pale, fine hands to take the fruit, to arrange the bouquets, to serve the chocolate, but they never speak to one another, the malicious child is the only one who says anything, pointing his finger from one to another, until he stops to dry his hair and wipe the grit from his eyelashes and shouts at them: Nuns! Whores!

They just eat and sip their cups of chocolate, except the woman who accompanied the child from the beginning. She sits with her elbows on the table and her head between her hands, perfectly still, staring into empty space, in despair. The others are lovely women, from Sonora or Sinaloa would be your guess if they were Mexicans, although you doubt it—Andalusian, Sicilian, Greek, their skin never touched by the sun or by the hand of man, the little boy tells you with a wink, they would rather die than be touched (you try to pierce the lowered gaze, the shadows of the thick eyelashes, of the woman dressed in orange silk, who briefly raises her eyes, looks at you, and veils her eyes again, after that single savage glance). That's it, that's it, says the child, look at her, so sweet and pure, she has always been accused of entering convents just to seduce the nuns. And the one next to her, do you like her? (the perfect oval of her cinnamon face has a single flaw, a five o'clock shadow above her lip), well, don't kid yourself, she has nothing to do with the work of man, as the priests say; she dressed up as a man to keep from being violated by men and ended up accused of fathering her landlady's son! That's why she wound up here, to give her old bones a rest—what a way to go!

This story amuses its narrator enormously, and he laughs until he sputtered and choked, pointing his finger at the girl with the mustache and the short chestnut hair. She serves the steaming chocolate while the child subsides; your drink immediately congeals in your cup; the bread turns cold at your touch. You seek the dark eyes of the woman with braids twisted like wagon wheels around her ears, who is dressed in a pink brocade dress buttoned up to the neck: that one would do anything to save herself from

men, continued the child. Look at the rolls on her plate: do they
resemble tits? Well, that's what they are, they're hers, cut off
when she refused to give herself to a Roman soldier. Agatha,
show the gentleman, entertain our illustrious guest. You lower
your eyes as Agatha unbuttons her blouse and reveals her scars,
to the hoarse laugh of the boy.

—Sometimes she carries bread, sometimes bells, it's terribly
symbolic: the tintinnabulation of toasted tits, get it? And look at
the next one, Lucía, you hear me? Look up, poor little Lucy!
Lift your veil, let our visitor see the empty sockets where your
eyes used to be, you preferred being blinded to being screwed,
didn't you? So now you chew your eyes, served up like fried
eggs on your plate . . .

He laughed like crazy, exposing his bloodstained baby teeth,
pointing with his finger, getting more worked up since he met
with no argument, like a precocious drunkard, commanding the
woman with long mahogany hair to open her mouth and show
her gums, Apollonia, not a tooth, see, not a single molar, ideal
for cocksucking (he laughed harder and harder), a second vagina,
the toothless mouth of the dentifrical saint, shake your bag of
teeth, Apollonia; which she does, and they all hurry to do something without his asking. The girl with the straw hat, instead
of putting the lizard she is holding into her mouth, tries to put
herself into the mouth of the lizard; the blind woman takes the
fried eggs from her plate and puts them in her empty eyesockets;
Apollonia takes the teeth out of her bag and puts them in her
mouth; and the child shrieks with laughter and shouts: They
just won't fuck! They just want to get away from men! From
repulsed suitors! From unsatisfied fathers! From raging soldiers!
Better dead than bed! The convent is their refuge from male
aggression, see, they tried to seduce me, I'd like to see them try
again; and one woman begins to play the guitar, another the
harp—beautiful women, women the color of spikenard and
lemon, cinnamon women and pearl women, lilting as an endless
autumn, silent as the heart of summer, silky and lacy as a con-

templative sea: they don't look at the child, the child points at them with his tiny finger, the finger injured by the needle; the woman who accompanies him holds her head in her hands, she lowers her arms, she makes me look at her, she is the only one who isn't beautiful, she is a dusky woman with moles on her temples, she reaches out and drops a thorn from the rose on the table. Come, she says to the child, and the child resists, he says no, she doesn't repeat her command, she just looks at him, he closes his eyes and puts out his hand, she gives him the thorn, he takes it, and without opening his eyes, he pricks his index finger with it.

His blood flows. The women around the table cry, their voices join in a mournful chorus, the guitarist and the harpist keep on playing, Sister Lucía raises her eyelids and reveals the endless labyrinth of her empty gaze, Sister Apollonia opens her toothless mouth, Sister Margarita tries to force her nose into the lizard's mouth, Sister Agatha shows the purple scars on her chest, Sister Marina licks her mustache, Sister Casilda places a rope around her neck, the dusky woman calls out their names, as if introducing them to me and the child, who is beside himself and runs to sit on his chamber pot; he makes a face, he stops crying, he screams with worn-out pleasure, and hurrying back to the table with the pot in his hand, he empties it among the roses and the bread. The shit is hard, the shit is golden, the shit is gold. Miracle! Miracle!

—Desire is like snow in our hands, says the melancholy woman who accompanies the child, gold is nothing to us. Look at the dog; he doesn't know what gold is. But he recognizes shit.

Carlos María: for a long time they hadn't looked at you, and you hadn't spoken to them, and in that indifference that combines silence and separation, all you see is a whirl of colors, taffetas, silks, roses, baskets, guitars, doe eyes, peach skin, and cascading hair, and you, too, feel distanced, as if you were watching yourself through opera glasses from the upper balcony of a theater, the *paradise* of the spectator, absent and present, seeing but seeming absent, tacitly ignored and yet represented, there and not there, part of a rite, a link in the ceremony being celebrated—you suddenly realize—with or without you, but which has been practiced a thousand and one times in preparation for this moment when you are there, absent and present, seeing without being seen, in a theater of the sacred, which seems cruel and bloody to you, the spectator, because it is caught between the style the work demands and the style the spectator provides, it is the midpoint—you stare intently at the child's pricked finger—between the conception of the sacred and its execution. One can conceive of God without a body, but action requires a body. The child looks at you and runs over to you to put his arms around your waist, growling like a little animal. It is only then that you realize that the floor of this refectory is not made of ordinary red tiles but of dried blood turned to brick.

9

The father and the daughter are going to look at two or three art books together, as they do every night, without discussing what they are going to look at, with the books open on *his* knees and *her* lap, pointing out one print or another, from time to time sipping a glass of claret or port, an old custom in the British Isles that has continued through the generations on this side of the Atlantic, *he* chooses a book of Piranesi prints, lord and master of the infinite, he tells Catarina, the author of engraving's most absolute light and shade: Roman landscapes and prisons, he points, prisons and vistas without beginning or end, *Santiago Ferguson caresses the head of his daughter*, the engraving as an infinity symbol lying on its side as you are, alongside my legs, an endless sleep, entrance and exit, liberty and prison, an imprisoned vista, a prison with a view.

—This is what I am offering you. How will you correspond?

She opens her own book, which is resting on her lap. She indicates a photograph of the Teatro Olimpico of Vicenza: she says she prefers Palladio's public architecture to his domestic architecture; he created uninhabitable Roman temples for the bourgeois of Italy, but for the public, poor and rich alike, he created imaginary cities, prosceniums that refused to be pure theater, instead they extended into streets, alleys, barely visible city vistas, urban mazes that, *Catarina Ferguson repeated*, as the professor had often said, gave the scene another, an infinite dimension.

—You don't see it?

—No. I don't see what you're talking about.

—It's the entrance. We are looking at the entrance.

—All I see is the same door as ever, bricked up, the same as always.

—Come with me. I will prove to you that the entrance is there.

—Will you? Has it happened to you, what sometimes happens, that suddenly we seem to see or feel something clearly, something that was there all along but we hadn't noticed until that moment, when everything comes together around it, and everything stops and falls into place . . .

—Do you see it, Catarina? Do you see that it's so? It is . . .

Later, in each other's arms, *she* told him to stop torturing her, it was so tempting to find out about it, but *she* didn't want to enter that hateful place ever again, and even though she detested it, and the people who lived there horrified her, still she couldn't seem to get over the temptation to return to it.

—You don't believe that there's a symmetry in all things? Santiago asked her.

—I believe things only happen once.

—In that case, we will never understand each other.

—Very well, Santiago.

—You have to learn to give things that have failed, that have been damaged or destroyed, another chance.

—But not at the expense of my health. I'm sorry.

10

The child falls asleep on the lap of the woman with the dusky face. The nuns wait on her silently, bringing her drinks, plates of rolls; they kneel before her as she sits in one of the low straw chairs surrounded by baskets of eggs and handkerchiefs, scissors and thread, corncobs. Some of the nuns fan her from time to time; others take handkerchiefs and moisten her forehead and bathe her eyes, her lips. The woman, sitting close to the ground, is stroking the child's hair, which is dry now; he is sleeping, his face calm. She smiles; she tells you that she sees a glint in your eyes which she recognizes; she knows what you were thinking, tell her if she's right, a nun is a woman, but not a woman one sees every day. Men don't get used to her in everyday encounters, so they desire her even more ardently; she is hidden, forbidden, veiled, in a convent, in a prison, in an infinite construction where every door conceals another, this one leading to that, and that, and yet another . . . like the nuns, doesn't it seem?

You say yes.

That is why they make that response you heard at the end of the meal, she repeats: Desire is like snow in our hands.

And you also repeat: *Yes*.

She looks tenderly at the sleeping child, and without shifting her gaze, she talks to you, there is never enough time for everything, maybe for animals there is, since they don't measure time, if they even have any, but for people, well, the ones who manage to become flesh, who possess a body, isn't it true that they never have all the time they want?

You return her look with your own uncomprehending one; you are sitting in a higher chair, staring down at the woman and the child; no, what she means—she speaks rapidly, in a sad but strong voice—Sister Apollonia takes care of wiping off the saliva that sometimes trickles from her lips—is that nobody ever has enough time for life, even if they live to be a hundred years old;

nobody leaves the world feeling they've exhausted life; there is always one last hope, an encounter we secretly wish to have, a desire that remains unfulfilled.

Yes . . .

There is never enough time to know and to taste the world completely, and the nun sighs, stroking the head of the little boy. —My son was denied things, there are things he never experienced. Does that seem incomprehensible to you?

No.

Abruptly, she takes your hand, her eyes shining, and asks, *But this time?* He could live longer than he did *the other time*, that's why he has come back to be reborn, she tells you, that's why I dared to do it again, they say I don't have the right, that my child has no right to be born twice, sir (the mutilated nun, Agatha, dries the sweat off her brow), they say it's monstrous (she squeezes your hand, this time her touch hurts), they say what I'm doing is monstrous, bringing him back into the world a second time (the blind nun, Lucía, carefully cleans the blood flowing from under the woman's skirts, forming a puddle on the floor), but you have to understand what I'm doing, you have to help me . . .

—Señora . . .

—You are a mason, or a carpenter, or something like that, aren't you?

You listen to her with annoyance, irritated, you don't understand her. But you agree, yes, you are, a manual laborer; and she sighs, perhaps the miracle can be repeated, despite what everyone says; she slowly opens her eyes, the blind nun wipes them with the bloody handkerchief, she doesn't close them, as if welcoming that stain, murmuring, If he has three fathers, why can't he have three mothers? And if he has three mothers, why can't he have had three fathers . . . ?

You look around you: the eight nuns are there, standing, surrounding the three of you, the woman with the dusky face, the sleeping child, and you, and one holds a harp in her hands,

another a guitar, one a staff, another a lead plate, the fifth's hand
has bells on every finger, the sixth a fork, the last a knife, a real
dagger pointing at your eyes. You have a horrible feeling that
everything unspeakable—sighs, sorrows, griefs—is about to find
a voice.

—No, says the woman, delicately lifting the head of the sleeping child, you don't have to say anything . . .

You manage to say something anyway, in a panic: —The child
is already alive. You don't have to do anything, look at him, he's
sleeping but he's alive, you babble on a moment before the eight
women begin to press up against your body, and you feel those
other bodies against you, an intimacy of smells and skin and
menstruation, a delicious sensation of bodies naked under green
silk, their saliva in your ears, the conch in your mouth; orange
silk covered your eyes and the breath of eight women had become
a single breath, as fragrant as your nights, as bitter as your
mornings, as sweat-drenched as your middays, and in the center
of the circle, reserved for you, untouched, immaculate, the
woman who was dusk itself, dark, desperate, the moles on her
temples tightening like screws, saying come, José María, it took
you a long time to arrive, but you are here at last, my love . . .
The woman and her companions speak in unison, pressing
against you, surrounding you, suffocating you, shutting you in
the tiled bathroom decorated in a pattern of foliage, with porcelain frogs set in the white bathtub that is like a vast bed of
water into which you sink . . . You are suffocated by unwanted
kisses, smothered in that bath of steam in which you suddenly
remember the maternal womb you have longed to regain before
you die, and that other bath floods over you, my brother, Carlos
María.

11

Those first days, Doña Heredad Mateos sat at the door of the
watchman's hut in a severe black dress, with her shawl sometimes
over her head, sometimes hiding her face, when a kind of willful

mortification made her hide her features, which nonetheless appeared about to slide from her face like pebbles from the wall of a ruin. At times she would drape the shawl over her shoulders to emphasize various attitudes: majesty, resignation, hope, even a hint of seduction. For all this and more, since its invention, the Mexican shawl, the *rebozo*, had served, and the aged Doña Heredad employed it with a kind of atavistic wisdom, seated at the entrance of her temporary home, on a rude woven straw chair, with her feet planted in the dust, the points of her black, well-shined shoes peeking out of her dark skirts.

Her breast was covered with scapulars commending her to all the saints, male and female. And by her side, though she never touched it, a cup decorated with flowers, ducks, and frogs silently inviting everyone to leave the contribution that she neither solicited nor, seemingly, touched. The cup was always half full and each twosome entering the hut added a handful of pesos to the pot, but later they began to leave coins and Doña Heredad assessed them out of the corner of her eye, fearing and confirming that some were mere coppers dropped from poor fists, but others—she didn't reveal her delight—were treasures taken from who knows what hiding places, flowerpots, mattresses, money boxes: testons, silver pesos, even the occasional gold piece.

So they came in pairs, a woman with a man, a woman with a child, a man with a child, two children, two women, almost never two men, and some left crying, others wearing beatific smiles, most in silence and with their heads bowed, some trying not to laugh, and they were the only ones Doña Heredad favored with a look of icy fury that was like a premonition of what hell reserved for the infidel, and the promise of paradise was reserved for those who left on their knees, repeating Miracle, miracle, miracle, and when the lines grew and began to snake through the construction site and down Calle José María Marroquí, a look of satisfaction appeared on her face, particularly when the aged mother of the watchman Jerónimo Mateos noticed scapulars like hers on the chests of the devout, and even cactus thorns piercing the breasts of the most faithful, and she tried not to feel

too happy about the trail of blood left by the knees wounded on
the painful climb from the excavations to the shack, since (as my
brother Carlos María Vélez would say ironically), in addition to
using the direct entrance to the shack from the street, where the
engineers had put the much-discussed traffic light, those who
felt they didn't deserve the vision without some penance decided
to crawl through the mud, the construction materials, the debris,
the barbed wire, the iron rods, and the clutter of the project, to
be rewarded with the divine vision inside the shack of Señora
Heredad: miracle, miracle, miracle, Madonna and Child, revealed
in the window of a humble shack, practically a manger, said a
woman to her husband, Bethlehem, O little town of Bethlehem,
how still . . . no, said another man to his wife, I happen to know
that they just put the glass in that window; but that doesn't make
it less holy, you heretic, answered his wife icily . . .

—Mexico is instant Fellini, I said to a group of engineers (I
am José María Vélez), not expecting them to understand me or
to see the irony of having discussed to death whether to put in
the famous traffic light in order to keep traffic from backing up,
and now look, you can't take a step into Calle José María Marroquí between Independencia and Artículo 123, first because
of all the curious and the penitent, and now because of the in-
creasing throng of ice-cream, popcorn, and hot-dog venders and
carbonated-water hawkers, competing with the stands that sold
tamarind, papaya, and pineapple drinks, and chunks of coconut,
and raspberries, and the piles of tricolor banners that began to
appear, the sweatshirts with stencils of the Child Jesus and
the Holy Virgin in various poses: the Child on the knees of the
Mother, the two embracing, he sucking the maternal breast; the
steaming sizzling grills with fried tortillas and meat pies and pig
cracklings, their spicy smells mixing with those of sputtering
candles and heavy incense, which were the prologue to the up-
right boxes on wooden sawhorses offering holy pictures, Sacred
Hearts of silver, novenaries, hymns, Magnificats and other prayers written in ancient, crude, almost archaic characters, on fragile

paper, and boxes containing statues of the Good Shepherd, Our Lady of Sorrows, the Immaculate Conception, the Sacred Redeemer, the Wise Child, all of them reflected infinitely in the mirrors of the boxes in which they were set and in the metal of the carts, the windshields of the automobiles, the windows of the stores . . .

Then one morning a thousand colored balloons appeared bearing the image of the Virgin and Child and a phosphorescent advertisement for Oasis Condoms proclaiming: Men, Be Prepared—Only the Virgin Conceived without Sin; but even this excess could not divert my attention, which remained fixed on the entrance and exit of the shack. I looked over the heads of the faithful, grateful for the way the penitents bowed low, so I could guard, from a distance, the purity of the wedding dress that lay on the cot, the painstaking, prolonged work of restoring it having been abandoned by the woman of the hour, Doña Heredad, mother of the watchman Jerónimo Mateos, the humble mother and son singled out for the blessing of the Virgin Mary and the Child Jesus, who had visited them and so allowed the people to taste, to savor, to share in the sacred glory, and only then the police appeared to ensure that order was maintained, and later the truckloads of soldiers arrived to impose it once and for all, when the crowds bearing placards claiming violations of the Constitution and championing a progressive lay society, free of superstition, were on the point of confronting other, Catholic crowds, crying: Christ the King Lives! Christianity Yes, Communism No! and the dialectic discourses were drowned out by Hail Marys in which hope was tempered with the benediction and that with the anticipation of the eternal, the celestial tower, ivory tower, tower of David, full of grace, the Lord is with thee, blessed art thou amongst women and blessed is the fruit of thy womb, Jesus . . .

But what really caught my eye, in the line waiting to enter and witness the miracle, was that pair of unbelievers, the engineer Pérez and the foreman Rudecindo Alvarado. Of course, the engineer could be playing doubting Thomas: until I see, I refuse to believe; and Rudecindo's agnosticism had already cost him an injured hand when he tried to capture the vision of the glowing child. Engineer Pérez and foreman Alvarado entered gravely, the engineer circumspect Rudecindo with his head bowed, into the shack of Doña Heredad Mateos.

—And the Day of the Holy Cross I did say a thousand times Jesus, Jesus, Jesus! Jerónimo Mateos struck his chest, kneeling beside his mother, who when she saw the television cameras coming told her son to guard her post and not let anyone by, she had to change fast so she'd look her best on television, and José María was afraid she would come back wearing the wedding dress, ruining it just so she'd be suitably decked out; but no, Doña Heredad Mateos reappeared, not in her black clothes, but in a pink jacket and pink running pants, a big Adidas logo on her breast and new white tennis shoes bearing the same trademark, and I, taking advantage of the confusion and of the sudden shower that disrupted everything and confused the couple inside the shack and the other people who went in to take refuge, I slipped inside, feeling less than a man and more than a god—I, José María, your brother—no more, no less than a fleeting drop, mobile, unattainable, of mercury; a winged thief, I hurried into the shack while Doña Heredad was outside cursing the heavens that had betrayed her with rain just as the television cameras arrived, and I, your brother, touched the wedding dress with incredulous fingers, then I clasped it passionately, embracing it, closing my eyes, as Catarina closed them in her embrace, repeatedly kissing the hem, caressing the jewels sewn to the dress, giving thanks for the miracle of having rescued that lost object of my desire, of my erotic memory. Who would take it away from me? You? Don't you have your own vision, brother, and your own object? And don't Professor Ferguson and Catarina and even Doña Heredad, and the absent mother of our unattainable love? You have your own vision and your own desire, brother; never give them up. And don't take mine away from me.

12

Exhausted, you wake up enveloped in a dripping skin; that is the first thing you notice, and your first question is whether it is your skin or that of some wet animal protecting you from the attack of another animal. That is what your sense of touch tells you. Your sense of smell detects the heavy fragrance of dried flowers, flowers that have withered and died.

Your soaked skin; the dry odor. The trembling of a pack of hounds that passed and pissed on you.

It tastes of gall; you spit it out and the spoon that the toothless nun forces between your gritted teeth falls out. You also smell the patched, urine-drenched, sweaty clothes of the group of nuns who surround you and take care of you; they buzz around like a cloud of bees in a hive, and you search in vain for the woman with the moles on her temples—she is the one you are looking for—but you hear instead—now you can hear it—a soft step approaching you, but the nuns, hearing that same step, seem to want to block out the voice that is getting closer, so they begin to talk animatedly, in no particular order, but keeping to a common theme: I left my house dressed as a man to keep my father from raping me, I begged my brother to kill me to avoid marriage to an old lecher, I threw myself on the soldier's sword and told him this is the only thing of yours that will penetrate me, they tore out my teeth, they gouged out my eyes, they cut off my breasts, so that I wouldn't fornicate, so that I'd be worthy of heaven, to preserve my sanctity, blind, toothless, mutilated, but chaste, brides of Our Lord Jesus Christ and mothers of the Baby Jesus and servants of the Holy Virgin . . .

Then comes a voice from within the circle of women, laughing.

He comes forward, still laughing, exclaiming: —Leave me alone with my father!

You see a familiar figure approaching, holding one hand up as if in blessing, but all the while smirking possessively; the other hand holds a curse, he has a whip, which he raises (still blessing with the other hand) to lash at the nuns, who moan and fly away like frightened bats.

When he kneels in front of you, you recognize the child who yesterday, a few hours ago, or perhaps only a few minutes, leapt, glowing, over the excavations on the construction site, who walked in circles around the convent patio holding the woman's hand, who ate in the refectory, who pricked his finger with a thorn . . .

You recognize his bloodstained tunic, but it seems shorter; you recognize his artificially waved hair, but it is not as blond, it's darker; you recognize his blue eyes, but they are smaller, it's just his makeup that seems to enlarge them; you recognize his sweet lips, but they are surrounded by the first traces of a nascent down, and when the boy raises his arm to stroke your forehead, he gives off the concentrated odor of armpits and damp hair like a nest waiting for birds to take shelter there; a burrow, you decide as he embraces you and kisses your lips and you are savagely assaulted by the memory of other touches both near and far, because you felt this same touch yesterday, last night, or a second ago, when the woman with the moles on her temples and the face of perpetual dusk kissed you and thanked you and told you . . .

—Thank you, says the grown boy.

Standing close to you, mild, fair, stinking of goat and shit and sweat and fried bread, a boy of the people, a farmhand or a laborer, he tells you that he and his mother are grateful for what you've done, and what's done is done . . . but now he offers you his hand to help you up, you shake off your drowsiness and try to hurry, we don't have much time, says the young man, who is strangely old, older every minute, there is never enough time, it's August and your son will be born in December—thank you— and in January they'll circumcise him, you know? and in April they'll kill him, and in May they'll celebrate him, recalling his death, putting wooden crosses over all the construction sites, you should know this, José María, you should be getting to work, come with me into the corral and the shed . . .

You take his hand with its black nails and follow him through the empty refectory and the already sunny patio, you hurry through the clean, dry bathroom, its stained-glass windows no longer steamy, its porcelain frogs dry and rough, no longer suffused with the warm moisture of last night . . . You and the aging boy go through the gallery of the house—the convent, the retreat, the maternity ward?

The stained-glass windows with twining floral patterns, the sideboards built into the wall, the bronze ornaments and the crystal drops, the mirrors, are suddenly behind you. The boy opens a door, the light is blinding, you cross another patio, and you have arrived at a shed full of hammers, boards, nails, files, saws, with a strong smell of sawdust.

Inside, sitting on a cane chair, surrounded by baskets of eggs and handkerchiefs, corncobs and embroidery, the woman with the face of dusk—her face even more shadowy, covered by a blue veil that hides the moles on her temples, which look less like flesh than like parts of the veil—she looks at you and smiles, but she doesn't put down the gold-trimmed tunic she's sewing.

—Thank you, she repeats, letting out a seam, and she gestures to you, inviting you to come into the workroom, pointing out the boards, the nails, and then makes an impatient gesture, telling both the boy and you that you should set to work.

He knows what he is supposed to do; he sits on the ground by the woman's side, takes the thorns, and begins to weave them into a crown.

But you don't know; she looks at you impatiently; she gets herself under control and again smiles sweetly.

—It's necessary to work. You will have to get used to it, she tells you in her gentlest voice, it kills time . . .

—If you like your time dead!—the irrepressible boy laughs, sitting by the side of the seamstress.

She gives him a light smack; he pricks his finger with a thorn;

he cries; he brings his bloody finger to his mouth and whines, but this time she does not make a sorrowful face, she has lost the look of despair that he knew . . .

—It doesn't matter, says the woman, it doesn't matter anymore. Now we will have him with us forever, and every year, when you die, my child, he will come back to make me a child to take your place, in December you'll be ready for the manger, my child, in April for the cross, and in May . . .

She looks up, between her appeal and its answer, to see you better:

—Isn't that so, José María?

—No, I'm not José María, I am Carlos María. José María is my brother, he stayed above, he chose not to accompany me . . .

First a thrush flies overhead, and its wings make a sound like metal in the hollow sky. Then the woman with the twilight face opens her mouth, the sweetness leaves first her lips and then her eyes, she looks at the boy who is sucking the blood from the finger he pricked with the thorn, and she raises her hands to her head again, her look of anguish returns, she whimpers, we've been deceived, we have been sent the wrong one, and the boy says it doesn't matter, Mother, taking her arm in his bloodstained hand, whoever he is, he has done what you wanted, the new child will arrive in December, don't worry, the child will die, Mother, and I'll be able to go on living, I'll grow old finally, Mother, isn't that what you want, look, I'm growing and I won't be killed in April, I will grow old, Mother, I will grow old with you, the child will take my place . . . *Mother, it doesn't matter who fucks you as long as I'm reborn!*

He embraces her and she looks at you without comprehension, as if her entire life depended on certain ceremonies that by being repeated had become in equal part wisdom and folly, and you try to say something to explain the inexplicable, you manage to mumble no, your brother, José María—I—was not deceived, I chose to remain because I was in love with a woman named

Catarina and, as I could not have her, I wanted instead to possess her wedding dress, her . . .

But they don't understand a thing you say.

—Mother, the name doesn't matter, what matters is what happened . . .

—What names do the gods use among themselves? Who knows?

—You continue conceiving, Mother, the boy said, almost crying now, holding the woman sitting on the cane chair, don't keep asking these horrible questions, the boy said, crying, pleading with his mother, begging her, and he shows his devotion by his tears, he's strung tight as a bow, sending the arrows of his misery in every direction, but he surrenders as well, trying to show that he's been overcome, that the true anguish lies in the son's breast, in his, not his mother's, that his sorrow and sense of disillusionment would outshine hers any day, that her tricks and her moods always fall on his shoulders, but it doesn't matter, he cries, if that's what it takes to make her happy, he'll just die again, and now she is the one who is sobbing, no, if it means you don't have to die every time the dog appears . . .

The woman calms down and picks up her sewing, she arranges it in her lap and looks at you, asking herself, asking you, can't miracles be repeated? How come it's a miracle to give birth without sin the first time and a crime the second? Isn't it possible to give birth to two gods, one good, the other bad? Tell me, then, who is going to save the imperfect and the bad, those who most need God?

Each time his mother asks one of these questions, the boy punctuates it by throwing an egg against the wall. In his face you see the rage of your country, which is the rage of the injured, the humiliated, the impotent, the insulted; you recognize it because you have seen it everywhere, all your life, in school, at work, among the engineers and among the masons, and you were its counterpart—your excessive self-confidence, the arrogance revealed in the ease with which you ignore the obstacles, and the

price of those powers, which is insensibility and finally indifference, the twin of death . . . And then you wonder if the only
people spared those destructive extremes were the architect Santiago Ferguson and his daughter, Catarina, if some quality possessed them, and if they possessed some quality that went beyond
the humiliation of some and the arrogance of others, and what
that quality would be called, that saving grace . . . It must be
something more than what my brother and I say we are: *reasonable people*. You and I, brother.

Another egg bursts hatefully against the wall and you think
of the walls of the architect Ferguson that structure space, opening and unifying it, but none of that concerns the seamstress
with the darkened temples. Instead, she's worrying about a name,
more than a man, a name; you had the man, the boy says; I want
the name, she replies, because the name is the man, the name is
what says what he is, the name is the same as the thing it names,
that is my faith, that's what I believe, what I believe, what I
believe . . .

But then she quiets down and reaches for two boards, which
she makes into a cross. She nails the cross together and hands
it to you. You cannot reject their gift, because they're giving you
something—now at last you know—that *they* expected from you.

13

Between the faithful and the doubting, between the troops and
the television teams, the engineer Pérez made his way toward
the shack where Doña Heredad Mateos was being filmed for the
evening news, dressed in her Adidas outfit, and he shouted to
the foreman, Rudecindo Alvarado, turn off the traffic light, and
to the believers who were inside the shelter, did they see anything
now, and yes, they answered yes, yes, because they were seeing
what they wanted to see, the engineer shouted, see if you can
find someone without mud in his eyes and a frog in his throat,
someone who sees and speaks clearly, you and you, look, they're

going by, and you two, don't say no, look, what do you see, frankly? nothing, nothing but a sheet of glass, right? just put in, and now, Rudecindo, turn on the traffic light that shines in the window of the shack, and now if I'm not mistaken, now the figures appear again, right? It's only an optical illusion, a reflection of the prints the old lady stuck on the wall when she moved in here to do her sewing, it's the candles under and in front of the prints, combined with the light of the traffic signal, which never goes off but is always changing from red to green to yellow, that's what causes the reflection of the Mother and the Child, are you satisfied? Now go back to your homes, break it up, nothing's going on here, and you, good woman, you can keep the proceeds from what you started, nobody is going to take them from you, don't worry, cash the check they gave you to wear that sports logo, and God be with you, señora, I tell you nothing has happened here, and you, Jerónimo, go back to work, nobody is being accused of anything, but we have to put an end to this farce and get back to work, we're way behind schedule.

—And my dress? said Doña Heredad, managing to look impassive through it all.

—What do you want, señora? Dress any way you like, pink pants or black skirts, it's all the same to me.

—My wedding dress, I mean.

—Ooooh . . . Aren't you a little old for that kind of game, you old flirt?

—The one I was sewing, where is it? Who took it? asked Doña Heredad.

She was about to cry Thief! Stop, thief! and Pérez the engineer was afraid that there was no limit to the capacity of the old woman, Señora Mateos, for inciting riots, when a silhouette appeared against the suffocating alkaline, midday sun that announced the approach of an afternoon storm; from the depths of the construction site the architect appeared, one of the Vélez twins, who knows which, it was impossible to tell them apart, walked toward them, followed by a dog. He carried a cross in his hands, two boards nailed together, and he reached the watch-man's shack and scrambled up some stones and planted the cross firmly on the roof.

14

When they led you out of the Art Nouveau house which looked Neoclassical from the outside, the toothless nun Apollonia, fol-lowed by the mutilated nun Agatha and the blind nun Lucía, dressed entirely in orange silk, Agatha with her braids entwined with flowers, Apollonia in her straw hat, and Lucía with a shep-herd's staff, you wanted to think that it was your teacher, Don Santiago, who led you here, asking you to view the ordinary with fresh eyes so as to make it yield its secret, which for the architect is the composition of a dispersed and hidden structure that only the artist knows how to see and reunite. You ask your-self if your brother—I, José María—couldn't or didn't want to see what you saw, or, seeing it, chose to pretend that he hadn't, that the lodestone wasn't there but in the watchman's shack, where Catarina Ferguson's wedding dress lay, waiting.

Before you answered your own question, you were blinded by the glare of the midday sun, as the door of the house swung open and the nuns said these parting words, my brother:

—Leave us. Don't worry about us.

—A nun is only a forgotten bride.

—And never bring us flowers.

—Do you know what the dead feel when flowers are put on their graves? The flowers feel like nails. The living don't know that. Only the dead know. Each flower is one more nail in the coffin.

—Don't ever come back. Please.

—Leave us in peace. Please.

—They are nails. They are sweet-smelling poison.

—Your work here is completed, said the blind Lucía.

—Things are as they are, said the mutilated Agatha.

—The dates can change, said the toothless Apollonia.

—But nothing can change the fatality of time, said the blind Lucía, and she opened the door onto the light of a Mexican noon.

It's true, you would have liked to say to the nuns, but I shall forget everything the minute I step out the door, except these four things: that nuns are only women who are rarely seen; that since they drink shadows they are always fresh; that flowers are like nails in the coffins of the dead; and that in December, perhaps, a child of yours will be born here. Only about this last do you have any doubts, just as the woman and the boy seemed to waver between two possibilities. Will a new child be born in December to prevent the other child you conceived from dying in April, the one who grows old or fades away before your eyes? But if the child you know is going to grow old and die much later and the new child is going to die in his place at the beginning of spring, will it be necessary to create a new sacrificial child each year who will assume, indefinitely, the death of the glowing child? Who will be the annual father of the sacrificial child? This year it was you, though they were expecting your brother, the carpenter José María. Does it matter who fertilizes the mother, how many pricks have entered and will enter the blessed and fertile belly of the dark woman? Or, perhaps, the boy you know will die, forsaken, in April, and each year a new child will be substituted, to be born in December and, growing rapidly, to die in April. In either case, the mother will be impregnated every year. This was *your* year . . . But of the dog you have no doubts; he guided you here and now he is showing you the way back. You realize that you had only noticed his injured rump, not his yellow body, streaked and stinking, not the melancholy eyes that perhaps give gold its value.

15

When I was young I made a trip to Scotland, my grandparents' country, Santiago Ferguson told his daughter, Catarina. *For me, that visit was both an inspiration and a reproach. In Glasgow, I encountered the past.*

—Is that where you want to die?

—No.

—Then do you know where you want to die?

—Yes, in Wells Cathedral, he told her, he told us, far from anything that reminds me of all the things I don't wish to remember, in the place that least resembles what we have created here. In a church without Virgins.

After his burial she told us a story: the day he visited the Mackintosh house in Glasgow, Santiago Ferguson left his companions and lost himself in the labyrinth of those three buildings that fit one inside the other, like stacked Chinese boxes: a modern municipal building made of concrete, a prison posing as an art museum, and, at the heart of the architecture, the reconstruction (*sorrowful, secret, shameful*, Catarina) of the home of the Mackintosh family.

But as he became more and more lost in astonishment (labyrinth: *maze, amazement*, repeated Ferguson, possessed by that astonishment), two things happened simultaneously.

First of all, he felt the various styles of architecture, infinite and wonderful, shifting before him: Palladian theaters, prisons designed by Piranesi, Jeffersonian lookouts above the clouds of Virginia, Art Nouveau palaces in the Chihuahua desert, all telling him (as he, always teaching, tells her, tells Catarina) that the word "labyrinth" also denotes a poem that can be read backwards and forwards and makes sense either way.

At the same time, he felt that he was losing control of his movements.

The first sensation filled him with the special ecstasy associated with one of his most singular notions, that of an ideal communication between all human constructions. In the bold, the adventurous mind of Santiago Ferguson (our teacher, our father, her husband, your lover), architecture was the simple and complex approximation to an imagined and unattainable model. Through these ideas, Ferguson flirted with the simultaneously tempting and horrifying notion of a perfect symmetry that would be as much the origin as the fate of the universe.

Then we remembered that in class, as we tried to comprehend the mysterious web our teacher had woven around our lives without our realizing it, Santiago Ferguson vigorously rejected the concept of unity. He called it the "ultimate Romantic nostalgia." But he considered equally detestable the notion of fragmentation, which he said was the devil's own work.

—The blithe Romantic identification of subject and object not only repulses me (it was as though we were still in his class, hanging on his every word); it terrifies me.

He made a sweeping gesture in the air. His blackboard remained empty. —It is a totalitarian idea, impossible physically, but enslaving mentally and politically, because it sanctions the excesses of those who would first impose it and then maintain it as the supreme, unassailable virtue.

Then he startled us, pounding his hands together twice, saying first—to see if we'd been dozing—that unity—now listen!—is no virtue, and, second, he scraped his chalk across the board to make our nerves stand on end, so we would be sure to hear:

—I fear happiness at any price. I fear imposed unity, but I have no desire for fragmentation either. Therefore, I am an architect. *Ab ovum*.

He turned to scrutinize us, with something approaching tenderness.

—Simply, a building allows me to regain the difference between things, aiming for symmetry as the concept that contains identical measures of identity and difference.

These arguments, communicated by the professor with his usual fervor, were the essence of his thought, the ideology behind his always imperfect and incomplete work. He explained them, we said, with words and gestures that were warm and fluid— but more than once we surprised him peeing in the faculty bathroom, merrily spraying the white porcelain and repeating "I want symmetry, I want symmetry!" And still his elegance and energy seemed undiminished.

But in the Mackintosh house, at the same time that his faith in the significance of his profession was renewed, he also felt, in that labyrinth, that he was losing his motor control. He told Catarina it wasn't that he felt paralyzed or that his limbs felt heavy. On the contrary, his movements were as quick and precise and fluid as ever. But they were not his.

Then Santiago stopped—Catarina continued the story—and he realized that there was someone mimicking every one of his gestures. Terrified, he wanted to seize him, but he couldn't because the being that was imitating him was invisible; and yet Santiago could distinguish him perfectly well: he was a man with a thick mustache, wearing mourning clothes, a black silk tie, and a serious expression. I couldn't see him, said Ferguson (to Catarina), because, since he mimicked me so exactly, that strange alien being *was* me—he was within me so he was me, transported, in a sort of vision, outside of myself, so that I couldn't see him.

He felt that being within him and at the same time beside him, simultaneously preceding him and following him, so that it was impossible to determine whether that perfect similitude of expression and motion was an imitation of Santiago Ferguson by that repulsive, mournful being (he began to smell decay around him— putrid water, damp skin, old flowers) or if he, Santiago Ferguson, were imitating his invisible companion.

He told Catarina, "I wasn't master of my movements. When I stopped abruptly in a corner of the Mackintosh house—a house that had three times been walled, displaced, disguised—and a shaft of icy light suddenly blinded me, I couldn't tell, daughter, if I was the one who had stopped or if that being who imitated me so perfectly had stopped me. Then a totally alien voice came from my lips, saying, *Take care of us. From this time on, dedicate yourself entirely to us.*

"I don't understand why, by what right, or on what whim, he dared impose that responsibility on me. I was blinded by the light but as my eyes adjusted to it, I could begin to make out a partly open door in one corner. Then the figure who had accompanied me pulled himself away from me and entered the space that could be glimpsed through the open door.

"Drawn in outline on the infinite whiteness within, two figures held out their hands to me, their arms open. The man who was and wasn't me went to join them, and then I saw that, like those two figures, one obviously feminine, the other a child, the figure of the man who had emerged from me melted into the whiteness of a white-tiled bath with porcelain frogs inset in a white bathtub and floral patterns that were barely visible through the thick steam of that architectonic belly.

"The man joined the other two figures, and then I saw how the woman and the child, she dressed in black, with her dark hair piled high, the blond child dressed in an old-fashioned suit with candy stripes, were wrapping themselves in fabric, in towels or sheets, I'm not sure, but only white material, wet, suffocating, and the man who had asked me to take care of the three of them joined his family, and like her, he began to change into a damp sheet, one of the sheets that stuck to those bodies I imagined foul, faded, savagely shrouded . . .

"They held out their hands to me, their open arms.

"From the child's little hands fell sweets wrapped in rich, heavy paper.

"The arms beckoned me, the sweets fell to the floor, and I felt myself surrounded by an intense, perfumed, unwanted love and I was about to succumb to it because no one had ever demanded and offered love with as much intensity as they did, that unlikely family, seductive, repugnant, white as purity itself but repulsive as the second skin, wet and sticky, of the shroud that covered them.

"I instinctively resisted the seduction, I decided they were the Mackintoshes, and that they were dead; you are a family of dead people, I told them, and with that a vista opened up behind them, behind their white, sticky redoubt, and there were all the houses of Glasgow, communicating with other structures that had been unknown before, almost unimagined, houses that had never been seen, perhaps had never been built, where other women wearing sumptuous capes of pale silk of the softest lemon and the filmiest olive walk through arcades and patios, carrying objects that I cannot recognize. Those women stood so erect, so sad, on a distant, precise, and horizontal world, that the effect—they were so far away yet I saw them so clearly—was to make me dizzy and nauseated.

"In the center of that distant horizon were two more figures, a woman clasping to her breast a child with an injured finger. The first group was hiding the other, but they were related, distant in space but near in time, symmetrical.

"I was afraid that they, too, would call to me and beg me: *Take care of us. Dedicate yourself totally to us from this time on . . .*

"Other houses, different spaces, but is it always the same trinity, the same responsibility? Everything telescopes back to the immediate, concealing the distance or the future, whatever it was (or perhaps it belonged only to the *other* and I was afraid it was *mine*, neither *time* nor *space*, at last, comprehensible, but only *irrational possessions*), and the figures before me returned to the foreground, I heard the tantalizing crackle of the cherry, gold, and blue wrapping paper that held the sweets, and I saw the swaddled heads of the figures smiling at me.

"Beneath the damp cloth, the blood ran from their gums, painting their smiles.

"I looked at those figures—now there were three of them— and I decided I preferred my vision of them, no matter how horrible, funereal and white, to my second vision of the incomplete figures behind them. The man was absent from that second scene. There was only the mother and child, beckoning to me. I had no wish to be that absent man.

"No sooner had I thought that than I saw them, the three figures in the closer group, huddled in the brilliant white light of the bath, their damp clothing removed, appearing naked, rapidly growing younger before me; I quickly closed my eyes, already driven out of my mind by the chaos of my sensations, convinced that their youth and their nakedness would overcome me unless I closed my eyes to negate both their youth and their seductiveness; if I didn't look at them, they would grow old as quickly as they had regained their youth . . ."

He never explained to me—Catarina resumed the story—what he meant by "regaining their youth" insofar as the child in the candy-striped suit was concerned. Returning to the womb? Disappearing altogether? But Santiago did tell me that when the guards in that little Glasgow museum found him prostrate in a corner and asked him what had happened and what they could do for him, he couldn't very well question them to find out if there was a family forever walled in, there in the corner where they had found him, by the closed-off door of a bathroom, so white and steamy, blinding and damp . . .

He just stared at the candy wrappers scattered over the floor.

16

—Catarina, I don't know what I said in class today or why I said it. I don't know if other beings have taken possession of me, daughter, talking through me, making me say and do things against my will.

—I am not your daughter, Santiago.

—They make me feel that my most private acts are public ones.

—You seem so tired. Lie down here.

—Abandon, for example; a careless cruelty.

—Can I make you tea?

—Have they been following me, constantly tempting me, imitating my movements as a kind of seduction so that I would imitate theirs? I will never know, daughter.

—I am not your daughter, Santiago.

—Do they inhabit the real houses that you and I do, Catarina, or do they live only in imagined houses, invisible replicas of ours?

—You ask so many painful questions, Santiago. Look, you will feel better if I sit down next to you. What did you say in class today?

—I addressed the boys.

—And not the girls? You have plenty of girl students—and some of them are quite attractive.

—No, I was talking to the two of them, you know, to the twins, the Vélez brothers.

—And what did you say?

—I gave a class on architecture and myth, but I don't know why I said what I said . . .

—Well, Santiago, in that case, the best thing would be for you to stay here by the fire with me and we'll look at some books, as we always . . .

—That it is myths that haunt us, not ghosts, which are only specters produced by an unexpected intersection of myths. A Celtic myth, for example, might intersect with an Aztec one. But what interests me the most is the syncretic capacity of Christian myth to embrace them all and make them all rationally accessible at once, and at the same time irrationally sacred. That was my class. But I don't know why I said all that.

—You have just explained it to me, Santiago. You were trying to reach those two, Carlos María and José María.

—Ah, yes. We think our actions are ours alone; an act of wantonness, for example: it seems entirely ours, but soon, Catarina, something else happens that completes, negates, and mocks the action we thought was ours, making it part of a much larger scheme that we will never comprehend. So maybe what we call myths are, finally, just situations that correspond despite their distance in time and place.

—Have something to drink. Look at the books. These are the prints you like the best. Piranesi, see, Palladio . . .

—That is the secret of the houses we build and live in. Tell the boys that. Tell the brothers, Catarina.

—They are my brothers, Santiago.

—*Take care of us. Dedicate yourself totally to us from this time on. Have mercy. Don't abandon us. Have pity.*

—What can I do for you?

—Bury me far from here, in a sacred place, but a place where there are no Virgins on the altars. The creatures who are pursuing me will leave me in peace if I deceive them, by leaving the places I've lived in and the people I've known. I'll make them think I've joined them permanently, joined their watery voice, their damp skin, their wilted flowers, after I returned from Scotland, my grandparents' home . . .

—You have reconstructed that bathroom everywhere, Santiago, the tiles, the recurring foliage, the porcelain frogs set in the white bathtub . . . Everywhere.

—They hold the secret.

—What secret, she implored, tell me, but he didn't answer directly:

—I chose them among all my disciples.

—You mustn't like them very much.

—Ask them if they, too, sense that others . . .

—You keep repeating that. Who?

—If the other beings are always there, or if they just sneak in between the stones and the bricks of all the buildings I've built since . . .

—Or what would be even worse, Santiago, in all the buildings you have imagined.

—So you finally understand what I'm saying.

—I'm glad, Santiago, that I will soon pass that burden on to the twins and let them puzzle it out.

—Someone must inherit the mystery of the dead.

That is what Santiago Ferguson said then, before he died.

Catarina looked at us with veiled eyes and said:

—I think that is Santiago Ferguson's legacy, twins. Now that you've heard it, and possibly understood it, you, like me, will never be free from the professor, as you call him . . .

We—José María and Carlos María—were going to tell Catarina, our unattainable love, that what she had told us might be a nightmare, but we were grateful for it anyway, if it allowed us to be near her at last, and to love her.

—To love you, Catarina.

—Both of you? She laughed.

We didn't know to what extent our intimacy and our love, as the father's disciples, meant the responsibility for his ghosts and his daughter.

The ghosts didn't worry us. We had heard the professor's lecture. An artist always creates an asystematic system, which he does not even recognize himself. That is his strength; that is why the work of art always says much more than the explicit intention of the author. The work—house, book, statue—*is* the ghost.

Love, on the other hand, blinded us again, though we hoped it would provide the final illumination.

But first there appeared, again, death and a journey.

III. LOVES

1

When Professor Santiago Ferguson died that autumn, his daughter Catarina called to tell us that her father had asked to be buried in Wells Cathedral in England. He had also said that he hoped his disciples, both old and young, who had dined at the Lincoln Restaurant, would accompany him to his final home. He didn't want it to seem an obligation, it was just a friendly invitation, a last sentimental request. We didn't try to find out how many others were going. We didn't call anyone: Say, are you going to go to the professor's funeral? Besides, those days nobody was doing any traveling except on business, on an expense account, or to get some money out of Mexico before it was too late. But our situation was different; we were associates in architectural firms in Europe and the United States, contributors to *Architectural Digest*, designers of some so-called residences in Los Angeles and Dallas, of the Adami Museum in Arona, on Lake

Maggiore, and of various hotels in Poland and Hungary. We were members of the class of Mexican professionals that had been able to create an infrastructure outside our country, so we could afford the luxury of buying our own airline tickets, if we wished. First class, because, as Professor Ferguson used to say:

—I only travel first-class. If I can't, I prefer to stay comfortably at home.

Well, now he was traveling with Catarina, but in a coffin in the cargo compartment of a British Airways Boeing 747, because we were flying first-class on Air France to Paris, where the Mitterrand government had commissioned us to design an international conference center in a district near the Anet Castle, owned, incidentally, by an old Mexican family: the sequel to an itinerant Mexico, sometimes dispossessed, sometimes in voluntary exile, sometimes engaged in professional and artistic activities that could not be limited entirely to the homeland; and as we flew over the Atlantic, we browsed through a book on English cathedrals and the itinerant world of the Middle Ages and the Renaissance, when religious and intellectual fervor caused people to travel more than they had before, though it took a greater effort and they faced greater difficulties than we do today, which puts us in mind of something the itinerant twelfth-century monk and educator Hugo de Saint-Victor said, that being satisfied with remaining in one's homeland and feeling comfortable there is the first stage in a man's development; feeling comfortable in many countries is the next stage; but perfection is attained only when a man feels exiled in any part of the world, no matter where he goes.

By that standard, our beloved teacher Santiago Ferguson had reached only the second stage, and we, his disciples, Carlos María and José María Vélez, brothers, might have shared that weakness; but we both knew well that it wasn't true, we had both traveled through extraordinary exiles, one of us to the summit of a tragicomic calvary guarded by Señora Heredad Mateos, the other to a place where nobody, not even its inhabitants, could ever feel satisfied. José María had traveled to a land of ritual; Carlos María to the subterranean discontent that fed it.

But we never told each other about our experiences. For each of us, true exile had been to be separated from the other, clearly making José María into a distant *I* and Carlos María into a remote *you*. If we were able to understand anything from this story, it was this: nowhere—not Glasgow, Mexico, Virginia, or Vicenza—was building a house enough to fulfill the human, professional, or aesthetic obligations of architecture. Someone had to actually *live* there. And those inhabitants were going to want what the Mackintoshes demanded of Ferguson, what the residents of the subterranean convent begged of Carlos María, what Doña Heredad Mateos asked of the Virgin and Child. Take care of us. Dedicate yourself totally to us from this time on. Have pity. Don't abandon us. What are the limits of creation? There is no artist who in his most private heart has not asked that question, afraid that the creative act is not free, not sufficient, but that it is prolonged in the demands of those who inhabit a house, read a book, contemplate a picture, or attend a theatrical performance. How far does the individual privilege of creation extend; where does the obligation of sharing that creation begin? The only work residing purely in the *I*, dispossessed of its potential *we*, is a work that was conceived but never realized. The house is there. Even an unpublished book, stored away in a drawer, is there. We Vélez brothers imagined a world of pure projects, pure intentions, whose only existence would be mental. But in that a priori universe, death reigns. That is, more or less, what happened to us when we separated—we lost the *us*; and now, flying over the Atlantic, we tried to regain it by avoiding all mention of what had happened: Carlos María never talked about what had happened to him when he went through the Neoclassical door, following the dog; José María never mentioned what had occurred at the shack of Doña Heredad Mateos. Only two mute objects remained as witnesses of those separate experiences: the wooden cross on the roof of the watchman Jerónimo Mateos's shack, which Carlos María had taken with him when he left the convent; and a wedding dress spread out as a temptation, as a remembrance, perhaps as a reproof, on the twin bed of José María in our family home on Avenida Nuevo León, by the Parque España, a house our father had designed in a style that was neat and sleek, or, as one said then, "streamlined" (or, another word: "aerodynamic"): in Mexican homage to Frank Lloyd Wright, circa 1938.

But we had lost the object that could have united our respective experiences—the porcelain frog—and now, perhaps, we were traveling secretly in search of that object that was so strongly associated with our love for Catarina, the object we had discovered one afternoon in her father's bath, and again in the secret convent on Calle Marroquí. Was there something that linked those two places and, consequently, those two experiences? The Mackintosh house in Glasgow meant nothing to us.

Perhaps, looking over the photographs of English cathedrals and sipping the Bloody Marys we had ordered, ignoring all the wise prescriptions against jet lag that advise forgoing alcohol at forty thousand feet, we were really looking back at our true home in Colonia Hipódromo, as if to compensate for the transitoriness of the shelter that carried us from Mexico to Paris in thirteen hours. And yet there was something more deadly about the maternal womb of aluminum and foam rubber now carrying us than about the immobile terrestrial home where we grew up.

An acquaintance of ours, a low-level Mexican bureaucrat, came into the first-class section and walked past us, nervously clutching a Martini wrapped in a wet paper napkin, grumbling:

—I feel like I was born in this thing and I am going to die in it. Bottoms up! She sighed, taking a gulp of her drink, and adding in a suggestive voice: —And that's all that's going down here, brothers.

She laughed, looking at us sitting there, identical, with our drinks and our art book, and said that our laps were already occupied anyway, get it? And she guffawed and turned away:

she was dressed for the long flight in a jogging suit with an Adidas logo, a pink jacket and pants, and tennis shoes. We looked at the photograph of the inverted arches that may not be the most subtle but are certainly the most spectacular element of Wells Cathedral; the double stone opening at the end of the nave creates perspectives similar to those of the interior of an airplane, while recalling the primogenial cave: two entrances to the refuge—the engines of the 747 were inaudible, a lap cat makes more noise—which safeguarded us and also, perhaps, imprisoned us. The home is a refuge that does not imprison, and in ours, our father taught us and made us what we are: gave us our love for architecture, the world, and its two geographies, natural and human. From our father, who died too young, we learned the lesson that Santiago Ferguson reaffirmed for us; we can't return to pure nature: she does not want us and we have to exploit her to survive; we are condemned to artifice, to copy a nature which will not suffer for us, which can protect us without devouring us. That is the mission of architecture. Or of architectures, plural, we said, quickly turning the pages of our book to the glorious images of York and Winchester, Ely and Salisbury, Durham and Lincoln, names that conjure up the glory possible in the kingdom of this world. Cathedrals with long naves, through which all the processions of exile and faith can pass; immense, intense pulpits out of which can tumble the most flexible and inventive rhetoric in the world, that of the English language; and yet, beside this splendor, rise the modest, infinitely varied sculpted façades of the towers; the wide arms of the monasteries embraced in the majestic hospitality of Canterbury and Chichester. Luxury liners, laden with souls, wrote the poet Auden: hulls of stone.

This is the place Santiago Ferguson has chosen for his burial, for if it was not in his power to determine the hour of his physical death, at least he was able to fix the place and setting for the death of his spirit, which, he always said, would be nothing less than the source of life itself. There is not a single life that does not spring from death, that is not the result of or recompense for the deaths that preceded it. The artist and the lover know that;

other men do not. An architect or a lover knows that the living owe their lives to the dead, that is why they make love and art with such passion. Our deaths, in turn, will be the origin of other lives, of those who remember or are affected by what we did in the name of those who preceded or followed us.

This was our secret requiem for our beloved teacher Santiago Ferguson. If the living Vélez brothers still retained a longing (and a memory as well, since we had lived there) for our own private cathedral, it was not a cave, not an airplane, but a house, a home, where our childhood possessions were gathered: toys, adventure books, outgrown clothes, a teddy bear, deflated soccer balls, photographs . . . Our father, the architect Luis Vélez, was nicknamed "The Negative" because his skin was dark and his hair white, so that, looking at him in a photo, one was tempted to reverse the image and give him a white face and dark hair. Our mother, on the other hand, was pale and fair; her negative would have been completely dark, the only exception, perhaps, the fine line of her eyebrows or the carmine of her lips. She died during the difficult delivery of twins. Us. We are the sons of María de la Mora de Vélez, so we were both baptized with the name of our lost mother.

The Mexican under-secretary again interrupted what we were doing, what we were thinking; in her high-strung ukelele voice she barked, Up and at them, boys, lift those curtains, we're about to land at Pénjamo, you can see the light of its towers, and she blinded us with daylight and the sight, at our feet, of the Abbey of Mont-Saint-Michel.

We were entering France through Brittany, we would spend two days in Paris, and Sunday was the event at Wells. We looked at each other, brothers, both thinking of Catarina, who was waiting for us there with the body of her father.

—Catarina is waiting for us with the body of her father, said José María, while the absurd under-secretary, plastered to the gills, sang "*Et maintenant*," no doubt to celebrate her arrival in Paris with a song from her youth.

—And her husband? asked Carlos María. Joaquín Mercado?

—He doesn't matter. Catarina and her father are the only ones who matter.

—*Et maintenant, que dois-je faire?*

—Just shut up, señora, please!

—What did you say? You bastard, I'm going to report you!

—Go right ahead. I have no use for your fucking bureaucracy.

—Never mind. She doesn't matter either. Only the father matters.

—He is dead.

—But you and I are not. Which will she choose?

—Her father was our rival, you know?

—Yes, yes, I knew he was the one Catarina was screwing that afternoon.

—You and I must not be rivals now, promise me that?

We didn't know which of us asked for that promise, as the plane began its descent to Charles de Gaulle Airport.

2

We had a tacit understanding that each of us would keep his secrets, but there was one, at least, that we had to share. Catarina had become irresistible to us the moment we saw her making love with her father. Then there was no rivalry between us, or jealousy of her father; once again, the professor had preceded us; he had done what we wanted to do; he did it first, he showed us the way, as he did in class. But now, entering the deep Gothic nave of Wells Cathedral, walking through the yellow and green, the white and red and olive lights, every color but blue, that were created by the great high stained-glass windows, we knew Professor Santiago Ferguson would do, would say, no more; never again.

She was standing by the casket. She saw us but didn't move. She knew as well as we: there would be only three mourners; no others would attend.

She was dressed in black, a severe silk suit, dark stockings, and flat shoes that could not relieve her exceptional height. She took our hands, kissed our cheeks: she withdrew one hand and touched the lid of the lacquered box. We did the same. We knelt. We heard a tape-recorded sermon, followed by a very brief Requiem.

The brevity of the ceremony was appropriate: the professor had no need for ceremony, he was at Wells, where he wanted to be, and the important thing was not to delay his solitary entrance, not to that marvelous English cathedral but to architecture itself, his true homeland, a place where he would never find peace, so much had he desired it, so much had he dreamed of it. Ferguson had to *become* architecture.

Here, with him, we felt that was how it should be, that all the places we could recall from our long friendship with him were here—the Mackintosh house in Glasgow, which was a delicate reflection of the professor's spirit, and which we knew better from his lectures than from photographs; or the projects on José María Marroquí, which we knew all too well; or our house on Avenida Nuevo León, where our impossibly fair mother died, and our father, dark like us; or the office on Colonia Roma, where we surprised the pallid architect Ferguson screwing his daughter, who was dark like us; or Ferguson's own house in the Pedregal, which contained not a single photo of Catarina's mother. If Catarina did not resemble her father, did she look like her mother, dead, absent, mute, unmentionable? Nobody ever dared mention her, neither us nor them, the father and the daughter, except once, when we heard Catarina say:

—When we moved here to the Pedregal, we got rid of a thousand old things, photos, dolls, dresses, records, all that, you know . . .

Here, our professor's wisdom was plain to see; here, he was equidistant from all his favored places, those of architecture and of his heart. This was the point of equilibrium—how well he understood!—on which his entire life balanced, and only in death could he occupy it.

Catarina knew this as well as we did; we could go now, leaving the casket to the work of time, and meet outside.

A pair of tall monks with light, graying hair and profiles like ecclesiastic Hamlets were walking through the cloisters in animated discussion, accentuating our melancholy mood, our feeling that every stone is a forgotten memory.

We were silent as we left the cloisters and went outside, to admire the incomparable façade of Wells Cathedral, which is the point of departure from the Middle Ages, just as Santiago de Compostela is its point of entry. But if grace welcomes glory in Galicia, with its arch of prophets in animated conversation, as if eternal life were a continuous, perfect, sacred cocktail party, and Daniel smiles at us with the enigmatic look of a thirteenth-century Mona Lisa, in Wells the inclusivity of its great entrance undermines the Gothic ideal; the Gothic of Wells is an imminent Baroque, a hunger for figuration that finds its expression in the tiers of three hundred forty stone figures that cover the façade and the tower of the cathedral, in vast horizontal groupings that proclaim the triumph of the Church: one line of prophets and apostles; another of angels; the intermediate ranks of virgins and martyrs, at the side of the confessors; and then the resurrection of the dead; and, at the very top, the faded majesty of Christ.

That is what you say, Carlos María, detaching yourself from us for a moment, but he, José María, does not agree with you, this is not the familiar Baroque of Mexico, Peru, and Spain, it remains Gothic, he says, faceted into multiplicity to increase our awe, when it finally reveals itself as pure void. The whole vast façade of Wells Cathedral, intoning a hymn to the triumph of the Church, offers infallible signs and absolute truths, which immediately demonstrate their fallibility and deceptiveness. He says that the Gothic loved that effect because it desired not what was revealed but what could not be revealed, what is only imminent, what . . .

—Isn't that so, Professor?

Then we looked at each other, with a little sadness and a lot of surprise. For a moment, we were back at our monthly meal in Lincoln Restaurant.

Catarina says that fewer than half the original statues remain; many have been mutilated; several—she smiles behind a veil that isn't there, because her dark skin is also a veil, accentuated by the deep eyes of her Indian and Spanish beauty—were decapitated; and all of them, without exception, are being devoured by the salt breezes from the nearby Irish Sea.

After a pause, Catarina continues. The three hundred and forty statues were born together, but they have been dying separately, one by one.

She asked us if the statues that have survived suffered, did they long to rejoin the ones that were gone.

She called us twins, *brothers*.

We didn't answer her questions, either because we didn't understand them or because we didn't think they were important: we were savoring the way she had addressed us, the Vélez brothers, Carlos María and José María, born at the same time but almost certainly doomed to die separately: one would survive the other—you? I?—as now, the three of us, together here beneath the sculpted sky of Wells Cathedral, facing its façade and its tower eroded little by little by the wind, we have survived our teacher, the father of Catarina Ferguson: *he*. The absurd undersecretary in the airplane had also called us brothers, and laughed—but what a difference in the way Catarina now said:

—Do you think, brothers, that the statues that have survived suffer, do they long to rejoin the ones that are gone?

She laughed and took two long steps with her slender legs, to stand face to face before us. Then she told us how she and Santiago Ferguson had spent hours talking about other homes, not only the ones where we had lived—together or separately: Ferguson's house in the Pedregal; ours in Avenida Nuevo León; his office on Colonia Roma where we saw the father making love to his daughter—but others, which Catarina and Santiago talked about and slowly re-created, she lying on his lap, he stroking her long, flowing black hair, freed from its prim bun: recollecting, reconstructing, caressing, just as they felt comforted and caressed by those houses, the Mackintoshes' in Glasgow, Jefferson's in Virginia, Palladio's in Vicenza, remembering that, though we make the houses, they outlive us, but a part of us remains in them, for they do not simply survive us, they keep our ghosts alive, they are the voices of our memory, dependent on us even after we are dead, as we are dependent on them when we are alive: Catarina and Santiago, holding large glasses of port in their hands, caressing, drinking, turning the pages of the architecture books, convinced that we will be received in the refuge we constructed only if we accept everything that occurred in it—crimes and punishments, births and deaths, sorrows and joys, sacrifices: Catarina and Santiago embracing in front of the domestic hearth, resolving to forget nothing, to destroy nothing, sometimes full of passionate humility, sometimes of a humble compassion before the world, sometimes inventing a married couple in Scotland, sometimes a father and child in Virginia, sometimes a couple consisting of a theater and its audience in Italy; exploring to their final consequences the comfort of refuge and the horror of openness, the capacity of a house to provide a space for love, life, death, the imagination, miracles; for a bath with porcelain frogs, a lead umbrella stand, for a rainy patio circled by nuns mutilated in defense of their virginity; a watchman's hut in which a traffic light was reflected, a rich woman's wedding dress passed from hand to hand, down to the dispossessed poor; for a violent desire to survive, for an imminent, unwanted birth, a once immaculate conception, which is corrupt and sinful the second time, for a . . .

—. . . so many little things, childhood toys, outgrown clothes, old movie programs, who knows why we saved them, old photos, so many objects, brothers, said the woman we had both desired so deeply, all our lives: Catarina took something from her jacket pocket and handed it to us.

It was a photograph, like the ones we kept in our house on Avenida Nuevo León, a photograph she may have kept in the drawer in a secret bathroom decorated with a floral pattern with frogs set in the bathtub, exposing it to moisture, perhaps in the hope that the steam would erode the image away, as the sea breeze eroded the statues on Wells Cathedral.

. . . Mackintosh; the Teatro Olimpico; Monticello; the house abandoned by the Gameros family in Chihuahua at the beginning of the Revolution: Santiago and I recalled all those, and out of our love we shaped the single, unbending resolve of discovering an architecture that would contain all those places that we explored in an effort to prevent their death, to keep them alive at any cost, or to bring new life to them, make them fertile again, brothers, as if houses were living bodies, with flesh, viscera, memories . . .

It was a photograph of the young architect Santiago Ferguson, instantly recognizable, holding the pudgy hand of a child with black bangs and deep-set eyes that had not yet known passion or remorse, the emotions that we saw now in the dark eyes our unattainable beloved raised to us.

The father was standing, holding the hand of the child, who was sitting in the lap of a dark woman dressed in a black forties-style suit, with the open-collar piqué blouse and padded shoulders that have been revived in current fashion; she was gazing intently at the child. The woman had a noticeable mustache on her upper lip, and a mole on each of her temples. She had a dusky face.

—Is she dead? asked Carlos María after a long pause.

—No, said Catarina, she is being taken care of. It's for her own good. I am telling you because it's our responsibility to keep her isolated, secure. Nobody must see her.

—Ah. We may never see her? Is that an absolute prohibition?

—Not everyone can be granted that privilege. Catarina smiled. On altars, perhaps, you may see her.

—And in memory.

—When memory comes fully to life, it can be an aberration or a crime. On altars—Catarina repeated—there, perhaps, we may see our mother.

—Not here. There are no Virgins on Protestant altars. Why did Santiago Ferguson choose this place to die?

—As you say, perhaps he felt that something was missing here. Perhaps he felt that there was a place for him in this cathedral. Perhaps this is the place that contains all others, or the place that excludes all others. Either way, he may have felt that this was the ideal architecture he had been seeking all along, an architecture without the burden of the maternal image. Santiago Ferguson was explicit about that. But if he wanted a resting place without Virgins, he could not wish for a place where bodies separated by death are reunited. We must respect his wishes. He wanted, really, to rest in peace.

—You loved him, truly, José María dared to say.

—I loved Santiago Ferguson, but not our father, Catarina replied.

—No, our father died very young, when you were a child.

Then, children of dark, loving parents, offspring of their dark love, of love between friends, we took each other's hands and walked away, vowing never to reveal what we now knew, what denied her brothers the intimacy of Catarina's body, what gave that right to Santiago Ferguson, what denied the death in childbirth of the fair María del Moral, or what opened the empty page of the mystery of her death, what removed Catarina's mother from the world forever, our mother, lover of our father, the architect affectionately known as "The Negative," our mother, shut away to protect the friendship between families, the memory of the father, or the love of Santiago and Catarina. We silently vowed never to speak of these things. We would never mention what gave our teacher the right to do what *we* could never do, condemning us to the separation of being three, not one, never one, and of never repeating what we saw and experienced separately, yet what brought us together, holding each other's hands, in passionate humility before the mysteries of life.

We left Wells Cathedral, each of us knowing that we could return only when we again had a thirst for miracles, and that our newfound kinship would depend on our continuing to believe in the miracle of the others. Apart from that, to all appearances, we would continue to be "reasonable people."

At that moment we lost the possibility of the couple, but we gained, behind the multitude of our ghosts, a fraternal trinity. Carlos María, José María, Catarina.

Had that been Santiago Ferguson's secret wish, after all?

3

Again last night the glow appeared.

Doña Heredad Mateos arrived at the convent hidden in Calle José María Marroquí, and in the hot white bathroom where the steam formed drops on the dried-up, wrinkled backs of the frogs, she presented to the woman who had just given birth an old patched wedding dress, which the old seamstress's art had made like new: pearls, organdy, and a whiff of naphthalene. The nuns thanked her for the gift and placed it, as though to try it on, over the stretched-out body of the woman who had just given birth, who did not smile. The mask of her immobile face, embellished only by the hair on her upper lip and the moles on her temples, broke as she asked, again, why the birth was a miracle the first time and now, the second time, it was a sin. The seamstress said she didn't know anything about that kind of thing, it was beyond her, all she had was faith. And, as always, she would gladly take care of the child. Yes, it was better, as always, for the father not to know about the child. She would take care of him.

—What a good idea it was to build this *temascal*—said Doña Heredad, looking around at the steamy white bath. —It's good here—she said tenderly to the woman who had just given birth.

Then the old seamstress, dressed in black, with her long skirt, her *rebozo*, her cotton stockings and flat shoes, took the baby and placed it in her crude multicolored shopping basket, hailed a bus on Artículo 123 and, after a long ride through the city of sorrows, got off on the broad avenue of La Esplanada, in Las Lomas de Chapultepec.

There, with the shopping basket in her hand, she went patiently from door to door, from one luxurious residence to another, requesting "an offering for this poor mother," and receiving, from time to time, a bottle of lemonade, the leftovers from a banquet, fried pork or seafood, dry tortillas, a bit of tossed salad. The assiduous woman placed it all in her basket, indifferent to the sounds of cars and trucks and helicopters and motorcycles; oblivious to the black clouds of exhaust fumes, because she knew that none of that affected the child; this child was born without lead in his lungs; each year when he was born, the child was saved from stain, sickness, and death. Presenting him at the doors of Las Lomas, Doña Heredad was oblivious to the noise and pollution. She received alms, but her memory went far beyond the limit of her travails, and in her head she heard the ancient sounds of organ-grinders, itinerant venders, old-clothes sellers, and knife sharpeners filling the ever-expanding, ever more immense terrain of the oldest city of the New World—another city, murmured Doña Heredad Mateos to herself, a pure city, in whose houses the living could rejoin the dead, a small city where people could tell their stories, a city of faith where miracles occurred, even if reasonable people never understood, said Doña Heredad, asking charity for the god child, charity for the newborn, showing the foam-rubber doll with his golden curls and his blue eyes and his white gown with gold edging and his bloody fingers—charity, charity for the child.

Varaville, Normandy, Easter 1987
Tepoztlán, Morelos, Easter 1988